Miracles

SERENA J. BISHOP

EOS
PUBLISHING

DEDICATION

A special thanks to my mom, and to Linda R. and Karen P.

To motherhood and all the forms it takes.

CONTACT THE AUTHOR

Website:
www.serenajbishop.com
Twitter:
https://twitter.com/SerenaJBishop
Facebook:
https://www.facebook.com/SerenaJBishop
Instagram:
https://www.instagram.com/SerenaJBishop

ABOUT EOS PUBLISHING

Website:
http://eos-publishing.com
Twitter:
https://twitter.com/eospublishing
Facebook:
https://www.facebook.com/eospublishing
Instagram:
http://instagram.com/eospublishing

Subscribe to newsletter:
https://eos-publishing.com/newsletter

CHAPTER ONE

LEELA TOOK HER first break of the day and watched the sunrise from the comfort of her kitchen window. It may have been early morning, but the temperature outside was already scorching. It didn't feel like summer would be officially over soon. She'd have to remember to bring water whenever she was out working on the farm.

And maybe a beer at the end of the day.

Yeah, that would be real nice. If that treat was in her future, she needed to make Aurora some lemonade ice cubes for her iced tea. Some time on the porch with a cold drink while watching the goats was how happy hour was done at their house.

Leela stood against the slider and held a bowl of maple cinnamon cereal under her chin. The mildly sweet, spicy aroma wafted under her nose, and she smiled.

Leela loved her growing goat farm, her expanding home, and the woman who ran back and forth from the bedroom to the bathroom and up the loft a dozen times in her small heels. Aurora's feet clicked and clacked about the house when she was about to leave for her day.

Their love had been going strong for three years.

Even with so much love, when Aurora moved in two years prior there was an adjustment period for Leela, to say the least. From two people living in a home built for one—because Leela never saw herself finding anyone who could put up with her—to the logistical fact that Leela started work at 5:30 a.m. She was accustomed to making a ruckus as she made her coffee and listened to wake-up music.

Aurora was not a fan of Oregon's most popular country radio station waking her up in the morning. But she and Leela had come to a compromise. Aurora could wake up a half hour earlier if Leela could wait to eat her breakfast a little later and make her morning coffee in her office, a few dozen yards away from the house.

"Have you seen my navy jacket?"

Leela continued to stare out the glass door while she chewed a hunk of pecan granola. "The one you let me try on before I went to the bank last week?"

"Yes!" Aurora appeared in her sleeveless, cream blouse with her long, black hair falling over each shoulder. "Where is it?"

"I put it back in the closet. At the far end against the wall."

Aurora's mouth dropped. "That'll smoosh it." She ran back, her small heels clicking along the way.

This wasn't their first early morning conversation about the location of clothing, but Aurora's frantic movements were atypical. Normally Aurora's calm, patient demeanor contrasted well with Leela's own occasional crazed and neurotic intensity. It was common knowledge among their friends that this was one of many reasons why they were the perfect couple.

"Why are you puttin' on the Ritz today?" Leela asked, and as soon as she heard Aurora gasp from the bedroom, she winced. "Oh, shit! Today's the day you're meeting with Milohila Resort."

As a sustainability and financial analyst with her company, Ever Green Grocer, Aurora worked with all of EGG's clients to improve their processes so they saved money while changing their practices to be more environmentally friendly. Aurora had been so successful in this endeavor that EGG had branched out to include consulting work. In the last six months, Aurora had met with dozens of businesses in Oregon, Washington state, and California who wanted to better themselves. However, Milohila Resort was a getaway on the big island of Hawaii that took advantage of the scenery and the geothermal power of an active volcano.

Leela continued to eat her cereal and admired Aurora's form. The navy skirt hugged her muscular legs right above the knee. Her slightly unbuttoned blouse exposed the tops of her breasts, and her long hair now cascaded down the back of the jacket.

It made her acutely aware that Leela herself wore grass-stained jeans and a t-shirt with a hole in it from where the fence had got her. At least her simple, shoulder-length hair was presentable. Kind of: "Your work clothes are so much sexier than mine. I'm a very lucky woman."

Leela sometimes wondered if Aurora got as much out of their relationship as she did. Aurora was smart, sexy, and gentle, whereas she was a bit immature and rough around the edges. But Leela looked for signs of unhappiness in her girlfriend and if she spied any, she was quick to either resolve or discuss the issue.

Leela refused to become as poor a partner as her parents—her divorced parents—had been to each other.

Aurora buttoned her suit jacket with an air of dissatisfaction. "I really wish this wasn't wrinkled but I know that wasn't your fault. The tiny closet is a problem which will soon be solved."

"It will be. Although, I question if the contractors will finish on schedule." Leela opened the sliding door and leaned out to see the framework for the house's addition. A bigger bedroom with a walk-in closet would fix most, if not all, their problems. No more wrinkled clothes. And Aurora planned to convert their old bedroom into an office so she could telework more and ride on her bike trainer.

Leela tipped her cereal bowl and drank the milk when a thought struck her. "I didn't think the Hawaii clients were coming into the office," she said as she went to the sink.

"It's a video conference, so I still want to look my best." Aurora gasped. "Should I wear my gray pinstripe instead?"

Leela finished soaking her bowl and approached Aurora. She looped her hands around her waist and was rewarded with the hint of a smile. "You look perfect. I don't know if you remember, but you and me together are like queer business superstars."

Aurora grinned and gave her a tiny kiss. "That's a very specific category."

"You know what I mean."

"I do. And…" Aurora leaned down and touched her nose to Leela's. "I know I'm a bit of a lunatic this morning. It's just that this is an entire resort we're talking about, not a producer of fava bean snacks or hemp purses."

In their few years together, Leela couldn't recall Aurora being this nervous over a client. Perhaps the resort was an even bigger deal than Aurora had let on. "Can I ask if there's something more to this that might have you nervous? I feel like I might not be getting the whole story."

"You know me too well." Aurora tightened her hold on Leela and sighed. "I have this feeling in my gut that this client is a real game-changer."

"Like a promotion?"

"I think so."

"You will be absolutely fabulous, and so you have less to worry about, I'll handle dinner tonight. I was already thinking that you need your special ice cubes for our happy hour later. Or, shall I say, celebration of your victory today?"

"That would be amazing," Aurora said with wide brown eyes but then skewed her brow. "But don't you have the farmers' market meeting for leadership nominations? I know you're extra busy these days too."

"Yeah, but when I said, 'handle dinner' I meant, 'pick up dinner'. I'll already be in town, so I won't be going out of my way."

Aurora sighed with a frown.

"What's that for?"

Aurora hooked her thumb under the waistband of her skirt to demonstrate the lack of space. Except there was space. "I feel like I've gained weight."

"But you still fit into the same clothes as when we met," Leela argued.

Aurora's downturned lips made Leela believe Aurora wasn't buying her words. "If it makes you feel less self-conscious, I'll get you something lighter. And maybe we can go on a bike ride together this weekend or something."

Aurora leaned her forehead against Leela's. "I would really like that. Maybe make it a date? I feel like we haven't been on date in a while. I miss it."

She wasn't wrong. The combination of new staff and the new filling and bottling machine required all of Leela's supervision during the traditional work week, which meant paperwork and marketing had been pushed to the weekends.

"You're right. I will erase tax planning and pencil you in for a date instead. That'll be much more fun." Leela pulled her into a hug but was careful not to further wrinkle her suit jacket. "Are you good for me to punch into the metaphorical clock now?"

"Yeah, I am. You don't want someone slipping on that latest super-secret Bakshi Farm lotion."

"That's right. I promise I'll send you encouraging text messages once I patch the east fence." Leela gestured to the tear in her shirt, then kissed her. "You're going to be great today. I love you, sweets."

"I love you too. And thanks for the pep talk." Aurora smiled.

Leela leaned closer, gave her a playful swat on the behind, and winked. "Anytime."

Leela stepped out of their home with a giggle and walked to the farm's office. Her commute was much shorter than Aurora's. When they'd first met, Aurora had lived close to town and rode her bike to and from work. Now, Aurora drove her company's hybrid and traveled thirty minutes each way. Even more if she had to wait for a train to cross. Leela logged into her computer and worked out the Aurora travel math in her head. Aurora missed approximately twenty hours of life every month because of commuting. Twenty hours during which she could ride her bike. Twenty hours of watching movies. Or sex! They could be having way more sex. But instead of riding her, Aurora was riding in her car.

That thought really sucked.

The only positive Leela could see regarding Aurora's commute was that Aurora used that time to talk to her best friend, Stacy, who lived on the East Coast, or her family who lived in Michigan's upper peninsula.

After Leela created the task list for each full-time employee for the day and verified the pick-up schedule for the latest batch of milk, she logged off and walked another fifty yards to the mixing and packing building. In the past two years, the operation of the business hadn't undergone many changes, but it was much busier due to the addition of another dozen heads to the herd. The farm produced more milk now, which she continued to sell to the local dairy pasteurizer, but she kept a significant quantity for herself. She had quadrupled the lotion and soap area of her business. Her "spa line" of products was the thing she cared most about, and within those products there was one lotion in particular she was very interested in at present.

Leela went to the scent experimentation table and pulled a small plastic jar labeled 'J5L2' from a line of ten. She unscrewed the lid and wafted the scent toward her as she sniffed. She bit her lip and made a small celebratory fist pump. It smelled just as good as it had the day before. And the week before that. She took a pen from the counter, crossed out the code, and in her nicest handwriting wrote its formal name.

"You look happy."

Leela spun around to face her friend, and now part-time employee, Jill. "This is it!" She shoved the jar of lotion under her nose. "What do you think?"

Jill shut her eyes and inhaled deeply. "Oh, that is lovely. What did you use?"

"Five parts jasmine, two parts lemongrass."

"Lemongrass! That's what that is. Is this part of the new fall line-up we're releasing this week? Because it seems kind of late to do that."

"One, we're still technically in summer, so it wouldn't be too late. Two, lemongrass is definitely a springtime scent. And three, this is only for Aurora. Think she'll like it?"

Jill tied her silver hair back into a bun. "She will love it. Does it have a name?"

She pointed to her fancy cursive writing. "Light of My Life."

Jill laughed until her faced turned pink.

"What? It's clever. Aurora is light and..." She sighed. "Shut up."

"I'm sorry; just work on the name a little more, please. What's the occasion?"

"Well, smart ass, there is no occasion. I just wanted to do something thoughtful in my own Leela way." She screwed the lid back on and placed it on the stainless-steel counter. "Aurora's working so hard lately, and I wanted to give her something that lets her relax and lets her know that I love her."

"I wish Viktor still did romantic gestures, but thirty years of marriage sometimes makes the spark fizzle," Jill said with a frown and a shrug. "When are you going to give Aurora her special present?"

"After I come up with a name that doesn't apparently suck, and after I do a really bang-up job on presenting it. So, to answer your question, I don't know."

The door to the building was flung open, and Keith, her second-in-command, practically jumped into the doorway.

"Morning, Jill," he said with a wave. "Leela, we got a situation at the east fence. Or, at least, what used to be the fence."

"Ah, shit." It appeared that her leisurely morning of smelling fragrances had ceased. She pulled the leather gloves from her back pocket and slapped them against her denim-clad thigh. "Guess it's time to do some real work."

#

"Here's to new contracts." Tonya, the CFO of EGG, handed Aurora a crystal flute of kombucha. "You are worth twice your salary and then some."

Aurora smiled and clicked her glass. "I can't believe they're going to fly us there. They're sending us to Hawaii! For free!"

"Correction. You and Leela are going to Hawaii for free."

Aurora nearly sprayed her drink on her boss. "What? You're not going?"

Tonya waved her hand like there was a gnat in the air. "Nah. I've been there before. Plus, I can't fly because of the blood clot in my leg. Flight risk, blah, blah, blah. But you and Leela should go together and have a good time."

"Me and Leela?"

Tonya laughed good-naturedly. "You heard the man on the phone. He wants us to see things from the point of view of his staff and visitors. I'm sure you'll find more new ways to improve their practices if you're actually there than if you only view pictures and reports at your desk."

She couldn't argue— hands-on exposure was the best way to understand a client —but the idea of a full vacation seemed unfeasible. "That's true, but I don't know if I can take Leela."

Tonya's ebony skin crinkled between her eyes as she narrowed them at Aurora. "I'm your boss. I'm giving you permission to take her. So, what do you mean you don't know if you *can* take her?"

"I know you're letting me but I don't know if she'll go. The longest she's been away from the farm since I've known her has been four days."

Tonya held up a manicured finger. "That's not true. There was that time she was gone for over a month."

"She was in a coma! That doesn't count as a vacation."

The car accident, which had incidentally precipitated Aurora and Leela meeting, had been the cause of Leela's longest stay away from work since she'd started running the farm immediately after college, thirteen years before.

Tonya pursed her lips and took a long sip. "For this argument, I think it does count. Why doesn't Leela want to go on vacation? It's not like you two don't have the time. You have unlimited paid time off, and she's the owner of the farm. And unless there's a situation I'm unaware of, it's not like you two don't have the money. Hell, she made Central Oregon's *40 Under 40*. She's practically a celebrity around here."

"And that's why getting her away from the farm is tough. Her success from the last few years has brought more responsibility. She has more acreage, goats, and employees. It's amazing really." She leaned back in her seat and took a long drink. Leela consistently worked twelve-hour days, and while she claimed to love it, Aurora worried if that effort was sustainable. "Having said all of that, I wish she trusted Keith more. He's certainly capable."

"Why do you wish that?"

"Because then we could go away for longer, and she would see. . . Never mind." She slumped back into her chair and took a drink.

"You don't get to weasel out now. What would Leela see?"

Tonya loved playing therapist, which would have been annoying if she hadn't been so good at it.

But Leela was incredibly sensitive, had issues with self-esteem, and a history of depression. That information was too personal for her boss to know. "I think Leela's afraid if we're together for a long stretch of time, I'll learn something new that will make me not love her, which is ridiculous, but it's impossible trying to convince her of that."

Tonya nodded with her fingers tented, as though she understood the full scope of the situation. "I guess that means she hasn't hinted at marriage or some other commitment ceremony?"

"We haven't talked about it since before my mom's operation. And Mom was *not* subtle when she asked."

Ani Okpik's checklist of items before she had gone into surgery had included asking both Leela and Aurora if they needed relationship advice in case she didn't make it out.

For a relatively routine procedure, the entire ordeal had been incredibly traumatic.

"If Leela had the same stable family history as me, we probably would get married, but Leela's terrified of becoming bitter and divorced like her parents. I understand that, because she's told me what it was like growing up in an environment like that. So. . . I mean we live together. We trust each other. We're basically married. But..."

"You want more," Tonya finished.

Aurora averted her gaze. She looked at the scuff on her shoe. The scratched wood on the floor. She looked everywhere but into Tonya's eyes.

Leela made her laugh, always gave her the last of everything, had hot water ready for her in the morning so she could make her tea. She was so caring and sensitive to her needs. Then there was Leela's physical beauty. Leela joked that with her petite frame and large eyes, she looked like an anime character, but Aurora thought she was anything but cartoonish. Leela was toned, bronzed perfection, with a face so expressive it gave Aurora no doubts as to how she felt.

Tonya was right. Aurora wanted Leela at her side for the rest of her life. "I do want more for us, and I used to think that I'd be okay with an arrangement like the one we have, but there's a part of me that wants that little extra."

"What do you mean by 'extra'?"

Aurora's gaze drifted to the clouds outside the window as she thought about how to best articulate her feelings. "I don't know, to be honest, because I've never experienced it. I just feel like there could be more. And I don't know how to tell Leela all of these commitment thoughts without scaring her or making her think that I don't respect her views. And," Aurora laughed, "I can't believe I'm talking to you about this."

Tonya grinned. "I think we crossed that bridge when we were both invited to Mya's sex toy party."

Aurora blew a breath out and nodded. She'd had no idea that her spin class friend was Tonya's cousin. Their professional relationship had shifted into friendship territory once they had ended up in Mya's living room, playing a game where they had to pass a dildo to their neighbor using only their knees.

The party had been a blast. And she'd bought the best harness ever for Leela.

"Please take my advice as someone who has been in your relationship shoes," Tonya said. "Don't make this trip an ultimatum. Rather, tell Leela how much you want to go away *with her*. To see a new place *with her*. Experience new things *with her*. And it wouldn't hurt to give her a symbol of your commitment either. Something that is private. That way, you both know how much you mean to each other, but other people won't make a big deal about it."

The post-meeting, celebratory kombucha had taken a deep turn. Everything Tonya had said was true. If Aurora wanted more, she had to vocalize it. She didn't want to fall back on old habits and just wish for things to happen. She had to take action. "I'll ask her about Hawaii over dinner and give you my answer in the morning."

"That's what I like to hear."

Aurora stood and smoothed out her skirt. "You wouldn't by any chance know of a jewelry store that's, you know. . . Leela-friendly."

Tonya grinned. "I'll text you the address."

#

Dozens of central Oregon's farmers and craftspeople left the fire station banquet hall in a mass exodus once the farmers' market meeting had come to a close.

Well, everyone except Leela and Jill.

Leela had remained motionless and quiet in her uncomfortable seat, breathing in stagnant air for several minutes after multiple people had put forth a nomination that she run for president of the market.

Jill had done just the opposite and had started acting as her PR manager, telling people she was shocked yet excited to receive the support of so many in the crowd.

"That was very unexpected," Leela said as she folded her metal chair.

Jill chuckled. "Then you've been re-experiencing head trauma. There have been whispers about someone nominating you to be president for over a year now. Or at least ever since you pushed city council to improve the traffic patterns and security. And found that band to play. That showed initiative and leadership."

"That showed I didn't like being hit by a truck and that I appreciate entertainment."

Jill directed an impatient gaze toward her.

"Okay, I'll consider it," Leela said. "God knows there could be more improvements to the schedule, the arrangement of vendors—" Jill's laughter caused her to cease reciting her growing list. "Okay, maybe I do have some ideas, but being the president would mean a lot more responsibility."

"True." Jill racked both her chair and Leela's. "You'd have to delegate more tasks around the farm, and your own stand at the farmers' mar— What am I talking about? I could do that!"

"What? Run my booth?"

"Yeah. Why not? It's not like I didn't run my own stand for years." Jill's daughter, Clarissa, had been progressively taking over the major roles of Jill's berry farm, including the stand at the farmers' market. "This way you can focus on bigger and better things."

Leela mulled the idea over. It was true she hadn't reached all of her business goals. There was still the dream of having her own pasteurization facility on-site and expanding her bath product line distribution to include all fifty states, Canada, Mexico, and India. Her cousin, Rashne, ran a hotel in Mumbai, and she knew if she pushed hard enough, he would cave and buy sample sizes for his two hundred rooms.

She'd have to come up with a clever way to justify all the shipping materials to Aurora.

"I'll see what Aurora thinks about it over dinner." Her eyes instantly popped open. "Dinner! Shit!" She scrambled to dig her phone out of her pocket. "I forgot to place our order." She went to her saved app and started to punch in her order.

Jill patted her on the shoulder and whispered, "You have a good night. I'll see you tomorrow."

While Jill walked away, Leela finished placing her order and headed toward her cherry red, extended cab pickup. She hoped stir fry with brown rice and tofu was light enough for Aurora, and that Aurora wouldn't be too jealous when she learned what she had ordered for herself. Maybe the talk of her running for president would distract Aurora from the smell of her eggroll. But probably not the General Tso.

As Leela drove home with the Chinese food nestled safely in her back seat, its fried and spicy-sweet aroma causing her stomach to grumble, her thoughts drifted to Aurora. What would Aurora think if she accepted the presidential nomination? It's not like Aurora would be directly affected too much, but their evening time together might change. Leela knew that would already be a strike in the minus column. However, Leela could make the argument that a little extra time now would save time and effort later. It was a time investment strategy.

Yeah, that's how she'd play it.

With the Chinese food under her arm, she opened the front door to their home. She expected to see Aurora with her hair braided, in her comfy nightclothes, reading from an e-book while she stretched on the sofa.

What she saw was Aurora still in her business suit, pouring a beer into a frosty pint glass.

Aurora looked up as she put the empty bottle down on the dining table. "Hi, dreamy."

This was leagues beyond their typical evening. Aurora had bought her beer, which she only ever did on the rarest of rare occasions. That was cause for alarm already, but it was Aurora's pose of her hands clasped behind her back, combined with her innocent smile, that set off the waving red flags and blaring sirens. "What happened?"

"Just a little something at wo—" Aurora sniffed the air. "You got General Tso tofu. And an egg roll! That's your stress food! Why are you stressed?"

"I'm not stressed! But you're up to something."

"Why would you say that?"

"Nickname, beer, work outfit." Leela counted them off on her fingers. "You are so up to something."

Aurora hustled over to her with a mischievous smile, gave her a kiss, and took the bag. "Okay, there might be something. But I promise it's great news!"

"I got that from the voicemail, but it still left a lot to the imagination."

"Well, I didn't want to ruin the surprise." Aurora beamed. "But I think you should tell me your thing first. The good news will balance the bad."

"Uh-uh. You first. Besides, my news isn't so much bad as it is…surprising and complicated."

Leela saw the perplexed look on Aurora's face and knew she had to spill it so they could at least get the conversation out of the way to enjoy Aurora's resort triumph. Leela began to divvy out the contents of their takeout. "Someone nominated me to run for president of the farmers' market."

Aurora's glass of iced tea stopped at her lips. "Really?" she asked with a smile.

"Right? I'm still in shock."

Aurora chuckled. "You shouldn't be. Your ideas have made that place so much better." She rounded the table to kiss and hug Leela. "I'm so proud of you. Are you going to accept it?"

Leela winced and took a seat at the table along with Aurora. "I don't know. There are tons of changes I'd like to see happen, but it would change our schedule. Our time together. You wouldn't see me as much in the evenings, at least initially, because that's when all the committees get together. But gradually," she shook her head while she spooned nearly the entire container of fried rice onto her plate, "the changes I'd like to make would make the market more efficient. After that has happened, you would see me more. Jill even offered to take over my booth."

A sour expression crossed Aurora's face.

"Are you mad? You seemed on board. . . I think."

"Huh? No, I'm not mad. But they did give me way too much broccoli and not enough mushrooms." She separated the offending vegetable from the rest of her food.

Leela waited for Aurora to comment further, but Aurora was too focused on de-greening her healthy plate. "So, what do you think?"

Aurora picked up a perfectly cubed piece of tofu with her chopsticks. "I think..." She chewed with her eyes raised to the ceiling while her head bobbed. "I think that if you accept the nomination, you should have a plan in place for what tasks you should delegate or you'll drive yourself insane. I'm glad Jill has volunteered to do the booth. That's huge. But I also think you need to delegate more tasks to Keith. He can do it. You just need to relinquish some control."

"But I hate that."

"I know, but that change will benefit you even if you aren't president. We could have more dates, and this opens the door for any possible trips we go on. You know...hypothetically." Aurora chewed with a smile.

Leela could feel her brow raise, as though it had a mind of its own. She needed to respond quickly but didn't have the words. To stall, she sipped her beer. "Oh, that's nice." She turned the bottle so the label faced her. The artwork was spot on. Tropical flowers, green mountains, and someone canoeing in crystal blue water. She needed that kind of marketing pop for her products. "I see your point," Leela said. "I'll start looking at what extra responsibilities

Keith can take on. If I do that, are you fine if I accept and potentially become President Bakshi?"

"If Keith agrees to take on more responsibility, absolutely I do. I'll even help you make campaign buttons because I totally support your success."

"Great!" Leela mumbled around her egg roll. That had been much less painful than she had anticipated. "Now, tell me about how you wowed these hotel people."

"Well, they simply loved the proposal we submitted and, based on our conversation, they want an even closer analysis." Aurora leveled her gaze to Leela. "So, I have to go to Hawaii, and Tonya wants you to come with me."

"Tonya wants me to go to Hawaii with you?" Leela asked around a mouthful of spicy, crisp tofu.

Aurora smiled. "She figures since they'll fly two people out, it might as well be you."

"And the resort is fine with this?" Leela asked, pleasantly surprised.

"Yes. They actually see it as a positive because then I'll feel more like a guest, and they'll get a more accurate analysis. So, this would be a working vacation for me. But while I do my thing, you could enjoy some Leela time, and then we could have time in paradise together. We've *never* been on a vacation like this together, and I think it would be really great for both of us to get away."

The wheels started turning in Leela's head about the work she could do while not working. She crunched on her eggroll thoughtfully. "When is the Hawaiian getaway?"

Aurora winced. "A week."

"A week! That's impossible! How am I going to get organized in that amount of time?"

"The same way I am: triage and delegation. Keith knows this farm and its operations better than you think he does."

Leela pursed her lips and looked at the tropical paradise depicted on the bottle. "He did run the farm like a boss when I became unexpectedly absent."

"See!" Aurora put her chopsticks down and reached for Leela's hand. "I love that you love your job and you're so successful at it. I really do. But I think it would do you good to step away from the farm a little bit. Who knows, maybe a vacation will relax your mind enough to come up with your next great business idea."

Keith had experience running the farm. A relaxed mind was a productive mind. Her parents never once did anything like that for each other. And Aurora looked so damn excited. "Just let me know if I need to pack anything special."

Aurora made a happy yelp, launched herself out of her chair, and into Leela's arms.

#

Aurora drove into work already feeling like she had put in her usual nine- or ten-hour day. After dinner, the conversation and planning for Hawaii had gone on for hours. Well past the time she and Leela usually went to bed.

Aurora had to resort to the unthinkable before she went to discuss the trip with Tonya. She ignored the tea bags in the breakroom, poured herself a coffee, and then doctored it with sugar and flavored creamer until her beverage was somewhat palatable.

"How'd it go last night?" Tonya sat behind her antique desk with a cocky grin and her arms spread. Her mouth quickly downturned and she pointed to Aurora's novelty mug. "Is that coffee?"

Aurora took a seat across from her and held up her cup in a cheers gesture. "It is, and it probably has enough flavored creamer to negate the healthy dinner I had."

"Sounds like a rough night. Were you able to convince her?"

"I was. She's using the opportunity to relax with me and then she'll market her brand while I'm doing my work."

"That's fantastic! I'll get your travel cleared and email you all of the information. Once you're there, you do your Aurora thing that makes the world a better place and makes EGG money. And," she drawled, "once you get back, there's another project you're going to lead."

"Hopefully, it's more local."

"Not so much. You're going on an East Coast tour to check out vendors for our new stores in New York and DC, and a few other consulting stops."

Aurora leaned forward in her chair, even though the sound of the new assignment added weight in her gut. "How long will this tour take?"

"I don't have everything etched in stone yet, but you'll be gone probably around ten days. However, you have a stop in Baltimore, so we can work in some time for you to see your friend, Stacy."

"I'll be gone for over two weeks straight?" So much for trying to go back to her healthy habits and spending more quality time with Leela.

"You'll have a down week or two in between your assignments. I realize you need time to determine your visitation strategy and tie up any loose ends."

"That's still *a lot* of time away from home." No more than twenty-four hours before, she'd asked Leela to rearrange her life to accommodate Hawaii. And she had told Leela she'd help her with the campaign. "I'm going to need to talk to Leela about this."

Tonya leaned forward on her desk and clasped her hands together. "Aurora, I'm going to level with you, if you come through on this like I think you will, I can see the board talking about making you Director of Finance and Sustainability. That would add twenty percent to your salary."

This was the promotion she had sensed, but news of the salary increase had her mouth gaping like a fish. "Twenty percent?"

Tonya nodded. "Who knows, maybe *you'll* be in next year's edition of *40 Under 40?*"

As someone who'd had to rely on scholarships, lived at home during college, and tutored when she'd graduated to save more money, Aurora was flabbergasted by the idea of making that much. "I...ah. . . Wow. That would be something else."

"Yes, it would." Tonya laughed heartily. "Now, I expect that you want to finish a few things before you leave next week. Reschedule some meetings."

"Yes. I should do that ASAP." Aurora stood, still shaky from her salary prospect.

"Oh! But before you leave town, don't forget to check out that jewelry store. Even a woman as rough and tumble as Leela would like a romantic present on a beach. She does have a girlie side."

That did describe Leela in a nutshell. "I promise to go when I leave today."

Aurora left Tonya's office and walked past several others before she entered the open-concept cubicles and settled back to her standing desk. She could have one of those offices someday. And someday soon by the sound of it. A large smile grew when she imagined reading *Aurora Okpik* stenciled on a door.

But that was the future, and now she had to focus on the present. She picked up her phone and called Leela.

"Sweets? What's going on?"

"So, there's no good way to say this, but after we get back from Hawaii, they want me to go on a trip to the East Coast."

"Seriously? Do you have a say in it?"

"I didn't say too much. I kind of got distracted with the prospect of a promotion title and raise percentage thrown at me."

"Those are two very shiny things." Leela paused. "I guess I can't use the 'we promised to spend more time quality time together' rebuttal when we will have just spent an entire week together in Hawaii."

"I was thinking more along the lines of how I promised to help you make buttons."

"I'm sure I can recruit someone to help me with that while you're gone, especially if this could mean a path forward that you want for yourself. So, I give my blessing, but when you get back, it's button city."

"Thank you for understanding. I promise to show my appreciation before and after my arrival," she said with a grin.

"I'm going to hold you to that. Thanks for letting me know, but I gotta go. I love you, sweets."

"I love you too."

Aurora hung up and opened her calendar. She began a series of communications to reschedule different vendor site visits and her weekly check-in with accounting. On a more personal note, she also had to reschedule her women's health exam. All of her commitments had to move for this opportunity.

By the time she buttoned up her obligations, it was essentially quitting time. That was another perk of her job. Not only did she love the mission, but she loved the flexibility. While there were weeks she sometimes worked as many hours as Leela, on a day like this, she could leave early, and that meant she had plenty of time to browse for jewelry before her spin class and then head home.

She found the store between a cluster of other antique shops in their quaint downtown. The thriving local economy, integrated greenery, and bicycle-friendly nature were one of the first draws Aurora had had to the city. Well, that and Leela.

It always came back to Leela.

The chime rang as she pushed open the chic glass door, and she was quickly confronted with an odor that reminded her of her father's workshop. A combination of wood shavings, oil, and a faint musky scent whirled around her as she began to peruse the items underneath the display glass, which stretched across the perimeter. No other customers or staff milled about, and the sound of a singer-songwriter with an acoustic guitar filled the room. She didn't recognize the song, but the melody was soothing and didn't distract her from appreciating the nuances of all the jewelry she viewed. She had her gaze on a wooden ring with malachite inlay when she heard steps approach.

"Hello, and welcome to my shop," a man with a bushy, strawberry-blond beard said as he came from behind a curtain of wooden beads. "I'm Joseph. Are you looking for something specific or would you prefer to browse in peace?"

Aurora immediately liked his friendly, no-pressure approach. "Actually, I'm looking for something very specific, and my boss, Tonya, thought you might have something."

He brought his calloused hands together. "Ah, you must be Aurora. Tonya said I should expect you sometime this week. What can I help you find?"

Aurora had rehearsed the meaning, but she still had no idea what kind of jewelry she wanted. "I want to give my girlfriend— no, she's more than that. I want to give my part—" She grumbled under her breath. "I love this woman who I've been with for three years, but rings and marriage talk freak her out. So, I want to give her a symbol that says, 'I love you, I'm not going anywhere, and I want to be with you forever, but we don't have to make a big public spectacle of it because I know you'd be uncomfortable'."

"That's a lot of words to engrave."

She scrunched her face in confusion. "What?"

He slapped his brown corduroy thigh and laughed. "I'm just joshing you. I think I have a few pieces— Oh!" He held up his finger, and his furry brows arched above the rims of his wire-framed glasses. "Would a necklace set be of interest to you?"

Aurora shrugged. She'd had no idea what she wanted before she walked into his store but she hadn't thought of a necklace. "I'll take a look, but it can't be too long or too short."

He waved her over to the opposite side of the store and went behind the counter. He pulled out the display and rested it on the surface.

Once she came closer, she saw the pendant of a necklace. The outline was the curvaceous form of a woman, her arms out-stretched over her head and her hands touching. The piece was carved from a dark wood but had occasional specks of red metallic luster. Especially in the concave region of the woman's figure.

Aurora placed the pad of her finger in the indentation. "What goes there?"

"That would be this." Joseph held out the companion pendant to a second necklace and allowed Aurora to view it from all angles. It was circular piece of the same wooden and metal materials but had a flat front and curved back. The red metal formed spirals on either side but went in opposite directions. "This is the heart of the woman."

Subconsciously, Aurora's hand began to gravitate toward the smaller piece. But then she retracted.

"Go ahead," Joseph encouraged.

Aurora held the piece and tested the weight. It was surprisingly heavy. "What is this made of?"

"I believe the wood is teak. I don't know what the metal is. No one I've asked knows either."

"Interesting," she said absently and placed the 'heart' into the woman's chest. It wasn't a perfect fit, but it came close. "Do you know what the spiral means?"

"I think it can mean anything you want it to. I like to think of it as never-ending love."

She could get behind that metaphor. The necklaces were unique, meaningful, and would drive home the point she needed Leela to understand. "How much?"

"Not that I don't appreciate your enthusiasm, but are you sure there isn't anything else in the store you'd like to see?"

"Nope. It's perfect."

She left the store four hundred dollars poorer but with a million-watt smile and her heart full. Now she had to think of the best moment to give Leela her gift and share with her that she was her heart.

Leela was her everything.

CHAPTER TWO

THE MINUTES TICKED by on the office clock as Leela quizzed Keith on emergency farm scenarios. She should have left the office already, but this was the last item Keith had to master. She knew he could do it! He simply had to focus and weed through the dozens of pieces of new information he'd received over the past week.

"I bet you're just overthinking it." She watched his expression shift from frustration to confidence and then back to confusion.

Keith rubbed the back of his modestly sunburned neck. "I'm not trying to complicate things. It's just that this calendar doesn't explain what happens if we need to change the order. There's no contact information anywhere."

It was times like this she knew that being with Aurora had made her a more patient individual. Three years ago, she would have literally beaten her head against a wall for dramatic effect. Now, Leela turned to the pygmy goat calendar on the wall behind her and gestured to it patiently. "This is the basic schedule for the part-timers to look at if they're trying to anticipate their hours for the upcoming weeks. You can see that next week, our monthly lye shipment is coming in, which means that Mike will request every single possible shift because of the massive crush he has on the driver."

"Oh," Keith drawled. "That's going to make Rosa sad. She really likes Mike."

Leela had to give it to Keith: he knew the employees well. "If you need more detailed information, then you need to go to the calendar on the computer, and double click on it." She demonstrated the process and pointed to the information on the monitor. "Phone number, email, and other kind of company information is there. If by some chance you need to alter an order, email them first, and if you don't hear back in twenty-four hours then call them."

He crossed his burly forearms and squinted. "Why are their birthdays listed?"

Leela smiled impishly. "I like to send people presents. It's nice and it helps grease the wheels if I ever screw up something or need a favor."

"Any birthdays while you're gone?"

"No. Any other questions before I go?"

"No questions." He nodded confidently. "I got it!"

"Great! One more thing, do you mind keeping an eye on the house renovation? I won't be here to give the crew stern looks when they are running behind schedule and taking a two-hour break."

"I might delegate that task to Jill. She has a look about her when she's mad that I never want directed at me." He shivered from the thought. "How's everything on the Hawaii end? Did the product samples make it to the hotel?"

"Yes! Finally!" She'd decided to mail a box of her lotion and soap samples to the resort rather than risk them being lost or stolen in baggage claim. "I have a list of stores I'm planning to hit up while we're there."

Keith bit his bottom lip and shuffled his steps. "I know this is a working vacation for Aurora, and I know this is a good opportunity to spread the Bakshi brand, but for the love of Jesus, please emphasize the *vacation* part of your trip. Let this be a romantic getaway. You made that specially for her." He gestured to a jar of lotion on the corner of her desk. "Make the whole experience once-in-a-lifetime. It's not like you've been to or will go to Hawaii again."

Leela actually had been to Hawaii before. When she was eleven, her father had attended a medical conference and had brought her along while her mother stayed behind because of an emergency surgery she had to perform. All Leela remembered from the trip was looking at the ocean from her hotel room as she read about the island's geology.

Her father had said it would be a fun book. He had been wrong.

She stood from the desk. "You're right, vacation comes first, even if it's hard to let work go. I know you'll have everything under control, but if something comes up—"

"I'll call the hotel. Turn your phone off." He pointed to the direction of her home and gave her a smug smile. "Now, go pack. I have a farm to run."

"Yes, sir." She grabbed the jar of lotion and left.

A cool breeze ruffled her hair as she followed the naturally worn dirt path that led home. There was one more thing to check off her list before she walked onto the porch and through the front door. She veered into the taller grass until she came upon the wood-railed fence that penned in her herd. She rested her arms on the top, a foot on the bottom, and watched them graze and meander. Keith was awesome, but her goats were her best employees. They were never late, talking back was unheard of, and they didn't ask for raises.

A doe picked her head up, looked squarely at Leela, and bleated.

Leela grinned. "I'll miss you too."

"But I'm coming with you," Aurora said softly from behind her, then brushed Leela's hair to the side. She kissed the spot under her ear, which made Leela's skin form goosebumps instantly.

Leela leaned back, feeling Aurora's warmth, and smiled. "Were you spying on me from the window again?"

"Can't help it. A cute girl watching goats is much more entertaining than watching the construction crew clean up their stuff for the day." Aurora's arms wrapped around her waist. "Did you have a good meeting with Keith?"

"Yeah, I think he'll be fine. It's me I'm worried about."

"Why are you worried?"

Leela stayed facing the herd. Talking about her feelings when she didn't have to look someone in the eye was always easier. It was one of the reasons she hated seeing a therapist; they liked eye contact. "I'm worried I won't be able to stop thinking about work. I love my job but I do want to be able to flip a switch so it isn't my entire life. I don't want to be my parents where everything was work, work, work all the time."

Aurora made a deep *mmm* that vibrated down Leela's spine. "I know you worry, but you're not them. I think the fact that you were willing to make so many last-minute changes so you could come with me says that you're not all about work. And I think that giving away samples at stores while I'm looking at water usage patterns and solar angles is a smart way of using your time. Instead of work, work, work, it's work, fun, romance."

"I think I can handle work, fun, romance." Leela turned to Aurora and saw the red-orange glow of the sun setting behind her. Two of the most stunning sights in the world combined into one. She rose on her tiptoes and kissed Aurora softly before taking her hand and leading her to the house. "Come on, I need you to stop me from packing jeans and flannel."

#

The company had sent a driver to pick Aurora and Leela up before the sun had greeted them for the day. After a three-hour drive through the dusty Oregon high desert and five and a half hours in the sky as they traveled to their destination, the end of the journey was almost in sight.

As Aurora read a novel on her e-reader, she was pleasantly surprised by Leela's relaxed attitude. She thought for sure she would have mumbled something about Keith or used the plane's WiFi to check the farm's web traffic statistics, but she seemed content looking out the window, listening to music, or watching a movie. Even if that movie was a tear-jerker about the journey of a child soldier in Sudan.

Leela took her earbuds out and wiped her eyes. "My childhood wasn't great, but at least it wasn't like that."

Aurora patted her thigh.

Leela's parents were the definition of high-achieving, high-pressure parents. To think they had mellowed considerably in the time Aurora had known them spoke greatly to the experience Leela had had growing up. Conversely, Aurora's parents were the definition of chill and had raised her to prioritize community and nature before herself. Someday the four would meet. Aurora didn't know whether to fear that time or to make sure she had plenty of popcorn available to watch the show.

The pilot came on the speaker and announced they were starting their descent.

"I guess that leaves out time for another movie," Leela said.

"But it does give us time to talk about the week. We haven't really done that."

"What do you mean?"

"Well, we won't be at the resort the entire time. We're allowed to go off and do our own thing. What would you like to do? Other than visit the stores that I already know you want to visit."

"I started to think about it, but then I got distracted. What do *you* want to do?"

"Helicopter tour."

"What?" Leela's eyes nearly bulged out of her head. "You want to give control of your life to an aerospace hummingbird?"

Aurora chuckled. "We can watch the volcano spurt lava…from the sky! It'll be cool."

"If you're making me do that, then I'm dragging you to the spa."

For anyone else that would sound like luxury, but for Aurora, the idea of a stranger touching her body gave her the creeps. "I'll agree to a facial. You'll have to be the one out of the two of us who has the whole-body treatment."

"You drive such a hard bargain," Leela said dryly. "Maybe one day I'll get a mani-pedi and the next day a massage? No. Wait. I should probably get a massage first. That'll help loosen me up for any sort of outdoor adventure we may have."

Aurora took Leela's hand before she pressed her lips to the back of it. "And what kind of outdoor adventures are you thinking about? Because if one of those things is skinny dipping…"

Leela inhaled sharply with a large smile. "For real? We haven't done that since…the only time we ever did that!"

Aurora still couldn't believe she had been the one who had initiated that excursion in her landlord's pool. She and Leela had been together a few months, the couple who owned the house Aurora rented from were gone, and Leela refused to do her physical therapy because she wanted to cuddle. Ergo: aquatic-based exercises.

Once the topic of activities, especially naked ones, had been broached, Leela unleashed a torrent of ideas. For the first time, Aurora felt like she might be the one who needed to back off work. But, then again, she was on a work trip.

"And at some point, I'd like to have a beer on the beach and look at the ocean, like one of those commercials," Leela said as the seatbelt sign turned off with a *ding*.

They patiently waited for everyone in front of them to exit before they grabbed their carry-on luggage, went down the steps, and walked across the runway's sunny tarmac to the official arrival area.

Aurora barely had time to enjoy the tropical breeze that tickled her skin and the island music that soothed her ears before she spied a broad-shouldered Hawaiian man in a suit holding a sign bearing her name. She waved, then adjusted her laptop bag while she approached him, rolling her carry-on luggage with her. "Hello, I'm Aurora Okpik."

He smiled warmly. "Wonderful to meet you in person. I'm Mac and your personal driver. And Ms. Bakshi, I presume?"

"Call me Leela."

"Well, Leela, I'm your ride for the duration of your stay as well. If there's anywhere you'd like to go while Ms. Okpik is at the hotel, I can take you."

She and Leela looked at each other with shared surprise.

Aurora wondered what other perks awaited them during their stay. "That's very kind of you."

"We know that the request for you both to come out here so quickly probably complicated your lives a bit. My employers are very appreciative of that and want to show their gratitude." He gave a small bow in thanks. "Let's not waste any more time. Do you have extra luggage with you?"

Leela raised her hand. "I checked a bag."

"I can retrieve it if you two want to use the restroom. What's your bag look like?"

"Dark orange and has the Bakshi Farm logo in white. Can't miss it."

Mac nodded his acknowledgement and walked in the direction of the baggage claim while they headed for the restrooms.

"Is that the only reason you checked a bag?" Aurora asked. "So that your logo could go round and round for all to see?"

"Partially. I also didn't want TSA to go through my stuff in front of curious on-lookers. Some things aren't meant for prying eyes." Leela grinned deviously at Aurora.

A thrill of excitement ran up Aurora's spine and caused a tingling in her limbs. "I really hope you're not referring to farm paperwork you want to work on."

"Definitely not." Leela held the door open for her. "But I promise I will share my secrets with you before the end of the trip."

"Interesting. I may have one to share with you as well."

Once they were done, they followed Mac through the throngs of tourists in flip-flops, colorful leis, and sunglasses to a VIP parking area, where he led them to a bright blue convertible among the other luxury cars.

"Is that our ride?" Leela asked, awestruck. "It's so pretty."

Mac flashed his perfect teeth in a broad smile. "It is."

Aurora watched amused as Leela admired the sports car from all angles. "That's a lot different than your truck."

Leela nodded with her mouth still open then hopped into the back seat via jumping over the closed door. Upon seeing Aurora's arched eyebrow, she grinned and shrugged. "I had to see if I'd be able to do it."

"I'm glad you could, because breaking your leg again wouldn't be the best way to start our vacation." Aurora joined her in the back seat and buckled her seatbelt. "We're ready when you are, Mac."

As they drove from the airport, Aurora was surprised to learn that the island wasn't overgrown with lush greens and colorful flowers. It was barren. Aside from the black rock, it reminded her of where they just were in Oregon. "I thought there'd be more palm trees."

"Remember, Ms. Helicopter Ride, that this island is an active volcano. Half of it is burned to a crisp, the other half is the green because it's on the windward side and it's had time to grow."

"You know your stuff," Mac said while he looked at them in the rearview mirror.

"I read a book once," Leela said casually.

He stifled a quick laugh. "Do you remember from your book that the big island has snow?"

"Seriously? Where?" Aurora asked.

"Mauna Kea," Leela answered. "Oh, we should do that! They have a huge observatory up there. Can you take us there, Mac?"

"Oh," Aurora drawled suspiciously, "that's sacred land where they're building that massive telescope."

"Yes," Mac answered. "So, you're aware of the controversy?"

Aurora nodded with tight lips. She may not be current with all science but she followed the news of Indigenous people.

Leela glanced at her with sad eyes. "Does that mean we can't go?"

Aurora could tell her disappointment was genuine. It wasn't a ploy to guilt her into compromising her values. "Well, we wouldn't be using the massive telescopes, right? Those are for the astronomers?" Aurora asked Mac.

"Right."

"Then, I think we should go. Maybe I can make offhand comments while we're there about how it's possible to appreciate nature *and* not destroy native beliefs."

"Nice twist," Mac said. "I can arrange a trip but not in this car. The terrain to get up there is very rough and, as you can imagine, it gets pretty cold at night at that altitude. Not really convertible appropriate."

"I'd really appreciate it if you could book that for us." Aurora saw the twinkle of childlike enthusiasm in Leela's eyes. She leaned over and whispered, "I want you to see everything."

The scorched earth progressively became greener until Aurora could have sworn she had been dropped into the middle of a jungle. A gorge made of every color green she'd ever imagined bordered one side of the road, and a great waterfall was in the distance, the pool of water at its base out of view. She pointed to the botanical garden sign they passed it and received an excited thumbs up from Leela in return. That was another item they could add to their itinerary.

A few minutes later they stopped in front of a stone path that curved into the dense landscape and then disappeared. There was no building in sight.

"Are we here?" Aurora asked over the chirping of a Saffron Finch.

"We are," Mac answered and popped the trunk. "Welcome to the Milohila Resort."

#

Leela's hammock swayed in the airy and tropical lobby as she sipped chilled, cucumber-infused water while Aurora talked shop with the resort manager at the more contemporary-looking check-in desk. Aurora hadn't been gone long, but it was just long enough to allow Leela's mind to start to wander. She hoped they would be able to go to Mauna Kea and have a day at the spa, but it was too perfect.

Leela shook her head. She did it again. The slowly whirling ceiling fans had hypnotized her into dark thoughts. Her therapist told her she made a habit of sabotaging herself. Whenever she felt truly happy, she would come up with reasons not to be, because deep down she didn't feel like she deserved it.

Sometimes her brain really pissed her off.

She needed to remind herself that everyone, including her, deserved to be loved, happy, and free.

Mac emerged from behind a large potted plant with leaves the size of a small child. "Hey, Leela." He held a cardboard box with a sticker of the Bakshi Farm logo on it. "Aurora asked that I bring this out for you."

"Sweet!" She clumsily pushed herself out of the hammock then took the box.

"There must be something very special in there."

He was wrong. The *very* special lotion had been packed in her luggage along with a toy she called Biddie. "These are samples of my products. While Aurora is off doing her thing, I'd like to go out to some stores and drop them off. I've already contacted a few retailers, and from what you said in the car driving over, you might be able to help me expand my targets."

"Absolutely." He reached inside his tailored jacket and pulled out a business card. "My business cell is on that. Text me when you want to go, but I would appreciate an hour heads-up. Although, you should be able to narrow down the times we can go based on your schedule. It's nothing too hectic, I promise. I just got a glimpse, and it follows a nine to five. In the mornings, Aurora will look at the employee behind-the-scenes and after lunch are from the perspective of a guest. I'll probably be getting those texts from you in the morning so you two can enjoy the afternoons and evenings."

This was an excellent plan. Whoever had made it would definitely receive a preview of her autumn blend lotion. "That's a yes regarding the morning texts. Does the schedule start today?"

"Tomorrow. We know how exhausting a day of travel is. Oh, looks like she's finished checking in." Mac pointed behind Leela.

Leela turned and saw Aurora saunter toward her in her summer dress with an extra sway to her hips. That was her sexy, confident walk. Leela loved that walk.

Aurora handed Leela a small envelope. "Here's your key copy, and I know what you're thinking—I'm going to get them off the plastic key cards and use wood fiber instead."

It wasn't the plastic that Leela found interesting. It was the two palm trees curved toward each other that formed the shape of a heart. "Um, are they putting us in a honeymoon suite?"

Aurora nodded with a sexy smirk. "And that's not all."

They walked behind Mac as he carried their luggage to the suite and pointed out the different buildings along the way: the gym, the restaurant, the open-air games room, and the spa. Aurora shared she had already booked time in the spa for their last day, but if Leela wanted more time there, she could go whenever she liked.

The guest rooms weren't found in a typical high-rise style, but rather spread across the campus as a series of two- and three-story buildings. As they passed, Aurora commented on the lack of a rain capture and solar panels.

While Aurora concerned herself with infrastructure, Leela looked down the grated metal bridge they walked over to see gigantic orange and white koi swim underneath lily pads of pastel pinks, oranges, purples, and blues. Once they stepped off the bridge, the gray stone path gradually transitioned into a dull red. When Aurora questioned it, Mac said that the cement had hematite sprinkled into it, which compelled Leela to explain the magnetic properties of the iron-based rock. She berated herself for her nerdy tendencies, but Aurora responded by giving her a wink. Leela never thought that reciting facts from a book she'd read when she was a kid would make her feel like such a stud.

They turned another corner and went through trees that formed a canopy over them.

"Holy shit," Leela exclaimed when she saw the outside of their suite, marked by a wooden sign with a palm tree heart that read, *Milo Hana*. The yurt-style suite used bamboo weaved onto the exterior to give the canvas shelter additional protection, strength, and design appeal.

"Wait until you see the inside," Aurora whispered and then turned to Mac. "Thank you very much for bringing our bags, but I think we got it from here."

"I hope you enjoy your stay, and Leela, don't be afraid to text me tomorrow." He pointed behind a bush with peach-colored flowers. "Right behind the hibiscus is your private saltwater hot tub. There are little solar lights lining the path in case you want to use it at night."

"Yeah, I'll be sure to let you know about the…um…car." Leela still reeled over the fact that there was a saltwater hot tub. Normally, she viewed hot tubs as massive petri dishes, but saltwater would kill most bacterial nasties that dared to live in there.

They could skinny dip in a hot tub. Score!

"Thank you very much, Mac," Aurora said. "We appreciate everything and we'll see you later."

Leela turned so Mac didn't see her trying to suppress her laughter. Aurora's words were kind, but she knew that tone and look. What Aurora really meant was *thank you, but go away now.* And based on the sexy signals she had received from Aurora ever since the lobby, the reason he needed to leave was because she was about to get lucky. And she actually had the energy to follow through!

Vacation was awesome!

Once Mac made his way back to the main path, Aurora waved her key card in front of the lock, opened the door, and pulled Leela inside where paradise continued. The interior walls continued the bamboo lattice design and were adorned with different watercolor paintings of Hawaiian life: a surfer, a fleet of people in a long canoe, and a waterfall. But the most impressive feature was the bed. A pure white comforter and pillows of different shapes and sizes covered a king-sized mattress with red petals sprinkled on top. The wind from the ceiling fan made them dance in place.

Leela adored watching Aurora take in their accommodations. "I think the last time I saw you smile this big was when Logan told you he was going to be a big brother."

Last fall, when they'd visited Aurora's family in Michigan, Aurora's brother, River, had allowed his oldest son, Logan, to make the announcement the family was expecting another child. It was the first time Leela had witnessed relatives learning for the first time about a new baby coming into the fold. It had been emotionally overwhelming, and no one had asked medical questions.

Aurora's family was so different to Leela's.

"I was pretty excited once Wade was actually born too." Aurora continued to look around the spacious interior and then ran to the door to toss their bags inside the room. She kicked off her flip-flops and grinned mischievously. "I don't know about you," she said and slowly approached Leela until her arms were looped around her neck, "but I'm exhausted from all of that travel, and I could really lay down for a while. Want to join me?"

"That sounds relaxing." Leela held Aurora more tightly and spun her onto the bed in a fit of giggles. "Very restorative." Leela picked a petal out from Aurora's hair.

Aurora brought her hand to gently cup Leela's face. "I love you."

Three words she would never tire of hearing. "I love you too." She looked deeply into Aurora's brown eyes and saw a hint of fatigue. "Did you actually want to rest?"

Aurora gave her a sexy smirk. "What do you think?"

"Oh good. We're on the same page then." Leela bent her head and grazed her lips against Aurora's. She didn't do this to tease her, Leela simply loved that she could feel Aurora smile while she kissed her with the lightest of touches. The perfect combination of joy and romance.

Just what she had hoped their vacation would bring them.

#

After an afternoon and evening of lovemaking, walking on the beach, and room service, a rare sight greeted Aurora the next morning: Leela.

Bright morning rays of sun came in through the windows and illuminated Leela's sleeping face and leg that snuck out from the covers. Her hair was mussed, and a group of strands covered the faint scar that ran along her temple. The surgical scar on Leela's thigh was more pronounced; it still gave Leela annoying twinges and pains every once in a while.

Aurora made a point to always kiss them when there was an ache.

She grinned as she reminisced about the first time she gave the scar on Leela's thigh that kind of attention.

"You're already up to something," Leela said with her eyes still closed.

"How do you know that?"

"Because I was watching you sleep, and then you started to wake up, so I pretended to be asleep to see what you'd do." Leela opened her eyes. "And the answer is nothing. You didn't even scamper out of bed to pee, and I was really hoping to see your ass again. It's a disappointing way to start the day."

"I'm very, very sorry I robbed you of your early morning entertainment." Aurora propped herself up on her elbow and looked down at Leela's smirk. She felt the sheet slide off her skin and the breeze of the ceiling fan against her bare breasts. "If you must know, I was thinking loving, sexy thoughts."

"About last night? If you were, you'll have to specify which time."

Aurora leaned down further and kissed her. The first time they'd made love had been fueled from the excitement of being in paradise, the second time had been prompted by stargazing in the hot tub, and the third time had been Aurora thanking Leela for suggesting they try sex in the hot tub.

Aurora tucked Leela's errant strands behind her ear. "Actually, I was thinking of the first time I ever kissed your scar." Aurora traced her fingertip up and down the shiny, pinkish-brown line on the outside of Leela's thigh.

"That's also known as the first time we went back to my place after my physical therapy, and the first time we ever got *down*," Leela drawled. "It took some confident ovaries on your behalf to do that move."

"It wasn't like I came up with the idea on my own. You literally raised your running shorts, pouted, and ask me to make it better. *That* took confident ovaries."

Leela sighed dreamily. "But you still followed through, which amazed me. But, then again, you're amazing, so it makes sense."

Aurora was drawn to Leela's lips again. "I can't get enough of *your* amazing self," Aurora said as she felt all of Leela's warmth beneath her and then heard her cell phone alarm of classic rock go off.

"Why is Led Zeppelin calling already? It's too early for your day in the 'office'."

"I thought I'd hit the gym before I start. This is actually the perfect place to maintain healthy habits. Between the gym, the outdoor activities, the vegan restaurant…"

"But we're not vegan."

"We already eat vegetarian, so it's not much of a stretch. And how did you not notice when we ordered room service last night?"

"All I wanted was French fries. I wasn't after cheese."

That was true. Leela hadn't ever bothered to glance at the menu. She insisted she was on vacation and could eat whatever she wanted. However, if her vacation diet only consisted of cheese and French fries, there may be problems later. "Feel free to go out for breakfast and get the cheesiest cheese thing you can find before you meet your first retailer. But I am detoxifying." Aurora punctuated her statement by kissing Leela and getting out of bed. She headed to her suitcase to gather her workout clothes and knew Leela's gaze was on her every move. And on her ass. "When we have lunch here, I think you'll be amazed at the quality. Dare I say, I think you'll even want to stay for dinner."

"But we don't have to, right?"

"Right. After five p.m. it's completely up to us. We can go wherever we want and do whatever we want." Aurora placed another tantalizing kiss on her lips. "So, do you want to be my gym?" Aurora waggled her brow.

"Can I have the morning to recover?" Leela asked. "I feel like this is a marathon, not a sprint, and I need to rehydrate. I lost a lot of fluids last night."

Aurora smiled. "You're not wrong. So, you don't mind if I get in some miles on the bike?"

"Nope. I can make my own fun while I properly hydrate for round four."

"*Mmm*. Can't wait." Aurora climbed out of bed for the bathroom and, when she shut the door behind her, she smiled and shook her head. She loved that woman so much. Aurora had been in relationships before, but no one other than Leela ever gave her that tickle in her belly. No one made her laugh or feel like a superstar the way Leela did.

She couldn't wait to give Leela her present.

After Aurora changed into her bike shorts and sports bra, rebraided her hair, and gave Leela a lingering kiss goodbye, she walked out into the warm September sun and jogged along the curved trail to the gym.

Given how vacant the rest of the resort seemed, she was surprised to see the fitness area well-occupied. A class of yogis in an open room on the far end were in their own version of downward-facing dog, while the traditional gym area had half a dozen individuals on the cardio equipment or lifting free weights. She recognized the manager's admin as she ran a steady pace on a treadmill and saw Mac lifting dumbbells over his shoulders with a series of grunts.

He saw her, removed his earbuds, and rested the weights by his feet with a *clang*. "Good morning. Did you enjoy your first night?"

She couldn't report that she'd had three orgasms and had slept like a baby. "It was relaxing."

"Glad to hear it." He picked up the weights and reracked them. "I like to get a good sweat in before my day starts too."

Aurora chuckled softly while she adjusted the seat on the high-end stationary bike. "Usually, I'm an afternoon person, but anything will work since I'm trying to find my workout groove again."

"If it helps, you look like fitness is important to you. You have that vibe, you know?" He said it so seriously Aurora could tell it wasn't a pick-up line.

"I'm doing what I can."

He nodded, put his earbuds back in, and picked up his next set of gigantic weights to resume his pump.

Aurora pushed his comment out of her mind and mounted the seat. She programmed the bike's computer for a virtual ride of one of the more scenic stages of the *Tour de France*. As she pedaled through vineyards and villages, she would occasionally slow her pace to type comments into her tablet about the resort. Whether it was something she had already observed, like the exterior lights still on in the outdoor yoga room, or reminders for later, the multitask was literally a good exercise for her.

Twenty minutes into her workout, Mac waved goodbye, and after an hour, she dismounted with wobbly legs and took a fluffy, white, oversized hand towel to dab the sweat off her face, neck, and chest. That amount of fabric would require a significant amount of extra water to clean and energy to dry. She added her observation to her tablet and then meandered back to the suite.

She came inside, saw the hastily made bed, and a folded note on the hotel's stationary propped on the nightstand. *I'm headed into town with Mac to work my G.O.A.T. goat products. See what I did there? I'll see you at lunch. I love you!*

Aurora was excited Leela had carved out time for herself and interests. By being strategic with their time, they could be successful both professionally and in their relationship.

After her shower and a change of clothes into a business/casual outfit of a khaki skirt and polo, Aurora headed to the main office to start her analysis. The morning's focus was utilities, namely water and electricity. She inspected different types of rooms, asked a variety of employees a series of basic questions, and made a note to inspect the grounds at night. That was technically part of her and Leela's couple time, but she could ask Leela if she minded an evening out where she made a few observations about the resort on their way to a romantic, moonlit stroll on the sand while they held hands.

The four hours of her morning flew by. The staff cooperated and there were no delays. She simply checked an item off and went on to the next until lunchtime rolled around. She looked forward to it because, if everything had gone to plan, Leela would meet her to eat together and exchange tales of their experiences so far.

When she walked on to the dining terrace, Leela was already seated at a small table, phone in hand. She tapped rapidly on the screen, so engrossed, she didn't react to Aurora's arrival.

"Busy day at the office?" Aurora joked.

Leela jumped then grinned as she accepted Aurora's kiss to the cheek. She put the phone away before giving Aurora her undivided attention. "I had the best morning!"

"Let me guess…cheese." Aurora sat across from her, grin in place. Leela was adorable when she was this enthusiastic, just like a jumping baby goat.

"No! Even better than that. Half of the people I saw were very interested in my products and one of them had actually heard of me. They'd heard of me!" Exuberance radiated off Leela.

"That's fantastic news. Congratulations!" Pride welled up inside of Aurora. That was her lady, rocking the goat-based products world.

"And Mac bought me a breakfast parfait made with coconut yogurt when I complained about a lack of dairy." Leela grinned, obviously aware of her obsession but only mildly apologetic. "How about you?"

"I had a great morning too, even if we didn't get to kiss good-bye." She produced a little pout.

"I agree, that was tragic, but I didn't know how long you'd be gone, and Mac said he had a good window to pick me up, so I took the opening." Leela folded her arms and sighed dramatically. "If only there was a way we could make up for that lost moment."

Aurora picked up the hint and shook her head with a smile. She rounded the table and gave Leela a proper kiss.

"That's what I'm talking about!" Leela watched her return to her seat with a pleased grin. "Now, back to you and your morning. Mac mentioned seeing you at the gym. I think he has a crush on you, by the way."

"No way." She was fairly sure he didn't but because she knew Leela had the occasional insecurity she added, "And even if he did, he's got nothing on you, so that's his issue." She reached for Leela's hand on the table and gave it a small squeeze.

Leela smiled. "All right, true," she said, with only a bit of inse-curity lacing her voice.

Aurora took that as a win.

Leela sipped her purplish and leafy drink from a straw. "This is really good."

"What is it?"

"Blackberry mint fizzy refresher. Want some?" She held her glass out for Aurora.

After making a mental note for the resort to ditch the straws or replace with reusable, Aurora sipped from the glass. Her taste buds celebrated in a dance of sweet, sour, and bubbly praise. "That's delicious. Do you have other drinks like that?" she asked the approaching waiter, who wore a standard black uniform.

"Only about a dozen." He rattled off an impressive list of mocktails, juices, and their lunch specials of the day.

Aurora ordered a drink and they settled on lunch.

As the waiter walked off, Leela leaned in. "Now, tell me what have you uncovered? How are they doing? Spill!"

Aurora smiled and leaned back. She was acutely aware Leela's phone was upside down on the table, and she seemed to have no attention for it, only for Aurora. It felt good to be the absolute center of Leela's attention, and she made a mental note to make sure she gave Leela's adventures the same level of attention. "Well. . . I need to check out the lighting when it's dark, so if you wouldn't mind accompanying me on a little work trip. Afterward," Aurora changed her voice to a sensual tone, "we can walk to the beach, under the stars—"

"Yes, please."

Aurora smiled, more than pleased Leela was onboard. "Aside from that, there are a few areas of improvement…"

Their drinks, entrées of enchiladas and pad Thai were mouthwatering, and the cupcake Leela convinced Aurora to split was divine. Aurora told Leela everything about her morning, from the gym to the moment she had spotted a natural beauty at her lunch table.

After Leela had protested that compliment, she told Aurora all about her morning, playfully slipping her own compliments in. Then she got serious. "I'm sorry I didn't react the best about the vegan thing," she said with the tiniest bit of white frosting stuck to her lip left over from the cupcake extravaganza before. "I can be open to new experiences, especially if those experiences are as good as lunch. And breakfast, actually."

Aurora smiled. "Thank you for that, but it's fine, really. I know dairy is your life." She grinned and took the nudge to the shin in stride. "We're both adjusting to being in a new environment."

"A magical environment!"

Aurora chuckled and dragged her finger through the chocolate drizzle on the dessert plate then sucked it off her finger with a moan. "You're right, this place really is magical."

CHAPTER THREE

WAKE UP NAKED in Aurora's arms, go into town with Mac to network, read an email or two from Keith about the farm, enjoy the resort's restaurant and amenities while she watched Aurora's brain work wonders, connect with Aurora via talking, playing, or fooling around until they were forced to sleep. Repeat. That was the basic schedule Leela had adhered to for the last five days, and she could honestly say she'd never had more fun in her entire life. She was determined to make their last day and night the most special yet, which was why she had insisted she and Aurora have their spa treatments in separate areas.

Aurora liked surprises, and boy was she going to get one.

Leela spun slightly in her swivel chair and looked around the salon. If she ever decided to venture into her own store front, this was the aesthetic Leela wanted. From the terracotta tiles to the stucco walls, this place was built from the earth. Although the chairs were modern, and the flash of extra sparkle in the granite countertops jazzed the room.

She loved sparkles.

Leela looked down at her toes and wiggled them, causing the gold metallic polish to reflect alternating bits of light.

A tall beauty with short, wispy blond hair, dyed pink at the tips, and large hoop earrings sat beside Leela and crossed her legs.

"I'm Quinn, your stylist, and rumor has it you want to make a bold change to your look."

"Yes, I do." Leela opened the gallery on her phone and showed her the celebrity haircut that she wanted. "I've come to the realization that I am more than a humble goat farmer. I can be the face of my brand. I can be President Bakshi. I need a haircut that says that."

Quinn nodded her approval at the picture. "A woman with ambition, style, and power. I love it."

Leela melted into her chair at the wash station as Quinn massaged her neck and scalp. She couldn't even imagine how good it would feel once she actually started washing her hair. While a significant portion of Leela's business was devoted to self-care, she didn't take advantage of it for herself. That was going to have to change. Once they returned from vacation, she would work her ass off but only during work.

Leela version 2.0 would have much more playtime. If their vacation had taught her anything, it was that they needed a much healthier balance, as hard as that would be to maintain.

Quinn turned on the spray, and perfectly warm water sluiced through her hair.

Leela briefly wondered what showers would feel like once her hair was shorter. Much shorter. "I hope Aurora is enjoying her treatments as much as me."

"What did she choose to have done?"

"While I was getting the stone massage, she had a reiki treatment. And now she's getting a pineapple facial."

Quinn's hands built a coconut-scented lather in her hair. "I can never say no to a deep tissue massage myself."

"Aurora hates those. She—Oh! I'm such an idiot."

Quinn's hands stopped working the bubbles.

"Sorry, everything's okay; it's just that I completely forgot to give Aurora this concoction I made."

"You realize that makes you sound like you're going to poison her."

"What?" Leela knitted her brow. "No! It's a lotion I made just for her. I buried the jar in between the pajamas I packed, but it slipped my mind because…" She hadn't worn pajamas once during the trip. "Of all the fun."

Quinn snickered while she washed away the suds and applied conditioner. "Well, I'm sure when you do give your concoction to her, she'll appreciate it. When I spoke to her, I got the impression she doesn't take anything for granted."

"She doesn't. She's like the best person in the entire world."

"That's funny, she said something similar about you."

"She did?" Leela turned instinctively, but the side of her face went into the wash basin. Quinn's gentle hand directed her to face the front. "How'd you two lovebirds meet?"

It was a question they were asked often, and they used the same story, which was mostly true, but left out the supernatural details.

"We became fast friends when she moved to town. After a few months, we were more than friends."

The spray shook as Quinn laughed. She squeezed out the excess water and wrapped Leela's hair in a towel. "Who made the first move?"

"I did. There were bold moves involved."

"That seems pretty consistent with your personality." Quinn turned her so she faced the mirror and adjusted the pneumatic chair into a higher position. "Okay, now it's time to use that *bold* attitude to turn you into President Bakshi, the face of your brand, and lover of Aurora Okpik."

Through the mirror, Leela watched Quinn as she gathered the upper half of her hair and bound it. Then, she took the electric shaver off its charger.

"Are you ready?" Quinn asked with the device near the base of Leela's neck.

"Let's do this thing." Leela watched a clump of dark brown hair fall to the clay tile.

While Quinn shaved her new undercut, Leela reflected on the new her. She was changing her attitude to go along with her hair. She would expand the confidence she felt about her products into her relationship with Aurora. She was awesome and could give Aurora everything she needed: love, security, and the BDE, when the occasion called for it. Occasions like later that night.

Biddie would make its Hawaiian debut. Otherwise, she'd packed it for nothing, and that was just frustrating.

"You look like you're having some very deep thoughts," Quinn said as she finished the hair fade and picked up the scissors and comb.

"I'm forming a plan." Leela was determined to make this evening the most special she and Aurora had ever shared. "Would you be able to get my phone? It's right there." She pointed to Quinn's organized workstation.

"Sure." She wiped the loose hair stuck to her hands on her black apron and handed Leela her phone.

Leela looked to the ceiling of skylights as she thought of what to say to Aurora, then her thumbs rapidly texted. *Can you leave our suite at six? I'll meet you at the restaurant shortly thereafter. Love you.* "Thanks," she said to Quinn as she placed the phone back.

"You're welcome. I'm a sucker for a grand romantic gesture." Quinn picked up the tools of her trade once more and grinned. "Now, where were we?"

While Quinn cut, styled, and coiffed, Leela worked out the details to her plan. She'd probably need to kill some time between now and dinner, but that could easily be done by checking her e— No, she wasn't going to do that. On the off chance something negative lurked in her inbox, she didn't want that to distract from her perfect evening. That was the enemy. First, she'd go back to the stone massage area and ask to have a few candles. Surely, they had a few to spare? Then, she'd burn several minutes by looking at baby goats on InstaPic. Because, duh, baby goats. Lastly, for the *piéce de résistance*, she would change into her latest purchase, a light cream, gauzy blouse with finely stitched flowers, paired with coral capris. And along the way, she would try not to mess up her hair by playing with its bouncy coolness.

Tonight would be epic.

#

Aurora twisted the linen napkin in her hands as she struggled to appear as though she were patiently waiting at the dining table. On the inside, her heart pounded, her gut twisted, and her mouth was drier than the tortilla chips on the table across from her. She wished she had braided her hair so she could fidget with its end, but she hadn't. She had decided to wear her hair long and straight, with a purple flower tucked behind her ear.

It seemed more island-like.

She gave a nod of appreciation to the server who filled her water glass once more, and then she drank greedily. She couldn't shake her nerves. Not only was it obvious that Leela was up to something, but Aurora planned to give Leela the necklace too. Their necklace. During her facial, she'd rehearsed what she would say and how she would say it but she knew once the moment was upon her, she'd probably forget all of it and have to speak from the heart.

But that wasn't a terrible idea either.

"Is this seat taken?" Leela whispered in a husky tone behind her.

"As a matter of fact..." Aurora turned, and her jaw dropped. "Your hair! You look..." She stood with the broadest smile her mouth had ever formed and began to feel the silky smooth and rough textures of Leela's new haircut. "I'm sorry. You look absolutely. . . I have no words." Aurora continued to stare dumbfounded. "Okay, I do have a word. Hot. You look very, very hot. And I love this shirt too." She felt the thin but exquisitely soft material between her fingers then closed the distance between them and kissed her. She restrained herself from giving her the kiss she wanted. That would have to wait until after dinner, when they were away from prying eyes. "You are beautiful. And so sexy."

Leela held her hands but took a step back and gazed in appreciation at Aurora's sarong-style floral dress. "You look incredible, and I swear you're actually glowing."

Aurora bit her bottom lip. "That's the pineapple facial."

"Did the slight burning sensation let you know the detoxification was working?"

"Pretty much," she said.

Leela continued to stare at her with sparkling eyes and a beaming smile.

"What?"

Leela sighed contently and touched the flower held in place by Aurora's curtain of hair. "I'm the luckiest person in the world."

"My thoughts exactly." Aurora gestured to the table, where a blackberry mint fizzy refresher awaited Leela. Once she was seated and had her drink in hand, Aurora raised her glass. "I'd like to propose a toast. May the magic in Hawaii follow us back home."

"And may our love grow and spur on more magic."

"I'll definitely drink to that." Aurora clinked her glass into Leela's. They both drank and stared deeply into each other's eyes.

"Are you ready to order?"

Aurora hadn't even noticed their server was at their table. She was so entranced by Leela. "Are you ready, dreamy?"

"Whenever you are, sweets."

Over drinks, macadamia nut and coconut risotto, and then a slice of carrot cake, they reviewed their favorite moments from the trip. The helicopter ride over Volcanoes National Park, the tour of the botanical gardens, and the astronomy lesson about the autumnal equinox as they stargazed on Mauna Kea. The resort itself had a private beach, spa, and gym, of which they were huge fans. Leela hadn't gone to the gym, but Aurora knew Leela still appreciated the spandex outfit she had worn.

After they finished their meal, each of them thanked the wait staff for the unparalleled service and headed towards their suite.

Once they were on the red path, Aurora raised Leela's hand to her lips and kissed her knuckles. "When do I get to see this surprise of yours?"

"Who says there's a surprise? Maybe my fancy butch hair and new shirt are all the surprise you're getting."

Aurora gave her a sideways glance.

"Jeez. Give a lady the third degree, why don't ya? Yes, there's another surprise."

Aurora waved the key card in front and opened the room to a cluster of small, unlit candles on each nightstand. "Looks like we'll have some extra romantic ambiance tonight. Thank you for leaving them unlit while we were gone."

"You're welcome. Burning the place down is not in my plans. Now, can you please go into the bathroom and put on the robe I hung up for you?"

Aurora came closer and playfully touched the tip of her nose. "I don't have a robe."

"You do now. So, go change and I'll get the mood lighting going."

"I'll change but I have a surprise for you too." Aurora reached into her bag and moved her pajamas to the side. Why she'd bothered to pack pajamas, she didn't know.

Leela whined. "Do you mind if I do my surprise first? I'm really excited about it."

Aurora would hold off on her own wants for now. "Okay. I'll be out in a minute." Aurora shut the bathroom door behind her and saw the robe hanging. "Wow," Aurora said quietly to herself.

The material was the same off-white color and texture as the new shirt Leela wore, but the hand stitching of ocean waves down the sleeves was exquisite. And much more elaborate. She unzipped her dress and let it pool at her feet. As she stepped out, she debated whether she was supposed to keep her bikini briefs on. "What's the rule with underwear?" she shouted through the door.

"It's stupid."

That was a clear answer. Aurora grinned and removed her lacy panties then glided the robe over her skin. In the mirror, she could see the robe was even sheerer than Leela's shirt had been. She could see the faintest outline of her areolas and the dark hair of her pubic region. Aurora had felt attractive at dinner but now she exuded sensuality. "Can I come out?"

"Yes, please. You're needed for this activity."

Aurora's grin turned into a smirk. Leela was definitely in mission mode, albeit a playful one. She walked out to the flickering orange glow of the candlelit room and saw Leela sitting on the edge of the bed in her clothes from dinner.

Leela played with a lidded jar that rested on one of her crossed knees. "You look like a goddess," Leela said with a smile. "Do you like the robe?"

"I love it. Truth be told, I feel like a goddess. Thank you." She sat beside Leela, kissed her softly, then pointed at the dish. "Is that a surprise too?"

"It is." Leela unscrewed the top and held it near Aurora's nose.

Aurora took a quick sniff and then repeated. The scent was faint but sweet and fresh, like she had passed by an aromatic flower. "That's really nice. Subtle. What is that?"

"It's my standard lotion base infused with a blend of jasmine and lemongrass oils. I know you're not a fan of strong fragrances, so I wanted to make you something lighter. I call it Light of My Life. I'm sorry I couldn't come up with a less cheesy name."

Aurora took the jar, closed her eyes, and inhaled the scent again. She could picture Leela at her experiment table mixing and taking notes until she reached perfection. There was no one on Earth who would ever treat her better, who would ever love her more than Leela did. "I don't think it's a cheesy name. I think it's a very romantic and thoughtful gift. Thank you." Aurora cupped Leela's chin and brought her closer for a kiss.

"I'm glad you like it. Would you allow me the pleasure of telling you more about it while I give you a Bakshi brand massage?"

To answer her question, Aurora gave her a sly smile and turned her back to Leela. "I find it amusing that you gave me this robe only to ask me to take it off."

"It's more dramatic this way." Leela moved behind her and swept her hair to the side so it fell across Aurora's chest.

Aurora anticipated the kisses on her neck and fabric sliding off her shoulders, but that didn't stop her from enjoying the attention. She felt Leela dab the cool lotion in a line of dots from one shoulder to the next then rub in the balm while giving her muscles gentle squeezes.

"I know that you know I love you," Leela said. "But I don't think you realize how much, and I'm not as articulate with my emotions as you are, so I thought I'd make you this as a way of trying to explain. Even with the terrible name, you are the brightest spot in my life. You saved me from a lonely existence and by loving me like you do, I've started to believe I'm worth it."

When Aurora started to turn, Leela directed her shoulder back.

"I promise you can talk once I'm done but I have to get this out now." Leela applied more lotion to the center of Aurora's back and continued to massage it in. "You make me so happy. Everything about you, from your attitude to your smile, is pure joy. I wouldn't be able to live with myself if I ever did anything to let you down. So, while a lotion sample might be considered an odd token of love, that's how I work, and I want to make these little jars for you—or big jars for you—for the rest of my life." She slid the robe back over Aurora's shoulders. "And I hope you can accept me giving you these lotion samples and massages for the rest of your life."

Aurora remained facing away from Leela. The moonlit palm tree she focused on outside the window was harder to see with the tears blurring her vision. Leela had committed herself to her and had done so in the most Leela way possible.

Leela moved to face her and brushed a tear away with her thumb. "Happy cry, sweets?"

"Very happy. I love you so much, and I'd like to give you something too. Return the sentiment."

Leela looked into her nearly empty dish of lotion. "I can make more at home."

"That's not what I meant." Aurora stood and went to her bag. After pushing her top-most t-shirt to the side, she pulled the square wooden box out of her bag. When she returned to Leela's side, she placed the box on her lap, and reached for Leela's hand.

"Pressure's on to say something crazy romantic," Leela teased.

Aurora appreciated the moment of levity and smiled. "I firmly believe there is no one on earth who is better suited for me than you. You respect my identity, encourage me, can make me feel like the most beautiful woman in the room, and make all of my bad days better. Being able to feel your love and love you in return is the greatest gift I could ever receive.

"I know because of your parents' history you have mixed feelings about the m-word, so that's not what this is, but I know, especially now, that you are as committed to me as I am to you." Aurora opened the box and revealed the two necklaces side by side. "If you'll accept this, we can each wear one as a reminder that we can function apart, but our pieces fit. It only makes sense for us to be together because, when we are, our love is powerful and infinite."

Leela's gaze went from Aurora's to the necklaces. She was silent.

"You don't have to say anything," Aurora said gently. "But I would be honored if you wore one of them."

Leela reached out and touched the polished dark wood of the feminine-shaped pendant and the red spiral of the circular heart. "These are so beautiful. Which one do I get?"

"Whichever one you want."

Leela pointed to the smaller, spiral piece. "This one is a little more me, I think, and the curvy lady is definitely more you."

Aurora placed the simpler necklace over Leela's head and adjusted the leather so the necklace wasn't too loose. "Does that feel okay?"

"Right now, I feel pretty incredible. Can I put the other one on you?"

Aurora freed the other necklace from the box and held it out for Leela. She ducked slightly, and Leela placed the larger necklace over her head. The pendant touched her skin, but the simple jewelry didn't feel unfamiliar. Much like the matching spiral Leela wore, it was like a piece of her that had been missing and was finally found.

Their lips pressed against each other in a series of brief but deep kisses.

Leela giggled and wiped away the tear that slid down her cheek. "Was this a commitment ceremony?"

"I think it was." Aurora had never felt so much energy. She was positively giddy with love and the knowledge that Leela only wanted a future with her in it. "Will our parents forgive us for not inviting them?"

"Yours will. Mine'll take some buttering up." Leela picked up her necklace and then Aurora's. "I can't believe this just happened. I was planning on a super romantic massage, not a life-defining moment. I love you so much."

"And I love you. Now and forever."

The sound of rain falling and the still flickering candles created the perfect atmosphere for them to celebrate.

Leela kissed her as though she tried to pour all of her love, passion, and commitment into one moment of contact. Aurora's pulse quickened, her thoughts clouded, and a familiar tension between her legs stirred. She reciprocated all Leela gave her and felt the weight of the necklace. The breeze of the room struck her skin as Leela untied the robe and slipped the fabric completely off her.

She needed Leela's touch to surround her and fill her to feel utterly complete. "You're everything to me."

CHAPTER FOUR

THE SQUAWK OF a bird called Leela out of her slumber. Without opening her eyes, she could feel Aurora's warmth pressed against her breasts, stomach, and legs. She also sensed something else while she was in the optimal, big-spoon position. She reached down to the side of her buttock and confirmed it was a strap. Leela's eyes shot open when she realized she'd slept in the jock-style harness.

That was a first.

Curious to what else she may have slept in, her hand went to her crotch, and found an empty o-ring, which was even weirder. She had absolutely no memory of removing Biddie and had no idea where it was.

Leela craned her neck to see over Aurora's shoulder but she paused and pursed her lips when she noticed Aurora's necklace had twisted in the night and rested on her upper back. It was attached to her own spiral pendant. That was so romantic. Even their necklaces could find each other in the night. Aurora hadn't mentioned the necklaces were magnetic, but there was so much they had shared, Leela understood how Aurora could forget to mention a minor detail like that.

Leela used slight force to pull the magnetic pieces apart and quietly slid off the mattress to use the bathroom. After she shut the door behind her, she jumped at her reflection in the mirror. She had forgotten about her haircut. The shorter strands along with the styling products had made her hair stand at several different angles. That, along with the hickies across her chest, made her giggle quietly.

After she shimmied out of the harness and relieved herself, she snuck back into bed and gently laid her arm over Aurora's waist.

Aurora took her hand and pulled her in tighter.

"You robbed me of watching you wake up," Leela said.

"I'm sorry. What can I do to make it up to you?" Aurora rolled toward her and laughed. "Wow. Your hair is...wow."

If she could cause that joyous sound to come out of Aurora because of hair humiliation, it was worth the sacrifice. "I'm happy I could make you happy."

"Not that I'm counting, but I think you made that happen a few times last night."

"If we're counting, I think the hot tub should count twice."

Aurora chuckled. "I'll give you that. All that activity did take its toll on you."

Leela cocked her head to the side. "How do you mean?"

Aurora attempted to smooth Leela's hair. "You basically passed out from exhaustion. It was pretty amazing, actually. I took the liberty of removing Biddie, but you made little grumbly, unhappy noises when I tried to slide off the harness, so I left it. Hopefully, you didn't wake up in the middle of the night from it pinching you or something."

All of this was news to Leela. She had slept like the dead. "No, I didn't wake up at all last night, and I have to say I feel awesome this morning."

"I'm feeling pretty refreshed too. I had this dream that was nothing but colors and energy, like slow motion fireworks."

"No wonder I'm exhausted, I made you come so hard I blew your mind."

Aurora giggled and spread her arms as she stretched. "Well, I feel awesome. Like a new woman."

"I'd like to meet this lady." Leela covered Aurora's body with her own and slowly leaned down when a guitar solo, courtesy of Aerosmith, blared from Aurora's cell phone. "I hate that thing."

"I know, but it's a classic." Aurora pecked Leela's lips. "Let's make a promise that we will go away with each other—and only each other—at least once a year."

"I'll make that deal and I'll add that as we become a powerful business couple, we play as hard as we work. I'm talking movies, outdoor fun, and getting one of those books where we try all the sexual positions at least once."

Aurora's body shook underneath her as she laughed. "That's a deal."

"Good. Now, would you like to share a shower? Rumor has it that you really like it when people save water."

"You know me so well. But don't you want to visit the beach one last time?" She watched the gears turn as Leela thought about it.

Leela kissed her quickly then scrambled off her. "Race you down there!"

They basked in everything vacation during their leisurely breakfast on the beach. Sun, sand, banana nut quinoa with maple syrup, and, for Leela, a beer.

And, of course, a photoshoot that captured all of those things.

After a shared shower, they packed their bags and tossed them into the back of the same blue convertible that had brought them to the resort.

As Mac drove them from the tropical, tree-covered area and back into the regions of charred earth, Leela held Aurora's hand tightly. She would savor every last moment of the best week of her life. And when she returned home, she would reflect on everything they had experienced. The food, the excursions, the weather, the hot tub, and even her trips to town with Mac. He was a little too into Aurora and her workouts, but she couldn't really blame him for that. Plus, he'd suggested multiple businesses for her to visit, so that was winning.

The idea of taking what she had learned and going back to work gave Leela a thrill. While it was good for her to step away and test Keith's management abilities, she was happy to get back to her goats, her business, and her presidential campaign.

#

On the flight, Aurora began her formal report, so Leela watched a movie and then dozed off. She dreamed she'd lost her necklace in the ocean.

After she confirmed it was still secured under her shirt, she remained wide awake for the rest of their journey. She could never lose that necklace. The symbol meant more to her than any diamond every could.

When she looked over at Aurora on the car ride back home and saw her thumbing the pendant at her neck, Leela knew she felt the same way.

Vacation was over, but her life with Aurora felt like it was just beginning, and they would do so in the home they shared, which made everything better.

The car pulled into the crunchy, gravel driveway and came to a halt. Aurora kissed her and then stepped out of the car into the musky farm air. Leela followed her to the trunk. A gust of wind ruffled the back of her head and made the rest of her hair stand on end instantly. "I didn't factor in how cold my neck might get with this haircut."

"Poor dreamy," Aurora said with a playful pout. "But at least now it feels like autumn. It was weird having warmer weather for the first day of the season."

Leela pulled her luggage out and removed her key ring. "Want to see what the addition looks like from the outside before we go in?"

"I am curious. Also, a bit terrified."

As they turned the front corner of their home, Leela was pleased to see the protective lining that had torn off the side during a windstorm had been fixed. Or at least she no longer saw a piece of plastic flapping in the breeze like a sail. They circled around their single level home and along the way noticed orange spray paint on the ground near their favorite juniper tree.

"I wonder if they started to paint," Aurora said while Leela opened the front door.

"Only one way to find out."

The house smelled like the lumber aisle of a hardware store. They walked through the living room, down the hall, and lifted the stiff plastic barrier that divided the new construction from the rest of the home. They walked inside the space that would be their new master bedroom and then shared an annoyed glance.

"What the serious fuck?" Leela asked rhetorically to the exposed studs and open soda cans laying on the plywood floor marked with orange letters and arrows. She had known painting was out of the question, but she'd expected drywall. And she definitely hadn't expected trash.

"I guess we're not in paradise anymore," Aurora said woefully.

Nobody made Aurora sad. Nobody!

"Don't worry," Leela assured, "I'm going to email the contractor right now and fix this."

Aurora nodded her thanks. "I'll start the first load of laundry while you do that." Aurora grabbed Leela's suitcase and headed toward the linen closet off the kitchen.

Leela continued to stare at the naked walls and junk that littered the ground. She took out her phone, snapped several photographs, and sent their contractor an email.

She walked to the kitchen where Aurora had begun sorting the laundry on the floor. "I sent a quasi-threatening email with pictures, so I'm expecting a phone call tomorrow. Do you need help in here? Or want me to move some of this to the bedroom?"

"No, I'm good. Go check on the herd and check Keith's notes. I know you want to." Aurora grinned and gave her a small kiss with the darks bundled in her arms.

"You're the best." Leela practically sprinted out the door and took the same path to the gate she had taken for over a dozen years. The farm would definitely take construction off her mind.

"Hello, ladies," Leela crooned as she passed the grazing herd and into the office. Upon first glance, everything was in its place. The employee tablet was charging on its sheet music stand. The snail mail had been sorted on the desk just as she'd asked. There was a note by the phone that said, *The only callers were robots.*

Since she had checked her emails on the trip, that wasn't a concern, so she turned and left the office for the packing area. But then she stopped. There was nothing critical that had to be handled right that minute. She was still on vacation and, since Aurora had started laundry, the least Leela could do was handle dinner. The food at the resort had been delicious, but there was something about the pesto pizza at Romo's that couldn't be beat. Even Aurora had to have a slice with her garden salad.

"Hey, buster! This is private property!" Keith yelled from behind her.

Leela slowly turned to him.

"Oh, shit! Leela?"

"That's me. The volcano didn't destroy me."

He stared, mouth agape. "I'm sorry. From the back it didn't look. . . Man, you look really different. You look like that lady who was in prison with the cool hair and neck tattoos. But not real prison, the TV prison, you know?"

"That was the idea."

He lightly scratched at the area below his Adam's apple. "And you're wearing a necklace. You never wear jewelry," he said, shocked.

She lifted the pendant off her skin. "This is a symbol of Aurora's love for me. It's incredibly meaningful and is now a permanent fixture of my being."

He came closer to get a better look. "Her love looks really swirly."

"Don't mock the necklace."

Keith put up his hands in defense. "I would never. I'm sorry."

She knew Keith meant it. Afterall, he was the type of person who thought 'buster' was threatening. "Apology accepted. And yes, it is swirly. Oh! Love Swirl might be a fun name for a Valentine's blend. We could do a half mix thing so you can see the swirls."

He arched a brow. "Wow. You're in a good mood."

"I'm in a great mood—except for the construction crew who are now suffering from my wrath—but aside from that, I feel great! Something about that place was really transformative, you know?"

He nodded. "Vacations can do that."

#

After her typical routine of a shower, breakfast with social media, and leaving for work, Aurora realized something was different. She felt different. The necklace she wore lay high on her chest, and she could sense its slight weight with every twist and turn. She wasn't annoyed by its presence, rather she just needed an adjustment period.

Most people got used to wearing a ring. With her it was a necklace.

While reflecting on the significance of the necklace and how it affected her life, she needed to tell the other people in her life whom she loved. She hesitated before she called because of the time difference in Michigan but, based on the time stamp of the likes and comments on social media, her mother was already awake. "Call Mom," Aurora instructed her car's dash.

After a few rings, the call connected.

"Boo bear!" Ani said with glee. "This is a nice surprise. I wasn't expecting to hear from you until my next treatment."

The reminder of her mother's chemotherapy treatment in a few days stung. It wasn't close to the punch in the gut she'd felt six months ago when she'd been first diagnosed with cancer, but every reminder still hurt and lingered. "I didn't want to wait anymore to tell you the good news."

"If the good news is that you had a great time in Hawaii, I'm afraid I already know. Your brother showed me how to get an In-staPic account."

Instead of quick pain, now Aurora had the anxiety of a teenager who just got caught. "So, I guess that means you saw all of our pictures."

"Yes! You look so happy and in love. And that bikini of Leela's really shows off her figure. I had no idea her upstairs ladies were so impressive."

"Boundaries, Mom." Her mother still hadn't learned what was too far in the sexuality department.

"I didn't mean to leave you out. Yours are looking very nice too." Ani giggled nervously. "I'm sorry. I think I'm just obsessed with boobs these days, for obvious reasons."

There was the sting again. "How are you feeling with everything?"

"To be honest, I just had to talk about everything yesterday at a potluck and I hate that our traditional medicine isn't progressing like I had hoped it would, so I'd much rather hear about your good news, if you don't mind."

After the surgery to remove her tumor, Ani had tried the cleanest diet and wellness plan she could, hoping that if she boosted her natural immunity, any remaining cancer would die. But it hadn't been enough.

Aurora understood why her mother wouldn't want to relive the potluck experience and continued with her good news. "Well, what Leela and I did isn't legal, but we basically had a commitment ceremony."

"Oh, boo bear, that's wonderful! We'll have to celebrate when you fly in for Irony Day."

It was difficult for a family who was Indigenous to celebrate Thanksgiving. Also known as Irony Day.

"That would be really great," Aurora said. "Just please don't tell people we got married."

Ani mumbled. "Leela still doesn't like that word, I gather."

"Well, when I asked her, I specifically didn't call it that because I thought it would ruin the moment. I wanted her to focus on how I felt without distraction. She was more than fine with how I articulated the commitment I wanted to give her, which was a marriage vow you'd hear at any wedding."

"Aw. I bet it was beautiful. Did you write it down?"

"Um, no."

Ani *tsked* in disappointment. "That's a shame."

A notification flashed that another call from Tonya's administrative assistant had come in. Aurora rolled her eyes. *And so it begins.* "I'm sorry, Mom, but I have to go. Work is calling. Literally."

"No problem. We'll catch up during my treatment on Thursday. I love you."

"Love you too. And love to Dad. Bye." She disconnected the call with her mother and answered the other. "Hello, this is Aurora."

"Hi!" Tonya's insanely cheerful admin assaulted her ears. "Sorry to call while you're on the road, but Tonya would like to see you before you settle in for the day."

"Okay. Do you know why?"

"Something about explaining what she needs in an email would take too long so she just wants to talk before you start your report."

It wouldn't have done any good to say that she had already started her report on the flight home. "Alright. I'll be there in about ten minutes. Well, fifteen if I get caught behind the day care drop-off line."

"Aw. But they look so cute."

Aurora couldn't disagree. There was an assortment of surprisingly cute moments the day care beside her office offered. "Please tell Tonya I'm on my way and I'll see her soon."

She drove the rest of the way in peace and only had to sit through the tail end of a few adults walking or carrying their tiny children into the day care. After she parked in her usual spot, she said a few hellos, dropped off her belongings at her desk, and then made a cup of tea before she went to Tonya's office. She knocked on the jamb.

"Hey! Welcome back to the mainland." Tonya beckoned Aurora into her office. "How was your trip?"

"I really don't think it could have been any more amazing. Top to bottom, both Leela and I thought it was fantastic. Almost a spiritual experience at times."

"It should have been. That place has been blessed by everybody."

"What do you mean?"

"It all started when a board member had the grounds blessed by a priest, but then the non-Catholic members felt excluded. Long story short: those grounds have been blessed by a rabbi, an imam, a Buddhist monk; you name it."

"Well, for me all ground is sacred, so they went a bit over-board. Tell you what, I volunteer to go back to the island with Leela and tell them."

Tonya tilted her head back and laughed. "Well, maybe if the resort implements your suggestions, we can convince them a follow-up report would be more accurate if you visited in person. That does remind me; how long do you think it's going to take to write your analysis?"

"I started it on the plane so…maybe seven more business days for the draft. I have a great pivot table idea that will add clarity and save time."

"Seven days," Tonya said thoughtfully. "Okay, that's reasonable."

Aurora furrowed her brow. Considering the normal turnaround time for a report of that nature was ten business days, seven should have had Tonya jumping for joy. "Did the clients ask for a new deliverable date?"

"No. I asked because of how the report delivery lines up with your East Coast tour. Since you left, we've expanded it a bit."

Aurora's suspicion meter rose. "How much is 'a bit'?"

"It's a full two weeks now."

Aurora's mouth dropped. "But Leela and I just agreed to a whole work hard, play hard philosophy. That's too much work hard! And it was hell trying to reschedule my doctor's appointment the last time I left."

"But I built in a full weekend of rest so you can play hard," Tonya said with a smile. "I can't do anything about the doctor except cross my fingers for you."

Aurora had missed Stacy to pieces but being away from Leela for two weeks straight was asking a lot. "Can't someone else do the second week?"

Tonya shook her head. "You know as well as I do that you're the only one with your skill set who works here, which we will have to change soon, given that the East Coast office will almost be identical to this one. So, I'm sorry to say that, for the time being, you're our woman."

Aurora's next suggestion was to divide the trip, but that would double the fuel and airfare cost. That would be feeding her enemy. Aurora decided to concede but only if she was generously compensated for the inconveniences. "I want a crazy high per diem and hotels with fitness centers. *And* I want my Baltimore visit to be at the very end so I can enjoy more time with Stacy without stressing about my next appointment."

Tonya typed something into her computer. "Works for me. Anything else?"

Well, if she could get more. "First class travel. No layovers." Considering she had just arrived from an all-expenses paid trip to Hawaii, Aurora withheld asking for a raise. "That's all."

"Done!" Tonya leaned back in her chair with her hands folded behind her head. "That's one of the things I love about you, Aurora. You're flexible but you're not a doormat."

Aurora nodded curtly at the compliment. "Is there anything else I should know?"

"Nope. Work on that report and I'll adjust your tour dates. Now, go work your magic."

Aurora returned to her desk and texted Leela. *Good news: you have more time to catch up on all those shows you want to watch but I hate. Bad news: in another week, they're sending me away for two weeks.*

She booted up her computer, opened her report template, and then paused. If she started work in a bad mood, that would affect the quality. She got out her phone again and texted Stacy: *This just in: when I come visit you, I can stay for the entire weekend.*

A few seconds after she pressed send, her phone rang. Her mood was lifted already. "Stacy!"

"OMG, smalls! Do you know when you're coming in?"

Aurora could practically see him bouncing on the other end of the line while she brought up her office calendar. "I don't have a date set in stone but I think it'll be the Thursday through Sunday, three weeks from now."

"Four days? Sweet!"

She saw an email notification with the subject line *Tried my best* pop up in the corner of her screen. She clicked on it to see that it was her entire East Coast trip itinerary. She should have known Tonya would have planned most of the trip before she discussed it with her. "I just got my details for the trip." She scrunched her brow as she read her Thursday and Friday evening schedule in Baltimore and let out an exasperated sigh.

"What's wrong?"

"I'm doing more consulting work than I thought—I was supposed to just be checking out vendors for our new stores. Looks like both are restaurants, one is called Paella Palace and the other is Fresh Fields."

"Oh! That's my buddy Stevie's restaurant."

"The baseball player?"

Through the charity organization Stacy did marketing for, he had met Stevie Fields at different events. They had started an immediate bromance, which he had been more than happy to tell Aurora about.

"He'll be so stoked to meet you. Do you mind if I have dinner with you both there?"

"If it's okay with Mr. Fields—"

"Stevie."

"Until he gives me the first name go ahead, he's Mr. Fields. Anyway, since Mr. Fields is paying me, I will have to work."

"Eh, work. He just likes to eat and talk about baseball or video games. That's why we get along so well."

Aurora chuckled. Stacy had grown as a person significantly since their college years, but his key interests hadn't changed a bit. "This is great! I'm more excited for my trip now."

"You weren't before?"

"It would have been more of an enticing trip had I not made a vow to Leela that we would work less and play more."

"You definitely played in Hawaii! Those pictures on InstaPic are crazy. Looked like an awesome time, and Leela—if you don't mind me saying—is in peak form in that yellow bikini."

She immediately conjured the image of Leela in that bikini on their last day. The water dripped from her new haircut, and she smiled at her from the surf. Her necklace glinted in the sunshine. "Oh! Leela and I did a commitment thing."

"Shit, smalls! You eloped?"

"No, but you could say we're married without the paperwork part. It wouldn't work for some people but it really works for us." Just thinking about Leela in that way almost brought tears to her eyes.

And an incoming text from Leela stated *Sigh. At least I know you'll make the East Coast a better place. I'll use the time to experiment with my new Love Swirl lotion. Details later.* Leela had punctuated the text with a winky face emoji.

"I don't think I've ever been so happy."

"Aw," Stacy drawled. "Congratulations! The two of you together are just the sweetest. You can hear the love in your voice. You sound...different."

Aurora cocked her head as she thought about Stacy's observation. "You know, I feel different."

CHAPTER FIVE

LEELA TAPPED HER pen aggressively against the desk in her office. "What do you mean there's going to be another week delay?" she asked the contractor in her calmest voice. "I was promised there would be electricity and walls by the time Aurora came back from her trip. *You* promised that."

"I understand that, Ms. Bakshi, but there was a delay in the permits. The electrician won't come in and do the work without the right paperwork."

She rolled her eyes and leaned back into the chair. "Is there any good news you can tell me? Like maybe the flooring we asked for is on a super sale. Or you've decided to give us a hot tub as an acknowledgement of how off-schedule this project is."

"Um. That's a no on the floors and the hot tub, but I was looking at the original blueprints and it would be very easy to build out a mudroom off the kitchen if you ever wanted to look into it."

That piqued her interest. If they had a mudroom, they would no longer have to sort laundry on the kitchen floor. "Would those plans have a price tag associated with them? And before you answer, remember my influence with the local business bureau."

"Ah, jeez. Okay. I'll draw up some plans for you."

"I like that answer." Leela gave Jill a quick wave as she came into the office. "I have to go but I'm looking forward to reading these plans under the light of a lamp in my new room by the end of the week. Bye." She hung up and mimed strangling her phone.

Jill rested a box on her hip. "I'm going to go out on a limb and say that you didn't get the news you wanted."

"I can't talk about it anymore. It's driving me up the wall. . . The wall that still doesn't have drywall." Normally, she'd have Aurora at her side saying calming words and giving her a little shoulder rub when she was upset, but with Aurora gone for over a week, she didn't have balance. Her yin had no yang. And because of it, she was lonely and sad and quick-tempered. "Please tell me you came for something not terrible."

Jill placed the box on the desk in front of Leela. "Then allow me to present to you with what I think is your button maker."

"Oh, gimme!" Leela grabbed her box cutter from the drawer and sliced through the packing tape with delight. She'd had so much fun in college when her microbiology club had made buttons to advocate testing for sexually transmitted diseases. Now, she could use her button-making power to campaign for her presidential run.

She took the directions out, read them, and then picked the large press out of the box. She reached inside to grab the remaining items, but there were none. "What the hell? Where are the parts?"

"What do you mean, 'parts'?"

"You know, the button parts." She picked up the directions once more and skimmed them rapidly. "Shit! 'Button pin-backs, covers, and rims sold separately'." She threw the directions down. "Dammit! All I want to do is make some fucking buttons and have a room with a light switch that works. Am I asking too much of the world?"

Jill sat in the chair across from Leela. "What's wrong?"

"I just told you!"

Jill wore a sad smile. "You miss Aurora a lot, don't you?"

Leela slumped back into her chair. "I do. She's been *so* busy on her trip. We haven't been able to talk as much as I'd hoped, and I'm really afraid Tonya's going to ask her to do more of it."

"You know, Tonya can ask, but Aurora can refuse."

Leela furrowed her brow. Somedays it was clearer than others that Jill had never worked for a corporation. "Not if she wants to keep her job. Besides, I think she's likes being a fancy executive. I swore I heard about first class leg room for a solid five minutes when she landed."

"You seem more agitated than just a case of lonely heart. What else is bugging you about this?"

It was a fair question she didn't know the answer to. Unlike before the trip, her feelings lacked any trace of insecurity and everything to do with a new drive she felt inside of her. Like a primal urge to make sure Aurora was close. "I think it's because I can't protect her."

Jill recoiled in her seat and blinked several times. "You know, if you were a man, I'd have the urge to yell at you."

"I know! It's completely ridiculous, but I have this fear something will happen. I think it started after this." Leela held her pendant up for Jill to see. "Maybe our commitment triggered some kind of mentality shift?"

"Have you told Aurora your fears?"

"No. Can you imagine me telling Aurora I need her home so I can keep her safe? I don't know whether she'd laugh her ass off or get seriously pissed."

"Hmm. Have you told *anybody* your fears?"

Leela knew what Jill was suggesting. "No, I haven't talked to my therapist in a while."

"Maybe you should think about doing that. Couldn't hurt." Jill shrugged. "When does Aurora come home?"

Just the thought of Aurora being home again made her heart fuller, and her fingertip ran over the different textures of the spiral in her pendant. "She'll be back in a few more days. I've missed her like crazy but I am glad she gets to spend some quality time with Stacy before she comes home."

Jill's face lit with surprise. "I didn't know she was able to visit him. God, they haven't seen each other in probably like a year."

Leela nodded. "I'm with it enough to acknowledge that even though I miss her, I know she needs to see him. They've been best friends since college, and video chat only works so well."

"Ah, college friends. I wonder what kind of trouble those two kids are going to try to relive?"

The idea of Aurora in any sort of trouble was laughable. "They're having dinner tomorrow at his friend's restaurant. Then Stacy's giving her a tour of the harbor, followed by goose pin bowling."

"I think you mean duck pin."

"Whatever. She's going bird bowling and, shortly thereafter, she's hopping on a plane. I'm picking her up at the airport." Just thinking about their reunion made her throat tighten and spirits lift. "I can't wait until she's home again."

#

Aurora had visited thirty businesses in five cities. She was mentally and physically exhausted but, much like her Hawaii assignment, she was sure she had collected enough data and observations to write a report that would please all parties involved. The only remaining work hurdle was the dinner at Fresh Fields, which would be more leisure than business. She even had time to slip out of her suit and into something more casual before Stacy came to pick her up from her downtown hotel.

While she waited, she settled in a stylish yet comfortable chair in the lobby and nursed a can of soda, hoping the bubbles and natural properties of the ginger would soothe her queasy stomach.

The stress of the trip had begun to take its toll a few days earlier. Her stomach had churned for most of the day, making food unappetizing, but at least she had learned her lesson and hadn't forced it. No more throwing up for her. At least now she felt semi-normal in the belly.

Of course, it might not have all been stress. Maybe the kombucha vendor hadn't had the right mix of microorganisms? She'd have to ask Leela about that.

Aurora sipped and caught the sports predictions for Saturday's gameday. She didn't really care about college football, but Stacy did. Stacy cared about all things sport, which was why she couldn't have been happier he worked for a non-profit that organized sporting events for children with special needs. It was a shame he had to live on the other side of the country in order to have the opportunity.

As the sports broadcaster explained his pick with zeal, her phone buzzed. She read the text and immediately groaned about the appointment reminder for her annual women's health exam. Scooching down a table in stirrups was the last thing she wanted to do. Still, she sent a reply to confirm.

When she looked up, she saw Stacy's huge frame come through the revolving door. They had known each other for nearly fifteen years, and he still looked the same: a tall, muscle-bound blonde with a complexion fair enough to have a farmer's tan year-round.

"Smalls!" He ran toward her.

"Stacy!" she squealed as he picked her up and spun her. The movement caused her soda to begin to bubble upward. "Oh, boy. Better put me down before I boot."

He lowered her back to the ground and gave her an extra tight hug. "Sorry. I'm just so happy to see you! There's like a ridiculous amount of news to tell you while we drive over. Unless. . . Do you need to power nap? You look exhausted."

"Just work stress and hotel noise is keeping me up."

"So, no weird dreams again?" he asked with a smile.

"Only a garden-variety, psychedelic one."

"Trippy. So, are you ready to go?"

"Yeah, but do you mind if I refill my bottle? I've been thirsty non-stop and I shouldn't have any more ginger ale. Too much sugar."

"Yeah, you want to save the sugar for the desserts at Stevie's place."

After she refilled her bottle, he drove them through the high-rises of the city and to one of the older but trendier parts of Baltimore. As the steel and glass towers were gradually replaced by cobblestone streets and brick buildings, he filled her in with the two pieces of news he had been bursting to share. The first was that he and Stevie had started a new campaign within his organization, which had gained the attention of the entire professional league. The second was that he'd found his one true love, a rescue puppy he'd named Griffey.

Pictures would be shown at dinner.

He pulled into a parking space overlooking the bay as she shook her bottle to confirm there wasn't any water left.

"Did you drink all that already?" he asked, shocked.

She shrugged. "Well, you did most of the talking and I told you I was thirsty." She exited the car and was immediately struck by the unique exterior of the restaurant. A large window advertised 'Fresh Fields' in gold stencil as a simple green awning covered the entryway. A rooftop garden with seating was visible from the street. "This is pretty cool."

"Wait until you get inside! Stevie's already at a table in the back."

Aurora nodded and followed him. She immediately noticed the hardwood floors, long booths, hanging plants, and framed pictures of different families dining hanging throughout. It was far from the pretentious farm-to-table establishment she had expected. This was homey.

At a round table in the back corner, she spied Stevie. Aurora recognized him from Stacy's InstaPic account and the video highlights her dad had made her watch when he'd learned he was two degrees of separation away from a professional athlete.

Stevie had Stacy's build but he had light brown skin and no hair, except for a goatee. On either side of him, he had a cardboard box, one with unsigned baseballs, one with signed ones.

He put a marker down on the table and stood as they approached.

"Hey, buddy!" Stacy said then went for the one-armed man hug.

"Hey!" Stevie finished the hug with a friendly punch to the shoulder. He extended his hand to Aurora and flashed a movie-star smile. "You must be Aurora. It's great to meet you."

Her hand disappeared inside of his. "It's very nice to meet you too. This is the first time I've had a business-friendship crossover. It's kind of neat."

"I'm glad you think so because when Stacy said he knew you would be coming to see my place I got really nervous that you might say no. He's said awesome things about you. Did you really finish a hockey game with a cracked rib?"

She didn't like to brag about anything but she did like it when her toughness was showcased. Even if it was a story from when she was sixteen. "I didn't really know it was cracked at the time. I'm just happy we won the game."

"That's some team spirit if I ever heard it," Stevie said. "Which is great because I feel like we're a team now, except you're the coach. I really, really want your input on what I can do to make this place as sustainable as possible. Not just for the environment, but as my long-term, post-baseball investment." Stevie was far from being a clichéd ballplayer.

"I can certainly help you with both of those goals, Mr. Fields."

"Stevie, please."

She looked at Stacy, who shot her a cocky grin in return. "Okay, Stevie. Considering that you're not currently the manager, do you feel comfortable enough showing me around?"

Stevie swept his arm out dramatically. "Right this way."

Aurora walked through the office, the kitchen, the storage, and the rooftop garden. She took notes and pictures and asked a few staff members about their procedures.

The rich and herbaceous smells made it difficult to focus.

Once they returned to the table in the back, Stevie unfolded his linen napkin and draped it over his lap. "Stacy told me you incorporate serving size into your analysis, so I asked the kitchen to make everything so you can, you know, assess it."

Aurora had glanced at the online menu earlier in the day, hoping that thinking of food would quell her nausea. It hadn't worked then, but her stomach was food-ready now. Even with an appetite, Stevie's announcement caught her off-guard. "That sounds like *a lot* of food for three people."

"It is, but any leftovers will be given to the staff." Stevie looked up to their server. "Water for me. Aurora?"

"Same."

"No more ginger ale?" Stacy asked.

Aurora gestured to her stomach. "Queasy feeling went away. I thought it was a combination of stress and bad kombucha, but now that I think about it, my seitan cheesesteak in Philadelphia seemed odd."

"That's weird." Stacy shook his head. "I'll have the pale ale on draft."

With their drinks ordered and the knowledge that food was on the way, the plain oatmeal she'd forced down earlier in the morning was suddenly not enough.

"I think you're really going to love this," Stacy said. "It's all the local free-trade stuff you like."

"What's your delivery range?" Aurora asked.

"Seasonal and local within four hundred miles."

Due to her recent tour, Aurora had heard of some of the farms he mentioned by name. At his mere mention of potato farms, her mouth started to salivate as she imagined the crisp and salty taste of homemade chips. She could hear the crunch reverberate through her jaw and up to her ear with each bite.

She was so hungry.

While she continued to daydream about salt, sugar, and fat, two servers—each carrying trays of food—placed six square plates of appetizers on the table.

Aurora wanted nothing more than to slather the fried pickle in homemade ranch dressing and devour it. Instead, she took pictures with her tablet once more and made her notes.

"You're killing me, smalls. Can we eat already?"

"Yes. And this looks amazing. Best day at the office I've had since Hawaii."

"Just remember," Stevie said as he added a crab-stuffed mushroom to his plate. "We have the entrées and dessert courses to get through as well, so pace yourself."

Aurora followed Stevie's lead and built a plate of epic proportions. She had eaten healthy for an entire month and would treat herself. Especially since the aroma of salty, fried food matched the fantasy she'd just had. The chips were as crunchy as she had hoped. The pickles in ranch just as tangy. And the mystery fritter had been made by the hand of the Creator.

"What vegetable is in here?" She pointed at a green speck. "It doesn't taste like zucchini."

Stevie stifled a laugh while Stacy stared at her with an amused grin. "It's called broccoli, smalls."

"But I hate broccoli."

"It appears that you don't anymore," Stevie said. "I'm kind of excited to learn if my restaurant's food gives you another change of heart. Or palate."

There was another glistening morsel on the table Aurora had been eyeing. Her brain told her it was wrong, but her taste buds screamed for it. There was no denying her urge. She wanted the cheeseburger slider in Stacy's hand. With a few exceptions, most accidental, she had been a vegetarian since college. But now, a primal instinct inside of her screamed for red meat. "Stacy, please don't judge me, but I need to taste your cheeseburger."

He held the last remaining bite of his miniature burger in front of him. "But it's made from a cow."

"But from a grass-fed cow that lived in a very open and picturesque field among other cows, right?" she asked Stevie.

"Yeah," Stevie drawled unsurely and then looked over to Stacy. "The lady wants some of your burger."

Stacy reluctantly gave her the rest of his slider.

Aurora's fingers sunk into the spongy brioche bun. The melted brie slid onto and down her thumb. A pink disc faced her from between the bread. She respected and honored the cow for giving its life so it could nourish her. She placed the slider in her mouth, tasted all of its warm, savory, fatty goodness, and moaned. It was everything. It was maybe the best bite she had had in her life.

She pointed at Stacy. "Don't tell Leela this happened." After he'd acknowledged her stern warning with a frightened nod, she turned to Stevie. "Are there more?"

Stevie smiled broadly, showcasing a dimple she hadn't seen before. "Can I get you to advertise my restaurant too?"

CHAPTER SIX

A LARGE YAWN escaped Leela as she sat in her truck outside the arrival curb at the airport. It was three in the afternoon and her energy levels were that of bedtime. Her fatigue did not shock her though. Two weeks straight of farm work, building her campaign, and not sleeping well because Aurora wasn't at her side was bound to make her more than just a little exhausted.

A message flashed across her truck's dash. *Hey dreamy, just got my luggage. Have to hit restroom then I'll be out.*

Leela's sluggishness vanished when she read her special nickname. She realized she hadn't appreciated it's deep meaning until now. The idea that she had once begged to have another nickname was preposterous. Aurora was her sweets, and she was Aurora's dreamy. That was the way nature intended it. To have it any other way would be a terrible way to live.

Might as well get rid of all the goats too and just call it the apocalypse.

Right as Leela was about to chastise herself for being completely, disgustingly in love, she saw Aurora come out from the automated doors. Her heart swelled immediately at the gorgeous sight of her love in jeans and a hoodie.

She didn't mind being disgustingly in love.

Leela shut the car off, opened the door to rush out, and was violently held back by her seatbelt. The strap dug into her breast like a punch. She shook off the discomfort, unbuckled herself, and jumped from the car.

Aurora saw her, uttered an excited yelp, and rushed toward her as fast as her baggage would allow.

As they reunited, Leela smiled uncontrollably and hugged Aurora with all her might. Everything felt right. Aurora's warmth, being, and love was in Leela's arms. She realized her reaction was more akin to welcoming someone home after they had been deployed to war overseas. She couldn't help it. When Leela realized she couldn't possibly hug Aurora more, she brought her hands to Aurora's jaw and guided her into a kiss.

She didn't even care that some cockwaffle's car alarm went off behind them.

"Wow, this is quite the greeting. I missed you too," Aurora said with a slight laugh then kissed her again.

There was nothing on earth like the tender and soft feel of Aurora's lips against hers. The only thing that distracted Leela from the joy her heart felt from being together once again was the intense spice of Aurora's breath. "That's some gingery breath you have there. Wow."

"I was sucking on some hard candies they sell for motion sickness."

Leela loaded Aurora's bags into the back of the truck and then opened the passenger door. "You don't normally get motion sick."

"I've had a weird stomach off and on since Philly. I'm starting to think I might be getting an ulcer."

Leela started the engine and shook her head. "Please tell me you're going to take it easy this week. I know you love your job, but don't let the stress literally eat a hole through you."

Aurora reached for Leela's thigh and rubbed it gently. "I know you worry, but you don't have to about this. I already told Tonya I'm taking tomorrow off."

"Really?" Leela glanced over with a smile before her attention went to the road.

"Yeah, the only thing I'm doing tomorrow is laundry, going to my doctor's appointment, and possibly going on a movie date with you."

"I completely support this plan, especially the movie part. The new steampunky sci-fi that came out last week is getting great reviews. Well, Keith liked it, and he hates most movies. Maybe we can go after your appoint—" Leela yawned, cutting herself off without enough time to cover her cavernous mouth. "Sorry, I'm super beat."

"Have you been getting enough rest while I've been gone?"

"I tried, but it's not the same when you're gone." Leela pouted. "I need my little spoon. My front has been very cold at night."

Aurora laughed and moved her hand higher on Leela's thigh. "I think a marathon cuddle session is in order. Oh! Then I can show you all the videos I took of Stacy's puppy."

"Yes, we must work pictures of the puppy into this agenda," Leela said with a grin. "How was your visit with Stacy? You started to tell me but then had to board your flight."

"Playing with Griffey in the park was a highlight. So, so cute, but training is definitely an obstacle. Hopefully, they'll sort that all out by the time he's one hundred pounds."

Leela gasped. "That's a person! I didn't know Stacy got a person-sized dog. Is the cute factor worth the person-sized messes?"

"At this stage, yes. He fell asleep while eating."

"Still talking about the dog, right?" Leela asked and received a loving slap on the thigh from Aurora in return. "How about the visit to the restaurant? Is his friend, Stevie, cool?"

"Very cool, and I think as far as pro athlete enterprises go, Stevie is taking this very seriously. It should be an easy analysis." Aurora dug inside her pocket and unwrapped a candy. "How about you? How's President Bakshi?"

Leela sighed. "Still without buttons but I finally decided on five main points, so that's a win. And in news related to my budding power, I was able to negotiate free mudroom plans due to the electrical delay."

"We're getting a mudroom?"

"Not yet, but I'm going to work all my mojo to get us one." Leela thought about her two weeks of lonely bachelorette living and placed her hand over Aurora's. "And, of course, I thought about you all the time. Starting thinking. . . Ah, never mind. It's stupid."

"Nothing you think is stupid. What's bothering you?"

Leela bit the inside of her cheek and shook her head. She dared to look over at Aurora, and Aurora's deep brown eyes looked into hers.

"Were you letting your brain torture you again?" Aurora asked gently.

Leela slowly nodded. "But this time it's a new torture. It's like…" She didn't think she could form the words to Aurora, even after practicing them.

"It's okay if you don't want to tell me or don't know how to, but have you let your therapist know what's been happening?"

"If by 'know' you mean communicated this information in some way then, no, I haven't."

"Leela," Aurora drawled.

"I know, I know. How about this?" Leela said upbeat. "I'll call her when you're at your doctor appointment. That way we'll both be attending to self-care at the same time."

"I like that plan a lot. I worry about you just as much as you worry about me."

Leela understood the sentiment but she knew it wasn't true. She had to protect Aurora and she would do whatever it took to do so.

"You okay?" Aurora asked. "You just got really quiet."

"Just thinking about our puppy-watching cuddles."

#

She had to pee so bad.

Aurora tried not to squirm in her seat as she waited for a nurse to call her to the back for her exam. It had definitely been a mistake to drink a ginger ale and an entire bottle of water before she even walked through the door. She took her mind off her bladder by briefly looking at the magazine covers in front of her that featured food, celebrities, world events, and parenting.

Such a waste of paper.

She turned her attention to the different women who waited in the room with her. Women of every body type. Every age. Every race. Every emotional state.

"Ms. Okpik?"

She put down her ignored e-reader and approached the receptionist desk.

"Can you please double check that your insurance is still accurate and update your medical information on the tablet?"

Aurora took the tablet and returned to her seat. Phone number, address, insurance, and emergency contact were all the same since her last visit. How was she feeling today? She checked the box for GI issues. When was the date of her last period? Aurora furrowed her brow as she did the math in her head. Normally, her cycle was like clockwork, but because of travel, stress, and the change in exercise routine, she realized she'd skipped. It wasn't unheard of for her but it was rare.

The last set of questions stole her breath: changes to family history. Aurora detailed as much information as she could remember in the text field. *Five months ago, my mother (57-years-old) had a mastectomy of the left breast to remove a stage 3 malignant tumor. Chemotherapy still ongoing.*

Aurora hadn't seen her mother since the procedure, but she and Leela would be visiting again in the next month for Irony Day. Aurora knew the reunion would be difficult. She just hoped she had the strength to keep her emotions together when they held each other in their arms once more. Just thinking about the scarf that covered her mother's head instead of her long graying hair caused Aurora's chest to tighten.

She finalized her form, returned the tablet to the front desk, and took the travel-sized roll of antacids out of her bag as she took her seat. Ginger candies weren't cutting it. After another few minutes of reading her e-book, a nurse stepped into the fringe of the waiting room. "Ms. Okpik, would you follow me, please?"

Aurora followed the typical routine. She slid off her canvas shoes and reluctantly stood on the scale. Her gaze went everywhere but on the weights the nurse manipulated to balance the measurement.

"You know what's next." She handed Aurora a plastic cup wrapped in more plastic and then pointed to a single-use bathroom. "Fill to the line and leave it on the counter. When you're finished, go to exam room three. I'll come in to do your vitals after I test that." She pointed to the cup.

Aurora gave her a quick thumbs-up then closed the door behind her to eagerly provide her urine sample. Life was instantly better. Of course, she wasn't looking forward to the next, more personal part of her visit.

She headed in the direction of the exam room.

This was only the second time she had seen Dr. Camila Aguilar, and while Aurora appreciated her bedside manner, the exam room was still like every other. Models and anatomical posters of breasts and the female reproductive system were scattered throughout the room, along with pamphlets about STI awareness, cancer prevention, and new pharmaceuticals. The mobile of crystals hanging from the ceiling was the only thing off theme.

She liked that it would provide a sparkly focal point for when her feet were in the stirrups.

She sat down in the visitor's chair and opened her e-reader once more, since she wasn't sure how long she was going to have to wait. It was so much easier to follow the story now that her bladder wasn't at full capacity.

Just as she learned the protagonist had been born into magic, there was a knock at the partially open door.

The short and stocky woman in the doorway surprised her. "Dr. Aguilar? I didn't think I'd see you yet."

"Neither did I, to be honest." She gave Aurora a kind smile and came into the room along with her intake nurse. She sat at the simple desk along the wall and looked at what Aurora assumed was her electronic chart. "How's Leela?"

"She's doing well. Business is great and she's running to be the president of the farmers' market. She says 'hi', by the way, and to let her know if you need any lotion or soap refills."

Dr. Aguilar nodded patiently but continued to stare at Aurora's chart. "I'm glad to hear it."

After a beat of silence that was too long for her liking, Aurora asked, "Is something wrong? Do you need more information about my mom or something?"

"No, the information you provided is very good—detail speaking, of course." She looked up at Aurora with a very serious gaze. "You know that while I'm friendly with Leela, you know that anything concerning your health is confidential, right?"

Aurora furrowed her brow at the odd question. "Yes, I know. What's going on?"

Dr. Aguilar bit her bottom lip. "You're pregnant."

"What?" Aurora asked with a half laugh. "No, I'm not. There is no possible way I could be pregnant. The urine test must have given you a false positive." She watched her doctor and nurse share a look. "It happens. I've seen it on TV."

"We know," Dr. Aguilar responded. "And that's why I asked Laci to run it again. And you're..."

"Still pregnant," Laci stated dryly and received a sharp look from Dr. Aguilar in return.

"Then maybe the entire box of test strips or whatever is off. Like a bad lot was released. That's a much more logical explanation than me being pregnant."

"I'm sorry but I don't believe the test is faulty," Dr. Aguilar said. "Now, I apologize in advance if this sounds invasive or judgmental, but it's important. On your chart, you indicate that you're bisexual."

Aurora nodded then felt heat rise into her face as the implication sank in. "I haven't had sex with a man in almost ten years! This is ridiculous. Can I just get a blood test or something to prove that I'm not pregnant?"

Dr. Aguilar turned to Laci. "Can you please get a kit prepped while I go through the rest of Aurora's form with her?" As soon as Laci left, she looked at Aurora's chart once more. "Under the current health field, you marked 'GI issues'; can you expand on that?"

It took a moment for Aurora to shift mental gears. She was still shocked she needed a blood test to prove she wasn't pregnant, and that her doctor had inferred she'd cheated on Leela. "I just came back from a two-week work trip. It was good but stressful, with a lot of city-to-city travel and looming deliverables, so my stomach's been acting up."

"How long?"

Aurora looked up at the shimmering mobile as she thought. "I guess it's been a little over a week now."

Dr. Aguilar added the detail to her chart. "And the date of your last period was early September. Do you normally skip cycles?"

"No. But, again...work stress."

Laci returned with the blood draw kit on a tray.

"Can you please take off your hoodie? We'll do your blood pressure and pulse while we're at it."

Aurora complied with their wishes and sat through the different tests. She shook her head while she watched her blood fill the vial but was somewhat less agitated when they covered the puncture with a bandage featuring Rosie the Riveter.

Once Laci left the exam room with her sample, Dr. Aguilar, said, "This could take a few hours, so—"

"A few hours!"

"Sorry. On the bright side, there was a cancellation just before you got here, so I can do your exam at that time. They can set you up with that appointment. Why don't you go home in the meantime and come back?"

Aurora rolled her eyes, catching the sparkly mobile again. If her home hadn't been filled with construction sounds and the trip wouldn't have been a waste of fuel, she would have considered going home. "I'll just go to the coffee shop across the street. I'll wait for someone to call me."

"Sounds good." When Dr. Aguilar started to leave, she added, "Please get something decaffeinated, just in case."

Aurora reached for her phone and texted Leela. *You wouldn't believe how my visit's going. I'll be home much later than expected.*

There was no response, but Aurora didn't expect one since Leela did the quality control checks around this time of the morning.

The only thing that could have make the experience more annoying was if the coffee shop had been was closed or they were out of decaf chai. Fortunately, they weren't.

Aurora tried to enjoy her warm, spiced drink and get back into her book's storyline, but it was impossible. Never in her wildest dreams would she have thought this would have been how her day would go. And she'd had some pretty wild dreams in her lifetime.

She put the e-reader away in a huff, propped up her phone, and watched a movie about a heist.

After her second cup of tea, a few rounds of unbraiding and re-braiding her hair, and three wrong guesses as to how the group of attractive thieves pulled off the robbery, a notification flashed across her tiny screen.

You have an appointment at Oregon Women's Care Associates. Please reply 'Confirmed' if you intend on keeping this appointment or 'No' if canceling.

She shouldn't have been surprised an automatic message would be delivered. Aurora replied 'Confirmed' and stopped the movie. Aurora caught the restroom sign as she put her ceramic tea mug in the wash bin. A quick visit probably would be in her best interest.

Aurora walked back to the women's center and was directed to Dr. Aguilar's office instead of an exam room. Aurora had never wanted a Pap smear so fast in her life. Her patience had reached its limit.

She followed the directions to the office and found Dr. Aguilar sitting behind her desk. A different woman sat in one of the two visitor chairs. Her name badge read, *Diana, Reproductive Thera-pist.* Aurora took the seat beside her.

"Thank you for coming back so quickly," Dr. Aguilar said. "I hope you don't mind, but I left Laci behind and brought in a differ-ent colleague. This is Diana, she normally—"

"What's going on?" Aurora demanded. "This is supposed to be my fun day off, but the only thing fun about today is that I've dis-covered antacids that taste like candy."

"Ms. Okpik," Diana started, "I want you to know that if you'd like me to leave at any point, I can."

"Okay, fine, but why are you here?" Aurora asked more loudly than she intended. "This whole thing is weird. I came in for a regu-lar appointment, you think I'm pregnant—which is ridiculous—

and now my intake nurse has been replaced by a reproductive therapist."

Dr. Aguilar sighed then her eyes softened. "Aurora, the blood test confirmed it. You are pregnant."

"But I can't be! I told you, I haven't had sex with a man in forever."

"Both Dr. Aguilar and I believe you," Diana said. "I'd like you to think back to about a month ago. Did you have any blackouts?"

"I don't drink," Aurora said firmly.

"I didn't mean to imply that it would be a blackout caused by alcohol consumption," Diana added. "Do you recall waking up disoriented? Waking up in a strange place? Or didn't know what you had done the night before?"

A month ago, Aurora had been in Hawaii and remembered every moment with crystal clarity. "Why would you even…?" Then, the reason for the questions dawned on her. "I wasn't roofied. I know the signs and I haven't experienced any of those. Did you test for that when you took my blood?"

"Unfortunately, a drug like that metabolizes too quickly to be detected in blood tests," Diana said. "It's possible but unlikely it would be detectable in a hair sample. However, I'm not a law enforcement officer. They would know much more about this than I do. If you'd like, I can escort you or call the police and act as a liaison. Your partner doesn't have to find out."

The serious tone and looks they both gave her caused her to suppress the snarky comment she was about to utter. They were convinced she was pregnant. A couple of botched urinalyses and a blood test were all it had taken. It wasn't even like she had symp—

Her missed period.

The queasiness.

The change in her appetite and tastes.

Realization, confusion, anger, and fear landed four forceful blows. Aurora couldn't talk, she couldn't move. She was numb.

There was a life growing inside of her and she couldn't fathom how it had gotten there.

The air moved into and then from her lungs faster and faster. Her vision began to blur and shrink.

"Aurora, you need to take slow breaths," Diana said in an almost melodic voice.

She did as instructed and gradually regained her sense of awareness.

"We understand you're shocked, but you're going to be okay," Diana cooed. "And we will do everything in our power to support you and provide what you need."

Aurora nodded slowly and leaned over, elbows on her knees. She needed a lot of things. She needed to understand how this had happened because, if she didn't understand, how could she accept it? And if *she* couldn't accept the news, how in the world would Leela?

She started to lose control of her breathing again as she began to sob.

"Focus on slow ins and outs," Dr. Aguilar reminded her and pulled several tissues from a box. "Leela doesn't have to know. The only people who know are confined to this room. Even Laci doesn't know it was confirmed."

"I have to tell Leela! How can I not tell her?" Aurora choked out. But how could she tell her? There was no possible way Leela would believe she hadn't cheated on her. There was no other explanation. "I don't understand anything that's happening right now."

"That's why I'm here," Diana said gently. "We can go to my office and talk about next steps, even if that next step only involves me sending you home with someone. Everything is entirely up to you."

"Do you want Leela here as we talk about your options?" Dr. Aguilar asked gently.

The word 'options' had never sounded so weighted before. She didn't know how to move forward with any choice that may have been presented to her. Despite the hurt Aurora knew it would cause, she couldn't move forward without Leela at her side.

"I need Leela. Please, get her here."

CHAPTER SEVEN

WHAT DO YOU think has prompted these feelings of fear? the online therapist asked her.

Leela's fingers paused over the keyboard. How could she succinctly articulate that she and Aurora were so madly in love that it felt like they exchanged pieces of each other's souls. Ergo, she knew that blissful feeling would be ripped away in the most tragic and horrifying way possible. Her fingers typed *I guess because I'm happy.*

She was about to add a comment about the political climate when her cell phone rang, drawing her attention away. Leela knew she had to finish the therapy session, but the caller identification piqued her interest. And concern. Why would Dr. Aguilar's office call her during Aurora's appointment? "Hello. This is Leela."

"Hi, Leela, this is Dr. Aguilar. I'm calling because Aurora is asking that you come to the office."

Leela's hunched shoulders went back and down immediately. "What happened?" There was a long pause on the other line, which caused her to stand. "Is everything okay?"

"We should talk about it once you get here."

Everything inside Leela went cold at her tone. "I'm on my way," she said with a shaky voice. The line disconnected and she typed *I have to go. Family emergency.* She ran from behind her desk and stopped right before she ran into Keith holding a box. "Move!"

"I just thought I'd drop off your button-making stuff. Where's the fire?" he said with a grin.

"There's an emergency with Aurora."

His grin disappeared and was replaced by steely focus. "You go. I have everything under control here."

Leela gave a nod of thanks and rushed to her truck. She fumbled with her keys and dropped them down by the pedals. "Shit!" She had to relax. She gripped the steering wheel and took a deep breath to calm her nerves. There could be a number of reasons why Dr. Aguilar had called and not Aurora. That reminded her that she had forgotten to read a text Aurora had sent while she'd QCed her outgoing shipment.

You wouldn't believe how my visit's going. I'll be home much later than expected.

That could have meant a dozen different things. There could have been a fight between baby daddies in the waiting room. Aurora could have been kept waiting because of staff calling out for the day. Or maybe they found a growth. A lump.

Leela's eyes started to water as she reached for the keys between her feet. If Dr. Aguilar had found a lump, no wonder Aurora needed her there. Leela swallowed her fear. She was letting her paranoia get the best of her again and, even if she wasn't being paranoid, she had to overcome her own mental baggage so she could be Aurora's rock.

She turned the key and sped out of her gravel driveway, leaving a cloud of dust in her wake. She knew the trooper who monitored the road between her farm and town only pulled people over for speeding if they went fifteen over the limit. She set her cruise control for fourteen over and hoped today wasn't a day the train crossing stopped her.

Once she had arrived at the office, the automated doors slid open, and she made a beeline for the receptionist's desk. "Dr. Aguilar asked me to come in."

The woman's eyes flashed with recognition and she stood from behind the desk. "Right this way, Leela."

Leela had been coming to this office for over ten years, but this was the first time she'd been down the physician's office hall. It wasn't all that different from her mother's cardiology office or her father's endocrinology office. Thin carpet, light gray walls, and a series of black and white artistically shot photographs that displayed different stages of womanhood hung between each office. Muffled voices came from behind the door with the placard *Camila Aguilar, MD, FACOG.*

"They're in there," the receptionist whispered and knocked lightly on the door before leaving.

Leela watched her depart and steeled a breath. The door opened, but the unfamiliar woman who stood to greet her barely registered. Her focus was on Aurora, who sat with a tear-stained face, a box of tissues on the desk beside her, and a trashcan at her feet.

Her heart, soul, and entire being broke at the sight.

Despite her unyielding resolve beginning to crumble, Leela rushed to her side. Their arms reached for each other. Aurora clung to her and spoke, but the words muffled in her neck were too incoherent to understand.

"Shh," Leela softly cooed while she stroked the top of Aurora's head. "Whatever it is, we'll get through this." In their time together as a couple, she had never seen Aurora like this. Not even when her mother had been diagnosed with cancer. Whatever had caused this level of devastation must have been life changing. A tightness and burn built in the back of Leela's throat, but she forced her own tears back.

The sound of the door's latch clicked behind her.

While Aurora clung to her, Leela locked eyes with the thin woman who shut the door behind her.

"I'm glad you were able to get here so quickly," Dr. Aguilar commented from behind her desk.

"What's going on?" Leela asked. "And who are you?"

"My name is Diana, and I work here as a therapist."

Why was her life suddenly filled with therapists? Although, she knew her own life needs were completely irrelevant. This was entirely about Aurora. "We'll get through this, sweets," she said softly as she continued to hold Aurora's shaking body.

"Aurora," Dr. Aguilar said softly. "Do you want to proceed the way we discussed?"

Leela felt Aurora nod against her shoulder and gradually pulled herself away. She finally had a clear glimpse of Aurora's face; she was terrified. Leela pushed a strand of hair that had escaped Aurora's braid behind her ear. "Your mom's getting through it and we'll get through this too. Dad knows the absolute best people doing hormone therapy."

Aurora shook her head. "It's not cancer," she squeaked out.

"Thank Gods." Leela rested her forehead against Aurora's. "Then whatever this is you'll be fine. I'll be right be your side for whatever you need." Leela kissed her and gave her a reassuring smile despite the confusion she still felt. If it wasn't cancer, Leela had no idea why Aurora would be so upset.

"I. . . I still don't understand," Aurora said. "Please don't be mad. Please don't leave."

The requests were so unexpected and, in a way, so ridiculous Leela could only stare and nod. "Okay. But why would I be mad or leave? I love you too much to ever leave you."

Aurora sniffed, bit her quivering lower lip, and looked at her square in the eyes. "I'm pregnant."

Leela knew what the words meant, but she'd never imagined them coming from Aurora's mouth. Yet they did. It was shocking, but she realized she only had herself to blame. She had been too caught up with her own world and, as a consequence, hadn't provided what Aurora needed, which had caused her to seek attention from someone else.

Despite the emotional blow, Leela would be true to her word. She would be there for Aurora. "Okay. It's okay. I'm shocked but I understand why and I still won't leave."

"What? You understand?" Aurora asked with a dozen emotions across her face before she broke down again, but this time, not into Leela's arms.

"Shh," Leela soothed and stroked her cheek. "It's not like you had sex with someone *after* Hawaii."

"I haven't had sex with anyone except for you since we've been together! I would never cheat on you! I've never, ever even thought..."

"Okay, okay." She held Aurora's face in her hands. "I'm sorry. I'm sorry, okay. I didn't want to think that, I'm trying to understand how." If Aurora hadn't had a fling with someone else that only left one other option, and that explained why Diana was in the room. Leela's blood went cold, her heart stopped, and she looked at Diana. "Are you with the police?"

"No," Diana answered, "I'm a—"

"I wasn't raped," Aurora said softly. "I know what you're thinking and I wasn't."

The urge to vomit stayed, and the mental war inside Leela began. She believed Aurora, so Dr. Aguilar or the tests had to be wrong. "Then, there's obviously been a mistake," Leela said to Dr. Aguilar. "Someone in this office made a mistake with the tests."

Despite the accusation, the doctor remained calmly seated at her desk. "There were two urinalyses from confirmed kits and blood tests. And before you ask, we ran those three times, by three different people. Based on those results, it places conception mid to late September."

Leela imagined the calendar from the past month. The time frame placed the conception during their stay in Hawaii. And there had definitely been one person there who had been keen on Aurora the entire time. "That son of a bitch," she mumbled as she looked to the ground.

"Who are you thinking about?" Diana asked.

"That muscle-bound, obsessive freak Mac is who. He was fixated with Aurora the entire time we were there and was alone with her multiple times. He could have easily slipped her something when she was at the gym and then…" Leela couldn't finished. Anger, sadness, and guilt crept in, along with the bitter taste of bile that started to rise.

Aurora placed a hand gently on her arm. "Mac couldn't have done this. I already told them I didn't have any symptoms of being roofied. I remember everything from that trip and I was on a tight schedule. Someone would have noticed if I had been gone for even five minutes." Aurora closed her eyes and sat in silence.

Leela knew she was processing. And she needed that time too. Aurora was pregnant, and that could only be the result of two things: egg and sperm. But Aurora was convinced she hadn't been assaulted and Leela believed her when she said she hadn't cheated.

The situation made absolutely no sense.

Aurora wiped away fresh tears before she opened her eyes. "Could Leela and I have a moment alone?"

"Of course," Dr. Aguilar said and rose from her seat. "Diana, let's go into your office."

Once she and Aurora were alone, Aurora reached for Leela's hands. "I know you're struggling with this. I don't know how this happened or even what I'm going to do, but I *need* you to believe me."

"I do. And I support whatever you want to do." Both of those were true; she wasn't just saying the words Aurora wanted to hear.

"Thank you," Aurora said just louder than a whisper. "Do you think I should go to the police?"

It was a direct question that required a direct answer. "Yes. But only because we don't know what we don't know, right?"

"I don't understand what you mean by that."

"Well, we don't know what happened, and letting the police know is the only way I think we're going to learn."

Aurora dabbed her eyes, blew her nose, and nodded. "Can you ask Dr. Aguilar and Diana to come back in?"

#

Aurora toyed with the end of her braid as she stared vacantly at the *Helping Survivors of Sexual Assault* pamphlet in Leela's hand and listened to the one-sided phone conversation between Diana and someone from the local police. They were sitting in Diana's office now and Diana was explaining that there was a woman in her office who may have been tranquilized with a new drug while on vacation.

That was wrong.

She knew she should speak up and tell Diana to hang up. Nothing nefarious had happened to her. There was no one the police could arrest. But she didn't have the mental energy to form arguments or to explain that she may be pregnant, but it hadn't been through any means that could easily explain it.

"Aurora?" Diana held her palm over the phone's receiver. "Do you feel comfortable talking to a detective? They can send someone over right now. You don't have to go to the station."

Aurora gave the faintest of nods.

"Yes, please send someone. . . Good. . . Yes, I've worked with Detective Garrison before. . . Bye."

"How long until they get here?" Leela asked, but she didn't strip her gaze away from the pamphlet.

"Only about five or ten minutes. Now, Aurora, while the detectives are here, at some point one will probably want to speak to Leela while the other is speaking to you."

"There's no way I'm leaving her side," Leela said.

"It's okay." Aurora reassured her with a sad smile. "They probably already think I've had an affair and will confess to it if you're not in the room."

"They don't think that, Aurora," Diana said. "No one is judging you."

Angry tears were now threatening to fall down her cheeks. "Just let them ask their questions and take their samples so I can go home. I just want to go home," she said to Leela.

Leela patted her hand and looked to Diana. "Will you stay with Aurora?"

"That's up to her. If she wants me, I'll be there, or I can call someone who specializes in this kind of advocacy."

"Wait. What kind of therapist are you?" Leela asked.

"I am a licensed sexual therapist, and while I do offer assault counseling, I mostly deal with infertility issues. That's why I recommend reaching out to these different groups if you want someone to talk to after today. I'm sure you'll each have your own individual feelings as well as how you feel as a couple."

Aurora had been so overwhelmed, she hadn't processed what her pregnancy would do to their relationship.

She was sure Leela loved her and would do anything for her. But could Leela's love go further? Could Leela love the being of mysterious origin inside of her? Aurora berated herself for even thinking such a question when she wasn't even sure if *she* could love it. How could she love something she hadn't even known existed less than a few hours ago?

There was a knock at Diana's door.

"They're here already?" Aurora asked, but then glanced to the clock on the wall. For ten minutes, she'd been recycling the same questions in her brain.

Diana paused in the middle of standing from her desk. "Have you changed your mind?"

"No. Let's just get this over with."

Diana went to open the door. She stayed in the hallway for a brief moment, mumbled a few words, and then ushered into the room someone who looked like he had once played linebacker in the NFL and a woman who looked like she had been born to be a cop. "Detectives Garrison and Malone, this is Aurora and her partner, Leela."

After the introductions, it didn't take Aurora very long to explain her side of the story. She was pregnant and not from an affair or from an assault. The detectives asked her questions about grogginess, confusion, and missing time. She consented to a hair sample and further blood testing. Then, they did what Diana said they would do.

Detective Garrison and Leela left for Dr. Aguilar's office.

Detective Malone waited until the door clicked to continue with her questions. "So, now that Ms. Bakshi's gone—"

Aurora met her gaze dead on. She wanted to say it only once and she wanted to be believed. "I didn't cheat on Leela, and I wasn't raped. I have no idea why I'm pregnant, but it's not one of those two ways. My answer will not change because that's the truth."

#

"Thank you," Leela said as Detective Garrison handed her a paper cup of water.

As the cool fluid touched her lips and traveled down, her dehydrated cells were relieved and the rawness in her throat disappeared.

"So, what do you think of all this?" he asked with his arms folded.

Leela took a glance at Dr. Aguilar's empty chair. Not that she would have been able to help all that much. "I think that this is crazy. I trust Aurora but, by trusting her, that means I have to believe one of the most heinous acts that could happen to a person happened to her. Happened to the person I love more than I've ever loved anyone else."

He nodded sympathetically and looked around the room. "So, you believe her? That she didn't cheat on you?"

"Yes. Now, when are *you* going to start believing that?"

"I just have to ask to cross the question off the list. So, you think she was drugged?"

It hurt so much to admit. "Yes."

He began to pace the room. "According to Diana, she didn't have any symptoms of being tranquilized."

Leela didn't care if the detective was twice her size, she crushed the paper cup in her hand anyway. "Look, I get that a drug without side effects is unprecedented and makes it harder to do your job, but all you have to do is check the tapes at the resort. There are security cameras all over the place, including the gym, which was the only time she was ever even close to being alone during that time period. And while Mac may not have done the deed, he could have slipped her something while they were in the gym so that somebody else could."

"What's the name of this hotel? And who's Mac?"

"The Milohila Resort. And he's their driver and gofer for VIP clientele."

He took out his phone, typed in the name, and flipped the phone's screen to face Leela. "Is this the place?"

The once beautiful but now ominous-looking resort faced her. "That's the one. Do you think they'll cooperate?"

"I tend to be optimistic, especially if it's a low-level employee who may be a liability."

Finally, the teeniest shred of good news. "Do you think I can go back and see Aurora now?"

"Almost. I have one more question. Do you know *anyone* who would want to harm Aurora?"

"No! She's a saint! She's the most loving, kind-hearted, perfect person on this planet. Of course, if you're evil and soulless then I guess you wouldn't like her. So, I guess your suspects are hate groups, big oil, and the NRA."

"I'll take that as a 'no' then."

There was a knock at the door, which was quickly followed by Detective Malone's head popping in. "Sorry to interrupt."

"It's fine. I think we're done." Detective Garrison stood and took a business card from the inside of his suit jacket. "Thank you for the lead. We'll keep you and Ms. Okpik apprised of our progress, but if you think of anything else…" He gave her the card. "Please call."

She took it and tucked it into her back pocket, where it joined the half dozen other cards Diana had given her.

Leela made the short walk back to Diana's office and saw that Dr. Aguilar had joined them. She was speaking to Aurora.

"You don't need to—and you shouldn't make any decisions right now," Dr. Aguilar said while Diana nodded beside her. "Read the pamphlets, call the numbers, and—" She made eye contact with Leela. "Please talk to each other. Your relationship will be better for it. Do you have any questions for me?"

Aurora shook her head but still said, "No."

With a nod, Dr. Aguilar left the room, but not before giving Leela a friendly pat on the shoulder. "Please talk to your therapist about this."

Since she was Leela's doctor too, Dr. Aguilar was privy to all of her medical history and had her best interests in mind, but the suggestion triggered the same rage that had caused her to crush the cup. But the last thing Aurora needed was for Leela to get emotional. Leela swallowed her anger, came behind Aurora, and rested her hands on her shoulders.

"What do we do now?" Aurora asked.

Diana gestured to a Manila folder between her and Aurora. "I would recommend you skim through the literature before you go, just in case it sparks any questions, but you can call me at any time. I'll give you two another moment alone so you can discuss."

Aurora nodded. Once Diana had left the room, she stood and walked to the window, which overlooked the park. Then, she turned to the embryo development-fruit comparison mini-poster.

Leela would have given anything to know what was going on inside her head.

"It'll be a blueberry soon," Aurora said.

"Huh?"

"According to this chart, the embryo will be blueberry-sized at seven weeks, but I'm not that far along. What's smaller than a blueberry?"

Leela wanted to scream at the absurdity of the question, but if this was what Aurora wanted to talk about then that's what they would talk about. "I think it depends on the farm and season. Jill's blueberries are pretty big, so maybe…a chickpea?"

Aurora nodded and returned to her seat. "How did it go with Detective Garrison?"

"I told him I believed you and that he should check the tapes at the resort. How about you? Did she treat you well?"

Aurora shrugged. "I didn't think about the tapes. I'm not thinking at all."

Leela kneeled on the floor in front of Aurora. She placed both hands in hers. "This isn't your fault."

"I don't know what to do. I've never felt so lost in my life."

If Aurora was lost, then it was Leela's job to provide direction. "How about I give you two options, and you just have to pick one?"

"Yeah, okay."

"Good." This was progress. "Do you want to stay here or do you want to leave?"

"I want to leave," Aurora said without taking a second to think.

"Do you want to go home or somewhere else?"

"I want to go home, but there's construction."

Leela hated that fucking construction so much. She pursed her lips while she thought. What wasn't home but were places Aurora felt completely comfortable and safe? "Do you want to sit in the truck at the city overlook or take a walk on the park's trail?"

Aurora cocked her head slightly and took a deep breath. "Let's walk. I haven't visited the ducks at the pond there in a long time."

The pure sweetness of Aurora's voice caused Leela's emotions to rise again. Why was the world so cruel? "Okay, sweets. Let's do that." She grabbed the folder and led Aurora through the office. She gave a quick wave goodbye to Diana and walked Aurora to the parking lot.

Aurora paused behind her truck. "Looks like you were in a hurry."

Leela looked at her truck parked crooked across two spaces. "Yeah, I pretty much drove like a bat out of hell to get here." She opened the passenger side door for Aurora and offered her hand as assistance to get in.

Aurora looked at the helping hand and leaned forward. Her lips were soft and reassuring. When Aurora's arms came around her body, the emotion Leela had pushed down slowly surfaced.

The hiccup of the first sob caught Leela by surprise. She tried to rein it back with sheer will, but Aurora tightened her hold and between her own tears said, "It's okay. You're allowed to cry too."

The floodgate opened.

They clung to each other in the parking lot, blocked by the open truck door, and gave in to their feelings. They didn't try to speak. They didn't have to.

Finally, Aurora began to say comforting words to her, and Leela knew she had to stop crying. If Aurora could gain control, so could she.

"I'm sorry," Leela said and wiped away her tears. "I need to be your rock right now."

"Leela, you're not a rock. You're my partner." After Aurora said the words, her face grew even more ashen.

"What is it, sweets?"

"You're still my partner, right?"

"Gods, yes! Please don't ever, ever doubt that." Leela embraced her harder and held on until Aurora's shaking body calmed. "I have what I feel like are hundreds of emotions and thoughts right now, but at the very top of my list is supporting and protecting you." Aurora pulled back from the hug enough for Leela to see her tears had stopped.

"That's good. I need to know that you're feeling a lot too. It makes me feel less alone."

"Like you have a partner?" Leela asked with a hint of a smile.

"Yeah," Aurora said with a tiny laugh. "And partners share, so can you tell me what you're thinking and feeling, other than being supportive and protective? Which you're doing a good job of."

"Thanks." As much as Leela appreciated the compliment, she didn't want to unload her emotions in a parking lot. "Can I tell you when we settle into our next destination? Maybe the park?"

Some of the tension that had been carried in Aurora's shoulders left. "The park's good." Aurora climbed in the passenger seat.

As Leela walked to her side of the truck, she realized she didn't know what choice to offer Aurora after the park. Or how to articulate how she felt.

#

The crisp fall day had less foot traffic at the park than Aurora had anticipated, but she supposed the middle of a weekday wouldn't draw much of a crowd.

Aurora never imagined how something so small could impact her—impact them—so much in a span of hours. And there had to be an explanation. As she thought about everything she knew related to sex and reproduction, she landed on a fact. Something plausible.

"Do you remember when we had dinner with your dad for your birthday?" Aurora asked.

"Yes, unfortunately."

Aurora rolled her eyes. Despite the rocky relationship Leela had with both of her parents, they really had made strides to become more involved since Leela's accident. "Well, remember when he was talking about some of the research he was being consulted for? The hormone signals or something when only an egg was needed for reproduction."

"Yeah, it's some sperm-less fertilization project. Two eggs and a shit ton of biomolecular technique and manipulation."

Aurora remembered that too, especially since she was pretty sure Leela's father, Sid, was pitching ideas her and Leela's way for a family. "In that conversation, he brought up some p-word. Pants...pants-o-gene-e-sis."

Leela's large eyes grew wider. "It's parthenogenesis and this is *so* not the context of what he was talking about."

When Sid had mentioned the concept over dessert, Aurora had been intrigued by the phenomenon that a single egg could naturally be triggered into developing into an embryo without sperm. He hadn't mentioned the event ever happening in humans, but it had happened in other animals. His examples included well-documented cases of snakes at the zoo and experiments with mice.

"You're really thinking asexual reproduction?" Leela asked with a skeptic tone.

"I can't help it. We have loads of DNA we don't use, right? But it's still hanging out because evolution hasn't gotten rid of it."

"You're not wrong, but to say that the chickpea is the result of parthenogenesis—something which has *never* been documented in humans—is beyond a stretch." Leela stopped in the center of the trail. "I understand that you want to come up with another way this could have happened. I do. Denial is a natural part of the stages."

"But I'm not in denial!" Convincing Leela would probably be impossible, but Aurora had to try. As far as Aurora was concerned, this was the answer that made the most sense. "Just hear me out. Maybe something inside of me or something I was exposed to in Hawaii made some sort of parthenogenesis switch turn on."

Leela looked at her, expressionless. She usually wore her emotions on her sleeve, so showing no emotion was possibly the worst reaction she could have.

Aurora swallowed the hard lump in her throat. "I need to believe that something like this could be the answer."

"Sweets," Leela said calmly and sadly, "if believing that helps you cope with it for now, okay, but I'm at a loss for what to say except that my brain doesn't let me believe that. I'm sorry."

"Fine," Aurora said curtly. "The police can analyze tapes, my blood and hair, and you can give them names of innocent people, but I know I wasn't drugged. The more time I have to process, the more I realize nothing about this feels violent, you know?"

"I believe you know you best. I'm not going to question how you feel but listen to your own words—'the more time you've had to process'. You've had *no* time to process this! Your biggest concern this morning was if you should machine dry your new cotton shirt. And now let's just say laundry is at the bottom of the priority list."

In a way, Aurora knew Leela was right. She had recently learned this news, but that didn't stop her brain from trying to make sense of it. "Put yourself in my shoes. How would you feel if someone told you that you were pregnant? Wouldn't you be reaching for an explanation?"

"Yes, but parthenogenesis is the most out-there explanation that exists." Leela closed her eyes and shook her head. "It's not possible."

Aurora needed more to convince her. Fortunately, the start of their relationship had been based on the fantastic too. "Okay, what made you finally believe we shared the same dreams? You said that was impossible at first too."

"Well, after I got over the 'being pissed at you for lying to me about it' part, it was the evidence that convinced me. The brain scans. The *really* personal information you knew about me."

"Okay then." If evidence was what Leela needed, then that was what she was going to get. Aurora got out her phone and began a search.

"What are you doing?"

"Finding evidence that supports my argument."

Leela guided her to the side of the trail, to a park bench, but said nothing.

Aurora looked up from the screen. "What are you doing?"

"Let's sit down while you do this. I don't want you to trip and twist an ankle." Leela sat quietly with her hands in her vest pockets while Aurora conducted her search of *parthenogenesis humans.*

Page after page of articles filled her screen. The amount of information overwhelmed her. "This is…"

"I know, sweets. I'm sorry. I know you want to believe this."

"I do believe this! Why didn't your dad tell us about this?" She handed Leela her phone that listed dozens of articles, the first being, 'Parthenogenesis and Human-Assisted Reproduction, Parthenogenetic Activation of Human Oocytes.'

Leela's brow raised significantly. "Well, Dad tends to shy away from the people-side of research. Plus, these are just the titles meant to grab attention; it doesn't mean they've concluded it's possible."

She knew Leela was naturally a skeptic and that her work to convince her had just begun. Aurora clicked on a link to review another article's summary. "Look here at 'A human parthenogenetic chimaera.' 'We show that parthenogenetic chimaerism can result in human offspring and suggest a possible explanation for this seemingly miraculous event.' Chickpea could be that miraculous event!"

Leela took the phone and began to read the summary. Then the introduction, the results, and the conclusion. Aurora didn't mind that fifteen minutes had passed, and her excitement grew when Leela clicked on the next article involving calcium oscillations.

Whatever that was about.

"This is…pretty amazing," Leela said as she looked at a four-cell stage human embryo that had been taken from a human ovarian tumor. "And a lot more impressive than a virgin snake giving birth at a zoo. I take back what I said about it not being documented in humans."

"So, you believe this could explain it?"

"Ah," Leela drawled as she looked at the ducks that paddled into view and then paused as if to choose her words carefully, "I believe that you believe this, but the odds of parthenogenesis being the explanation are infinitesimal. So, while I'm open to the discussion, I'd like to talk to Dad about it—which I can't believe I just said—and read more. I need to understand how this would be possible because you don't have a tumor anomaly."

Even with Leela's doubts, Aurora was grateful. She leaned into Leela and, when Leela put her arm around her shoulders, Aurora snuggled into her. "Thank you."

"For what?"

"For not running away. For believing me. I don't think I'd be able to do any of this without you."

"Like I said back in the parking lot, I'm your partner and I'm not going to leave your side." Leela held her a little tighter.

"It's hard to imagine myself pregnant, let alone with a baby. The two of us with a baby. That'll be an adjustment."

Leela dropped her head and shook it.

Aurora pulled away enough to look up at her. "What?"

Leela bit her bottom lip. "I don't know how to say this without upsetting you."

The glimpse of brightness was suddenly covered by a dark cloud. Aurora moved away to better face Leela's downturned mouth.

"The past few hours have been an emotional rollercoaster for you and me," Leela said. "I can't fantasize about our potential new life until we've both had more time to process."

Aurora didn't follow Leela train of thought. "What fantasy?"

"You're talking about our lives changing with a baby and...I can't do that right now. I feel completely overwhelmed ri—"

"You feel overwhelmed?" Aurora said flabbergasted. "I'm the one who's pregnant! And it's not like we never talked about having children."

"First of all, in the extremely brief conversations we had regarding kids, we talked about shopping at a sperm bank for a nice Indian or Pakistani man who didn't mind ejaculating into a sterile cup and then putting a bun in your oven via IVF. We did not talk about you getting surprisedly knocked up by mysterious circumstances! It would also be a planned event! There would probably be a selfie of us in the room pre-insemination."

Aurora knew Leela's outburst wasn't directed at her but she shrank back into the bench.

Leela sighed and laid a hand on Aurora's leg. "I'm sorry. I didn't mean to raise my voice. I'm just trying to process the impossible. Drunk calculus is easier than this."

Aurora turned her head to watch a duck swim in a circle and then dunk its head in the water, leaving its bright orange feet in the air. "I promise that no matter what you're thinking about the baby—"

"Please don't use that word. At least not yet."

"Why not?"

"For one, this so early, I'm not entirely convinced you have a viable, organized ball of cells inside of you. Too much bad can happen early on, even with a typical pregnancy conceived under typical means with all of the preventatives."

"You're worried I'll miscarry." Aurora didn't say the words as a question. It was a sad possibility she had forgotten amidst all of the other medical talk. "I can understand that."

"So, that's why I think we should be careful how we refer to our ball of cells. 'Baby' should be reserved when chickpea looks person-like. Let's just use chickpea for the time being."

She liked how Leela said 'our ball of cells.' "That's fair. But say chickpea is growing the way she should. Can you tell me what you think about *chickpea*? Or starting a family? I really, really need to know what you think."

After several moments to collect her thoughts, Leela began. "While we're completely unprepared, and I'm not anti-parenthood, I do want to know how to explain said parenthood. I don't think that's asking much."

"I don't follow."

"Basically, what are we going to say when people ask us who the father is?"

"That's none of their business."

"Okay," Leela said with a sarcastic laugh. "You say that to Ani Okpik and see how that far that gets you."

Leela was right. Her mother would be relentless.

"And how about chickpea? They're going to want to know where they came from—which they have a right to know—and I doubt 'your bio mom had pineapple water in Hawaii and that switched on her parthenogenic snake genes' is going to work."

"I'll admit that sounds bad. But we have time to learn more and come up with answers for these questions. I promise no secrets. I know how you feel about those." Aurora glanced back to Leela and saw her gripping the bench with both hands. "What else?"

Leela kicked a twig on the ground. "I need the cops to say nobody slipped you anything to be as accepting as you are of this."

"Well, I have good news. That's what they're going to say," Aurora said matter-of-factly.

"How are you so calm about this?" Leela exclaimed. "Maybe that's my bigger problem. In the doctor's office, we were both on the same emotional page and now you're cool about the whole thing. Like, 'Oh, I guess I'm going to be a mom now. By the way, if we hurry, we can still make the movie.'"

Leela's words gave Aurora pause. She had gone from scared crying, to confusion, to hope, and to excited in a staggeringly short period of time. "That's fair, but this is how I'm processing. I haven't landed on one particular emotion just yet."

A thoughtful look passed over Leela's face. "So, you're just telling me everything you feel as you feel it?"

"Pretty much. I don't know what else to do other than get everything off my chest. How I feel an hour from now could be a one-eighty from how I feel now."

"And what do you feel right now?"

Aurora cocked her head. Given the situation, how Leela felt, and the still unexplained nature of chickpea, how did she feel? When she'd settled on her emotion, Aurora smiled. "I feel ready.

We love each other, have flexible jobs, and our home is getting bigger as we speak. I think chickpea would have happened within the next year or two anyway. Life just sped up the clock for us."

Leela blew a long breath. "Fuck me. We're going to do this, aren't we? If this is actually a thing that happens?"

"I think so."

Leela pursed her lips and rocked as if she were psyching herself up. "Okay, so we're doing this."

"Yep."

"I still don't think we should tell anyone. This is super secret. Most people don't share the news about a baby until after the third or fourth month anyway because of the risks. You haven't been on prenatals. We need to go to the store ASAP and get stocked up."

The intensity which took over Leela's features surprised Aurora. "Agreed."

"Good. I'll get a water filter while I'm there too. I don't know off the top of my head how effective the one in the well is."

Aurora scrunched her brow. "I think that may be a bit unnecessary, but okay."

"Cool. I want to make sure I'm doing everything I can do."

"So far you're doing great." Aurora leaned in until Leela's arms wrapped around her once more. "Although, promise me you'll talk to your therapist about this? I know you won't feel comfortable telling me everything, and you do have to talk to someone."

"I promise. Now, in terms of the immediate future, I'm going to have to tell Keith and Jill something given the way I left today."

Aurora closed her eyes and enjoyed the security of Leela's arms. "How did you leave?"

"Like you were on fire in the gasoline store."

"Oh." Aurora hadn't really thought of what Leela must have looked like at the farm when she had received the called from Dr.

Aguilar. "Well, tell them the doctors found something. I need further testing, and leave it at that."

"I can do that." Leela took a deep breath, as if she were trying to convince herself. "We can do this."

Aurora might have been on a public park bench, but when Leela was at her side she always felt at home. She rested her head on Leela's chest to listen to her heartbeat, and the two arms around her brought her in closer. A kiss on the crown of her head completed the sensation.

Her family would be fine.

CHAPTER EIGHT

EVERY TIME LEELA thought she had come to terms with Aurora's pregnancy, she came back to a place of doubt and fear, even after two weeks. Knowing Aurora's toxicology screens had been negative for any sign of tranquilizers, and that the security tapes showed no wrongdoing, had taken the edge off, but it didn't stop the cycle.

Mostly because that meant the pregnancy culprit was science-fiction.

Every so often, the thought of infidelity still crossed her mind, but those were her own insecurities talking more than a true lack of trust in Aurora. Aurora wouldn't have cheated—especially not during their magical trip to Hawaii.

Also, the word 'magical' had taken on a completely different connotation since this discovery.

Leela watched Aurora take her feet out of the examination table stirrups one at a time. It was so cute she had left on her penguin knee socks. "How are you feeling?"

"Like a woman who's just had a pelvic exam in front of an audience." Aurora made eye contact with both Dr. Aguilar and the nurse then looked back to Leela. "And I'm freaked out by the fact that chickpea will eventually be much, much larger."

Dr. Aguilar stifled a laugh. "Everything looks and feels normal, but I want to go about this by the book. Regular appointments, prenatal vitamins, the whole enchilada. I don't think we want any more surprises."

"Mm-hmm," the nurse in the back muttered.

Leela shot her the meanest glare she could muster. "I'm sorry? I missed part of that."

The nurse sheepishly looked down to her tablet and wrote with the stylus.

"Yeah, that's what I thought," Leela said, a bit more forceful than intended. Everything when it came to Aurora and chickpea brought out her strongest urges to come to their defense. More calmly, she added, "Also, Aurora is stocked with prenatals and washes them down with ultra-filtered water."

Aurora grinned, laid a gentle hand on her arm, then turned to her doctor. "Actually, if you have a minute, Leela and I would like to talk to you about the 'surprise' part. Alone."

Dr. Aguilar dismissed the nurse with a pointed chin, who left with an eye roll. "Okay, shoot." She tossed her blue gloves in the biohazard bin.

Aurora sat up, causing the thin paper blanket over her lap to crinkle. Then, she paused. She closed her eyes and began to breathe deeply.

"Are you okay?" Leela asked and rubbed a small circle on her lower back.

"Just waiting for the nausea wave to pass."

Leela waited for Aurora's face to lose its green before they began the conversation. When Aurora gave her the go-ahead nod, she started. "So, Dr. Aguilar, you know how my father is into hormone research?"

"Yes, I'm familiar with him; he's one of the top endocrinologists in the country. Why do you ask?"

"Because he's involved in a project now that, in a way, we think relates to our situation. He's part of a team looking at parthenogenesis in the context of assisted reproductive technologies."

"He's doing what now?"

She looked positively floored, but Leela didn't blame her. She had been exactly where Dr. Aguilar was two weeks ago when Aurora had first suggested the idea. "Dad brought it up at dinner fairly recently, but Aurora remembered and suggested it to me after we received the news about her pregnancy. It's all I've been reading about. Parthenogenesis in snakes, Komodo dragons, mice…and humans." Leela reached into the bookbag she'd brought, pushed Aurora's bag of ginger candies to the side, and pulled out the two-inch binder of literature she had printed. She handed Dr. Aguilar the binder of scholarly research. "We think this explains it."

"What she said, and I insisted she print double-sided," Aurora added. "Oh, can I have a candy?"

Dr. Aguilar took the binder and arched a brow at the tabs.

"It just made sense to divide the research into categories," Leela said as she gave Aurora a wrapped ginger.

"What has your father said about the pregnancy?"

Aurora shook her head. "We haven't told anyone I'm pregnant, and you're the only one right now who knows about what we've discovered."

Dr. Aguilar's eyes grew wider as she continued to flip through the pages. "Are you two serious?"

"Yes," both she and Aurora answered in unison.

"But…that's not possible. That's not how this works." Dr. Aguilar's eyes went back to the pages.

Leela gripped the sides of the chair to keep herself from standing in a rage. Her scientific literacy was being challenged in front of her partner and unborn chickpea. She caught the subtle shake of Aurora's head and then the mouthing of the words *Calm down.*

Part of her didn't want to follow that directive, but at the same time she did acknowledge her point couldn't be made if she threw a plastic ovary at Dr. Aguilar's head. It was best to cool her jets and deliver her comment without too much agitation in her voice.

"Dr. Aguilar." Leela waited until they resumed eye contact. "I appreciate that you're a medical professional but I would like to remind you that I graduated with a degree in microbiology from one of the top colleges in the country and was accepted to every medical school I applied to. Please do not patronize me when it comes to how asexual reproduction—which is what parthenogenesis is—works. I know my stuff."

"Dreamy," Aurora said calmly and with a gentle hand on her forearm, "I'm sure Dr. Aguilar didn't mean to offend you."

Dr. Aguilar pursued her lips and nodded. "That's right, and I'm sorry if I did."

"Apology accepted. And I understand that you've never had parents with a parthenogenetic conception story before, so I understand this was a surprise, but once you read the research, you'll definitely reach the same conclusion I did."

"This will be part of my nightly reading, that's for sure. And it's so helpful that you've made a table of contents." She took her eyes away from the article and looked at them both. "Have either of you shared your research will anyone else?"

"No," Aurora answered.

"Our plan is to tell no one until Aurora's reached the three-month mark."

"Good. This should remain our little secret because you do not want this story getting out. The press would have a field day with the story of a virgin birth, especially coming from two women."

She was one hundred percent correct. Leela had already been in the papers once for her coma-brain anomaly. They did not want it to happen a second time.

Dr. Aguilar flipped to the red tab. That was the mice section. "Have either of you spoken to a therapist or counselor about what's happened?"

Aurora shook her head.

"I mentioned 'difficulty coping with significant life changes out of my control' in the patient portal but I haven't heard back. That's healthcare in America for you." Leela shrugged. "But it's okay since I kind of lied. I think I'm coping fine," she said as she looked to Aurora.

Aurora nodded. "Once we both got over the surprise, I think we've handled it really well. We're doing our research together now, which I think has brought us to a new level in our relationship."

"It really has," Leela agreed.

Dr. Aguilar seemed unconvinced. Or at least the abundance of ridges between her eyes that accompanied an intense squint made her appear unconvinced.

"What's wrong? You don't like our binder?"

"Ah," Dr. Aguilar drawled. "Well, this research certainly is interesting. And, you know what? Once the time comes, it'll be easy enough to confirm."

"How do you mean?" Aurora asked.

"Well, for starters, a parthenogenetic baby would mean a clone. So, if it's a boy or has a different blood type, there's another explanation for the pregnancy."

If Dr. Aguilar sent that subtle, judgmental look at Aurora one more time, Leela was going to have to tear off her arms. She would just have to. "If you flip to the green tab and go to article eight, you'll see the haploid versus diploid parthenogenetic pathways very clearly," Leela said with confident sass. "So, chickpea could be different, and have XX chromosomes."

Dr. Aguilar closed the notebook. "I think we should schedule that next appointment. And, um, I think Aurora may also benefit from making an appointment with a counselor to do a mental health onceover. Just to be on the safe side. I'll get some more cards from Diana."

#

Leela felt Aurora's gaze on her the entire way to the parking lot. "What?"

"Given the chance, I think you might have pummeled them both with your notebook. I was surprised by both how angry you were and how fast you got there. That's not like you to have such a quick temper."

"I'm sorry if I went overboard. It's just. . . It's my job to protect my family. If someone is judging you or questioning chickpea's development or my intellectual skills, I have to step up."

"Okay, but you do remember that I'm capable of defending myself if I think someone's crossed a line?"

"I know that and..." Based on Aurora's expression that said, 'there are no exceptions to what I just said,' there was only one way for Leela to respond. "You're right, I'm sorry. I didn't mean to feminize the patriarchy."

"Thank you." Aurora kissed her on the cheek. "That's good to hear, but I'm also worried about chickpea."

Stress was very bad at any stage of pregnancy. "You heard Dr. Aguilar; you're pretty textbook right now with your symptoms and hormones levels. Your cervix is a champ."

Once they reached their vehicles, Aurora reached for Leela's hand. "No. I'm worried about us. We've researched how chickpea came to be but we haven't really talked about what we're going to do about chickpea."

Leela furrowed her brow. "You lost me. She has a nickname and medical appointments. That's definitely something. My parents never even gave me a nickname."

Aurora sighed. "What I'm trying to say is that we haven't talked about anything other than the fact that we are going to have her and fantasy scenarios of when she's a little kid. I'm getting to the point where I need to prepare. We're going to be parents! You're not going to like this, but I really want to call my—"

"You cannot call your mom! Not yet."

"But we need to—"

"Slow down there." Leela rubbed both of Aurora's arms in an attempt to soothe her. It was a tactic she'd started using rather frequently during her mood swings. Which were things she was also apparently suffering from in her own way. "We have a long way to the finish line. That's plenty of time to figure some things out and kick some contractor ass to finish the addition."

"I know, but maybe we can start testing the waters of how other people will react? Like, if something comes up in casual conversation related to families, could we mention it? Or maybe talk about shifting responsibilities at work?"

"How do I subtly do that? 'Hey Keith, you're doing a bang-up job with that schedule. Oh, by the way, I've been thinking about giving you more responsibility.'"

"Yes! That's perfect!"

"Oh. Okay," Leela said with a shrug. That hadn't been too hard. "How about I bring in the extra whiteboard from the office and we do some serious planning tonight?" She gasped from an idea. "I can make a chart. Like a month by month what we need to do, and you can be one color and I can be another." She saw the board clearly in her mind's eye. Aurora would definitely be green, probably purple for herself.

Aurora kissed her with a grin. "That sounds great. But you know who would be an even better resource?"

Leela sighed. "I understand why you want to tell your mom. I do. But I think we should stick to our plan of getting out of the first trimester. Your mom and dad will be ecstatic when you tell them, but if something bad happens, I'm worried about that extra emotional toll on you." Leela opened Aurora's car door for her.

Aurora didn't get into the car. "And take a second to think about the emotional toll *not* telling my parents has on me. My mom is the only person in the world who will believe us *and* has experience having children. I can only learn so much from online message boards. I could really use her advice."

Shit. Aurora had a point. Two points, actually. And those message boards were great examples of people who did not have scientific literacy, unlike herself. "How about this: we stick to the first trimester reveal plan for everyone else but we tell your parents *in person* when we see them in a few weeks. That gives chickpea even more time to incubate and, I'll be honest, I really want to be there too when we tell them."

Aurora smiled broadly. "That...is...a...deal," she said between parking lot kisses. "Thank you so, so much. I love you."

"You're welcome and I love you too," Leela said as Aurora got into her car. "Have a great day at the grindstone."

Aurora blew her a kiss and then drove away.

With a smile and wave, Leela climbed into her truck and tried to think of how in the world she could make good on the promise she'd just made Aurora. The Hawaii trip had been an excellent practice run for Keith, and it had given her confidence that she could take a week of vacation without the barn exploding, but this was a serious change to how the farm would be managed. Which meant she knew she had to change her approach.

Leela knew she had a tendency to micromanage, and that was something she would need to let go. She hired good people, trained them well, and trusted them. She just had to remind herself of that.

She flipped on her radio, caught the middle of a public radio segment, and tried to pay attention to the interview while she drove home. But she was going to be a parent! With parent responsibilities and a job! How the fuck was she going to do that? She had been asking herself that question for a few weeks and still didn't have a clear answer.

When she walked into the farm office, both Jill and Keith were huddled around the employee tablet.

"What are you two up to?"

"Just entering my hours for the day," Jill said. "How's Aurora? Any additional news?"

Leela walked past them and settled behind her desk. "All things considered, there's not too much to worry about. We have to go back in a few weeks for another follow-up."

"That soon?" Keith asked, alarmed.

Jill placed a hand on his arm. "I'm sure Leela would like some work to distract her."

"Thank you, Jill," Leela said. "I appreciate that."

"But it would be nice if you gave us a little more. We're like a big family around here and we're worried about Aurora."

So much for having Jill on her side. "It's because of lady stuff. It's complicated."

Jill and Keith shared a look.

"I'm immune to 'lady stuff' ever since you asked me to order feminine hygiene products while you were in Hawaii."

"I'm sorry but I can't tell you anymore. Besides, they're more like research trips than actual appointments."

Jill pursed her lips and cocked her head. Then, her jaw dropped, and she gasped.

"Ah, shit." Leela recognized Jill's elation, but at least Keith was still confused. "Can we please not make a big deal out of this?"

Keith's gaze darted between she and Jill. "What aren't we making a big deal about?

"She and Aurora are looking into fertility treatments," Jill said smugly. "Aren't you? That's why you asked me so many questions about how 'lifelike' the teat suction cups were last week?"

Aurora's words from earlier popped into her head. *So, what if we were looking into fertility things? How would you feel about that?*

Keith and Jill were mirror reflections of each other: broad smiles and bright eyes.

"That would be fantastic!" Keith shouted. "And it makes so much sense given the responsibility changes around here. Hawaiian practice run my behind; you were testing me." Keith puffed out his chest and hooked his thumbs into his pockets. "Making sure I was up to the job."

Leela laughed nervously. "You caught me."

"The addition to your house makes more sense now too. Needed more space for your clothes," Jill said with a chuckle. "You've been planning this for ages! How far are you in the process?"

"Um. Really depends on how you want to look at it, but can we please not talk about it anymore? I'm still uncomfortable with certain parts of it."

Jill frowned. "Why are you uncomfortable?"

"Maybe because I know nothing about babies—the human kind—and then there's the issue of the donor."

"You have a donor picked out already?" Keith asked.

"You could say that."

"But you're uncomfortable?" Jill asked. "Does Aurora know?"

Leela didn't know how much more dancing she could take. "I'm pretty sure she understands how I feel. It's tough for me, you know? Since I'm not carrying."

Keith crossed his arms and then rubbed his short beard. "My brother-in-law had a tough time coming to terms that he and my sister needed a donor. Then he couldn't decide whether it would be better knowing or not knowing the guy who donated."

"Really?" Leela asked, intrigued. Maybe there was something to this talking with close friends. "How does he feel about it now?"

"You've seen the family holiday card. They look pretty happy, don't they?"

"I think they do. I'm going to leave you two now to talk shop or sperm," Jill said with a mischievous grin. "I have to rush home. Clarissa and her friend are coming by for dinner, and the house is a mess."

"Please don't say anything to anyone," Leela said. "I'm not ready."

Jill turned her grin into one of patience. "Of course not. That's your business to tell."

As Jill left the room, Keith stayed and, with his thumbs hooked in his pockets again, rocked in his boots.

"What?" she asked with healthy doses of suspicion and nerves.

"I know I'm not who you go to when you have personal stuff, but if you need to talk to me, you can."

Part of Leela wanted Keith to go and tend to the afternoon shift, who had just arrived. But she knew she could trust Keith and he had a perspective unique to most of those around her. She could do more than test the waters. Keith could be her sounding board, even if she might have to fib a little.

"I tell you what, Keith, this fertility planning is way more stressful than I thought. Sometimes I really wish Aurora and I could just do our thing and have an 'accident' like you folks who have the man-lady sex."

Keith rubbed his beard. "I don't know about that. I've never told you this but I've had two pregnancy scares and both times I felt like I was absolutely losing control of everything."

"Really?"

"Oh yeah. The idea that I could be a father completely turned my life upside-down. Everything became a 'how will this change with a baby?' Eventually, that kind of thinking drove me crazy. Plus, I felt bad I couldn't do anything for my girlfriend. I was a complete spectator."

Leela focused her energy on appearing calm. He understood everything! "That's how I imagine it would feel to all of a sudden have this *huge*, but *tiny,* thing you didn't plan for. You must have been relieved when the final result was negative."

"Eh, fifty-fifty. I wasn't emotionally mature enough the first time and wasn't financially secure the second. I wasn't capable of supporting a baby; I was barely supporting myself but I would have gotten a second or even third job if I'd had to." Keith paused and bit the inside of his cheek. "Do you remember Skye?"

"Um, I think I do. Wasn't she the one you were seeing right before you moved to Oregon?"

"She's the one. What you don't know was that when I was dating her, she was pregnant with her separated husband's baby."

"Holy shit! Seriously?"

"As a heart attack. She didn't tell me until we were together two months and, by that point, she was four months into her pregnancy."

"Four months!" she shrieked. "That's like halfway there."

"You're telling me. I figured I had three choices: be one hundred percent supportive, gradually get myself out of the relationship, or run for the hills. I'll be honest, there were parts of me that wanted each of those options, but I knew I had to step up and, if I didn't, I'd be judged. So, I was honest with Skye and told her that even though our relationship was still pretty new, I wouldn't leave because of the baby."

"Didn't it bother you that it wasn't even yours?"

"That was the weird thing. It really didn't. Now, that might have been because I didn't know my dad very well. I was raised by my mother and grandparents so I was comfortable with the idea that sometimes stuff happens and kids aren't raised by their biological parents.

"But then, Skye decided to try and make it work with her husband. I really don't know what happened to them after that since I took my broken heart and moved here."

It was like Keith had just poured his soul into the office. She knew he was a good man, but she had no idea he was *that* good. "I'm sorry things didn't work out with her, but I'm really glad you came here. You're my rock around here, and when there's a little one scampering about, I'm really going to need your help."

"Then you'll get it," he said with a kind smile. "You need to talk about anything else?"

"No, I think I'm good. Thank you, Keith, for everything."

He tipped his ball cap goodbye and walked out of the office, leaving Leela alone for the first time since four o'clock that morning.

She felt better than she had in the past two weeks. She didn't have all of her issues worked out but at least she knew her feelings were normal.

Now, if she could only wrap her head around the idea of herself being a parent.

#

"I'm glad I caught you before you left for the day." Tonya sidled up beside Aurora and then pointed to her candy dish. "You are addicted to those ginger things. Every time I see you, you're sucking on one."

Aurora swallowed the spicy yet soothing juice. "They are pretty tasty. What's going on?"

"I wanted to ask what your schedule looked like next week."

Aurora pulled her calendar up on her monitor. Every day was populated with multiple colorful bars designating the different types of meetings.

"Whoa! You're busier than me. No wonder you look so tired." Tonya scrutinized her face. "Are you okay?"

"I'm fine."

Tonya folded her arms across her chest and pursed her lips.

Aurora hated getting the silent third degree. "Okay, there are some personal things that are distracting me right now."

Tonya's arms fell to her sides. "Is Leela okay? Your mom?"

"Yeah, they're all fine. It's just...the house construction has my nerves living in my stomach."

"House stuff can definitely add stress. As can all the other balls you're juggling here." Tonya nodded and glanced at Aurora's calendar once more. "You're only taking two days extra for Thanksgiving? Sorry, Irony Day."

"I'd like to take more time off but, with the year-end coming soon, I have extra work."

Tonya took a candy out of the jar and sucked on it thoughtfully. Fortunately, Tonya was a reasonable person and whenever she had one of these moments it usually worked in Aurora's favor.

"This is what I want you to do," Tonya said. "I want you to open a new email and address it to me. Go ahead, I'll wait."

Aurora did as instructed.

"Now, subject line: request PTO. Body of the email: Hi Tonya, I would like to utilize my unlimited PTO and request two additional days off for my November holiday." Tonya waited patiently while Aurora typed the message away. "Now, send it."

Reluctantly, Aurora hit *send*, but she didn't want to fall back on old habits of being a doormat. "But what about year-end?"

"It's called delegation. While you are excellent at what you do, there are interns and junior analysts who can do some of your work. You don't have to call businesses and set visitation appointments or do data entry. Let them do that."

Tonya was right. There were elements of her job she did out of habit. She didn't need to do the same tasks she had done when she'd been just starting out in finance. "That does make sense."

"That's why I'm the boss," Tonya said with a wide grin. "Why don't you head home? Ride your bike or do some yoga. You need to manage your stress. I don't need you developing an ulcer."

It was moments like this when Aurora was infinitely happy she worked for Tonya and not the soulless corporate entity she used to. "I appreciate all of this, but didn't you come here to ask me to do something?"

Tonya spoke as she backed away. "It can wait until tomorrow. Go home!"

Aurora leaned back in her seat. While the uneasy feeling wasn't completely gone, it had significantly lessened after the exchange. And now with two extra days free, she didn't have to stress about laundry or groceries when they came back from Michigan, or packing the day before. She could even make time to see Stacy when he came to Oregon to see his family.

With that thought, she smiled, saved her work, and left the office. Once she got to the car, she connected her hands-free set and dialed Stacy's number.

He picked up on the second ring. "Smalls! To what do I owe the honor of this phone call?"

"When do you fly into Portland for the holidays?"

"I learned my lesson last year. I'm supposed to land Tuesday morning."

Aurora clenched the steering wheel in celebration. "How would you like to have breakfast before you drive off to see your family? I could meet you halfway."

"Are you serious? That would be awesome! But…wait. Aren't you going to Michigan?"

"We are, but I just took some extra time off work and I thought this would be a great way of using my time. I miss you."

"Aw, are you feeling sentimental?"

She cursed her pregnancy hormones for making her tear up. "I guess so. How's Griffey? The last I saw on InstaPic he made a meal out of your cleats."

"Aw, man. That was a day. I think I bought fifty bucks of bitter apple spray after that. But it worked; he hasn't eaten any more shoes. How have you been? You've been radio silent on social media since your trip here."

"You know how it is. Lots of work lately." Time for a swift topic change. She didn't want to run the risk of even having to skirt around the chickpea topic. "Oh, by the way, I checked in with my editing department today about the report I wrote for Stevie's restaurant. I should be able to send it later this week."

"OMG! It's so funny you brought him up. He came to the office yesterday to do some holiday press for the foundation and he asked about you."

"He did?" Aurora asked with a grin.

"Yeah! He had some of those cheeseburger sliders the other day and thought of you but, get this, he asked me—" His own laughter interrupted his speech. "Because you were so...I don't know, food-crazed?"

Aurora's heart stopped then rabbited in the span of time it took for him to get his laughter under control. She could see where this was headed, and it was nowhere good.

"He asked me if you were pregnant. Isn't that hilarious?"

"That's so, so funny," Aurora said, trying to keep humor in her voice. "How did you respond?"

"Um, that there was no possible way and, if you were, you would've definitely asked me to be a donor."

Her discomfort increased to a full wince as she drove. "You know, not to hurt your feelings, but Leela and I have actually talked about that and if I were carrying, we'd want a donor with her ethnicity."

"What if Leela carries?"

Aurora laughed heartily. The idea of Leela pregnant immediately caused her to think of her small-framed love with a huge belly and a t-shirt that read *Everything Hurts and I'm Dying.* "I think we've ruled that out, but in that case, I think we'd ask River first. Regardless, you get honorary 'uncle' privileges."

"That's cool. And speaking of River, you must be excited to see the new baby soon. What's his name?"

It seemed she had dodged a bullet, and she realized she should focus on the road a lot more than she had been. "Wade. And every single thing I see online is adorable." There was no denying it, her life was all about babies now. She couldn't avoid thinking about them. She couldn't escape their tiny smiles or toes. Or their baby-scented heads as they rested on your chest. The pure beauty of it all made her misty.

"Aurora? You still there?"

"Sorry." She wiped a tear away. "I zoned out for a bit. I'm by the train tracks and about to lose signal anyway. I'll touch base with you next week about breakfast, okay?"

"Sounds good, smalls. Catch you later."

The phone line clicked off as she exited the city limits and drove onto the open road that led to the country. The country that didn't have a twenty-four-hour pharmacy, daycare facility, or baby gym. There were suddenly so many more pressing things to figure out that weren't her baby's miraculous conception.

She finished her drive while she bounced different scenarios and ideas around her head. There was no way she'd have that kind of quiet at home. She expected to walk into a noisy house filled with construction where she could change into some workout clothes for a run in the peace of the outdoors.

Aurora opened the front door and heard the high-pitched whirling of drills. She gave a slight nod of acknowledgement to the workers outside the slider who worked on the early stages of the mudroom and walked toward the back of the house to their bedroom. She didn't expect to see Leela there making a list on the whiteboard.

Leela turned to her, purple marker in hand, and smiled. "You're home early!"

"So are you." Aurora walked closer, gave Leela a brief kiss, and read what was on the board: *Chickpea's Priority List.*

Leela had written different parent and child-related issues on magnets. She had taken Aurora's concern from the morning seriously. Very seriously.

"This is impressive, but when I talked about planning this morning, I didn't mean it all had to happen today."

"Think of what is going to happen during the next year." Leela waited a beat. "Are you thinking it?"

"Yeah," Aurora drawled.

"Good. Chickpea will be here in less than that. You were right. We have to get cracking on this!" She turned to her magnetic strips. "Which do you think is a higher priority, finding a midwife or establishing childcare?"

"I think midwife," Aurora answered with uncertainly.

Leela slid the magnet so that it was higher on the board.

"Why does that have two colors?" Aurora asked.

"Because we're both involved in that responsibility."

Aurora skewed her brow. "Shouldn't we both be involved in everything? Also, if we're trying to keep this a secret, maybe we shouldn't write our plans on a gigantic board for everyone to see."

Leela looked at her elaborate, colorful board, and threw her hands in the air. "Ah, shit."

CHAPTER NINE

LEELA TRIED TO keep the impatience off her face as she listened to why her therapist needed to reschedule. She knew the receptionist couldn't see her, but patience was something she needed to practice. At least that was what Aurora had told her. Children required patience.

Or something like that.

"I understand why he canceled the appointment. All I'm trying to say is that I can't come to your suggested rescheduled one." Instead, she was going to Aurora's appointment to close out the first trimester. "Can't I just use the online system to touch base with him? I've really liked doing that so far." Between the occasional talks with Keith and actively reaching out to an almost always available online therapist, she finally felt comfortable with herself and with the idea of her expanding family.

Aurora came into Leela's office with a smile and pointed to the clock on her cell phone. It was almost time to leave for the airport.

Leela nodded her understanding. "I have to go catch a flight. I'll call back when I figure out a good day to come into the office." She hung up the phone with a violent poke of her finger. "Argh!"

"Therapist?" Aurora approached her.

"Yes! I've really been able to get a lot out of our last few tele-sessions but I made the mistake of saying that I've lost—" She wanted to avoid mentioning her weight loss as much as possible, especially since Aurora was sensitive about her own body image. And Leela'd had an eating disorder in college. "Time! I've lost so much time. And now he wants to see me in person because he's afraid I'm as depressed as I was in college. I'm not depressed! I'm just busy as fuck!"

Aurora smirked. "Speaking of that. . . Are you off the clock?"

"Yes. I am ready for—"

Aurora laid a kiss on her that made her forget all about her therapist.

"Family fun. What was that for?"

Aurora hooked her fingers in Leela's front jean pockets. "You said something to the contractors. We have a motion sensor light in the master closet and tile down in the mudroom."

Had she known she would have received a response like that, Leela would have pulled out her biggest weapon a month ago. "I told them if they weren't done by December fifteenth, I was changing the logo on my products from my barn to pictures of my unfinished house."

Aurora's lips were a fraction of an inch away from her ear. "You're amazing and deserve something for your trouble." Aurora cupped an ass cheek. "Also, we have expedited boarding, so we have a few extra minutes here at home."

Every muscle in Leela's body tensed from the clear sex move. "I don't know if that's a good idea."

"I...think...it's...a...great...idea," Aurora said between kisses on her neck.

"Is this the pregnancy libido I read about?" Aurora responded by chuckling in that deep, diabolical way that Leela found irresistible.

But she had to resist.

"No, it's too early for that. This is just an I'm-not-stressed-out-about-life-right-now and we-haven't-had-sex-in-a-month libido."

She took Leela's hand and started to lead her out of the office, but Leela's feet were planted.

Aurora bit the tip of her tongue and smiled. "You want to do it in here?"

"No. I don't want to have sex in here. To be honest, I don't want to have sex anywhere right now. I feel weird."

"Like you're sick?"

"No." Leela knew no matter how she described her feelings it would come out wrong. Aurora had already told her that she could defend and protect herself and chickpea. But her pause to carefully select her words backfired.

"Am I becoming less attractive to you?"

"No! Absolutely not. I promise it's not that. If anything, I love that your boobs are getting bigger." When Aurora crossed her arms across her chest, Leela cupped her face and stroked her cheeks with her thumbs. "You are absolutely stunning and I'm not the only one who thinks so. Keith asked me the other day if you switched workouts because your legs looked so toned."

Aurora lowered her arms. "Really?"

"Yes. Come here." Leela held her close and felt Aurora's head fall onto her shoulder. While she held Aurora, Leela began her second attempt to explain her feelings without hurting Aurora's. "I didn't mean to make you feel bad. It's me; I just feel weird because of chickpea."

Aurora lifted her head and gave her a skewed glance. "We're not going to dislodge her from her cushy home if we have sex."

"I think I know that. But I'm unsure. I've been able to give you some very powerful orgasms. Now, that might be like an earthquake or something, and chickpea's still so vulnerable."

"So…" Aurora chuckled softly. "You're afraid you'll create an internal hazard for chickpea because you're so skilled at giving me orgasms?"

"Yes!" Thank the Gods Aurora understood. "It's just…you and chickpea are so fragile right now; I don't want to do anything to risk it."

Aurora's eyes widened, and her jaw dropped.

"Oh shit," Leela muttered in a whisper.

"You think I'm fragile?"

Leela had wanted to interject an apology but couldn't find space. Physical space was also an issue. She slowly backpedaled in her office as Aurora inched closer with a fire in her eyes. Once Leela felt the metal handles of the file cabinet against her back she knew she had to apologize. "I'm really, really sorry. I didn't mean fragile. I know you're perfectly capable of protecting yourself and chickpea. I mean, you're so strong. Much stronger than I am," Leela added with a grin.

Aurora didn't find it humorous.

Leela gulped. "I think I should stop talking and let you finish your thought. I can tell you need to get more off your chest. Out with it."

Aurora nodded but kept her pissed-at-the-world expression. "I hate this stupid societal rule that just because a woman becomes a mother, she's weak. My body is preparing itself to give birth to a person. A person! And if that isn't the definition of tough, then I don't know what is!"

Between Aurora's breath for air, Leela took another shot at an apology. "You're completely, one hundred percent right. Society has even convinced me, a complete ecofeminist, that a pregnant woman is somehow less than capable. That's stupid! And I thank my lucky stars every day that chickpea has a woman as resilient and strong, yet sensitive, as you as her birth mother." Aurora's aggressive posture softened, but Leela needed to add one more piece to her apology. "I'm an idiot."

Aurora steely gaze softened. Then, she closed her eyes and shook her head. "I'm sorry. I didn't mean to make you feel bad.

It's just I'm going through these huge changes to my body. And my brain. Did you know that earlier this week I spent five minutes at work trying to find my jacket? Guess where it was."

"I, ah…" Leela shrugged.

"On the back of my chair." Aurora reached out to hug her.

Leela returned the embrace, not completely surprised by the turn in Aurora's emotions. "I know, sweets. It's okay. Just please know that I think you're gorgeous, strong, and so, so sexy." When Aurora returned the hug with an extra squeeze, Leela knew it was an appropriate time to follow through with why Aurora had come into the office in the first place.

Leela kissed her gently. Then used her tongue to sensually lick her bottom lip.

Aurora pulled away with a giggle. "What are you doing?"

"Um, foreplay?"

Aurora scrunched her face. "I'm really not in the mood anymore. Sorry." She turned and headed to the door.

"Where are you going?"

"I'm going to go through the packing checklist one last time. I love you, dreamy."

"I love you too, sweets!" Aurora might not have been at the enhanced libido stage, but the mood swings were definitely in attendance. Leela hoped Aurora could keep them in check while they visited her family in Michigan because they would be a dead giveaway. Ani Okpik had an uncanny ability to read anyone's emotions, but the way she was attuned to her only daughter's was downright freaky. But Ani was the least of Leela's worries.

Leela had eight hours of travel time with Aurora at her side with the potential for dozens of emotional provocations.

#

The drive to Portland followed by the flight to Michigan couldn't have gone better in Aurora's opinion. Leela had offered to get her more ginger candies at the airport and had gladly switched seats with her in case she needed to use the plane's restroom. And Leela had asked if she'd put her bag in the overhead compartment for her, since Aurora was taller and stronger. At first, she thought Leela might be patronizing her but she realized Leela was trying her best to traverse a murky field of hormones, insecurities, and her own drive to make sure she was being the most supportive partner and parent possible.

It was plain as day how much Leela cared for her and chickpea. She simply needed more time to adjust to their new roles.

"You're sure you feel fine from the change in altitude? No additional queasiness, headache, cramping?" Leela asked once they left the gate.

Aurora gave her a patient smile. "Chickpea and I are fine."

"Just need to make sure."

Once they'd taken the turn for Transportation, Leela asked, "Is your dad picking us up at the usual place?"

"Of course."

Niq Okpik had insisted, for as long as Aurora could remember, that by walking to the far end of the local airport, they'd save a potential ten minutes of travel time because they could avoid the long-term parking exit.

It was the ultimate Dad Move.

They weaved quickly through the much colder Michigan air and throngs of holiday travelers. They walked past all of the arrival areas and then stopped at the employee-only entrance.

"Would you like me to give Niq the cue?" Leela asked.

"I got it." Aurora dug out her phone and texted her dad.

When she heard a car horn, she looked up to see the family's burgundy sedan parked by a mini-mart with its lights flashing.

Aurora pointed to the car. "There he is."

They hustled across the street to meet him, their suitcase rattling across the abused pavement along the way.

Niq hopped out of the car with spry steps as his mostly gray hair ruffled in the wind. "There's my girl!"

Aurora hadn't prepared for a bear hug. Why did every male figure in her life need to greet her like this? "Hi, Dad. Easy on the hug, please. The plane ride made me a little queasy."

He rested her on the ground immediately and looked at her with concern. "Do you need me to stop at the pharmacy on our way home?"

She held up one of her ginger candies. "I'm set."

"You're always so prepared," he said with pride and turned his gaze to Leela. "And how's my other girl? Can I pick you up?"

"Please." Leela showed her the brightest grin Aurora had seen all day. Her father picked Leela up and spun her in a circle while she giggled. When her father had done that the first time, Leela confessed that she had only ever seen it in the movies, and that it was even more fun in real life.

Sid Bakshi had very different ways of showing his affection.

"Your spin move's improved since last time, Niq. Are you working out?"

He made a show of flexing his muscles. "I think lifting Wade has woken them up."

Once Niq had loaded the luggage into the trunk and had turned the car onto the recently salted highway, he cleared his throat. "I know you're probably pretty tired from all the travel but I'm hoping you're up to a little extra company at the house. And when I say 'little', I mean it."

Instead of feeling a niggle of disappointment from their post-dinner chickpea announcement plan being ruined, Aurora beamed. "Are River and Becky there with the kids?"

Niq nodded. "They're trying to get in as much time with you two as they can since they'll be spending part of the holiday with

147

Becky's family. Traveling back and forth might be tough with the wintery mix we're supposed to get."

Aurora loved the cold weather but had to admit she was okay living five months out of the year without freezing temperatures in Oregon. She turned around and saw Leela in the back seat, on her phone, wearing a scowl. Aurora didn't know what had put that face there but she didn't like it. "You're okay with a little more socializing tonight than anticipated, right?"

"I'm going with the family flow, sweets."

Aurora knew she meant she was fine with a little more catching up.

"Plus, the time change is on our side," Leela said and then turned her phone so Aurora could see a snow accumulation graph. "How can this place already have two feet of snow for the season?"

"I bet you're glad I told you to wear your ski jacket now." Aurora turned to face her father again and asked a question that sprung to mind. "How's Mom taking the cold?"

His wind-burned face contorted into an uncomfortable wince. "She's adjusting. The house is like a furnace. She has the wood stove burning all the time and she still wears a bandana or cap at all times to stave off the chills."

Aurora nodded at the news. "I take it she hasn't gained the weight she lost yet?"

"Not yet but she's working on it. Even now that she's stopped chemo she has some herbal assistance," he added. "She wouldn't mind if you and Leela wanted to join in."

While Aurora had partaken with her mother a few times in her lifetime, that activity was off the agenda for this trip. "Sorry, Dad, but I'm on a cleanse...of sorts."

"I'm *not* on a cleanse," Leela said with cheer. "I'll be happy to keep Ani company."

Niq slapped the steering wheel and laughed. "She'll be glad to hear that. Her energy's better now, so she's been a real hoot. And maybe while Leela's doing that, I can show you the new bike I'm putting together."

"I'd like that." Aurora grinned and turned to the window. She allowed her thoughts to wander as her father drove them to her childhood home. She was pleased her mother had found some sort of comfort and that her health had improved but she worried about her own reaction to seeing her mom. She had seen plenty of pictures since the surgery, but there was something different about seeing someone in person. The hollowness of her cheeks. Her bones as she hugged her.

Aurora hoped she wouldn't become a weeping puddle as soon as she saw her mother.

"Home sweet home!" Niq called out when he'd pulled in front of the steep-roofed, ranch-style home. "I'll get your bags. Go ahead inside."

Leela had gotten out and opened her door before Aurora even had a chance to unbuckle her seat belt.

Aurora gave her a nod of thanks and lowered her voice. "I'm nervous about seeing Mom."

"I know but I'm right here for you. If you start feeling too emotional just say 'comfies', and we can go into our room and change out of our travel clothes."

"That's a good plan," Aurora said as the door to the tan house swung open.

"Boo bear!" Ani rushed out of the house in her cream cardigan with a red bandana around her head.

Aurora gently squeezed her mother's frame as they embraced. She did feel smaller, but the heavy knit of the sweater prevented Aurora from learning how thin she was. "Hi, Mom."

"I've missed my baby girl so much." Ani placed a kiss on her cheek and then turned to Leela. "You're next."

"I hope so. Otherwise, I'm going to feel left out." Leela gladly hugged her and received her kiss as well. "I like the bandana. Very biker gang."

Aurora watched the sweet exchange and listened for voices as they made their way into the house. "Where's River and his brood?"

"He took Logan down to the creek to look for tracks. Niq," she said as he came into the house with all their luggage, "do you mind going down to get them?"

Aurora watched him nod diligently and take their bags into the back room. "What about Becky and Wade?"

"She went to get him from his nap a few minutes ago." Ani sniffed the air in front of her and crinkled her brow. "Do you smell ginger?"

"That's me. I have a little bit of an upset stomach— Oh, hello," Aurora said in a baby voice as she saw her nephew use his chubby fists to rub the remaining sleep out of his eyes. He was more than a baby. He was the most precious being she had ever seen.

Becky rested him on her hip and pointed. "That's Aunties Aurora and Leela. Let's go give them a hug." With the infant in her arms, she half hugged each of them while he made attempts to grab them. "I love your new haircut, Leela, and so does Wade, apparently."

Leela played with the longer side. "I think I'm due for a trim soon, but my hair's been low on my priority list as of late. Got a lot going on." She shot a smile at Aurora.

Aurora tried to subtly convey with her eyes that she needed to retract or explain before her mom jumped all over it. But based on her mother's inquisitive expression, it was too late.

"Oh, really?" Ani said, concerned. "Is work overwhelming you?"

"Yes," Leela drawled. "Work is so, so busy."

"I bet you are busy, Ms. Oregon-Forty-Under-Forty," Becky said to Wade in her baby voice. "How about you?"

"About the same," Aurora said. Okay, the small talk was over, and it was time to get to business. She needed that baby. "Can I hold him now?"

"Didn't take you long to ask." Becky passed her young son over to Aurora with a "whee!"

Apparently used to this game, Wade smiled and outstretched his onesie-clad limbs.

Aurora took him with a swoop, causing him to release a tiny giggle. A quick glance at Leela confirmed something she suspected may happen.

The look in her wide brown eyes could only be described as terror. Aurora wasn't just holding an infant. She was holding a replica of what chickpea would be at that time next year. Except Wade was beiger.

"Are you okay, Leela?" Becky asked.

Leela's gaze quickly shifted from Wade to her quasi-sister-in-law. "Um, yeah. I just..." She unzipped her jacket and pulled her shirt away from her skin to fan herself. "I'm really warm, so I think I'm going to change. Be right back."

Aurora was about to turn Wade back over when her mom recruited Becky to help finish setting the table for dinner. With a sigh, she bounced with him into the guest room, which was her former bedroom. She found Leela still wearing her jacket and pacing. "I think the first step to changing out of your travel clothes is taking off your jacket."

"I freaked out."

"Really?" Aurora asked sarcastically. She wasn't surprised by the reaction, given how many times Leela had commented about her lack of knowledge regarding human babies. "What could have caused that, I wonder?"

"I'm sorry. It's just I knew Wade would be here and mentally I was like, 'oh, Wade's a baby and we're going to have a baby,' but I didn't fully get the fact that we're having a *baby* like him." She pointed at the tiny culprit. "And the way you're holding him. That's such a perfect way to hold a baby. I know nothing about holding babies. I'm going to be terrible!"

"You've held babies before."

"Most of my experience is with goats. A very different type of kid."

Leela had such an interesting mix of skills and perspective. But there was only one way to get her over this hurdle. She walked toward Leela.

"What are you doing?"

"You're going to hold Wade."

"No, I'm not!" Leela backed into the bed and sat when her knees hit the mattress.

Aurora sat beside her and turned Wade so he faced away. "It's easy. See how I'm holding him with my forearm, supporting his butt and the other hand across his chest?" When Leela nodded, she stood from her seat. "And see how I can move while I'm doing it?"

"Yeah."

"Good. Prepare to receive." Aurora placed Wade on Leela's lap.

Her hands immediately went to where they were supposed to be.

"Ta-da; you're holding a baby."

Wade turned around slightly and reached for Leela's chin. She looked down at him and her shoulders relaxed. "It's a little less terrifying than I remember. Probably because he has neck muscles and isn't screaming like I'm trying to eat him."

Aurora kneeled on the shag carpet and rubbed Leela's knees. "Okay, I'll admit that can be pretty uncomfortable. But this is doable, right? Not too scary."

"I'd say I can successfully hold a happy baby and it isn't absolutely terrifying." Leela avoided Wade's hand as he attempted to put it in her mouth. "Sorry I got weird. It's just making the leap from picturing chickpea to seeing you hold Wade, who once was a chickpea, was a little jarring."

Aurora shrugged with a grin. "It happens."

Leela leaned over to kiss her while their lips were poked at by tiny fingers. "Now that I've established I can hold a baby without freaking out, can I please take off my coat? It's a thousand-billion degrees in here."

It was stifling hot, even though the wood stove was in the living room. Aurora happily took Wade back and returned to bouncing him on her hip. While Leela took off her coat, Aurora answered the soft knock at the door.

"Aw," Ani drawled. "You are such a natural. But do you mind if I interrupt your baby time? Becky wants to feed him before we all sit down at the table."

Aurora passed Wade one more time. "I think I'll change too, then we'll be out." She softly shut the door and pouted.

"You'll be able to hold him more later," Leela said. She unzipped their largest luggage and sorted through different garments until she pulled a black short sleeve out.

"While you're in there, can you hand me my turtle tee? It's the blue one wedged into the side."

Leela found the shirt and tossed it to her.

While she quickly changed her own clothes, Aurora watched Leela get into hers.

Leela did so much physical labor on the farm, she didn't need a gym. Her back, arm, and ab muscles were lean and well-defined.

"See something you like, Peeper McStare?"

Aurora enjoyed her ogling, but then the guilt struck. "Yeah, I do."

Leela's amused face left. "What's wrong then?"

"I'm going to become less attractive to you as time goes on."

"Lies!" Leela said without missing a beat. "You're the most gorgeous person on this planet, and that t-shirt makes your boobs looks amazing! Not that I'm minimizing your beauty to a single body part, it's just that, well…they're awesome. Even in that sucky bra."

Aurora threw her arms around Leela's neck. Leela knew just what to say to make her feel better. "You're the best."

"I try," Leela said as she squeezed her gently. "Bodies change all the time. Remember that I couldn't walk without crutches when we first met, and now look at me. But even if I still needed them, I know you'd love me and appreciate my body."

She was right. Smart and gorgeous and all hers. "Maybe later I can show you how much?"

"I don't hate this idea."

"Great!" She kissed Leela softly. "Let's be social before dinner."

"Wait," Leela said as she held her back. "When are we going to tell your parents? I want us to be a united front."

"Hmm." Aurora crossed her arms as she thought. "Well, River and his family could be here a long time, and I don't want to tell Mom and Dad too late in the evening. So, breakfast?"

"Works for me."

They walked out into the living room together where Becky was in the process of guiding Wade's mouth to her exposed and prominent nipple.

"Aren't you girls cold in just those t— Wow!" Ani said with a smile. "Boo bear, where did *those* come from?" She gestured to her chest.

"New bra," Leela answered quickly and touched Aurora's arm. "Are you cold?"

"No," Aurora said absently as she stared at Becky, fixated on her feeding Wade. She had seen a multitude of women breastfeed in her lifetime but had never thought about what it meant. Becky nourished Wade via her breast. Food came out of her. It was surreal. "Does that hurt?"

"Not anymore," Becky answered and adjusted Wade's body while his hand gently touched the side of her breast. "Although, he does have teeth coming in now."

Aurora couldn't help the reflexive wince. "But the suction?"

Becky shook her head. "Not after the first week or so. Although, I did learn from several mistakes I made with Logan. No chapped, bleeding nipples this time."

Aurora fully recoiled and crossed her arms over her chest. She hated chapped lips; she couldn't imagine what chapped nipples would feel like. "How do you prevent that?"

Becky laughed, her blond hair shaking over her shoulder and Wade. "Do you want me to write it down for you?"

Leela gently grabbed Aurora's upper arm. "I'm thirsty. Can you show me how to use the water filter in the kitchen?"

Aurora didn't answer but felt herself get pulled into the kitchen of steaming, savory smells.

Leela turned on the kitchen tap, letting the sound of water dominate the room, and whispered, "What are you doing in there?"

"What do you mean?"

"You're asking your sister-in-law for breastfeeding advice."

"If you had chapped nipples in your future, you'd want advice too!" Aurora said in an intense whisper.

Leela took two glasses from the cabinet, turned on the filtration, and filled them. "Okay, I'll admit that was probably alarming for you to hear, but if I can get my goats through it, I can get you through it."

"I'm not a goat!"

"You sure aren't!" Becky yelled from the living room.

Leela took a long drink from her glass while she pushed the other toward Aurora. "Fair point, but we both have to be cooler about this. People with literally no training and very little life experience successfully have babies. That's what you keep telling me, at least."

Aurora leaned against the tan, laminate counter. "You're right. I was okay with holding Wade, but we have to get used to more. There's more than just holding and bouncing." She paused as a thought struck her. "We need books."

"Agreed. That's why it's number two on the whiteboard at home."

Aurora thought of the insane list Leela had compiled at home. "What's number one?"

"Threatening the contractor one more time."

Aurora rolled her eyes. She couldn't wait for that drama to end.

"We need those rooms done. And I just know we can get that mop sink beside the washing machine."

The back door slammed shut, which was promptly followed by the whine. "But I want to take more pictures!"

Clearly, their eight-year-old nephew was not happy, but as soon as he saw his aunts, his mood drastically changed. "Aunt Aurora!"

The force at which he came at her set her off balance. "I'm happy to see you too, and now I can understand why you're spending so much time in the penalty box this season. Show Leela what you're made of."

As Logan greeted Leela with a tackle-hug he'd picked up playing sports, her brother gave her a much gentler greeting. "Thanks for resetting his mood," River whispered. "I didn't think coming in for dinner would be such a huge deal."

"Aunt Aurora, do you want to see the picture I just took?"

"Absolutely, but I bet Aunt Leela wants to see too."

He nodded enthusiastically while River gave him his phone. He opened the gallery and went to his latest series. "Look! It's an eagle."

Aurora took the phone to view the image. The bird of prey was front and center, making inspecting it easy. The feathers were every color of brown and gold with the occasional highlight of white, its hooked beak was the shade of dark honey and black at the tip, the yellow of its beak matched its eyes and talons, and while one foot had all four talons intact, the other foot's front and center talon was damaged. Only a stub of the digit remained. Above the foot, the eagle had visible scars where it had lost feathers. "You either have one heck of a camera on that phone or this eagle was crazy close."

"He was so close! Wasn't he?"

River nodded. "He was probably only twenty feet away. Saw him on the way in. Well, technically Dad saw him, but I got out the camera."

"Didn't even drop it in the snow," Niq said with a friendly punch to his arm. "Logan, let's get that bike grease off your hands before dinner."

"That's our cue," Ani said. "And thank the Creator I feel like I can eat. Aurora, if being around the food smell doesn't help your queasiness, you can visit more with Becky. I'm going to put the finishing touches on the soup."

Much like her mother, Aurora was pleased her stomach had calmed itself. "I'm better now, so I can help." She knew as long as Becky was breastfeeding Wade, that was where her gaze would be drawn. "What can I do?"

"If you can cut up the broccoli into tiny pieces to stir into the broccoli cheddar, that would be wonderful. I thought adding in some veggies at the end would give it a fun crunch."

Aurora moaned. The idea of warm, creamy soup sopped up with fresh bread was the ultimate cold weather pleasure. "That sounds amazing. Good idea about the broccoli."

Ani placed a hand on her hip and viewed her daughter suspiciously. "Since when do you like broccoli?"

"It's a recent discovery."

Ani smiled as she reached for the chef knife. "You are so much like me. I don't know if you know this but I used to hate broccoli too but then I got pregnant with River and that completely reset my taste buds. You're not pregnant, are you?" Ani asked with a chuckle.

Aurora froze. If she lied, her mom would know. If she told the truth, her mom would definitely know. She risked a glance over to Leela, whose eyes looked more like a surprised cartoon character than an actual human. The already warmer kitchen became a furnace. She felt a bead of sweat roll down her arm.

"Boo bear?" Ani put the knife down. Then her gaze drifted down to Aurora's breasts and then her waist. She gasped.

How could she possibly know? Aurora remained speechless from her mother's sixth sense.

Leela swiftly took Ani's hand and started for the hallway. "This conversation should be held elsewhere."

Aurora followed.

Once the door to the guest bedroom was shut, Aurora led her mother to sit on the bed and stood facing Leela. She hoped Leela understood her well enough that she needed a moment to collect her thoughts.

"Here's the thing, Ani, I think I speak for both Aurora and myself when I say that we *need* the information we're about to tell you to not leave this room."

"It's true?" Ani asked in wonder.

"You have to *promise*," Leela emphasized.

Ani sat at attention and mimed zipping her lips and throwing away the key.

"I am pregnant." Aurora gave her mother a moment to squeal and tap her feet. "However, how it happened is through rather unique circumstances."

The dancing feet stopped. "What do you mean 'unique'? You didn't use a donor?"

Both Aurora and Leela shook their heads.

"Aurora, you didn't…?"

"No, she didn't cheat on me," Leela said.

Aurora was appalled that her mother thought she would commit adultery. "I would never…" Leela's calming hand on her arm made her pause.

"I'm sorry, boo bear, I didn't mean to upset you. But if it wasn't a donor or…*that*, then what can it—" Her normal happy face transitioned to one of horror.

"And there's no evidence of something bad happening either," Leela said quickly. "It just…happened."

"When? How?" Ani asked, amazed and surprised.

"Conception was in Hawaii. We were planning on telling you and Dad tonight but we wanted to keep it a secret to everyone else until my first trimester was over."

Ani nodded. "That makes sense. But how it happened doesn't make sense at all."

"We have that all figured out," Leela said with confidence. "This is clearly a case of parthenogenesis in humans."

"Oh! I know what that is. It's like reptiles at a zoo. I read about it in my blog."

Her mother's favorite blog, while ridiculous, did seem to expose her to a number of different topics.

"Leela and I have found some interesting research about it happening in humans and mice, but we haven't talked to her father about it yet, who's researching the phenomenon. In animals, though. No human ethical dilemmas," she quickly added. "We were planning on asking him questions when we told him."

"Are you telling Sid and Tanha soon?" Ani asked.

"We'll tell them in person too," Leela said.

"I see." Ani's gaze zeroed in on Leela. She stood from the bed, approached her, and lifted the pendant at the hollow of her throat. Then, she went to Aurora, pulled the leather chain of Aurora's necklace from underneath the neck of her shirt until she viewed her pendant. "*Mmm hmph*. This makes much more sense than parthenogenesis."

There was a knock at the door, and all sets of eyes turned to it at once.

"Yes?" Ani said.

"Can we eat soon, Mom?" River said through the door. "Logan's about ready to have a meltdown."

Ani turned to them. "We're returning to this conversation immediately after dinner."

#

The side smiles and little looks Ani sent her during dinner drove Leela mad. It was bad enough she had to try to keep up with a conversation about hockey for fifteen minutes, let alone knowing that, as each moment passed, she was closer to having what would be a completely bonkers conversation with her partner's mother.

What other explanation did Ani have for Aurora being pregnant? Anything from space aliens to shapeshifters was a possibility. And while Leela wanted an answer more than anything, she wasn't sure she wanted Ani's take on it. Especially if it somehow involved their necklaces. That was next level out there and she knew Aurora felt the same way. She could sense her growing frustration. If Ani asked Aurora one more time if she liked the broccoli cheddar soup, Leela thought Aurora might start throwing bread. And then cry.

There was always the crying.

After dinner and then a dessert of sweet potato pie, River and his family wished everyone a good night and left.

"Here we are, alone at last," Ani said, giddy to start the conversation. "And about to discuss my latest grandbaby. I'm so excited; you have no idea!"

Based on the manic smile and legs that wouldn't stop bouncing, Leela had a pretty good idea. "Do you want me to go get Niq from the basement?"

Ani took a moment to think. "As much as I want to get into this and talk with just us girls, yes. Go get him. Hopefully, you've caught him during a commercial break."

Leela gave a dutiful nod and headed to the basement, where Niq was fixing a bike derailleur with the hockey game on in the background. The game clock quickly counted down the last remaining seconds.

He looked up from his bike parts. "Decided to learn about hockey?"

"Um, no. Aurora and I were hoping we could steal you for a second. Looks like it's almost over."

"Well, the period's almost over. I'll be right up. I need to degrease my hands."

She gave a nod and headed back up to where Aurora and Ani smiled at each other. "He'll be right up."

They waited in silence until he arrived. Which must have been the first clue something was up.

He stood at the entrance of the living room with a suspicious look. "What happened?"

Aurora stood, no doubt anticipating the hug she knew would come her way. "Dad, Leela and I are pregnant."

"No way," he said with a surprised and delighted grin. Niq rushed toward Aurora and—thank the Gods—he embraced her much more gently than he had at the airport.

That was an external pressure chickpea could handle.

Leela watched him pepper Aurora's head and cheeks with rapid kisses. Then, Aurora teared up from her father's attention. This was why telling Ani and Niq over the phone wouldn't have been right.

"I can't believe it," Niq said as he cradled Aurora's head to his chest. "My little girl is going to have a little one of her own."

"Believe it. Mom guessed right away."

"She does have a sixth sense about these things." He released her, and Leela could have sworn he did a little hop. "Is it too early to start looking at tricycles I could fix up?"

"I don't know a lot about babies," Leela said, "but I think you have plenty of time for that."

Niq folded his arms across his chest and grinned. "This is so exciting. When are you due?"

"June fifteenth," Aurora and Leela answered in unison.

Niq continued to smile like he had received the earth's greatest present. "When are you going to tell your brother?"

"Right after we tell Leela's parents, when we wrap up the first trimester."

"We'll keep your secret safe. Isn't that right, Ani?"

"I promise I won't say a word," Ani replied then took a sip of tea.

Niq's smile faded into a slight awkward grimace. "Am I allowed to ask about the donor?"

"Before we get to that," Ani said, "are you planning on keeping the placenta? You know, Becky turned hers into vitamins."

The slight discomfort it appeared he felt turned into full aversion. "If you're going to talk about that, is it okay if I go?" Niq asked. "You know how squeamish I am when it comes to medical stuff. I promise, we can celebrate properly tomorrow."

Aurora gave her mom a suspicious glance. "Yes, Dad, that's great."

When Leela turned, she saw that Ani had a devious smirk. She didn't want him to be told about the parthenogenesis. Once the basement door shut again, Leela asked, "Why'd you scare him away with placenta talk? You know he almost passed out the first time I described my leg surgery."

"Because you were going to tell him your theory, and I don't think that's the correct explanation." She made a little twirl at the hollow of her throat. "Those are."

"What do our necklaces have to do with me being pregnant?"

Ani blew the steam away from her teacup. "It's a fertility necklace. Leela's represents the baby, yours represents the vessel."

"They do not," Aurora said and picked up her necklace, looking at the pendant upside down. "This indent is where the heart should be that is missing, but Leela has it. The spiral is the never-ending love. At least, that's what the guy at the store said."

"You let a man try to tell you about the parts of a woman's body? I taught you better than that." Ani tsked. "No, the indentation is an empty womb, and Leela's piece is the baby. Spirals are often used to represent fertility."

Leela looked at her piece skeptically. "No way."

"Way," Ani answered. "I bet they're magnetic."

"How...?" Leela's interest was piqued. "How did you know that?"

Aurora turned to her, confused. "What do mean? They're not magnetic."

"Yes, they are," Leela countered. Why Aurora thought they weren't, baffled her.

"Oh," Ani drawled. "Now, this is getting interesting. Why are you giving different answers?"

"Because when I bought them, I fit Leela's piece inside mine and it wasn't magnetic."

"But when I woke up on our last day in Hawaii, yours and mine were stuck together, like magnets."

"What?" Aurora asked, stunned by the information. "You didn't tell me that."

Leela shrugged. "I didn't think it was a big deal. I figured you knew they were magnets. See." Leela placed her spiral pendant into the concave space of Aurora's necklace.

And then it fell out.

Ani's eyes grew wider. "This is even more fascinating than I suspected. Such powerful medicine. It's not magnetic anymore but it was the morning after you made love?"

"Whoa!" Leela said with an awkward laugh. "Who said we had to have done *that*?"

Ani's whole body rocked as she chuckled. "Leela, I know you and my daughter make love. It's a beautiful thing so please don't feel embarrassed. Besides, I hear you're quite good."

Leela turned to her partner with horror. Aurora had spoken to her quasi mother-in-law about their sex life. "Why are you talking to her about that?"

"She asked," Aurora said matter-of-factly. "Mom just wants to make sure you're meeting all my needs, and, like she said, what we have is beautiful and special. There's nothing to be ashamed about. Plus, this is a much more romantic origin story for chickpea."

Ani placed a hand over her heart. "You call the baby 'chickpea'? That's adorable."

Aurora nodded with a smile. "We don't want to upgrade to baby until—"

"Let me guess," Ani said, "you're out of your first trimester."

"It just seems like the right thing to do," Leela added.

Ani gave a thumbs up and then looked up at the ceiling. "Let's see if we can make sense of this. You have a fertility necklace that was activated—for lack of a better term—immediately after you made love. You must have done some kind of ceremony."

"We did not do a ceremony!" Leela stood and started to pace. She fanned her face with her hand to decrease the actual and metaphorical heat she felt. While her parents were often emotionally unavailable, at least she never had to endure this. "After a week at a spectacular resort, we had a truly fantastic last evening there, and I think Aurora was exposed to something that may have changed her inability to genetically imprint, which led to asexual reproduction. I need to check with Dad about that."

Ani looked at Leela and then to Aurora before bursting out in laughter. "That is the most ridiculous thing I've ever heard."

"It could be possible," Leela defended.

Ani shook her head. "No way. Now, if I recall the bits Aurora told me, and what I saw on InstaPic, in the middle of September you spent a week at a vegan resort that also had a saltwater hot tub. True?"

Both she and Aurora nodded.

"Good. And Leela made a lotion just for you and applied it. Then, Aurora gave you one of the two pieces of the necklace and she put on the other."

"Yes," they answered simultaneously.

"Excellent," Ani said. "Now, let me summarize all of that information in a different way. The two of you spent a week detoxifying your bodies. Then, you anointed each other with oil; you followed this up by professing your feelings for each other while exchanging pieces of the necklace; this led to you making love during the equinox."

"What?" Leela asked. She couldn't believe what she was hearing. The borderline science-fiction of the parthenogenesis explanation was one thing, but the idea that chickpea was conceived via a fertility ritual was pure fantasy. "No way."

"I don't know," Aurora said. "That does sound pretty accurate."

Ani nodded and tapped the side of her teacup. "Was the sex different?"

"Whoa!" Leela shot up from the couch. "Pump the brakes, Ani. I really, *really* don't feel comfortable discussing this."

"But it's starting to make sense!" Aurora argued.

"No, it's not! This is crazy!"

Aurora set her jaw, looked at her with defiance, and turned to face her mother. "The sex was incredible. And yes, it felt different too."

Leela wanted to slip back into her coma. At least then she wouldn't be mortified.

"Was the sex being incredible the only way it was different?" Ani asked.

Leela turned and leaned her forehead against the dry wall.

"Leela, your experience is just as important as Aurora's here. So, you're going to need to get over this hurdle of self-shaming when it comes to sex."

"I'm not ashamed! I'm just weirded out. You're her mom and you want me to tell you about the sexy stuff we do."

"Was it consensual sexy stuff?"

"Of course!"

"Then, don't worry about it," Ani said with a wave. "If it makes you feel better, I'll tell you some of my past."

"Mom, please, is that really necessary?"

"I think it'll make Leela feel better. Besides, I won't say anything you don't already know."

Aurora tilted her head to the side as though she were thinking about it. "Okay. That makes sense."

Leela made a grunt of frustration. "Fine! First, I gave Aurora a sexy robe. Then came the lotion rubdown, which was immediately followed by the necklace exchange. During that, we each said very loving and meaningful words we'd never said before. We had sex for hours, and at some point, we even managed to orgasm at the same time without even trying."

"At the same time? That's amazing." Ani couldn't have looked more pleased. "Even Niq and I have never pulled that off and we've been having sex since Reagan was in office."

Aurora winced.

Leela supposed they'd both just learned something new about Ani.

"If you can't tell, I'm very jealous," Ani said. "All of that power, both physical and emotional, all at once. It must have been incredible."

"Yes. It was very nice." Leela would leave it at that. Ani didn't need to know that she had been so spent afterward, she didn't remember falling asleep while wearing her harness. And Ani certainly didn't need to know that she still remembered the sensation of Aurora's rippling and contracting muscles as they orgasmed.

"Um." Leela shook her head and gulped. "Ani, would you mind if Aurora and I spoke privately for a few minutes?"

"Absolutely! I can already tell this is going to be good. While you chat, I'll hop online and see what I can find out about this."

#

While her mother sat in the sweltering living room and sipped hot tea, Aurora sat on the bed in the guest room and heard the latest piece of information that rocked her sense of reality. "What do you mean you felt me?"

"You know how before and during orgasm there's extra. . . tightness?"

"Yeah," Aurora answered matter-of-factly. "But I don't see how that relates. Your fingers were," she cupped her breasts, "other places."

"My point exactly! I felt you with Biddie. . . I think."

That didn't mean. . . did it?

"Hold on," Aurora said with her hands waving. "There's a big difference between thinking and knowing here. Thinking implies doubt, but knowing implies, well, you know what knowing implies, right?"

"That Biddie came to life like a pornographic snowman. And I know how ludicrous I sound. But..." Leela placed her hands on her hips and shook her head. "I felt you. I'm sure of it."

Aurora agreed that this idea was even more out there than her parthenogenesis theory, but unlike that event, with this, there had to be some kind of proof. "Do you remember feeling anything other than me?"

Leela skewed her mouth. "I had some muscle cramping, but then you got on top and I was fine."

She remembered changing positions very well. There had to be something else. "Did Biddie look different?"

"Um, not really visible. And then you took it out of the o-ring. Did it look or feel different to you?"

Aurora shook her head. "The room was dark. But in the morning when you cleaned and packed it?"

Leela shrugged. "Looked the same. In all its ridged, purple glory."

She thought about what else could explain Leela's observation, but she hit another roadblock. Luckily, there was someone close to her who was an expert at thinking outside the box. Aurora slapped her thighs and stood. "We have to tell Mom."

Leela rushed to the door and blocked her exit. "No, no, no. That's next-level sex information. I don't want her to know I'm the top."

"Do you want answers or not?" Aurora asked with her hand on the doorknob. "Besides, everyone already knows you're the top."

When Leela sighed and stepped to the side, she strode into the living room, where her mother had her laptop open on the coffee table. "There's been a revelation of sorts."

"Oh?" Ani said and closed the laptop. "What did you learn?"

Aurora looked to Leela, who shook her head. "I can't be here. I'll be in the bathroom," she said and then turned away.

Once the door to the bathroom latched shut. Ani turned to her. "Leela's much shyer about sex than I would have imagined. I guess her parents weren't very open with the topic."

"That's one way of putting it."

Early in their relationship, Leela had shared that there had been no sex talk. Rather, when she was eleven, her parents had arranged office visits for a gynecologist and a proctologist so they could give her a sex talk. She had learned a tremendous amount about anatomy and diseases, but that was the extent of her formal education. Leela had explained that all of her other knowledge and skills came from self-study and field work.

"Well, I guess not all parents are as cool as your father and me." Ani sipped her tea. "So, what's this discovery you two figured out? Because I found some great stuff on my own."

Aurora was about to speak but stopped. She could always talk to her mother about anything; relationships, emotions, the dreams that had led her to Leela, but this was as intimate as it got. She pretended she wasn't about to talk to her mother, but rather a friend who happened to be older and struck an uncanny resemblance to her. "So, Leela thinks she felt me with the toy we were using. Almost like it became a part of her."

Ani gasped. "A ceremonial phallus. This is excellent! As far as I'm concerned this isn't even a mystery anymore."

"But I. . . I still don't understand. Babies aren't made this way! It was a stretch to believe that my cells did this on their own, let alone this. How can I tell people, tell chickpea, when I don't understand?"

Ani set her teacup down and cradled Aurora's hands in hers. "Boo bear, you and Leela are together because of a miracle. In three years, no one has ever been able to explain how or why you dreamed about her the way you did. Leela's doctors and even the one in Seattle tried. Brilliant minds with millions of dollars of equipment couldn't explain why you were called to her. And back then, you didn't believe it at first either, but you had faith and went to her. Aren't you glad you did?"

Aurora nodded, her mother's words bringing tears to her eyes.

"And look at you two now. Your love for each other is so deep—it's so profound—that the Creator has given you life. In fact, maybe your chickpea is why you and Leela are together? Maybe chickpea is the key to saving the world or something?"

"Mom, that's a giant leap you're making."

Ani shrugged. "I think of it more as a grand duty you've been given?"

She supposed her mother had a point, even if it was one that she had difficulty contending with. Through the walls, Aurora heard water running from the bathroom. She hoped Leela would come out soon. Any type of support she could provide would be welcomed.

"The more I think about it," Ani continued, "I can't help but be reminded of Nanabozho."

"You think Leela, a non-native, is an Anishinaabe trickster legend?" Aurora asked skeptically.

"Oh, don't be ridiculous. I know she's not, but she could have shapeshifted like Nanabozho."

Aurora blinked several times, but each time her eyes reopened, her mother held the same tightlipped, serious look.

"I know that sounds a little woo-woo, but the stories of Nanabozho aren't limited to shapeshifting into an animal. There are also some that portray a shift of sex. Kokopelli has a detachable penis, according to some. I wonder…" She drifted off thoughtfully then opened her laptop again and typed.

"This is crazy," Aurora mumbled in a whisper.

"Legends come from somewhere, usually rooted in some fact. There!" Ani spun her laptop so it faced her. "Cultures from around the world have embraced this."

170

Aurora read the bold word at the top aloud, "Tiresias." She continued reading until she reached the part that explained Tiresias was a man until the Greek Goddess, Hera, changed him into a woman.

"I didn't even get into the virgin birth stories yet." Ani typed away again as Leela emerged.

She joined Aurora on the sofa.

"Feeling better?"

"Still confused and embarrassed, but at least I don't have to pee anymore."

"Here we go," Ani happily announced. "There's an entire list here. The Hindus have Devaki and Krishna, the Christians have the Virgin Mary and Jesus, the Chinese have Jiang Yuan and Qi. And now we have the two of you and chickpea. The next miracle birth."

"What if I don't believe in miracles?" Leela asked.

"You don't have to believe for the Creator to gift you. Your love has been acknowledged and honored in a way that happens once in a millennium. This is the grandest of big medicine."

"What do you mean by that?" Leela asked.

"Somehow both you and Aurora are chickpea's biological parents. I have no doubt."

"I do," Leela said with a dry laugh. "Parthenogenesis made some sense, me being a genetic contributor makes none. I'm not. . . I couldn't be a bio mom too."

Aurora recognized Leela's sharp tone immediately, but instead of seeing her teeth gritted, her lips were tight and she shook her head.

Leela was on the verge of becoming emotional.

"Dreamy," Aurora said. "Even though it's difficult for me to believe Mom's idea too, I want it to be true. I want you to be a part of chickpea."

Leela inhaled deeply and nodded. "I want to have a DNA test that says that too. But it can't be real."

Ani smiled sweetly. "I know you will love this child with all your heart regardless, but when you see chickpea with Aurora's nose and your eyes or with a beautiful blend of your skin and hair colors, you'll see how real it is.

"Of course, this is something other people don't have to know. I imagine you'll say you used a donor?"

"Yeah, that's our plan," Aurora said without taking her eyes off Leela.

Leela wrung her hands and her chin quivered. Some kind of emotional switch in Leela's mind must have turned on.

"Why don't we go into the room and talk?" Aurora gently suggested.

When Leela quietly nodded, she turned to her mother.

"I understand. I can't imagine what you two have gone through trying to wrap your heads around this." Ani closed her laptop again and stood. "You need time together to process this. I think I'll check on Niq. Give you two some privacy."

Once her mother had left them alone, Leela stayed as still and silent as a statue. The openness of the room only increasing her vulnerability. Neighbors could see in through the windows. Her father and mother could reappear any second. They were too exposed for the conversation Aurora knew they were about to have.

No words were spoken as they moved into the bedroom. Once the door clicked shut behind Aurora, she reached for Leela and held her. Or rather they held each other.

"You've been through so much." Aurora kissed her forehead and then pulled away so see could look Leela in the eyes. The eyes she hoped chickpea would inherit.

"Even though it could never, ever be possible, the mere suggestion that chickpea could be part of me makes me indescribably happy. And that makes me worry because I'm afraid I'd love chickpea more if she was genetically mine."

With all the scenarios Aurora had run through, this was not one of them. "I don't think that's how it works. Think about all those parents who adopt or who have stepchildren. They love those kids because of something greater than biology. At the same time, some biological parents want nothing to do with their kids."

"True. I just—even though I don't believe it—I feel more connected now. Is that wrong?"

"No." Aurora sat beside her and framed Leela's face in her hands. "Regardless of how chickpea came to be, we are both her parents. We'll be the ones who will tuck her in at night, teach her how to ride a bike, or help her with her homework."

"Milk a goat?"

Aurora grinned. "Yeah. Although, I'm putting that responsibility on you."

Leela sat in silence for a beat and then nodded. "Okay, I promise I won't think less of myself or my love for chickpea because of a silly thing like genetics." Leela leaned forward and kissed her gently. Then slinked down her body and raised the bottom of her turtle shirt. "Do you hear that, chickpea? I'm your mom too, and I love you. Also, you have to love me back because I'm going to be a super parent. Way better than mine. And I'd really appreciate it if you accept a generic donor answer until you're older and can understand the nuances of genetics." Leela quickly lifted her head. "Do you think chickpea heard me?"

Emotion welled inside Aurora, and it wasn't because of her hormones. Leela's commentary was the first time Leela had spoken to their child, and she'd done so in such a way that was quintessentially her: honest, funny, and tender. "I think the message got through clearly. Come here."

Leela kissed the skin at Aurora's waist before moving up her body.

Aurora giggled into her lips. "You're going to be as great a mom as you are a partner. And you're a pretty damn good partner."

"I think I could work harder then. I need to turn that good into great, like attending to *all* of your needs." The second time Leela lowered her mouth, she sensually moved her lips and tongue.

A rush of heat flushed Aurora's skin. Especially the spot under her ear where Leela kissed her. "I'd really like my needs attended to, and it's hotter than the sun in here so I really like the idea of stripping off my clothes."

"I think we should start with your shirt." Leela gave a small tug to the material in question. "It's in my way."

"It is rather cumbersome."

"Well, then so long shirt!"

Leela stripped off her tee and then pulled her in for a kiss so deep Aurora thought Leela had entered her soul.

There was nothing more arousing that having her entire being wrapped and filled by Leela.

Aurora felt Leela's fingers at her back and then the sweet freedom of her bra being unclasped.

Leela didn't wait for her to shrug out of the material before her hands went to both breasts and used her slight fingernails to scrape at her hardened nipples.

She covered Leela's hands with her own and broke their kiss.

The fire in Leela's dilated pupils turned her on further, but she wasn't nearly as aroused as Leela seemed to be.

She pushed Leela back onto the bed and sucked at her pulse point.

When Leela urged her for more, Aurora's fingers went to the button of her jeans. Aurora couldn't wait to taste how excited Leela was. But then she paused. After their heart-to-heart about one of the most serious conversations they would probably ever have, shouldn't they go slow?

"Why'd you stop?" Leela asked while panting.

"You've been on an emotional rollercoaster. I thought maybe we were going too fast and you'd rather talk about it."

"No. No talking. That speed was just right. Please continue with that pacing."

Aurora crushed her mouth against Leela's as she worked her hand inside Leela's jeans. "You are so w—"

"Boo bear," Ani called through the door, "I'm sorry to interrupt your bonding, but I kind of made an oopsie and now your brother knows. I'm sorry."

Aurora pulled herself away from Leela's kiss-swollen lips. She could be aggravated with her mother's lack of secrecy later. She had to focus on Leela now. "We're not done talking, and Leela really needs me."

Leela nodded emphatically while her chest heaved. "This won't take long," she whispered. "I'm really turned on."

Aurora pushed Leela's jeans and panties down by way of acknowledgement. "We'll be out in five minutes or so! We have to collect our emotions!" She kneeled between Leela's legs. Aurora began with long, firm licks through her slick warmth. She craved her taste and couldn't believe they had denied themselves this pleasure for so long. That was complete nonsense. "We'll be out soon, alright?"

Leela opened her legs more and drew in a sharp breath. "Oh, yeah. This won't take long at all."

"All right," Ani said through the door, the teasing quality to her tone obvious.

Her mother knew they were having sex and Aurora couldn't care less. Aurora was in absolute heaven. To be able to touch Leela so intimately was a gift she never took for granted. She could have stayed where she was, pleasuring Leela for hours, but time was of the essence and Aurora did enjoy the challenge of getting Leela to orgasm as quickly as possible.

Based on the grip Leela had on the comforter, she wasn't going to have to wait much longer. "Oh, so close," Leela said a few decibels too loudly, but she must have realized it, because she reached to the head of the bed and grabbed a pillow.

Aurora swirled her tongue and, over Leela's heaving chest, watched Leela place the pillow over her face.

Leela's lower body quaked as she let out a muffled scream into the pillow; the reward of a job well done.

Aurora grinned, kissed Leela below her belly button, and traveled up her body. She did the honors of moving the pillow off her lover's face. "Was the pillow really necessary?" Aurora asked.

"I didn't want to take the chance." Leela held her close. "Think we have enough time for you?" she asked with an eyebrow waggle.

Aurora shook her head. "Not unless you really want to be teased by Mom." When Leela looked at her with a furrowed brow, she explained, "She knows we were having sex in here."

"She does?"

"Yes. But I promise I won't let you get away with being a pillow princess." Aurora kissed her and then started picking up their clothes. "I'm dying to find out how Mom slipped the news to River."

After they redressed, Aurora headed into the bathroom while Leela ventured back out into the scorching heat of the living room.

"Where's my little girl?" she heard her father ask and then clap through the door.

"Bathroom," Leela answered. "We had an emotional moment. She wanted to wash her face."

Aurora chuckled and turned on the faucet. She didn't hear the conversation as clearly for the next minute, but she knew it was all smiles and Leela was probably picked up and spun again. Once her face was dry, she walked out to her father's laughter while he hugged Leela and the sight of her mother back on the computer.

"There she is!" Ani said. "I'm so, so sorry. When I went into the basement to check on Niq I was still a *little* excited—"

"She practically sang at the top of her lungs, 'Boo bear's baby' repeatedly, while I was talking to River about the end of the game. You didn't hear her?" Niq asked.

"It was difficult to hear with the emotions," Aurora said.

"I'm a loud crier," Leela added.

"Well," Niq continued, "it was a complete accident, but now he knows."

"I'm sorry," Ani said but still smiled. "He wants his family to hear it from your mouth though."

Aurora sighed. It was impossible to be upset with her mother if that was the reason why her brother found out. "Okay. Do you want to ping him for a video chat? That way *everybody* is there."

"I'll text him now and see if he's available."

While her mother texted and waited for a response, Leela came up beside her, reached for her hand, and rested her head on Aurora's shoulder. "I hope he doesn't have any theories about aliens," Leela whispered.

"Okay, River's going to gather Becky and Logan," Ani said. "Why don't you two take my spot on the couch? I need to make more tea anyway."

They took their seats in front of the laptop and waited for River's family's faces to pop up on the screen, which only took a minute.

"Hey, Mom says you and Leela have big news." River winked and then whispered, "Becky and Logan don't know."

"Know what?" Logan asked, suddenly more interested in the family call.

Leela gave her the go-ahead nod. "I'm pregnant."

River smiled, Becky gasped, and Logan's eyebrows crinkled.

"Congratulations!" Becky said and hugged River. "Now your staring at me while I breastfed Wade makes so much more sense!"

"None of them's a guy," Logan said in a curious non-whisper to his father.

River waved off his son's comment. "This is amazing. Why didn't you tell us before?"

"Leela and I were waiting until I start my second trimester to make the announcement, but Mom guessed."

"This is so wonderful," Becky said. "I didn't even know you were trying. Did you use a donor?"

"Yes."

"Did you use a friend or go to a bank?"

"Why would they go to a bank?" Logan asked, even more confused than he was before.

Aurora was happy River told Logan he could go choose a movie to watch instead of staying on the family call. She didn't know if she could deal with questions coming from both him and Becky.

"Donor wants their identity private," Leela blurted. "We want to honor that."

"Oh," she said. "Did you do IUF?"

"Um…" Aurora stalled.

"Yes," Leela said.

"At home or did you go somewhere to have it done?" Becky said, and Wade started crying in the background. "I have to go but start thinking about keeping the placenta. They might not offer that option and Leela could integrate it into her products."

Aurora and Leela shared a knowing look while Logan yelled in the background about the TV not working.

"Be right there," River said. "Sorry, do you mind if I see what's wrong and come right back?"

Ani must have caught how overwhelmed they felt by the onslaught of questions because she quickly answered. "You know, it's pretty late now. Aurora looks exhausted."

"I bet. All that travel and the new mom hormones making you sleepy. I'm really, really happy for you two."

Aurora looked at Leela who was giving her a sappy grin. "Thank you."

"And Leela," River added, "take good care of her and let me know if you want any clothes or toys. I'd love to get rid of some of that."

"Always and that would be great," Leela said. "Thanks."

"No problem. I'll give you all a call tomorrow. Bye."

Ani looked at them both once the virtual chat was over and closed the lid to her laptop. "Well, that was fun."

Niq raised his eyebrows and went to Aurora and Leela. He embraced them in a group hug and kissed them both on the cheek. "I'm so, so happy for the both of you, but you do look tired and you're both going to want to sleep as much as possible now, because you're going to miss it later."

"You're right," Leela said. "Let's hit the sack. Significant festivities tomorrow."

Aurora wished both her parents a good night and retreated to the guest room once more. Leela locked the door behind them.

"That went well," Aurora said. "And I have to say I'm relieved River knows."

"So, you're feeling happy? I know I'm happy."

Leela was in a good emotional place, she was in a good emotional place, so it was time to pick up where they left off. She stepped in and gave Leela a long, sensual kiss. "Happy, but slightly unsatisfied."

Leela smirked as she tucked her fingers inside the waistband of Aurora's jeans and pulled her closer. "If I recall correctly, you called me a pillow princess."

Aurora looped her arms around Leela's neck. That wasn't *exactly* what she had said, but if that riled up Leela more, then that was what she'd go with. "You literally orgasmed into a pillow as I serviced you and you laid there doing nothing. Very passive and princess-like, if you ask me."

"You think by antagonizing me you're going to get it extra hard?" Leela slowly backed her into the room. "Well, it's working."

Aurora loved the playfulness and stifled a chuckle. "Like you could ever give it to me extra hard."

The little spark in Leela's eyes turned into an inferno. "Don't think I can?"

Aurora already knew this was going to be incredible. "I'll believe it when I feel it."

In moves fueled by love, passion, and play, Aurora was naked and on her back with her legs wrapped around Leela's waist in seconds. Leela's fingers teased her with barely there caresses. "I think you could do better," Aurora said with breathy hitch.

Then, she felt it.

Leela's curved fingers thrusted inside of her, faster and harder, until she wasn't sure her pleas for more were actual words or unintelligible moans.

"I can feel how close you are," Leela said and then kissed her neck.

"N-No, I'm not," Aurora lied. But she knew Leela knew she was lying. The tension and blush across her body were obvious. She didn't know how, but Leela's power increased. And then, once her orgasm came, that power sent her from a place of tension and heat to calm and. . . Well, it was still hot. But she was very relaxed.

While her body came down from its high, Leela placed a loving kiss on her lips.

"Thoughts, comments, opinions," Leela said smugly.

Aurora took a few more breaths to calm herself. "That was. . . okay."

Leela gave her a side-eye.

She laughed with goofy bliss and then kissed Leela. "Just kidding. You. Are. Amazing."

Leela patted herself on the back. "And you. Are. Welcome. Ready to go to sleep now and call it a day?"

"Yeah. Let's get ready for bed."

CHAPTER TEN

PATIENCE WAS A tricky thing to get used to.

"Let me try to explain it differently," Leela said to small group of employees in the office. She drew a quick block on the whiteboard representing her current schedule and then the new schedule.

"Why are we doing this again?" Rosa asked.

"Because I want to spend more time with Aurora, especially when it comes to the fertility treatments." Ever since returning from Michigan a few weeks ago, it had been difficult to keep the secret, but at least this way she could plan openly and with feedback. Once her parents knew about chickpea—which was quickly approaching—then everyone could know.

"I think it's sweet you want extra time together," Jill commented, "and you're being so supportive. Viktor was never this supportive."

It was so much more than the extra time and support. It was also a feeling—no, it was knowledge—that as long as she was with Aurora and chickpea, they would be safe. "So, like I was saying, the new schedule won't affect your weekly hours—unless you want more hours—in which case, I can schedule you for one of my former blocks."

The group nodded their approval.

"Okay, now—" Leela's phone vibrated in her pocket. The days of her checking texts and calls when it was convenient was over.

She was on-call 24-7 for Aurora and chickpea. That was her new job, even more important than business owner and presidential candidate.

She took the phone out of her pocket. It was a call from Aurora. "I have to take this," she said and left the office into the chilled December air. "Hi, sweets, what's going on?"

"I'm trying not to freak out, but there's blood," Aurora said in a tight tone.

It was like the ground beneath her had just moved. She leaned against the siding to help keep her balance. But panicking wouldn't help Aurora. Or chickpea. "Okay, we both read that this happens sometimes. Did you call Dr. Aguilar?"

"Yes. I'm driving there now."

"Good. I'll be right there. I love you."

"I love you too, but Leela. . . I'm scared."

Aurora was on the verge of tears, Leela could hear it in her voice. "I know you are, but let's stay optimistic and remember that spotting is normal." The words were meant to help both Aurora and herself.

"You're right. Okay, I'll see you soon."

Leela hung up and walked back into the office where Jill and Rosa had added different colorful lines to her new schedule. She didn't know what they were doing and she didn't care. "Meeting's over. I gotta go." She grabbed her keys from the hook on the wall and left.

She sped through the countryside and prayed everything was okay. She wasn't even religious. She didn't know if there was a god or gods listening to her, but if any of them did have their ears open, they had to see to it that chickpea was fine. Because if chickpea wasn't...

Leela couldn't even finish. It was the most devastating thought that had ever entered her mind. Life was a rollercoaster, and they had been riding high for far too long.

Once she and Aurora returned from their Michigan visit, Aurora had become more comfortable delegating work, Keith had begun to take more initiative with administrative aspects, the contractors finished the remodel, which included a mop sink, and she had ideas for the farm and campaign.

Now there was this moment of absolute terror.

Everything had been going so well, and even though they had been waiting to tell others the announcement, Leela had forgotten the reason. She had started a delusion where the sad reality of a miscarriage didn't exist.

But that was wrong too. Just like she knew Aurora and chickpea would be safe if she was there, she *knew* someday chickpea would enter the world.

After an agonizing drive that felt like it took an eternity, Leela rushed into the waiting room and saw Aurora sitting with her knees bouncing.

She was playing with her braid. Her eyes were glassy and unfocused.

The sight broke her heart.

Rather than say something, Leela sat beside her and placed a hand on her back.

Their gazes met, and Aurora's arms went around her in an instant.

"I don't know what I did wrong," Aurora softly said.

"You didn't do anything wrong. You've been textbook momming this whole pregnancy."

"But what if I did and something bad happened?"

Leela gulped. She had to be strong. There was no room for her own paranoia or hurt. "Then we'll get through it, but I want you to think positively."

"Ms. Okpik," the registration nurse said. "You can follow me, please."

Leela felt Aurora's white-knuckle grip all the way to the examination room. After a short wait, Dr. Aguilar explained the need to use a transvaginal ultrasound for heart rate detection, since Aurora was still in her first trimester, but they shouldn't worry.

Leela continued to worry and held Aurora's hand throughout the exam. She felt a slightly firmer grip when Aurora squeezed from the wand placement. "You're doing really well, sweets."

"Yes, you are," Dr. Aguilar said in a calm voice as she turned her attention to the monitor. "And chickpea is too."

"What?" Aurora's eyes shot open and to the fuzzy black and white screen. "How do you know?"

Dr. Aguilar pointed to the screen. "See all this black space? That's the fluid surrounding chickpea. And the gray irregular shape with the flicker is—"

"That's chickpea!" Leela gave Aurora the best sideways hug she could.

"Chickpea's alright," Aurora said, relieved, with tears starting, and she held Leela's arms closer to her body. "All I do is cry now."

"You're allowed to." Leela kissed Aurora's temple and thanked the being or beings who had listened to her in the car. "Do you see something else on there?"

Dr. Aguilar continued to study the screen. "Their heartrate is. . . *Hmm.*"

This was not the time for suspense.

"What does 'hmm' mean?" Leela asked.

Dr. Aguilar shook her head. "Nothing major, it's just that fetal heartrates, like everything else, have a range, and chickpea's is a little low. So, not a bad thing, but it does mean we should pay extra attention to it going forward."

Aurora sighed a heavy breath beside her. "Is there anything else?"

"Just your picture."

"We get a picture of chickpea?" Leela asked, overjoyed, and then smiled at Aurora.

"You sure do, but chickpea is more plum-sized now," Dr. Aguilar said. "Also, your twelve-week appointment was originally scheduled for next week, but this pretty much takes care of that, so feel free to cancel it."

"Okay, but what if I bleed again? Why did I even start bleeding in the first place?"

"A dozen of different things can cause that, from rough inter-course to exercising too vigorously."

Leela shot a concerned look at Aurora, who shook her head in return. Thank the Gods it wasn't her fault.

Aurora bit her bottom lip. "Maybe I should ease back my workout intensity?"

"Maybe. But don't get rid of exercise completely, that's very important. In fact, you might want to consider couples yoga if you haven't already."

"Oh no," Leela whispered.

Dr. Aguilar laughed. "Just give it a try. It really helps prepare the birth mother, it's great for your relationship, and it gives the partner not giving birth a chance to commiserate with other people in the same situation. And while I have given you a few midwife suggestions, it can't hurt to ask there too."

Leela was impressed by the sales pitch, even if it did mean she might have to downward dog in a room full of people. "Sounds reasonable. But only if Aurora wants to."

"I want to, and there's something else I want to do too." Aurora turned to her, jaw set. "Since this is functioning as chickpea's twelve-week visit, I want to tell your mom at dinner next week."

Dr. Aguilar smiled. "I'll make sure the tech prints an extra pic-ture then. Your mom will be thrilled."

Leela's mother, Tanha Mitra, pain-in-the-ass and cardiologist extraordinaire, would love that.

"Are you okay?" Aurora asked. "It looks like you drifted off there for a second."

"Just thinking about how Mom will take the news. She might actually squeal."

Aurora's brow knitted together. "I've never heard your mom squeal."

"Which goes to show you how rare it is."

"Being a first-time grandma is squeal-worthy." Dr. Aguilar took Aurora's chart and then paused at the door. "You two have a wonderful holiday. I'll see you in four weeks."

Leela sat patiently while Aurora changed back into her work clothes. Part of her was pleased Dr. Aguilar treated the visit just like she would have for any other couple—she imagined—but another part of her wanted her to admit Leela was right about the parthenogenesis theory. Which still made loads more sense to her than Ani's idea.

"What's wrong?" Aurora asked. "You have that little crinkle between your eyebrows."

Aurora was also on board with Ani's idea, which Leela didn't want to spend the energy arguing about, since, ultimately, she was happy that Aurora and chickpea were healthy. "Just thinking about how I don't want all the questions like last time we told people the news."

"It wasn't that bad. But I do understand where you're coming from. Let's just come up with answers to the questions Becky asked."

Leela scoffed in disgust. "I do *not* need to keep the placenta for my products."

"You know what I mean. It's a good way to prepare for the nosiest of people."

It would almost be like creating a practice test. She excelled at tests. "Okay, so we have to come up with information about our 'donor'—"

"I think we already have a clear answer for that," Aurora said with a chuckle.

Leela treaded lightly. "I think we need to be on the same page, because if our baby comes out looking *really* close to you, I don't know what I'll say."

"I know what you're suggesting, and that won't happen," Aurora said confidently. "I *know* chickpea is yours."

"Can we at least narrow down the traits of mine we looked for in a donor? Then, if they aren't in chickpea, I feel comfortable saying the genetic wheel of chance wasn't in my favor."

"That's fair."

"Thank you. We also have to figure out some answers to a few things already on the whiteboard." There was so much on the whiteboard already. It seemed like every day one more item was added. "Do you want to figure it all out tonight?"

"It doesn't all have to be tonight. Let's just make sure we finish before we see your mom for her holiday dinner." Aurora furrowed her brow. "What holiday is it this year?"

"Hanukah." While Leela criticized her parents for many things, the one part of her childhood she couldn't fault them for was how they acknowledged different religious holidays. She wasn't raised with any spirituality, but they did want her to understand that different cultures had different beliefs, traditions, and foods. "I hope there's latkes."

Aurora nodded enthusiastically. "And chocolate babka."

#

Leela held a large gift basket as she and Aurora ascended the elevator to Tanha's upscale Portland apartment. She glanced at Aurora while she bounced from side to side. "You wouldn't be excited by any chance, would you?"

"How'd you guess?" Aurora answered with a smile.

There was so much excitement.

Not only were they going to tell Leela's mother the news, but they were going to do so in the most precious way. In the congratulations card Aurora held, the sonogram picture was on one side and the heartrate data on the other. "I bet this will rank in her most exciting moments of all time."

"Agreed. Chickpea might be tied with her divorcing Dad."

Aurora *tsked*. "That's terrible!"

"I'm kidding! This will be very exciting," Leela said seriously as the elevator doors slid open.

Aurora silently rolled their overnight suitcase over the plush carpet of the long hallway to Tanha's corner suite and rang her buzzer. The door opened, and an aromatic wall struck Aurora. She was thankful her nausea was limited to the refrigerator smell at work these days.

"My favorite girls!" Tanha, dressed in black evening pants and a bright pink blouse, hugged each of them tightly.

"Hi, Mom," Leela said unenthusiastically and scrunched her face like a child when her mother kissed both cheeks.

One of the most wonderous parts of her relationship with Leela was watching Leela's relationship with her parents evolve over the past few years. It was beautiful to watch Leela become more open and her parents become more affectionate.

Even if they still sought to find the appropriate balance.

Tanha gestured to the basket in Leela's arms. "Is this my yearly spa package?"

"It is. And this year there's an extra present too," Aurora said with a mischievous tone.

"I can't wait! Now, why don't you put your bag away, and we can get settled at the table. Dinner will be done soon."

Aurora's eyes followed her nose to the source of all the delicious smells coming from Tanha's top-of-the-line kitchen.

She saw a young man in an apron who had tattoos covering both of his forearms.

"Is he joining us?" Aurora asked in a whisper.

"Oh!" Tanha said with a smile and rushed to the kitchen. "This is DJ. He's in his last year of culinary school and does catering on the side with a specialty in Jewish cuisine. He is excellent, and his father is almost as good a surgeon as I am."

DJ smiled warmly and stirred a pot before putting on the lid. "The applesauce and matzo ball soup are finished. The salmon and latkes are on warm in the top oven. The sufganiots are covered on the counter. Did I forget anything, Dr. Mitra?"

"The wine?"

"I chose a pinot noir. It's breathing on the counter. Would you like me to plate?"

Tanha clasped her hands together, clearly pleased with his work. "Just excellent. No need to plate, we'll get to it. Thank you very much for everything, DJ." She went to the kitchen table to fetch a plain white envelope and handed it to him.

He looked inside, and his eyes grew larger. "I can't take this. You already paid me."

"You can and you will take it." Her tone made it clear he had no say in the matter.

"Well, thank you very much. I'll add this to the food truck fund." He folded and tucked the envelope into his back pocket. "I'll let you all get to your dinner. Have a great night."

After the door was shut behind him, Aurora turned to Tanha. "He seems nice."

"He is such a delightful young man. DJ's father was almost exactly how Leela's father and I used to be when it came to her future plans, but I was able to convince him that just because DJ doesn't go into medicine or become a scientist, doesn't mean he's a failure," she said with a pleased smile.

"Thanks, Mom," Leela said. "I like how you always have my back."

Tanha shrugged happily and went into the kitchen while Leela took their bag down the hall.

Aurora caught up to Leela outside the powder room. "When do you want to tell her?" Aurora whispered.

"Let's do it soon, but after we eat. I'm starving."

Aurora hung their coats in the guest room closet while Leela paused to view the shopping district of Portland directly outside their window. The hustle and bustle outside matched the lively tones of the showroom replica they would sleep in. When they returned to the dining room, they discovered Tanha had begun to serve the beverages. Starting with herself.

"Would you girls like some wine?"

"Beer?" Leela asked without pause and a hopeful smile.

"This isn't a cookout," Tanha answered. "Wine or no wine."

Leela stuck out her lower lip. "Yes, wine."

"Just water for me, thanks." Aurora pulled out her seat.

Fine China etched with gold and polished silverware was placed at each of their seats. They sipped their requested beverages while they watched Tanha make different trips for the appetizers and soup. Rather than a prayer or moment of silence, Tanha referenced the lights of the Menorah and led a toast to celebrate all of their Jewish friends.

Especially DJ, who created their feast.

Tanha tasted the soup. "Hmm."

"What's wrong, Mom? You have an inquisitive and annoyed face."

"I just remembered that the matzo ball soup is made with chicken," Tanha warned.

"It's okay, Mom."

"I don't mind either." Aurora draped the napkin over her lap. "Especially if it's something to celebrate other cultures." Although, there was that one time a few months ago where it wasn't a cele-bration of culture but rather a ravenous, zombie-like hunger that had taken over. Guilt gnawed at Aurora. She needed to confess now, or she'd be forever a two-face. Plus, Stacy knew, and he was a fan of blackmail. "When I was in Baltimore, I had a cheeseburg-er," Aurora blurted.

"You did not!" Leela stared at her in shock. "Really?"

"I needed it *really* bad."

"Oh," Leela drawled in understanding. "That must have been quite a craving?"

"You have no idea." Aurora sampled the soup. It was divine. And DJ seemed like the type of person who would have made sure the chicken had a good life before he turned it into a rich broth.

Tanha shook her head. "Had I known this, I would have told DJ to make brisket. I guarantee it would have been better than a cheeseburger."

She couldn't have been more wrong, but Aurora kept her rebut-tal to herself and filled her mouth with bits of matzo ball.

Leela picked a thick fried patty off a center plate. She bit into it with a crunch then her eyes rolled back. "Sweet Moses. What did he do to this falafel?"

"I actually caught him making those. He mixed cilantro in with the chickpeas."

Aurora gasped and slapped Leela's thigh under the table. She couldn't have asked for a more perfect segue.

"You don't like cilantro?" Tanha asked.

"I love it!" Aurora said. "It's just that I love chickpeas more." She made eye contact with Leela and then slid her gaze to the bright purple envelope she had set down beside the basket on the sofa table. Hopefully, Leela would catch the hint.

Leela nodded and stood from her seat.

"Something I said?" Tanha chuckled at her joke and sipped her wine.

When Leela handed her the card along with her bifocals, Tanha looked at them quizzically.

"What is this? We never exchange cards?"

"It's a special occasion," Leela said. "Go ahead, open it."

Tanha pulled the card out of the envelope and read the front.

Aurora wasn't sure how Tanha would react to the cartoon of a child congratulating an adult, but the sappy grin and hand at Tanha's heart gave her confidence she chose wisely.

"Aw. This was so sweet of you. You know, being published in the Ventricle Times was nice, but I don't know if it was card-worthy."

"Well, Mom, this card is kind of a two-fer. While we were both very happy about your latest publication, there's much more on the inside."

"Oh?" Tanha open the card, squinted, then looked over the card to both Aurora and Leela. Her gaze returned to the inside. "I don't understand. Are you…?"

"Congratulations! You're going to be a grandma," Leela said with jazz hands while Aurora clapped quietly.

A loud and surprised *ah* escaped Tanha's lips before she covered her mouth and clutched the card to her heart. "You're serious? You're having a baby?"

"We are." Aurora placed her hand low on her abdomen. "And due June fifteenth."

"I can't believe it! This is so unexpected! I'm so. . . gah!" Tanha rushed out of her seat and hugged Leela and Aurora before they had the chance to get out of their chairs. "I thought maybe someday you would want children, but I had no idea you were actually trying."

Leela straightened her necklace, which had become askew from the hug. "What can I say? Someday is now, and we didn't have to try very hard. Aurora is very fertile."

Aurora appreciated that Tanha loosened the tight hold she had on her. "I hope you don't mind we kept it a secret. There's just so much extra pressure when you tell people, so Leela and I figured we would just keep it to ourselves until it happened."

"That's such a sound and logical approach," Tanha said as she returned to her chair. "The extra stress can harm fertility, but Aurora should have no problems. You're built for this! Your hips alone, and I mean that in only the most complementary way possible. I've always thought you had an excellent figure."

She supposed that was something else Leela and Tanha had in common. "That's actually what my Mom said too."

"When did you tell your parents?" Tanha asked without a tinge of jealousy.

"My Mom guessed at Irony Day. Then we had to fess up."

"Our plan was to wait three months so we could be sure chickpea was okay," Leela said seriously.

Tanha put her hands to her heart again. "Chickpea? That's the most adorable nickname, and now I know why the falafel had you so excited." To prove her point she took a bite of the fried appetizer. "Tell me about the donor."

Aurora chewed matzo and gestured for Leela to explain. She hoped their tactic of vague nationality and ethnicity played well.

"Well, the donor was adopted, so he isn't one hundred percent certain of his ancestry, but he's fairly certain he's Indian."

"Oh, that's tremendous. Any idea what area?"

Leela shook her head. "We just know Indian."

"Hmm." Tanha swirled her wine while she pondered other questions to ask them. "What about phenotype? You know, his physical attributes."

"Just around average height, athletic build, and successful," Leela said.

"A doctor?" Tanha asked with bright eyes.

"Could be," Aurora answered to take some of the pressure off Leela. "You know how donors are on the younger side. The standardized test scores were very impressive."

Tanha smiled broadly and tipped her glass to them. "You must have searched for a long time trying to find a donor who matched Leela so well? Did you know her MCAT score was in the ninetieth percentile?"

Both of Leela's parents were so proud of her academic accomplishments, but the pressure of those accolades was the genesis of her self-esteem and depression issues.

Aurora gestured to the card again. "At our last obstetrician visit, we asked for the heart rate data. We thought you'd think it was neat."

"That's right!" Tanha looked inside the card. "I saw the picture and got so excited I forgot there was another." She had a second look. "That's odd. You said chickpea is due in June. So, you're twelve weeks pregnant, correct?"

"Just about."

Tanha shook her head. "No, that doesn't make sense. The heart rate is much too low."

"Dr. Aguilar said chickpea was on the low side, but it's nothing to worry about."

Tanha pursed her lips as she continued to look at the electrocardiogram. "It's true that there's a range, but this exceeds that. How are you feeling, Aurora?"

"I think like most women who are just about ready to go into second trimester: tired, nauseated, new food cravings. Anything else?" she asked Leela, but the terror in her eyes informed her of another symptom. "Mood swings have been a thing."

"Hmm." Tanha left the table to go in the direction of her office.

"What's she doing?" Aurora whispered.

"I don't know," Leela said as she took another appetizer.

Tanha came back out with a small black bag.

"An exam?" Aurora shouted in disbelief. "Why?"

Tanha calmly walked over to them and set the bag on the table beside the menorah. "I need to make sure the mother of my grandchild is well, especially when chickpea may have bradycardia."

"Oh, my Gods, she's right!" Leela said with a mouthful of falafel, and immediately both her mother and Aurora looked at her flabbergasted.

"Are you. . . agreeing with me?" Tanha asked, still stunned.

Leela nodded vigorously. "Absolutely! If your radar is going off that something's wrong, we should probably check. Right?"

Tanha wanted to do an exam. Leela *needed* her mom to do the exam. But she really wanted to get back to eating, which wouldn't happen until she relented. Aurora's hands fell at her sides. "Fine. If it'll make you feel better."

"Thank you," Tanha said. "All I want to do is check your vitals."

"Is there anything in particular you're worried about?" Aurora asked while Tanha secured the blood pressure cuff around her upper arm.

"Mostly hypertension, possibly gestational diabetes, but I don't have tests for that here. Do you remember what you blood pressure was at your check-up?" Tanha asked as she secured the earpieces of her stethoscope.

Aurora shrugged. "I don't remember."

"Her BP was 115 over 75, but I don't think they checked for glucose," Leela said immediately and walked away from the table in a huff. "I knew Dr. Aguilar wasn't checking all the boxes!"

Aurora had seen Leela protective, but this was a new level. "I'm sure she did. And let's take it down a notch."

Tanha whispered to her, "Someone's 'daddy hormones' are high." She used the pump to tighten the cuff and then studied the numbers of the blood rushing inside her veins.

Aurora watched Tanha's face go through different expressions as she listened and kept an eye on her Rolex. "Am I good?"

"Yes. Please unbutton your shirt."

Aurora undid the first few. It was better to get it over with. She retracted a bit as the cold metal touched her skin above her camisole.

When Tanha finished and looped the stethoscope around her neck, she reached into the bag and took out a pen.

"You're going to record— Ah!" A retina-frying light beam went into Aurora's eyes.

Tanha clicked off the pen light. "Everything seems fairly normal. It's just that…" Tanha left Aurora's side and went to the congratulations card. With her hands on her hips, she looked at chickpea's sonogram image and shook her head.

Then, she left the room and headed toward her study.

Leela rejoined Aurora at the table. "I just know she's getting a book."

"She could be getting a sweater. Or your baby album for comparison?"

"You're funny," Leela said and kissed her cheek. "We'll take care of you and chickpea, don't you worry."

Daddy hormones, indeed! The evening had taken an unexpected turn, but it was easier to go with the flow for now. She'd have to have a private conversation with Leela later.

They both listened to the sounds of rustling, various thuds and *smacks* on the floor from the other room as they sipped their drinks.

"Where is it?" Tanha asked loud enough for them to hear in the dining area.

"I'm starting to think she's not getting a sweater." Aurora picked up the half-eaten falafel from Leela's plate and sampled a bite. "That is really good."

Leela nodded and then poured herself another glass of wine. She leaned back into her chair, crossed one arm over her chest, and looked at Aurora thoughtfully. "You really ate a cheeseburger?"

"Here we go!" Tanha stepped out of the study carrying a paper journal and smiling broadly. "I *knew* I brought this home from the office. This edition was one of my favorites and I didn't want any of my colleagues getting their sticky fingers on it."

Aurora caught the subtitle, *Special Edition: Endurance Athletes*. As a former high school track and field star, and current cyclist, the unique physical characteristics of long-distance athletes was something that piqued her interest.

Leela quirked a brow. "You think chickpea's running a marathon in there?"

"That's ridiculous. It's far too aqueous in there to run," Tanha answered while her gaze rapidly scanned the table of contents. "Do you know anything about the donor's health history?"

"Um."

"Hmm." Leela was just as perplexed. "We just know he is in good enough health to donate."

"That makes sense, and I'm assuming a history of arrythmia wouldn't be an attractive feature of a donor. Still," she flipped through the pages, "I'm sure I read something which included fetal and pediatric data of athletes. Most subjects were from the summer games, but still, it was an impressive data set."

"I think it's great chickpea has an efficient little ticker. That'll probably mean chickpea'll be calmer and cry less."

Tanha and Aurora shared a confused look with each other and then directed it to Leela.

"What? I'm trying to be optimistic here."

"Yes!" Aurora blurted. "Now that we know I'm healthy and chickpea's doing great, can we celebrate chickpea over dinner like most families?"

Tanha's eyes softened, and she closed the journal. "You're right, I'm sorry. Old habits, you know?"

"We know." Aurora patted Leela's thigh under the table. She knew Tanha meant well, and her natural curiosity took over sometimes. But mostly, she was relieved Leela had returned to her less-stressed self.

Tanha pushed the journal to the side and placed the napkin back on her lap. "Does your father know?" she asked while she broke off a piece of matzo.

"Are you kidding? Dad will have even more questions than you."

"You're right about that." She gestured with her spoon toward Aurora. "You didn't take hormones, did you?"

"No. That was not necessary in our case."

"Good. Sid would be all over that, especially now that he's found his way into the double oocyte fertilization research." Tanha chuckled to herself. "I recommend you tell him after you have as many questions answered as possible."

Aurora's brow knit together. "What do you mean by that?"

"Well, just off the top of my head: gender, names, your jobs, childcare, private versus public school—"

"School," Aurora said with a laugh and looked over to Leela to see that she wasn't sharing her joy. "Oh, she's serious."

"I'm very serious," Tanha confirmed. "He'll want to know so he can start writing letters of recommendation. But I have to say, I'm curious too about what you plan on doing with your jobs. After Leela's accident, I did a lot of reflecting on how Sid and I raised her, and I have to say that I regret not being at home more when she was a child."

"Leela and I haven't really discussed the whole childcare thing yet."

"But it's on the whiteboard!" Leela said proudly.

Tanha's silence was enough to communicate her feelings regarding their lack of conversation.

"Well," Leela rolled her eyes to the ceiling, "it's not like we haven't discussed work stuff. I laid the groundwork for my employees and they'll all get the big announcement next week. Aurora's going to tell her boss next week. I think how flexible they are will dictate how we move forward with leave and childcare."

"I don't know if I like that plan anymore. Why should we let other people decide how we raise our child? In your case, you can set the rules and the schedules. And in my case, I think I've proven that I'm valuable enough to the company to set my own terms."

"Good for you! You just have to figure out what those terms are," Tanha said with a sage smile.

CHAPTER ELEVEN

OVERALL, SHE AND Aurora had a pleasant visit with her mother—although Aurora reminded her again that she was perfectly capable of speaking for herself—but Leela still couldn't believe her mom had bullied them into starting a baby registry. She didn't know so many baby products existed! It was simply ridiculous that a child could have five different versions of a bathtub.

And now that her mother knew, it was time to tell the world. Except her father. She didn't have enough questions answered for that conversation yet.

The door to her office opened, and Keith came in along with a cloud of snow flurries. "People are already driving like idiots out there." Keith dragged his boots across the mat and took off his gloves. "We're only supposed to get two inches."

"And then another four to six tonight. People need their bread and their milk."

"They need chains on their tires and some common freakin' sense."

She wasn't going to disagree with his opinion. In fact, it made her reflect on Aurora and chickpea's safety. Aurora's company car lacked chains and four-wheel drive. That wasn't acceptable. They would need to have a serious conversation regarding family transportation.

Argh! She was doing it again. Aurora just told her to ease back on the protectiveness, but she couldn't escape the need. The new urge wasn't even a thought, it was a primal drive.

Therefore, transportation was going on the whiteboard.

But, for now, the moment was all business. "Keith, have a seat. We need to have a talk," she said in a dropped tone.

Keith stifled a laugh. "Okay. What's up?"

The door swung open again. This time, Jill came in along with the snow.

Jill looked at Keith and then to Leela. "What's going on?"

"I don't really know," Keith said. "But right now, I'm feeling like I got called to the principal's office."

Jill hitched her thumb in the direction of the door. "Maybe I should leave?"

"No," Leela said with a sigh. "You can stay. I was planning on telling you both today anyway—albeit in different ways. Jill, you should sit down too."

"Okay." Jill slid the stool hesitantly over that currently functioned as a snowwoman display. She relocated the holiday decoration to the edge of Leela's desk. "What's going on?"

The role-playing with Aurora had not prepared her for this. Jill was like the fun, wise aunt she'd never had. She'd have questions and want to hug. Keith was. . . Well, Keith. He'd smile, accept responsibility, and then go about his day. Now, she'd just have to roll with both of them being there. "I've been lying to you two just a *tiny* bit lately."

Jill gasped. "We're not moving forward with the lilac scent."

"Oh man," Keith said. "The girl I've been seeing, Cassie, really liked that."

"Oh," Jill drawled. "Looking out for her lilac, are you? What about the Love Swirl?"

Leela rolled her eyes while Jill playfully nudged Keith. "We're moving forward with lilac. People like lilac, including Cassie, apparently. Love Swirl is still a work in progress, but I don't want to talk to you about products right now." Both of their eyebrows rose in surprise. "I've been lying about the fertility appointments with Aurora. We're not trying to have a baby because we're already pregnant."

Keith's mouth dropped open, but he still wore a huge smile to go with his beard scruff.

Jill screamed and rushed to the other side of Leela's desk to hug her. "This is incredible news! When's Aurora due?"

"June."

"Who's the father?"

"Athletic, smart, Indian-type person."

Once Jill returned to her stool, Leela continued her planned speech. "Aurora and I are very excited, and I will be an equal partner in raising our little chickpea. Keith, you've taken on responsibility like a champ, and you're going to get more of it."

He shifted in his seat. "Does this mean I have to wear a tie?"

"If you have to go to the bank or meet with a larger client you should wear a suit, which includes a tie."

"I don't have a suit."

"I'll buy you one." It seemed like a fair compromise, since she couldn't possibly offer him another raise.

"What about me?" Jill asked.

"To be honest, I haven't gotten that far in my planning. The first step was to make sure he was on board."

Keith had suddenly found the laces of his boots captivating.

"You are on board, right?"

"I don't want to wear a suit."

Luckily, Jill slapped his arm so she didn't have to. "Suck it up. It's not like she said you have to shave off your beard."

He grabbed his chin protectively.

"Calm down, you can keep your beard. As far as I'm concerned, most of what's happening right now can stay the same, but after June, I'm not going to be around as much. I'm thinking of a twenty-hour week schedule for the first four months."

"And what about after that?" Jill asked.

Leela sucked her upper lip and let it go with a *pop*. "We haven't really thought that far ahead yet. We're hoping there's room at the childcare place near where Aurora works."

Jill's face contorted into a grotesque version of itself. "Seriously? That place is terrible!"

"But it looks so cheerful!" Leela said. "And they have that awesome playground."

"Yet I've never seen a child play in it," Jill said ominously.

"That is creepy," Keith added. "Those empty swings give me horror movie vibes. Do you have any other ideas of what you and Aurora might do?"

Leela had absolutely no other ideas. "Well, we also need to wait and hear what Aurora's boss will say. Who knows? Maybe they'll offer some 'Bring Your Baby to Work' plan."

Jill and Keith shared a skeptical look.

"Why not bring your baby here?" Keith asked. "You could wear one of those front backpacks."

She held thought about that, but the images she conjured chilled her. An accidental goat kick. Slipping on lotion. Tripping over a box in the packing area. Chickpea's curious hands reaching into the lye at the soap making station. "No. It's too dangerous."

"Okay. You could take full maternity leave then," Jill suggested. "Keith can manage this place."

"Hold on right there! No, I can't."

"Yes, you can," Jill said, disgusted. "And why are you surprised? You knew this would be coming."

"I don't know. I guess it didn't seem real yet. Plus—and pardon me on this—Leela's more like the dad and they don't take leave a lot of the time."

Leela stared at him.

"Allow me." Jill smacked him in the arm. Not enough to hurt, but just enough so he knew how wrong he was. "Leela, what doesn't he know that would prevent him from running this place completely?"

"Off the top of my head: payroll, keeping track of business expenses for taxes—"

"Taxes?" Keith exclaimed. "I can barely do my own taxes."

"You wouldn't have to do the taxes, just keep track of receipts from the vet, the farmers' market, visits to interested stores. . . It's not that bad. You can do this, and, more importantly, I need you to do this."

His shoulders were more relaxed, but he was still seated as though he were sitting on a tack.

"And remember my house is literally right there and I'm very invested in the success of this place. I might have an infant strapped to me, but I will help you in the office. I won't go into the other buildings though. I can't risk chickpea getting a chemical burn."

Jill contorted her face in horror and confusion.

But he finally returned to his natural posture. "Okay, that doesn't sound too bad."

"Great! We're a team and we can make this work!" Leela beamed and made a mental note to cross this item off the whiteboard.

"When's Aurora telling her work people the big news?" Keith asked.

"Today."

#

Aurora started her day as usual. While her computer booted up, she put her lunch away, made herself a cup of decaf tea, and chatted with a few coworkers about their weekends. Then, she wrote the email to Tonya. Subject line: *personal news to share*. She fig-ured by the time Tonya got to it she'd have time to confirm her cli-ent visits for the week. If the Mom-and-Pop convenience store re-ally did invest in a charging station for electric cars she might weep from joy.

"Boo!"

Aurora did a startled dance and turned to see Tonya amused with herself. "I just sent you an email."

"I know." Tonya smiled and held out her wrist to display her smart watch, which showed the notification. "You have personal news, huh? Could it be what I think it is?"

Aurora scanned her immediate area. It was like she was sur-rounded by ears, which meant she wouldn't be able to stop the conversation once the news was out. Then nothing would get done in the day. "Can we go to your office?"

Tonya cocked her head in that direction and started walking. Aurora grabbed her tea and followed until they were inside. Aurora closed the door.

Instead of Tonya's casual lean behind her desk, she opted to sit in the other visitor chair beside Aurora. "Something tells me that this isn't so you can go backpacking in Europe."

"No. Not backpacking." Aurora took a deep breath. "I'm preg-nant and due in June."

"Congratulations!" she said with a move that was both a dance in her chair and a shake. Tonya's excitement mellowed after a few seconds. "I'd hug you, but HR hates that."

"How about a high five hand clasp?"

"Yes!"

The hand clasp that followed the high five lasted longer than Aurora had anticipated. "I'm happy you're happy for me—us—happy for us."

"I am! And all of those ginger candies you were eating make sense, because they were god awful." Tonya cocked her head to the side. "Wait. So, if you're due in June, you must have just started your second trimester. That means you were never 'trying', you were already pregnant."

"You caught me. But I'm sure you can understand why Leela and I wanted to wait."

"I do, but damn, we have to figure out a plan ASAP." She tapped a pen on her desk. "Hopefully, you've thought about some kind of maternity leave transition."

"You're right." Aurora had thought long and hard about this. She didn't want to present her boss the news without also having a solution to her leave. "I thought that perhaps we could bring in an outside consultant."

Tonya barked a quick laugh. "Sorry, but that's an extremely remote possibility. The only way that would happen is if we were on the verge of landing a huge client and we couldn't wait for you to return. Try again."

"Okay. Well, since we're expanding the East Coast, I thought maybe you could bring someone in for me on a temporary hire, and then if they work out, offer them a full-time position out there. We can release the announcement and interview during the next few months, and then I still have time to train them."

"Now, that's a good idea! But damn, do I have a lot to discuss with HR. Leela's lucky she's her own HR. Is she taking maternity leave?"

"Yes, but to what degree depends on the arrangements she can make with Keith and the rest of the staff."

"You decided to spill the beans on the same day, huh? That makes sense. Just do me a favor and don't incorporate that childcare place in our business park. Those walls have seen everything from porn video rental to a vape store. Who knows what has seeped into the drywall."

#

Everything is fine. Aurora is not in a snow-filled ditch. She'll be home soon.

Aurora had texted her almost an hour ago with the message she left work. She should have been home half an hour ago.

Leela tried to push the paranoia out of her mind by focusing on dinner, but rigorously stirring sautéed mushrooms into her pot of quinoa didn't help.

When headlights finally arched through the kitchen, Leela dropped her wooden spoon.

Putting chains on that hybrid was now priority number one.

She exhaled a large breath, moved the pot off the burner, and used the balled hand towel on the counter to quickly clean her hands.

"It smells amazing in here," Aurora said as she walked in and unzipped her parka.

There Aurora stood with a smile and snowflakes sprinkled in her hair. The greatest gift she had ever received. Leela had to hug her immediately. "You didn't answer your phone."

"I'm sorry, I got caught behind the train, and I was on the phone giving Stacy the news, which was *not* a short conversation. Fortunately, he couldn't have been happier. Unfortunately, I had to answer the same questions everyone else has asked us."

It was like Aurora didn't even know there was a blizzard outside. "I was really starting to worry. There's a squall out there."

Aurora chortled. "I grew up in northern Michigan. Learning how to do everything in the snow is pretty much a requirement."

Leela kissed her and cradled Aurora's face in her hands. "But those other people out there can't claim that! They don't know what the fuck they're doing."

Aurora brought Leela's hands to her heart and smiled patiently. "We discussed the excessive worrying. I'm fine."

Leela dropped her gaze to Aurora's waistline.

"Chickpea's fine too."

There was a force inside of Leela that had to embrace Aurora again. "I'm sorry I got a little crazy. It's just talking to Jill and Keith today and the snow. . . It's really in my head now about how—"

Aurora firmly pressed her lips against hers, but Leela broke the contact, which left Aurora looking puzzled. "You like it when I do that," Aurora said disappointed.

"I do, but this is important."

"Let's take a breath, maybe sit down, and you can explain what's got you so befuddled. Does that sound fair?"

Leela nodded, watched Aurora take off her coat, and joined her on the couch. "First thing, you need an appropriate winter car with chains or air bags all over the fucking place to ensure both yours and chickpea's safety. Second thing, this house is nothing but sharp corners. It's kind of amazing neither of us has been maimed. Third thing, given how much sex there is in the world, there is a surprisingly small number of resources about how to be a support-ive post-pregnancy partner. Fourth thing, we need another place to send chickpea after our maternity leaves are over. We absolutely cannot send chickpea to the childcare center in your business park. From what I read online it's riddled with splooge and toxic fumes. What do you think?"

Aurora didn't respond immediately, which was a trait Leela appreciated. She took the information and then created a thoughtful response. "We need to talk."

"Yes!" Thank the gods Aurora understood. "Where do you want to start? The car, the house, the resources, or the toxic child-care?"

"Um, I'm mostly I'm worried about you."

Leela chuckled. "Of all the things to be worried about, you're worried about me?"

"Yes. The items you've listed are all reasonable action items. However, the intensity with which you're concerned. . . I don't think it's good for you." Aurora took her hands and held them in her lap. "Have you told your therapist about this?"

"He says it's normal for partners to be protective of their partners and chickpeas."

"Yes, I've read that too. It's just. . . I don't want you so fixated on what bad could happen when there's so much good. Instead of seeing snow as an instrument of vehicular destruction, think of when we'll teach chickpea how to make her first snow angel. And as far as the house, we have *months* after chickpea is born to childproof, so in the meantime, let's enjoy a fire roaring in the woodstove and not think about the protective gate we'll have to put up around it."

Leela hid her face in her hand. "I'm sorry. You're right, you're right. This is a joyous time and while it's good to prepare, I shouldn't go overboard or let my paranoia run wild."

"Exactly. I know nobody will look after chickpea as well as you, but let's watch the helicopter parenting."

Leave it to Aurora to bring her back to reality. "I think I needed that talk. Thank you."

"You're welcome." Aurora leaned forward and brought their lips together. "Don't forget you're the best."

Leela grinned bashfully. "Takes one to know one."

Aurora kissed her again, but this time Leela allowed herself to linger and enjoy it.

The light touch of Aurora's lips disappeared and was replaced by a skilled tongue licking the crest of her ear. This was the second time Aurora put the moves on her in three days. The libido stage of the pregnancy had officially begun. "You were horny when you came home, weren't you?"

"Don't blame me. Blame the bumpy road."

"I need to point out that if we have sex, dinner will get cold."

Aurora revealed a sexy smirk. "That's why we have a micro-wave."

Rather than head to the bedroom, Aurora covered her body and went straight for the drawstring of Leela's lounge pants. She untied the knotted bow with record speed. Cool air rushed at her legs as her comfy pants were slid down. Once they were thrown to the floor like an offensive article of clothing, Aurora reached for the zipper at the side of her skirt.

"Oh, can you leave that on?" Leela asked. "It's really hot."

Aurora removed her black tights instead. In the middle of the cotton that fell to the ground was a splash of purple bikini briefs. Leela's arousal increased ten-fold when she realized Aurora strad-dled her commando.

"Is leaving my sweater on part of your fantasy too?"

"Is it wrong if I say *mostly* on?"

Aurora grinned and unbuttoned her sweater just enough to ex-pose the cleavage coming out of her camisole. "Any other re-quests?"

It amazed her that Aurora could still turn her on in an instant. From neurotic mess to a complete sex fiend in seconds. "No." Leela slipped her hand underneath her skirt and stroked her once to see how ready Aurora was. She was damn ready. "I have every-thing I need. Now, what do you need?"

"Something I was thinking about the last ten minutes of my car ride. I need you to relax and let me take control."

Power bottom time was some of Leela's favorite time.

"Okay," Leela said, "tell me what to do."

Aurora guided two of Leela's fingers inside of herself. "Just watch me."

She loved it when Aurora said exactly what she wanted. Grant-ed, she also liked it when there was trial and error, but it was extra titillating hearing the words come out of her mouth. "Yes, ma'am."

Leela watched Aurora's eye close and listened to her breath hitch as she felt her inside and out. It was so familiar but also never the same. Always full of surprises but never questioned how much love she felt when they were together.

Aurora gently rocked herself on Leela's fingers. "What do you see?"

Leela stripped her gaze away from Aurora's cleavage. "A strikingly gorgeous woman pleasuring herself. Who also has awesome tits."

Aurora laughed, not changing her rhythm. "I love how honest you are."

Leela smiled. How could she not? "Would you like a little more participation from me? Or are you good?"

"Maybe a smidge more."

When Leela moved to a more seated position, she had the angle to give Aurora just that little bit extra. And Aurora had the angle to dip her head and kiss Leela like she needed to consume her soul.

Leela kept her new pace even as Aurora no longer held eye contact and pumped her hips faster. Based on the look and how Aurora felt, Leela could practically keep a countdown for how long it would take her to orgasm.

But then, there it was.

Leela held Aurora tight as she shuddered and moaned. There was no greater feeling or sound on earth. It was so pure and something Leela knew only she got to experience.

Aurora collapsed on top of her. "I love you so much," Aurora mumbled into her ear.

"I love you back. And just think, I made dinner too."

Once Aurora stopped giggling, she looked up and placed a tender kiss along Leela's jaw. "Not that we have to dive into that right this— Hey!" Aurora looked down their bodies.

The surprised and confused look on Aurora's face did not give Leela comfort. "What's wrong?"

"I think I feel chickpea." Aurora sat back.

"Something's wrong with chickpea?" Leela bolted upright. "Did I go too hard? I was really trying to be mindful of that."

Aurora's hands went to her belly and she scrunched her brow. "I don't think so, but something is definitely happening."

"Is it gas?"

"No, it's not gas! It's like. . . popcorn. Little, tiny bursts of energy from inside." The bright smile Aurora flashed at her was one of the happiest expressions she had ever seen. She took Leela's hand and placed it low on her abdomen. "Can you feel it?"

Leela focused on the sensation under her palm, but all she felt was the rough texture of Aurora's skirt. Leela hadn't been envious of the nausea, the mood swings, or changing taste buds, but she wanted more than anything to experience this moment with Aurora. "So, popcorn and not butterflies?"

"Yeah. Little bursts as opposed to a tickle."

Leela continued to keep her hand where it was, hoping she could feel the tiniest movement. "Do you think we woke chickpea up with our, you know, sex?"

"I don't know. I'll have to look that one up, but it wouldn't surprise me. I would probably get all squirmy too if I was in a water balloon and someone started squeezing me."

She was about to agree when the most minute force pressed into Leela's hand. "Wait a second." Leela tucked her hand under the waistband of Aurora's skirt and stayed motionless. Their gazes locked as Leela concentrated. After a few breaths, Leela felt a ripple. It was akin to the most distant ripple from throwing a pebble in a lake, but it was still a ripple. She jumped as she pulled her hand back. "Holy shit!"

"I know," Aurora said with a laugh. "Isn't it amazing?"

Leela moved her hand and reached for their clothes on the floor. "I can't believe chickpea is big enough now for me feel movement."

"According to our fruit chart, chickpea is lemon-sized now." Aurora looked at the tights in her hands, shook her head, and headed to the bedroom.

Leela pictured their citrus-sized baby stretching and followed Aurora still, grabbing her phone off the coffee table along the way.

As Aurora sifted through her bureau drawers to find her evening comfy clothes, Leela needed confirmation that what just happened was possible.

She sat on their bed and conducted her search. She quickly learned that not only was it possible, but enough pride swelled through Leela to the point where she needed to do a small dance in her underwear.

"Why do you look so pleased with yourself?" Aurora asked in her favorite college sweatshirt and pajama bottoms.

"Because I'm such a stud!" Aurora joined her on the bed and she passed the phone to her. "My favorite part is when it says intense orgasms cause the uterus to contract. I made that happen! I made it intense."

"Yeah, that was all you. Had nothing to do with me." As Aurora read further, she bit her lip and cocked her head. "It also says that partners usually can't feel anything until around twenty weeks. I'm over a month away from that."

Leela's pride drained and was replaced with worry. It was only two weeks ago when Aurora bled and they had their emergency visit to Dr. Aguilar. "You and chickpea are on bed rest."

"What?" Aurora asked in a much higher tone. "You can't be serious."

"I'm totally serious. You should lie down until we learn this is okay."

"I feel fine! Also, we *just* talked about this!"

Leela sent Aurora her most intense puppy dog eyes. She was defenseless against the tactic.

"I will sit down like a reasonable person and wait to hear what our doctor says. Your puppy dog eyes don't work all the time. I've built some immunity."

"Since when?"

"After year two, the effect started to dwindle."

Leela gritted her teeth. So much for her secret weapon. "I'm still calling." She opened her phone directory and called Dr. Aguilar's personal phone. She wouldn't normally do such a thing outside of business hours, but the invitation had been extended.

The phone rang. And rang some more before she was informed that her mailbox was full. "Dammit! No one is picking up and I can't leave a voicemail."

"Well, if you're really worried, there are other doctors you can call."

"Like who?"

Aurora arched her brow. "You're kidding, right?"

It took a moment for the connection to register. "No! I'm not calling Mom. She's already obsessed with the heart rate thing. She keeps sending me scholarly articles."

"I was actually thinking about the other parent. The one who does fertility research and doesn't know about chickpea."

"Ah, shit. That one."

#

Aurora filled their dinner bowls while Leela psyched herself up for calling her father. She really didn't understand what the big deal was. Yes, Sid approached life much like a robot, but because of that he was always honest and never intentionally hurtful. That had to count for something.

"I can't believe I'm about to do this." Leela stared at her phone one last time before dialing her father. "He's probably in a meeting anyway. Or at the driving ra— Hi, Dad! You know me, I'm choc full of surprises. I'm going to put you on speaker so Aurora can say hi."

"Hello, Aurora," he said in an enthusiastic tone that crackled over the speaker. "How are you? Did you like your holiday present?"

"I'm great and the slippers are very cozy, thank you." She could picture him smiling proudly on the other end of the phone. It was the same smile as Leela's.

"Oh, good. I thought the way the feet came together to make the face of a moose was very charming and comical."

He really was a misunderstood, sweet man. "Yes, they are very funny moose feet."

Leela nudged her and whispered, "What did we get him?"

Aurora rolled her eyes and kept her voice down. "A round of golf at that place Stacy recommended."

"How'd you like your present, Dad? I hope the water hazards weren't too treacherous."

"I have not been able to play yet, but it is only because I want the weather to be perfect when I go."

"I understand," Leela said. And then said nothing.

Aurora pointed to the phone and whispered, "Now's when you tell him."

"So, Dad, we called to thank you for your presents, but also to share some news with you. Aurora's pregnant."

"Yes! That is fantastic. Tanha told me the news! It is very exciting, but I do not think you should worry about chickpea's heart rate issue. Your mother has a tendency to overreact."

Aurora and Leela stared at each other with their mouths agape.

"I can't believe Mom told you! We were supposed to do that. And I can't believe you talked to Mom!"

"Yes, we talk every now and again when we need professional advice. In this case, the topic of your relationship came up organically. She said you used a donor who was practically identical to Leela and you are due in June."

"I can't believe you know," Leela said. "And I can't believe that you knew and started the conversation with moose slippers!"

Aurora motioned for Leela to calm down. "We're glad Tanha told you, but I'm sorry if it hurt your feelings she found out first."

"No, of course not! I am just happy to be included."

Aurora placed her hand over her heart at his bittersweet words. He was a perfect example of someone who had turned over a new leaf and had made attempts to reconnect with his family. "I'm glad to hear that, Sid, but to make up for learning about it secondhand, we have an update to share with you." Leela gave her the go-ahead nod. "I felt chickpea move for the first time just a few minutes ago."

"Hmm," he uttered then paused. "Are you sure it wasn't gas?"

What was it with Leela's family and gas? "No, Sid, it was chickpea. I'm positive."

"That is wonderful! Much earlier than most women, but wonderful all the same. I am curious, were you doing anything that provoked the response?"

Leela shook her head emphatically.

"I was. . . exercising," Aurora said.

"Interesting," he said. "That must have been quite the workout."

Leela gave herself a pat on the back.

"It was okay. I've had harder workouts," Aurora said while she smiled sweetly at Leela.

"So, Dad," Leela jumped in while Aurora challenged herself to keep her laughter silent. "We have a question for you. None of the articles we've found have said it's possible for a partner or someone else to feel the baby move at this stage."

"That is correct."

"But what if someone could?" Aurora asked.

"That is impossible."

"Dad, I want you to go to that hypothetical, theoretical place you like to live. What would cause someone who isn't the biological mother to feel a baby move at the beginning of the second trimester?"

A long pause on the other end of the phone created even more uncertainly.

Aurora leaned down to the phone as if that would help him hear her better. "Sid?"

"I am thinking. That is a very interesting question. At that stage, the limbs are too small to push against the tissue in a meaningful way, but I suppose if the fetus moved quickly it could cause the amniotic fluid to move. To cause waves. But I feel that I need to stress how unlikely that is. A fetus of chickpea's age would only have limbs that are a centimeter long. For something so small to do something so powerful is not only unlikely, it is highly illogical." A muffled noise carried over his words. "I am sorry to tell you that I have to get off the phone now. My plane is ready to board."

"Well, thanks for you input, Dad. It was very helpful."

"You are so welcome. Love to you both and to chickpea. Goodbye."

They looked at each other when the phone went dead.

"Chickpea is illogical," Leela said.

"But also powerful."

CHAPTER TWELVE

IT WAS TIME for Leela to say goodbye to a friend she hardly got to know.

She placed her button maker into the cardboard box it was shipped in and folded the flaps down to secure its closure.

"You couldn't have made all of those buttons already," Jill said. "You bought a kit of one thousand."

"No, I didn't make them all." Leela rested her arms on top of the box and regarded Jill seriously. "I've pulled myself out of the running for president."

"What? Why?"

"I had to decide what my priorities are, and while I do think I could incorporate changes that would be easily implemented and benefit everyone, I don't have the time or the patience to convince people. Any extra time I have has to go to prepping for chickpea. Aurora's showing now, so every time I see that little bump it's a reminder."

Jill nodded politely and turned to leave, but she paused. Her gaze went to what Leela had been browsing on her computer. "Motion light security?"

"Yeah! Do you know a good system? My problem right now is that I can't find one that detects motion from as far away as I'd like."

"Why do you need that, exactly?"

Asking why she needed motion lights was akin to asking her why she needed locks on her doors or chartreuse poison stickers on the cleaning products. "Because we need something that will detect coyotes and mountain lions out here!"

"Isn't that what the gun's for?"

Jill made a good point, but the rifle in question was kept in the upright safe behind her desk. That would only be useful in a situation where she was in the office, not if she were in the house.

She definitely needed another gun.

But weapons still wouldn't protect chickpea from all incidents. "Hypothetically speaking, say a mountain lion is drawn in by the goats in the early evening, which is the same time I have to take chickpea to karate practice. Little do I know, there is a legit lion skulking about in the shadows." Leela inhaled deeply as fear began to overwhelm her. "And chickpea doesn't see it because there is no motion light. That is unacceptable!"

"That's one word for it," Jill mumbled as she looked over her shoulder. "How are you feeling?"

Leela moved her button box to the bottom of the closet. "What do you mean?"

Jill grimaced slightly. "You seem stressed. Like even more than usual. Would you like to get a drink in town and talk about it? I'll drive."

It had been ages since she and Jill hung out as friends, and while she could talk to Aurora about almost everything, she couldn't talk to Aurora about Aurora. "That sounds nice, actually. Do you mind if we make some stops while we're in town?"

"Not at all."

"Cool. Let me just tell Keith where I'm going, and I'll meet you in your car."

Leela took her winter vest off the back of her chair and headed out to the mixing and packing building. As soon as she walked in the door, an overwhelming citrus aroma struck her nostrils. "What the hell happened in here?"

Keith turned, clipboard in hand. "Oil jar broke. Got the windows open and I'm writing the incident report about it now."

The incident report idea was Keith's. One which she didn't feel was entirely necessary at the beginning, but once he explained the tracking system, she was all for it. "I'm going into town with Jill for a bit. You're in charge."

The small smile she received was enough of an indication that he was fine with it.

Leela walked across the icy gravel, her footsteps crunching along the way to Jill's car. She sank into the cushy seats, but there was a gnawing at the back of her mind that prevented her from relaxing.

It was incredibly rare that she wasn't home when Aurora arrived from the end of her workday. Sure, sometimes Leela had a meeting or appointment around that time, but Aurora always knew about it. She could plan accordingly. This unexpected change in schedule would add stress to Aurora, which in turn would aggravate chickpea. "I'm sorry, but I can't do this."

Jill's hand paused on the gear shift. "Why not?"

"Aurora doesn't know I'm doing this. She's coming home and expecting cauliflower crust pizza, and now I'm going to have to bring home take out."

"She's still getting food."

The situation really wasn't that difficult to understand. "But it's not food that's on our menu."

"So, you think Aurora will be upset you didn't make dinner and instead brought home dinner because it wasn't written down that way?"

Finally, Jill understood. "Yes!"

"Leela, do you hear yourself right now? Only someone completely unreasonable would get mad about that, and Aurora's a pretty rational person."

"But she likes that the crust has less carbs. Then, she can eat a cookie."

Jill sighed. "You know what? I know how to get to the bottom of this." Jill pressed the address book on her touchscreen and scrolled until she reached Aurora's name.

"What are you doing?" Leela asked.

Jill smiled mischievously.

After the first ring, Aurora answered. "Jill? Is everything okay?"

"Everything's fine. I'm kidnapping Leela for happy hour. She'll be bringing home dinner instead of making a sorry excuse for a pizza. Is all of this okay with you?"

"That sounds fun! Have a good time. Anything else going on?"

"Nope. Goodbye." Jill disconnected the call and turned to Leela. "Do you feel better now?"

"Knowing that Aurora's fine with it helps a great deal, yes." Leela swallowed a lump that consisted of her pride. "Is this what you meant when you said I seemed stressed?"

Jill shot her a sideways glance. "Um, yeah." Then she started down the long gravel driveway, swerving around a few snowy patches that remained. She flinched and did a doubletake in her rearview mirror. "There's a huge bird back there. Did you see that?"

Leela shook her head as she looked at her snow-covered farm. She didn't see anything but Aurora and chickpea. "I don't know what's come over me lately. Aurora keeps telling me not to be so worried all the time, but I can't help it."

"In your defense, you do have some major life changes coming. The most important thing is to be supportive and plan to a *rea-*

sonable degree. You're letting your imagination get the best of you when it comes to the latter."

"But that's what good planning is. I have to be prepared for anything." Nothing or no one would harm a single hair on her family's head. She couldn't expect Aurora to be in her third trimester and lift the heavy boxes that were sometimes accidentally delivered to the house or scare away mountain lions. Those were her jobs. "I'm terrified beyond belief that something could happen to them, so I'm just doing what I have to do to keep them safe. There's like this new voice in my head that whispers, '*Protect them.*'"

"I see. Have you shared this with your therapist?"

Leela didn't possibly see how she would have time for that. In the last few weeks alone she had started test driving new cars with Aurora, researched and bought every baby proofing supply on the market, looked at a boat-load of midwife resumes, applied for five different childcare locations, and was now in the process of determining the best motion sensor system. "I may have skipped my last session."

"Hmm. What would you say to Aurora if she ignored her health like that?"

Leela scoffed at the question. "This is different."

"No, it's not! You have to take care of you. If you fall to pieces physically or mentally, then that will put a real damper on trying to protect your family, won't it?"

Shit. Leela buried her face in her hands; not from shame, but from pure confusion. The voice in her head was so strong. She couldn't just ignore it, and while she wasn't one to self-diagnosis, it wasn't a symptom she had ever had before. Leela owned her history of depression and neurotic tendencies, but this was completely new and different. "What I'm thinking doesn't feel wrong." When Jill didn't respond, she added, "Okay, how about this? I'll call now to reschedule the appointment I missed last week, and then once we're at the bar, I give you permission to pry into all the little things I've been hiding away."

"You have yourself a deal."

After spending five minutes on hold and another five explaining her situation, Leela tucked her phone away. They hadn't reached the outskirts of town yet, but they were close enough for Leela to see it in the distance. All Leela had to do was follow the river, and she could see the downtown area cozied against it.

This would be a great place to raise chickpea.

There were mountains, rivers, and lakes to explore. Shops, theaters, and museums for cultural exposure. And, she supposed, being only a few hours drive away from her mother was an advantage. While she and Aurora hadn't discussed the topic, she knew Aurora wished her family was closer.

"Drifting off to la-la land already?" Jill asked.

"A little bit." Leela shifted in her seat to look at Jill head on. "How did Viktor feel raising your girls so far away from his family?"

Jill took a moment before answering. "I guess the short answer is that he thought it would be easier. That we'd go over to Russia every five years or so and his family would come here once in a while. But that didn't happen." Jill took the turn for downtown. "Are you worried about Aurora?"

"Is it that obvious?"

"Only because you seem to be worrying about everything else. Look, times are so much different now. There're video chats for crying out loud. My girls had photographs and letters, which was nice, but it's far from being able to hear someone's voice or see them smile from something you said. If I were you, I wouldn't worry about it. Remember, I met Aurora's parents that one time they came here and got a pretty good sense of who they are. And they will *not* allow Aurora to keep them out of the chickpea loop."

Jill eased herself into a prime parking spot right in front of Leela's favorite bar. Although, speakeasy was a better term.

Leela smiled broadly. "I was hoping you'd take me here."

"It's only because now I'm going to start asking the tough questions."

They walked in, and the abrupt darkness of the bar always came as a mild surprise. Once Leela's pupils adjusted, she could make out the distinctive 1920s theme. Framed newspaper headlines proclaiming prohibition and the women's right to vote hung above the bar, and a mannequin wearing a flapper dresser had a permanent seat.

Jill cozied into a small booth, took the cocktail and wine menu leaning against the wall, and passed the beer list to Leela. "Oh, Valentine-themed drinks! I'm going to have the chocolate cherry cha-cha."

Leela mimed gagging while she read the rotating tap list.

Jill waved her off her exaggeration. "Speaking of Valentine's Day, what are you and Aurora doing?"

"We promised each other we'd present five possible names for chickpea then have a romantic dinner, cooked by yours truly, followed by gifts and sexy time. You?"

"Viktor's out of town doing some scouting for the university," she said with a shrug. "Back to you. Are you sure there'll be sexy time this year? I thought she was still queasy."

Leela stifled a laugh. "The queasy period passed and was immediately replaced by the horny one. We haven't had this much sex since the first few months when we started having sex."

"I can come back if you want," their server said nervously.

Jill bit the inside of her cheek and pointed to the cocktail menu. "I'll have this, and the love machine across from me will have…?"

"The double IPA."

Their server left with the order and Leela looked at Jill with an annoyed stare. "Thank you for that."

"I try. So, Aurora's keeping you busy in the boudoir. Viktor was so weird about that when I got pregnant the first time. He was insistent we would hurt the baby."

"I'll admit that I was hesitant, but I got over it."

"Did it take you *months* to get over it?"

"Months? Seriously?" Leela asked and shook her head. The sex she and Aurora had in the past month was beyond great. It was actually euphoric. Every time Aurora had an orgasm, it was like a wave of comfort washed her brain. It was like a love hug for her mind. "I'm glad I got over it, because it's brought Aurora and I closer, you know, emotionally."

"I honestly didn't think that was possible."

"I know, but it's true. It's like before chickpea, I loved Aurora. I wanted to share my life with her. But now it's all that, plus this intense, primal need to protect her and chickpea. And my rational brain knows that Aurora is completely capable for caring for herself and chickpea—more than me, probably—but I can't help it. Everything I do comes back to her and chickpea."

"Everything?"

"Everything. Which is why my Valentine gifts this year are going to be especially epic."

"Are you going to greet her at the door with a smoke detector and flannel lingerie?" Jill asked with a grin.

"Um..." Their server held a pint of beer with a thick head and a martini glass of crimson liquid. "I'm just going to leave these here." He placed their drinks down and scurried away.

Leela picked up her beer and took a sip. "My lingerie is not made of flannel, I'll have you know, and my gifts are centered around a certain theme."

"Let me guess, you want to protect them."

Leela nodded and tasted her cold and pleasantly bitter IPA. "But I feel like it's more than protection. It's the caring aspect too.

I don't want chickpea growing up even thinking for a moment that she's not the most important part of my life."

"Hmm," Jill uttered with a slow nod. "Leela, you're not your parents. I don't think you have to try so hard to be the perfect parent. For one, there's no such thing as the perfect parent. And two, just make sure your basics are covered. Will chickpea have a roof and food to eat?"

"Yes. Although, we haven't painted the nursery yet. Aurora and I are still debating themes."

"Chickpea won't even be able to see color until she's five months old." Jill left her pinky out while she took a dainty sip. "How about your midwife search?"

Leela grimaced. "That's not going so well."

"Okay! There's where you need to focus your energy. Why isn't it going well?"

"There's like two ends of the spectrum. Completely hippy dippy or too clinical. Aurora and I are trying to find someone in the middle. We did have a great lead! But he already has two women who are due around the same time as Aurora."

"He?" Jill asked with a quirked brow.

"Men can be midwives too, you know." Leela took another sip of beer and thought about what Jill said. *Make sure the basics were covered.* "Childcare is still a bit up in air too. They're all crazy far away and expensive! I have no idea what we're going to do in that department."

Jill placed her drink on the table. "I might be able to help you with both of your problems."

"Really? How?"

"About your midwife, Clarissa has a friend who technically isn't certified yet but has a ton of experience. I have no doubt she passed her certification test. She's waiting for the results."

Experienced and her *daughter's friend* seem contradictory. "Not to sound like a jerk, but how much experience can a twenty-three-year-old have at being a midwife?"

"Her mother was one, and she has assisted her since she was fourteen."

Okay, that counted as some experience. "Tell you what, if she passes her certification, give me her information. Now, what's the second thing you can help me with?"

A gloomy expression took over Jill's features. "I like working for you part-time, but some of the things are a little too physical for me."

Leela couldn't believe her ears. "There are plenty of people who can do the heavy lifting—"

"It's not the lifting. It's the dexterity work. Just today I was trying to unscrew a bottle of orange oil, but I dropped it. The smell was ungodly strong!"

Rather than respond, Leela took a long drink from her beer.

"But I don't want to leave. I love the farm and you, so why don't I become chickpea's childcare?"

Leela drank again, but this time it wasn't to avoid responding, it was so she could think. Jill had plenty of experience. Her schedule would be open. Aurora trusted her as much as she did. And there would be a consistent figure in chickpea's life.

"And you don't have to pay me a lot, maybe just enough to cover my groceries."

Jill's proposition could work. "I'll ask Aurora tonight," Leela said with a grin. "I didn't know you were having trouble in mixing. I could have changed the scheduling to accommodate you."

"I know you would have, but I think this is better. Plus, I can't stand the music they listen to over there. I'm so glad I have that weight off my chest. It's been bothering me for some time now."

"I'm very glad you told me. Now, my only short-term worry is if Aurora will like her Valentine's gifts. They're a little outside the box."

\#

Aurora and Tonya ended their last phone interview of the day with a high five. After two weeks of searching, they had found someone who could make it past the phone interview. And hopefully once Bobby interviewed in person, they could consider him Aurora's mentee and future East Coast analyst.

"I definitely think this is a case for celebratory kombucha," Tonya said as she reached into her minifridge.

"Can't, sorry."

"Oh, right. Don't want chickpea getting tipsy and jacked up on caffeine at the same time."

Aurora smiled good-naturedly. "Well, that and I have to pick up Leela's present before I get home. Otherwise, the exchanging of Valentine's Day presents will be less of an actual exchange. I promise, though, I will gladly raise a cup of decaffeinated tea to Bobby tomorrow."

"You have a good night then, and happy Valentine's Day."

"You, too."

Aurora shut down her workstation, left the office, and headed into town. Aurora was still amazed the framing shop accommodated her last-minute request. She normally wouldn't do such a thing, but she had to rely on a third party for the picture, and Dr. Aguilar's tech was slower than she would have liked in delivering the image. Hopefully, the quality of the double-framed picture wouldn't suffer because of the rush.

Once Aurora laid her eyes on the present in the store, her eyes misted over. Aurora knew that her gift was perfect. Her other gift was less sentimental, but Leela would still love it.

She achieved the perfect balance of presents. Much like her life.

Aurora had begun to refocus her priorities in the past few months. Yes, she wanted professional success and a life with Leela. But now she needed Leela. She needed her family more than she ever thought imaginable. She liked her job, but the desire to put in the extra hours was gone. Plus, she was certain she could still get her own office someday without sacrificing her family.

Aurora pulled into their driveway, and, on cue, Leela opened the front door and greeted her with a smile and Aurora's favorite outfit: jeans and a fitted flannel shirt with a white camisole peaking underneath. It was the same outfit Leela wore on their first date. "Why, don't you look nice."

Leela ushered her inside, placed her bag on the floor, removed her coat with a flourish and spin, and then planted a hello kiss on her waiting mouth. "Happy Valentine's Day, sweets."

Aurora leaned in for another. "Does this mean I get to change into my first date outfit of yoga pants and a hoodie?"

"You can wear whatever you'd like, but I'm partial to the third date outfit myself."

"That was appropriate swimwear for your aquatic therapy session," Aurora patiently said.

"You and your appropriate swimwear teased me relentlessly." Leela playfully poked Aurora in the center of her chest. "I loved it! And it really greased the wheels for our fourth date."

Aurora grinned. "Well, for tonight, I think I should wear something that doesn't distract you from the ability to form words. At least initially."

"I can't wait. Okay, you change into whatever you'd like, and I'll set the stage for our romantic evening."

Aurora gave her a quick peck and walked down the hall, but before she reached their bedroom, she paused in front of the nursery door. They had finally finished painting the room. Most of the walls were cream, but the wall with the window gave a colorful splash of sage green. Despite the finished look, the theme of the room was still debated: forest friends or rainforest friends. Aurora leaned more rainforest friends since they already lived in Oregon.

Aside from the walls, the room was bare.

They really needed to get on that.

There were no tiny clothes in the closet or a rocking chair in the corner. She doubted that Stacy would want to take the lead on a baby shower, but maybe her mom and Tanha could work together. Surely, they could put together a simple party.

Once Aurora settled on a comfortable ensemble of yoga pants and wispy shawl—a dressed-up version of the first date—she heard the crackle of a small fire in the woodburning stove and the soothing sounds of the rain that had begun to fall outside. The smell of something tart and savory filled the air.

Aurora inhaled the kitchen's aroma. "Now that I've had a few moments to settle from my day, I can tell you that whatever you're making smells delicious."

"I thought about going fancy, but when I saw the forecast, I thought I'd make your favorite, which motherly instinct tells me will probably be chickpea's favorite too."

Tomato soup and grilled cheese! "I need to kiss you again. Come here." Leela laughed while Aurora kissed her lips, cheeks, chin, forehead. Anything she could possibly kiss.

"Given your enthusiasm for dinner, would you rather eat first?"

"No. We have to do presents, but let me go first." Aurora brought a canvas bag over to the couch and pulled out a box the size of a hardback novel. It was wrapped in cream-colored paper dotted with hearts.

Leela accepted the present and tested the weight. "Hmm. Wonder what this could be?" She ripped into the thin paper and gasped at the gold sticker in the center of the box.

Aurora had no idea what the message in French said, but she did know they were Leela's favorite chocolates. "Shipping made me go a little bit over our agreed upon budget, but I figure you wouldn't mind."

"Mind? Are you crazy? These are the best!" Leela opened the box of fancy French-Canadian chocolates and took a bite from one of the square pieces. "So very great," she mumbled around a caramel. She fed Aurora the rest of the first piece. "Now, tell me that's not worth the extra shipping. Chickpea agrees with me, that much I know."

"You two are going to be two peas in a pod, aren't you?"

"That's my plan," Leela said with a mischievous smile. "What else did you get me?"

Aurora picked a red and silver gift bag out of the larger canvas one and rested it on Leela's lap. She watched anxiously as Leela sifted through the pink tissue paper and eventually pulled out the hinged, wooden picture frame. Leela opened it and her upturned lips disappeared behind her hand.

Her gift struck the emotional chord she had hoped it would. "I thought it'd be nice if we had a family portrait. Even if there are two pictures required to make it."

On the left side was a photograph of her and Leela during their last day in Hawaii. A server had taken their picture while Aurora was mid-laugh, and Leela, with her freshly cut hair, smiled with her head rested on Aurora's shoulder. The picture on the right was an enhanced photo from chickpea's latest ultrasound. It was a four-dimensional image, which showed chickpea's closed eyes, button nose, and a hand rested against their forehead.

Leela embraced Aurora while she held the frame. "I love this so much."

She hugged Leela back with all that she had then released her grip when she felt Leela start to pull away. She grinned when she saw Leela's large brown eyes shimmer from unshed tears.

"This is amazing." Leela held the photo so Aurora could see as well as she could. "For one, we both look super hot, and then look at little chickpea. It's like she's trying to take a nap but these adults around her won't stop talking."

"How do you figure?"

"Other than the pose that screams, 'Go away, I have a headache,' look at the other hand. The middle finger is definitely sticking up."

Aurora took another look at the picture. It definitely looked like their child was flipping them off. "That wasn't very nice, chickpea," Aurora said as she looked at her bump.

Leela's shoulders bounced with laughter beside her. "We really have to start thinking of actual names."

"We can do our name trade during dinner."

She watched Leela trace her finger around chickpea's face.

"I'm glad you like it."

"I love it, but now I'm clearly going to lose the game of who gave who the best Valentine's Day gifts."

"Oh, does that mean I can get my presents now?"

Rather than get off the sofa, Leela held Aurora's hand on her lap. "I went with a bit of a theme for your gifts. And. . . I also went overbudget. But I figure now that Jill is our daycare, we've saved some money! So, it's okay."

For Leela to venture into a level of justification that detailed, she must have gone more than just a little overbudget. "Can I ask what the theme is?"

"It's not the most romantic theme, but my heart is in the right place, and Valentine's Day is all about the hearts. The wrapping paper you gave me suggests as much," Leela said while she backpedaled into the kitchen. "And my heart told my brain that I needed to start to think about different ways to protect the family."

"Did you buy even more fire extinguishers?"

"No, but that reminds me we need a fire blanket for the kitchen." Leela took a manila envelope and small box off the dining table and then handed them to Aurora. "These are presents number one and two. Three is within the theme but very different."

"Is it Love Swirl?"

"No, that didn't work out. The thing about red swirls made with natural dye is that they tend to stain people's hands. But I promise you'll still like gift number three."

More than a little perplexed, Aurora took the envelope and pulled out the paper inside. She did a double take of the title on the photocopied paper. It was Leela's application for a marriage license.

Aurora threw her arms around Leela's neck. They had their own private ceremony in Hawaii, but Leela hadn't seen the need to make their relationship legal. She must have changed her mind. This was something Aurora never thought would happen, and now that she was essentially proposed to, the feeling was more amazing than she even could have dreamed of.

"You're sure?" Aurora asked with a smile.

"I am absolutely one hundred percent certain." Leela took the box from Aurora and opened it to expose a ring made from wood with an inlay of lustrous black and green. "I know that we love each other and we're committed, but say something terrible happens to you and the patriarchy comes through and writes a law which makes it difficult or impossible for me to have custody of chickpea. This," she shook the ring between her fingers, "protects the family legally. So, want to have an old-fashioned shotgun wedding? Be my spouse listed on forms and all that jazz?"

"I would love to." Aurora punctuated the end of each word with a kiss.

"And related to this, I found an adoption attorney. If we plan well, I'm thinking we can get married at the courthouse and have that meeting on the same day since they're in the same district downtown. And afterward, maybe some fine dining downtown to celebrate?"

"All of that sounds perfect."

How long had Leela been thinking of all of this? Marriage, adoption, courthouses. . . Aurora hadn't had so many ideas run through her mind since the day she learned she was pregnant. And there was still the third present. "Wow. I didn't see this on the whiteboard."

"I wanted these particular items to be a surprise. I think it worked." Leela smiled proudly and kissed Aurora again. "Are you ready for your last present? Although, to be honest, it's more of a family gift."

"Absolutely," Aurora said. "Do I get a hint?"

Leela took a moment. "Well, let's put it this way, you can't have a shotgun wedding without a shotgun."

"You bought a shotgun?" Aurora asked in disbelief.

"Sure did! If something's out there lurking, trying to hunt us down, we have to be prepared. Want me to go get it?"

Aurora didn't have a chance to answer before Leela left the couch.

"I hope you like twelve gauges," Leela said down the hall.

Leela's behavior surpassed bizarre. The gun issue wasn't what troubled her. It wasn't as if the gift was an automatic weapon or Aurora was unfamiliar with long-barrel guns. Her dad had taken her out at a young age to learn the basics about hunting, fishing, and trapping. But still. A shotgun for Valentine's Day?

Leela returned with a weapon that was nearly half the length of her body. The walnut stock gleamed, and the barrel was a standard matte gray. "As far as guns go, it's very versatile. I bought four shot ammo." She presented the gun for Aurora to take.

Aurora's arms dropped slightly from the weight. The chamber was open, and as far as she was concerned, it would remain that way. "This is a very. . . surprising gift. We need some kind of case or cabinet to keep it locked in."

"Oh! I got that covered. There's a locked case under the bed. The combination is sixty-nine, sixty-nine."

Aurora rolled her eyes.

"I had to make sure I'd remember it!" Leela grinned and returned to her seat. "I can tell you're warming up to the idea. I thought we could go the range with Keith sometime to shoot."

Aurora looked at the weapon in her hands once more. Leela's drive to protect chickpea at all costs had taken Leela's neurosis to a place that exceeded concern. Now, it was an obsession that consumed Leela's thoughts all the time. What had Leela said earlier? It was like a voice told her to protect chickpea?

Something else was at work.

Leela squinted and then looked down at Aurora's bump. "You're feeling overwhelmed, aren't you? Chickpea feels what you feel."

"I think you're projecting my emotions onto chickpea a little too much."

Leela bit her lower lip and took a breath. "No, she really does. That's why she's moving around so much now."

Aurora gripped the couch to stop from swaying over. It was one thing for Leela to know chickpea was moving when her hand rested on her belly, but it was completely different when Leela's hands weren't near her. "How do you know chickpea's moving?"

"So, here's a new thing that I didn't think was real, but now I *know* it is. I can sense her," Leela said with hesitation.

"You. . . sense her? You know what she's feeling?"

"I don't think it's emotional. Ever since the popcorn belly started, sometimes I get this restless sensation." She pointed to her temple. "Up here."

What Leela described couldn't be possible. "Are you sure you're not just being perceptive of my emotions?"

"I don't think so. And I know I sound delusional—I didn't even want to tell you—but what I have is only getting stronger. And you just confirmed it. I couldn't keep this a secret from you."

"How long has this been going on?" Aurora asked, even though she was afraid to learn the answer.

"I think it's been gradual, but I really started feeling different a few weeks ago."

Before she could accept Leela's claim, she wanted some kind of proof. Aurora needed to think of an experiment she could do that would have immediate feedback from chickpea. "Can you go into the bedroom? I want to try something."

"Okay," Leela said unsurely and stood with the shotgun. "What do you want me to do?"

"Nothing. Well, for one thing, you can put the gun away. I'll tell you when to come out, okay?"

Leela nodded and left.

Aurora quickly stood up and went the freezer. She jimmied a few ice cubes loose from a tray and dropped them into a glass that she filled with water.

"What are you doing? I know you're doing something!" Leela hollered.

"I'm doing lots of different experiments." She rattled the kitchen drawers while the water dropped its temperature. She dipped the tip of her pinky finger in. It was much colder than she liked. Her teeth were really going to hate her for what happened next. "How do you feel?"

"Not much of anything."

Aurora picked up the glass of frigid water and chugged it in the most uncomfortable gulps her body could take. When her lips touched the ice, she put the glass down and placed her tongue on the roof of her mouth to get rid of her non-dairy ice cream headache. Chickpea stirred inside her like she was trying to escape the cold river.

"What did you just do?" Leela yelled. "I know you're doing something!"

"How do you know that?"

"Because my brain feels agitated."

"Shit," Aurora muttered to herself as she wandered into the seat of a dining chair. "You can come out now."

Leela came into the kitchen and eyed the glass of ice cubes suspiciously. "Did you put that on your bump?"

"No. I drank it very, very quickly, which really, really sucked, but. . . you felt that?" Leela joined her at the table with an ashen expression. "How can you feel what I feel?"

Leela shook her head. "I think I feel what chickpea feels. Again, I know it sounds impossible, but think about it. Maybe how you communicated with me in my coma has been passed down to her?"

"Or maybe you passed the ability to her? That's another tick in the column for Mom's idea versus parthenogenesis."

Leela's eyes grew larger. "Fuck," she drawled.

"Exactly." The conception wasn't normal. Chickpea's heart rate was that of an endurance fetus. Chickpea's strength and activity was well above average. Now, chickpea was psychic. "Do you think Mom was right about chickpea? That's she's, you know, meant to save the world? Because I don't know how I feel about that."

Leela relaxed in her seat and thoughtfully look skyward. "I don't know either, but if it is true, chickpea's unique qualities make sense. Has she given you any supernatural symptoms?"

"No. At least I don't think—" Aurora gasped. She hadn't connected the dots, but now everything was clear.

"What? What?"

"Do you remember the last morning in Hawaii I said I had a dream with colors?"

Leela nodded. "Yeah, I blew your mind with my love skills."

"Every once in a while, since then, I have another color dream, but each time it's become less abstract and senses have been added to it. I had one the other night and I could have sworn the colors moved in perfectly rhythmic waves. And there was sound. It's like..."

"The more chickpea develops the more detailed your dreams are. You're dreaming of her experience!"

Aurora couldn't even pretend that was impossible. In the world she and Leela—and chickpea—lived in, this was logical.

"What if your mom is right," Leela said, "and that's why I have to go above and beyond to protect her? Because she's destined to protect others with her skills or something?"

Leela's idea made sense. When chickpea was conceived, Leela had been rewired to protect them at all costs. If chickpea was uncomfortable, Leela knew and could intervene. If chickpea was in danger. . . Well, motion lights and shotguns helped.

Aurora sighed. "We can't tell anyone about this. If people find out— If that blog finds out..."

"Fuck."

CHAPTER THIRTEEN

WHAT HAD STARTED as an occasional nudge in her brain was now a constant but gentle squeeze. It was like chickpea was giving her little hugs all the time. It was adorable.

"Leela!" Keith shouted from the other side of the field.

"Huh." His expectant expression and impatient body language bewildered her. She knew there was something they were supposed to do, but she couldn't think of what it was. The goats seemed fine. The delivery van was on schedule. Why was he looking at her like that? It was too hard to concentrate. "What?"

"You said you wanted to go to the shooting range after we finished the morning milking, but now I'm thinking maybe you should use that time to take a nap."

"No, I'm good." A tiny white lie wouldn't hurt. "Just a headache I can't get rid of."

"You don't need to see that neurologist fellow again, do you?"

Sure, the constant reminder of chickpea was distracting, but what bothered her the most were the secrets. Neither she nor Aurora had told a soul about the connection she and chickpea shared. Initially, Leela thought the pact wouldn't cause any issues, but once Aurora started her sixth month, Leela's mental connection matched Aurora's physical. And sometimes it wasn't all hugs. Sometimes they were like kicks to her temporal lobe.

Leela created a new definition for "sympathy pain".

"The only doctor I'll be seeing is Dr. Aguilar when we have chickpea's appointment this week. I'm good to go to the range."

"You're sure?"

"Yeah, I'm sure." Keith's arched brow led her to believe he was unconvinced. "Do you need me to start shooting for you to believe me?"

"No, ma'am. I'm ready to leave when you are."

With a terse nod, Leela left the barn and headed in the direction of her home. It was the same route she had walked for ten years. Almost everything from that first step to now was the same. The worn path. The mountains off to the west. The sounds of the goats while they milled about after their milking. It was the perfect environment for chickpea.

Or Megis. Or Kallik. Or Rajata. Or Qushi.

They were still narrowing down the names—which mostly consisted of their grandmothers' names—but whatever chickpea's real name was, Leela knew she would have a shadow in the form of a curious, probably clumsy, little girl.

She couldn't wait.

On the way to get her shotgun, Leela crossed the threshold and staggered to the couch as a giant, invisible finger burrowed in her cushy brain. She threw her head back as colorful, temporary dots clouded her vision. This was the worst one yet.

It really sucked.

The vibrating phone in her back pocket would have to wait for just a few more moments, even though she knew it was Aurora. When the last spot disappeared and her mind was free from the paralyzing drill, she reached for her phone and, with a quick tap, called Aurora back. "What in the frilly hell was that?"

"I'm so, so sorry. Are you okay?"

"Let's put it this way, I'm glad if the chickpea punch had to happen, it happened now instead of when I was at the range with Keith. What caused it?"

"I added too much siracha to my Thai leftovers."

"It's ten o'clock in the morning!"

"I was hungry! But as soon as I felt little Megis Rapinoe kicking around in there, I knew you'd feel some sort of consequence. I definitely did," Aurora mumbled.

Leela pushed aside her problem immediately. "What happened to you?"

"My organs are definitely getting some penalty kicks. Especially my bladder. I almost peed while I explained a pivot table to Bobby."

She closed her eyes in relief. Everyone was okay. "Sounds like everything's under control. Although, the almost wetting yourself part is a bummer. I bet you're glad you've done so many Kegels." Leela chuckled as she reached under the bed for the gun case but didn't hear any laughter in return. She made a note: no more Kegel jokes. "I should let you get back to work."

"I really should. I'm already probably going to come home late."

"Please don't be late to yoga." It surprised Leela how much she enjoyed prenatal yoga. Although she understood why now: chickpea liked yoga. "I'm really excited a rep from that baby spa product place will be there."

"Oh, that's right! I completely forgot."

"Which is why I'm here." Leela didn't like to point out Aurora's occasional pregnancy-induced forgetfulness or overly emotional responses. Mostly, because the few times she did, Aurora almost cried. "Then, after yoga, Jill's also coming over with Fiona."

"Who's Fiona again?"

The forgetfulness was in peak form. "She's Jill's daughter's friend. The midwife."

"Oh, that's right! I really hope she's better than the last two."

Leela grinned while she relocked the house. She had no issues with the prior midwives Dr. Aguilar recommended, but Aurora found them either aggressive or inexperienced. "Jill knows you pretty well. I don't think she'd suggest someone you or I would hate. Anything else you need to tell me before I try out the bang stick?"

"No, but I promise I'll stay away from the siracha if you promise not to shoot yourself or Keith."

"That seems like a very extreme deal, but okay. I'll see you at yoga. Love you." She waited until Aurora returned the sentiment before she hung up.

Keith leaned against her truck with his arms folded. "Finally. I was beginning to think maybe you were getting cold feet."

"Like hell I am. I'm ready to blast the shit out of some clay pigeons." She rounded the truck, placed her case on the back seat along with his, and stirred up the gravel as they left. She could be a yoga-going, wife-supporting baby mama and wield her shotgun like a boss.

#

A dimly lit room and the soothing melody of Sanskrit chants relaxed Aurora's muscles and thoughts. She stayed reclined between Leela's legs as their joined hands rested on top of her baby bump. With each one of Leela's breaths, she subconsciously took hers.

She hadn't felt this at peace in ages.

Aurora imagined chickpea's arms and legs curled inside her. Warm and cozy in what Leela called 'the Aurora spa'. Yeah, the water birth approach was definitely the way to go. She and Leela would return to that conversation later.

The yoga instructor's voice brought Aurora out of her thoughts. Leela's resting hands began to slide away, but Aurora held them firm. "Where do you think you're going?"

Leela leaned forward enough to whisper in her ear. "My leg is falling asleep, and— Oh, that's a new one."

Aurora tried to turn, but her bump provided resistance. "What's new?"

"I think she's hungry or something. Did you have your snack before coming here?"

"Didn't think I needed it. I had a late lunch after my pad Thai snack." Her meal planning was much less of a concern to her than Leela's growing connection to chickpea. Yes, there was an advantage to knowing chickpea's needs, but Aurora worried about Leela's mental well-being. If they stayed connected like that for the duration of chickpea's lifetime, surely there would be problems. Leela was still learning how to properly express her own emotional needs.

"Is she giving you low blood sugar vibes?" Aurora asked.

"No. It's like there's a new corner of my brain that's shimmying. It doesn't hurt at all."

As the couples around them started to stand and leave, Aurora thought more about the concern she tossed around at the end of their meditation. "Are you worried that you'll always feel what chickpea feels?

Leela scoffed. "Why would I worry about that? That'd make me like the best mom ever. No offense. You will also be a very badass mom."

"You don't think it'll be too much up here." Aurora gently tapped Leela's forehead.

Leela took her hand and placed a kiss on her palm. "I promise I'll be okay. And I promise I'll always let you know if I'm feeling overwhelmed. And I could ask you the same thing. Are you worried you'll always be dreaming what she dreams? Or vice versa?"

That was something she thought and remained torn about. On one hand, that kind of mother-child connection was amazing, but on the other hand, having that kind of tether could be unhealthy.

"I'm hoping what we both feel is temporary. Face it, if she does have powers of some sort, she's not going to need us looking after her."

"That's a really good point."

"I still have some moments of clarity." Aurora kissed her quickly then began the challenge of standing. If six months felt like this, she didn't want to know what the seven, eight, and nine would be like. "Want to grab a birthing tub pamphlet before we leave?"

"No, thanks. I know where to buy petri dishes."

"That was uncalled for."

Leela regarding her seriously. "I know you want the gentlest childbirth possible for you and chickpea. And so do I, but do you want me to list the things that can come out of you during that experience?"

"Joy?" Aurora said innocently.

"Yes. A warm tub of brownish-red joy."

"Gross."

"That's why you love me," Leela said and smiled.

Aurora swatted Leela on the behind as they left the studio together. Leela stopped in the middle of a cluster of empty parking spaces and searched for something in the early evening light. "Do you see something over there?"

"There's a *huge* bird perched on the streetlight over there."

Aurora turned and saw the outline of a raptor. "That's pretty cool. Almost looks like a hawk or an eagle. Not sure what it's doing here in the city."

"Maybe it's sick of rodents and giving fishing in the river a try." Leela quickly pecked her on the cheek. "I'll see you at home where Jill has promised to feed us."

"I'll take it." After a better return kiss, Aurora got into her new fully electric SUV and headed home. She wasn't in the mood to interview another midwife, but knowing that Jill trusted Fiona set the majority of her concerns at ease. Plus, Jill only knew how to make vegetable lasagna, and there was no way she'd turn that down.

The thought of food caused her stomach to rumble and chickpea to stir. "Don't dance around too much in there. You'll make Mama Lee crash."

She grinned at the nickname Leela had created. She wasn't sure if she was completely on board with Mama Roar since it made her sound like a lion, but that wasn't necessarily a terrible thing. Lionesses were very protective of their cubs.

Even if the Creator had assigned Leela to be her primary protector.

Ahead of her, the two blinking red lights flashed to warn traffic about the oncoming train. Leela would definitely beat her home. To pass the time, she pressed the call button on her steering wheel and dialed her mom.

"Hi, boo bear!"

"Hey, Mom. I thought I'd give you a call since I'm driving home from yoga."

"I know. You texted me that yesterday, plus I just saw Leela's pictures on InstaPic."

Aurora could feel the skin of her forehead bunch. "When did I text you?"

Ani chuckled. "Has the pregnancy brain gotten to you?"

"I guess it has." Aurora gritted her teeth. Of all the pregnancy symptoms she had, the occasional lapse in memory was the one she had the least humor over. Well, that and the gas. That was just embarrassing. "How have you been feeling?"

"Better! My hair has grown out enough where Logan thinks I can pull off a fauxhawk."

"How about—"

"I'm fine, boo bear. I really am. Tell me about yoga! It looked like you had fun."

"It was good. I like the exercise and bonding with Leela. Plus, she was able to network with a baby lotion rep."

"She must have been busy. Networking and acting as a photographer."

Leela rarely single-tasked, yet she hardly ever made mistakes. "And she still participated in the couples' portion of the couples yoga."

"Just wonderful. Tell her to keep those pics coming! You have the cutest little belly. How have you been feeling?"

"My belly doesn't feel so little. Even Dr. Aguilar was surprised by the jump in chickpea's length, which also explains why her kicks feel like they're reaching my kidneys. I swear I haven't felt this beat up since that time I tried to play rugby." Aurora expected her mother's next words to be criticism from that single attempt in college that left her with a nosebleed. "Are you still there?"

"Yeah, I'm still here. It's just a little odd that you're feeling the kicks that intensely. Usually, the sensation of your internal organs being assaulted doesn't start until month eight or nine. What's your doctor said?"

"I haven't told her yet. Our next appointment is in two weeks."

"Okay," Ani drawled. "But promise me if it gets more intense, you'll call."

"I promise. And I'll bring it up at dinner with the prospective midwife. This one comes highly recommended by Jill, so maybe she'll have something insightful to say."

"Have Sid or Tanha said anything about you using a midwife?"

"I don't know what Sid thinks, but Tanha's on board. Overall, they've been incredibly supportive of our plans. I think they feel like they can make up for being less than stellar parents by being fantastic grandparents. They've basically furnished the entire nursery."

"They didn't buy blankets or clothes, did they?"

"No, Mom, those are still yours to knit and River's to give."

"Oh, good. I'm making one that's kind of like a cape with a frog headpiece. It has the biggest eyes."

Aurora grinned, and chickpea must have been fine with the conversation too because the movement inside of her had stilled. "Any chance you can make one that's a goat?"

"We'll see how the frog turns out. If it's not too scary-looking, I'll work on a goat."

"That'd be great." Aurora saw her home in the distance along with Leela's truck and a new car in the driveway. "Mom, can I call you back tomorrow? Jill and Fiona are here already."

"Sure thing. Love you, boo bear."

"I love you too. Bye."

The motion sensor lights flooded her vision as soon as her car reached the fifty feet threshold. She had to admit that initially she thought implementing the lights was a little ridiculous, but they had been handy to avoid stepping on icy patches or in puddles. The lights also allowed her to read the bumper stickers on the young midwife's car. Based on the stick figure family of six and the slightly aged election sticker, Aurora was fairly certain Fiona had borrowed the family car.

Maybe Kamala would be a good name.

Aurora entered her home to the enticing aroma of warm, buttery garlic. While Jill and Leela smiled, Fiona nodded shyly. She still looked like a teenager who had long, red hair that fell around her small shoulders.

"Hello, everyone," Aurora said and hung her coat. "Sorry I'm late to the party."

"Got caught behind the train, huh?" Leela asked. "Jill and Fiona already have dinner set up."

"I hope you don't mind," Jill said. "I figured you'd forgive me if the reason I used the emergency key was to make sure the lasagna and garlic bread were hot when you got here."

All was forgiven when there was food. Especially garlic bread.

"Are you kidding? That's not a problem at all." Aurora approached the group and looked at Fiona. "I'm Aurora, and this is chickpea." She motioned to her belly and extended her hand.

Fiona smiled softly and returned the handshake. "That's an adorable nickname. Have you chosen their legal name yet?"

Aurora and Leela shared an annoyed look that only couples direct toward each other.

"Don't get them started on that," Jill said, keeping her smile in place. "Or we'll spend the next thirty minutes listening to it. I'd much rather eavesdrop on all of this midwife business. So, let's eat and chat. I hope you're hungry."

"I'm always hungry," Aurora said as she walked to the dining table.

As Jill began to cut and serve the gooey dish, Leela placed a hand on Aurora's thigh. "Jill told me that in addition to being Clarissa's friend, she was also Fiona's gymnastic coach."

"Really?" Aurora asked as she took a steaming plate. "Jill's known you for a pretty long time then?"

"Since I was six, so. . . seventeen years."

Twenty-three years old! Aurora didn't know if she could handle a twenty-three-year-old delivering her child. She acknowledged that she was far from being a wise elder herself, but Fiona's youth gave her cause for concern. "When did you graduate from nursing school?"

"I got my BSN and passed my boards two years ago. I received my certification to be a midwife a week or two ago," Fiona explained and picked up her fork. "Please start eating, I can tell Aurora probably needs to."

Leela nodded emphatically.

As they began to eat, Leela sighed contently, loud enough for all to hear, which forced Aurora to suppress a laugh. The surge of sugar in her blood stream must have been making chickpea happy.

Jill smiled. "Another satisfied customer."

"You have no idea," Leela said and gave Aurora a piece of garlic bread. "Eat up. Someone else is hungry."

"It's nice to see a partner be so supportive before the birth," Fiona said. "If you don't mind, I have a few questions for the both of you. I think the midwife-parent relationship needs to understand all the expectations—on both sides— in order to be as successful as possible."

None of the other candidates had bothered to ask them questions. That was a refreshing change. "Okay," Aurora said. "What would you like to know?"

Fiona looked directly to Leela. "How much of a role to you want to have in the birth?"

"Ah," Leela drawled and stared at Aurora for help.

Aurora smirked. "Actually, I don't know the answer to that."

Fiona's brow raised. "None of the other midwives you interviewed asked?"

"No," Leela and Aurora said simultaneously.

Both Jill and Fiona scrunched their faces and shook their heads in disgust.

"I'm still very interested in the answer," Aurora said.

While Leela squinted and looked skyward, Aurora kept eating.

"I would say," Leela began, but then trailed off. "I can hand you things or hand Aurora things. To be honest, I didn't see myself doing much more than thing handing."

"Don't you want to cut the cord?" Aurora asked. Even the most distant partners participated in that ritual.

"Oh, yeah! I can do that thing too," Leela said proudly. "Just consider me an assistant to all your needs and if that requires action south of the border, I don't mind. I've seen a few goat births in my day, so I know what's up."

"I have to say that's the first time I've heard that," Fiona said with a smile.

The window was open for Aurora to ask the question she had been dying to ask. "How long have you been doing this?"

"I assisted my mother who is a midwife from the time I was fourteen to basically a few weeks ago."

Fiona may have been young, but she had probably been present at more births than any paramedic. "How many babies have you helped deliver?" Aurora asked.

"Three hundred and twelve. I have a counter."

Leela and Aurora shared an impressed look.

"Told you she was experienced," Jill said while she grabbed another piece of garlic bread.

Based on the gentle thigh squeeze Leela gave her under the table, Aurora knew how Leela felt. "I'm assuming most of these were home deliveries."

Fiona nodded.

"Any in birthing tubs?"

Fiona winced. "A few. I don't recommend it."

Aurora's spirit deflated. "Why not? They seem so natural."

"They sound nice in theory, but if there is meconium or any of your stool that is pushed out during the delivery then it's in the water along with you, the baby, and me. It's. . . unpleasant, and if it were me, I wouldn't want to take the chance of my baby's first breaths being bacteria-filled water."

"Told you," Leela said under her breath in a smug voice. "How about emergency situations? Breech? Surprise twins?"

"Yes. Yes. And yes. While everyone wants a smooth labor, I assisted in dozens of deliveries which had surprises and quick changes to the birth plan." She paused as if to collect her thoughts. "There was one situation where we were in a small apartment building..."

Aurora listened intently but her focus was lost when Leela tapped her knee under the table. Aurora looked over to Leela, who subtly scratched her temple and dropped her gaze to the bump.

Chickpea was up to something. As soon as the thought registered, Aurora felt. . . not a kick, but almost a whirl inside of her.

Fiona leaned to the side, presumably to see past their heads. "I think you may have another visitor. Your motion lights just turned on."

Aurora turned to see that through the living room windows the front of the house was bathed in light. She knew the activity from outside and chickpea's movements weren't coincidental.

"I'll go see what it is," Leela said, stood from the table, and went straight for the doorknob.

"Wait," Fiona said. "Don't you want to at least look through the window. There could be a mountain lion out there."

"See," Leela said to Jill. "Lions are a valid fear, but in this case, I don't think that's what it is."

Aurora watched as Leela pushed the curtains to the side for a cursory look. "What do you see?"

"Uh," Leela drawled. She opened the door and walked out, not bothering to close it behind her. "Sweets, can you come out here?"

Curious, she joined Leela on the porch and followed her finger to where Leela pointed. On the roof of her SUV, in the center of a spotlight, was one of the largest golden eagles she had ever seen. Based on the height of the windshield, she estimated it stood three feet tall. The bird of prey stared at her and outstretched its enormous wings. Their tips stretched beyond the width of Aurora's car.

It was immense. It was also familiar.

Aurora slowly approached her car and the animal. Chickpea's somersaults ceased. "This. . . This is the same eagle Logan took a picture of back at Mom and Dad's."

"No way," Leela said. "How do you know?"

To verify her suspicions, Aurora focused on its feet. "One of its talons is gone."

"I think this is the same eagle I've seen around here for the past month," Jill said. "Are you saying it flew from Michigan to be here. Why?"

Without thinking, Aurora whispered, "Chickpea. It's here for chickpea."

As if providing an answer, the eagle flew silently toward them and banked over the house.

The four of them stared in silence as it disappeared.

"This is one of the most amazing things I've ever seen," Fiona said, awestruck. She ran off the porch and spun in a slow circle as she scanned the higher landscape. "There! It's in the tree."

The three women followed Fiona to the tree then her finger, which pointed upward. The bird stood regal and calm, camouflaged in the branches of the juniper tree outside of Aurora and Leela's bedroom window.

A flash of light beside Aurora drew her attention away.

Fiona, with her phone acting as a flashlight, approached the base of the tree, inspected the ground, and then picked up what looked like a dark egg with dark straw covering it.

"What's that?" Jill asked.

"Pellet," Fiona answered. "There's easily a dozen of them down here. If I had to guess I'd say your friend has been living here for quite some time. I wonder if it's watching over you," Fiona said with a laugh.

"Maybe," Aurora said in wonder. She turned to head back into the house, shaking her head. This was too much. She couldn't keep this a secret any long. She touched the back of Leela's shoulder. "Once they leave, we need to talk to—"

"Yeah, I know," Leela said. "We'll call your mom after they leave."

Aurora nodded and started back to the house to hopefully enjoy their meal with limited distractions.

Hopefully, was the key word.

The rest of dinner was a challenge. There was not letting Jill know something was awry. There was being pleasant and conversational with Fiona, who did seem like she would be an excellent midwife. There was the throwing of subtle hints at Leela that they should wrap up as soon as possible. And there was the lasagna. The delicious lasagna Aurora could have devoured by the panful once everyone was gone.

"You're going to want plastic barriers between whatever padding you decide to use and the cloth," Fiona advised. "That way you still have a level of comfort and you don't risk staining everything for all of eternity."

"That's a good point," Aurora said politely, even though the point had been made five minutes earlier.

It was so hard trying to have a focused conversation. Outside of their home was an eagle that had flown halfway across the country to be with chickpea. Not to mention that eagles were associated with healing. Was chickpea a healer? Did she need healing? They needed to finish now so she and Leela could call her mother.

"Anything else?" Jill asked.

Leela sent Aurora a glance that suggested she was less interested in the answer and more interested with getting them out of the house too.

"Regular medical supplies," Fiona said. "I'm sure you have all of that here already given the dangers of farm work."

Aurora elbowed Leela gently.

"Yes, I have everything," Leela said then looked down at everyone's empty plates. "Well, this was fun, and very educational, but we should wrap up. Aurora gets so tired these days. Don't you, sweets?"

"Yeah," Aurora feigned a yawn. "But we'll reach out soon so we can formalize everything. Fiona, you're the woman for the job."

"Fantastic! If it helps, I can send you a packet. Some standards of care, a few forms."

"That'd be great!" Leela stacked all four plates on top of one another, a fork falling to the tile with a *ding* in the process.

Jill picked up the fork. "We can stay and help clean up."

"Not necessary," Leela said. "Now, be careful getting home. Don't want any eagles dive-bombing you or something equally crazy like that."

Jill waved to Aurora to come closer and whispered to her, "I'm worried about Leela."

"I know you are, but we're making strides to talk about her protective streak. She's made a big improvement."

Jill cocked an unconvinced brow toward Aurora. "Well, I know I had a lovely time, and please keep the rest of the lasagna."

Once they left, both Aurora and Leela both waved from the door with large smiles. When Jill and Fiona's taillights disappeared in the distance, they went back into the house and Aurora grabbed her phone. "I thought they'd never leave."

"Seriously. So, how much talking should I do?" Leela asked. "Because I don't know what to say."

Aurora dialed and placed it on speaker. "Just fill in the gaps."

"Boo bear?" Ani's voice projected from the phone on the coffee table. "I didn't expect a call so soon."

"Something kind of weird happened at dinner." Aurora laughed nervously. "And we thought of you."

"I'm all ears!"

Leela gave Aurora the nod and took a seat on the couch.

She joined her and figured she might as well make herself comfortable and draped her legs over Leela's lap. "Well, Mom, it goes like this."

Aurora launched into the details of Leela's ability to sense chickpea. When it started. How it felt. The experiment they ran with the ice water. The unfortunate incident with the hot sauce. And her latest dream experience.

"Let me get this straight," Ani said. "You both have a psychic connection to chickpea and you didn't tell me?"

"We didn't know how," Aurora defended while Leela gave her a foot rub. With all the nervous energy Aurora felt, receiving a massage from her partner's hands was much better than pacing. "Plus, Leela doesn't know how to articulate what she feels beyond what we've already told you."

"Sorry about that," Leela said and applied more lotion to her hands.

Ani made a long and exaggerated sigh. "You really can't do better than, 'mind hug' or 'hangry brain worm'?"

Leela shook her head.

"She really can't, Mom."

"Hmph. Well, I'd say it's pretty obvious that the psychic ability Leela was only able to tap into during her coma is hereditary, and she passed it on to chickpea. But chickpea can't control it yet. Makes sense to me."

Aurora lifted her other foot, indicating it was time to switch. "Do you think chickpea is trying to communicate with everyone or only us?"

"I would think she's trying to communicate with everyone, but they don't have the ability to understand. That might be why she kicks you so much. It's the only way you'll pay attention."

"Yeah, that definitely gets my attention," Aurora mumbled.

"Are you going to tell her about...?" Leela said quietly and cocked her head to the window.

Aurora nodded. "There's something else we need to tell you. I. . . I think chickpea has an eagle looking after her."

"Not just any eagle, a gigantic freakin' eagle that followed us home from Michigan and made its home in the tree outside our bedroom window."

Ani gasped. "Logan's eagle?"

"The same." Aurora attempted to sit up, but she required a helping help from Leela. "And what's even weirder is that we know chickpea sensed it."

"I bet it's a guardian. Another sentient being sent to protect chickpea."

"But that's my job!" Leela winced. "Sorry, our job."

"I think while chickpea is too young to defend herself, she might have several different protectors. Don't be surprised if a bear comes stumbling along too."

"Why all the protection?" Aurora asked. "She's a baby. An innocent baby."

"I think you know by now the Creator has big plans for your little chickpea."

As Aurora stretched her back, Leela stood to pace. "We've talked about that, but what I don't understand is why tonight was so special? This eagle has been around for a few weeks now, but tonight chickpea was all the sudden excited to see him."

"Well, chickpea's developing, so maybe she finally honed into the fact that she has a friend. Oh! That's so cute! I'm going to take that frog pattern and turn it into an eagle."

"So, you don't think we should worry?" Aurora asked.

"Not any more than most first-time parents. If anything, now you have a warning system if something goes awry. You can't pay enough money for that."

CHAPTER FOURTEEN

LEELA'S SMALL BLACK heels clicked against the sidewalk outside the courthouse as her leg bounced in place. She pushed her suit jacket slightly up her wrist to look at the time on her mother's hand-me-down Rolex.

Aurora was ten minutes late.

What if she had changed her mind? She had been so excited about them legally getting married. Or at least that was how she had seemed when Leela proposed, when they scheduled the appointment, and this morning when Aurora kissed her goodbye, promising she'd see her in the afternoon.

"Look, there she is!"

Leela's ears perked, her head turned, and she stood in her designer suit. "Dad!" Leela looked on, stunned, at her father walking alongside Aurora. She barely had time to register Aurora's wedding outfit. She wore a white dress with large black roses with a red shawl. And red lipstick. She loved it when Aurora wore lipstick.

The admiration of her bride slipped into the background as her father hugged her in almost the same dark gray pinstripe suit she wore.

"How are you here?"

"When I received your text message yesterday notifying me of the event, I cleared my calendar and booked a flight," he said with a broad smile. "I would not miss this for the world."

Aurora took her hand and squeezed. "He's offered to hold up his phone so my mom and dad can watch via video chat."

"That's…" Her father was here on her wedding day. If you had asked her the probability of that five years ago, she would have said having a psychic link with her miracle child inside her dream woman would have been more likely. "I'm…" At his exuberant experience and Aurora's presence at her side, Leela smiled. "I'm glad you're here, Dad."

"Tanha wishes she could be here too but had to perform emergency surgery." He whispered to her, "She said she will see you soon."

Leela winked at him then looked over to Aurora. "Any other special guest stars I should know about?"

"No." She gestured to Sid. "I didn't even know about him. We ran into each other in the parking lot."

"She means that metaphorically," he said. "I would not want anything to happen to Aurora or chickpea."

Was there a more serious man on the planet? Leela didn't think so. "Okay, then. Ready to get hitched in the eyes of the law?"

Aurora kissed her on the cheek and smudged the lipstick away with her thumb. "Absolutely."

#

"So, you two are now legally wed," the adoption attorney said from behind his highly lacquered, grand desk.

"Yes, we are." Aurora held up her left hand, showing her ring. The ring which had gotten tighter in the two weeks since their wedding. Her pregnancy swelling was out of control now. Pretty soon she'd have to wear the ring as a necklace to join the other one and her ankles would be completely gone. "Although, we had a private ceremony in September."

"So, now it's very real," he said with a smile.

Leela shifted in her seat and gripped the end of her arm rest. "I assure you, it was very, very real the first time."

Ever since she and Leela had their official courthouse ceremony, suddenly everyone had treated their relationship seriously. It didn't matter that they had been together for years. Lived together for years. Had committed to each other in private. Apparently, that wasn't enough to show society they were a serious couple.

He had the decency to slink back in his seat a little. "Let's get down to business then. You—" he gestured to Leela "—are interested in adopting—" he gestured to Aurora's bump "—her baby."

"No, that's not correct," Leela said in an even tone. "I *want* to adopt *our* baby. There is no 'interested'. I'm not picking out a car. I did that already, and it is very safe."

Aurora smiled sweetly. She loved it when Leela broke out the butch. "You see, without Leela there would be no chickpea, so this, much like our legal marriage, is simply a formality because we continue to live in a patriarchal system that denies *us* the ability to parent *our* child in the way *we* see fit."

"Be that as it may," he said, "at this point there's not much you can do since there isn't a child to adopt yet. You'll have to wait for little. . . Do you have a name?"

"No," they both said.

"But Okpik-Bakshi is the last name," Leela said. "So, we got something going for us."

"I suppose. My recommendation is that you place me on retainer for when the time comes. You'll want baby Okpik-Bakshi's adoption handled ASAP in case something were to happen to Aurora."

"That's why we're here in the first place!" Leela said.

"There's no need to raise your voice," he said in a patronizing tone.

Both he and Leela stared each other down. Clearly, she'd have to be the cooler head. "I'm sure you can give us something to work with before chickpea is born."

He started to laugh. "Chickpea? You've nicknamed it chickpea." He cackled some more.

Aurora felt the heat rise from her chest and to her face. No one made fun of their baby. "We're so done here. Let's go, Leela."

He *tsked*. "You're making a mistake."

Aurora stood. "And you're not making money off us." She stormed out of the office. Her arm shoved open the doors as she exited the building and stomped her way into the mini-mall parking lot. When Leela placed a gentle hand on her back, she turned. "Can you believe that guy? Such an asshole!"

"I was thinking cockwaffle, but asshole is good too." Leela put her arms around Aurora. "I'm sorry we went there. Usually, my farmers' market crowd is better with their recommendations."

"It's not your fault." Aurora pulled away and kissed her. "I just want this part to be easy, you know. Chickpea has been the happiest of happy accidents, and all I want is for her to be both of ours in the eyes of everyone. It's not fair we have to jump through all these hoops."

Leela wiped away a tear Aurora hadn't known was there. "I know, sweets. But it's a hoop that adds extra protection for chickpea. Or baby Okpik-Bakshi."

"I know. It's just hard."

"Can you take the rest of the day off? I think both you and chickpea need it. Plus, I'm getting a little cramped in my brain space."

Aurora felt chickpea's extra twitches and closed her eyes. "I'm sorry, I didn't even think about that. But yeah, I'm at a good spot to come home. I think Bobby knows what he's doing for the rest of the day."

"Good. Then I'll take some time off too and use the rest of the day to spoil you and chickpea."

Leela was a perfect partner, and she would be an absolutely perfect parent. "Lead the way."

#

"A table for two, please?" Leela asked the hostess with a smile. "Outside."

Aurora was certain she had the same bewildered expression as the hostess from Leela's request. The region wasn't experiencing the brutal cold of winter, but spring had yet to kick in. "Um, isn't it still a little cold for outside dining?"

"Is it?" Leela asked pleasantly. "There's not a cloud in the sky. I know you're not cold, because you hardly ever are, and I have a jacket. Plus, there is no one else out there. It'll be like our own private dining experience on the river."

Those were all excellent points. "Can we, please?" Aurora asked the hostess.

"Sure, go to any table you'd like. Your server will be out shortly."

They followed their hostess outside to an elevated deck that was only a few feet away from the river rushing over the rocks and the smell of pine from the trees on either side of the water filling the crisp air. She felt more relaxed already.

Leela pulled out a teak chair at their table for her.

"Thank you," Aurora said as she sat. "You're very chivalrous."

"Just wait until later when I use my jacket to cover a puddle for you."

Aurora laughed and reached for Leela's hand on the table, who took it with a small squeeze. "This was a great idea. I love that it's just us right now."

Leela cocked her head and pursed her lips. "You do realize we live together, right?"

Aurora chuckled. "You know what I mean. There's this extra thrill because we're playing hooky."

"You know, I never did that and always wanted to know what it's like."

"It's like this. Except I'm not terrified my parents are going to find out."

"You played hooky when you were in school?" Leela asked, clearly surprised by Aurora's adolescent behavior. "How am I just learning about this now?"

"I like to keep some of the mystery alive in our relationship."

Leela *tsked* with a shake of her head. "You are a bad, bad boo bear. What made you skip school?"

"I only did it once. We had a substitute teacher for gym class. As soon as attendance was taken and we went outside for whatever it was, my girlfriend and I went back in, changed, and then left for the movies. It was the last class of the day anyway."

"Was there making out in the locker room?"

Aurora grinned. "Why do you want to know?"

"Because I can't be outdone by your high school sweetie."

Aurora knew Leela was playing up her jealousy for a mild ego boost. "We conceived a cosmic love child together and I married you, so I'm pretty sure you can't be outdone by anyone."

Leela sighed with a grin. "I do love being reminded of that," she said as their waiter brought out their linen-wrapped utensils and wine glasses filled with ice water. "We could go to the movies after this, if you wanted?"

Aurora smiled again. She felt that she hadn't stopped doing that since they had arrived. "I think that could be fun. What's playing?"

"I have no clue."

"If you like space opera sci-fi, there's one I saw last week that's pretty good," their waiter said and got out his miniature notepad. "But it's *really* long."

"Sweets, you game?"

"I am." Every minute that passed lifted her spirits from their disastrous time at the lawyer's office more and more. She looked up at their waiter. "Do you think your bartender could fix a mocktail of seltzer water, some kind of juice, and basil or mint muddled in?"

"I'm sure we can fix up something like that."

"I'll have the same," Leela said. "And we'll share a plate of truffle fries to start."

When he left, Aurora grinned at the thought of them recreating some of their Hawaiian experience by the Oregon river. To a stranger, it probably looked like two women having a bite to eat in the middle of the day. Of course, she rarely felt like a stranger in their smallish town. When Aurora had moved three years ago, she had felt excited about the new opportunities a new town offered, but part of her had never thought she'd have a family and community outside of Michigan. Yet here she was with both.

"You have a sentimental face," Leela said.

"It's hard not too these days." Aurora took a sip of water. "Okay, now it's your turn."

"My turn for what?"

"Tell me something I don't know about you."

"You know all the important stuff."

Aurora rolled her eyes. "I'd like to think so, but I'd like to know a cute, little Leela fun fact. Something completely random, like how you just learned about me playing hooky."

"Can you at least give me a theme?"

She supposed she could show Leela a little mercy given the broadness of her request. "Okay, the theme is. . . musical theater."

"Come on! Seriously?"

Aurora tipped her head back and laughed at her annoyed reaction. "Yes, I want a Leela fun fact involving musical theater."

Leela sighed and then looked off into the river like the answer was going to come floating by on a raft. "Okay, but I don't know if this counts because it's hearsay and also a movie."

"Movie counts. Hearsay?" Aurora folded her arms across her chest and took on the most serious look she could muster. "Maybe I'll allow it."

"Okay, the story goes that when I was a baby and would cry at night, my dad would sing *Somewhere Over the Rainbow* to me until I fell asleep."

"Aw," Aurora said with her hand over her heart. Sid could be such a sweetheart sometimes. "That's a really nice fun fact."

"Yeah," Leela drawled with a smile. "I just learned that. I guess he's an okay guy after all. But I really wish I would have known these stories when I was younger. I would have thought they had more compassion."

"Alright." Their waiter came back with two highball glasses of pink, bubbly liquid. "This is what we invented, but if you want a second round, I don't think we'll be able to make it again. Fries will be a few more min— Holy Moses!" He pointed on the other side of the river. "Do you see that eagle?" He dug into his pants pocket and took out his phone.

"Oh, my Gods!" Leela said, but she then secretly smiled at Aurora while he snapped several pictures.

"Do you mind if I go in and show them this before I take the rest of your order? I don't want it to fly away."

He reminded Aurora of a grown version of Logan. "Sure, go ahead."

They watched him scurry inside while Leela held her drink up. "To Scout. May he be swift when the need calls for it and not fly into any windows."

"To Scout," Aurora said and clinked her glass against Leela's. "Do you want to see what times that movie is playing?"

#

Aurora lay naked on the ground in a humid, black void. She uncurled her body and stood. "Hello!" she yelled with hands cupped around her mouth. Her voice echoed off walls she could not see.

A colorful stream of lights surrounded and pulsed around her. Then disappeared.

She interpreted the sign as a form a communication. "Do you understand me?"

The lights returned, as did a loud, "Whooom!"

Aurora dropped to a knee and covered her ears. The powerful noise was deafening and caused the bones in her body to vibrate. When the rattling stopped, a warm liquid surrounded her feet. Then her ankles. Her knees. Her hips.

She wasn't frightened, and by the time she felt the mystery bath around her shoulders, she lifted her feet and floated on her back. From above, a dancing rainbow of lights greeted her eyes. A dark silhouette of a hand, foot, and rope-like object occasionally overlaid the wavy prism.

"Oh," Aurora drawled. "So, this is what it's like for you."

Whooom!

#

Aurora bolted upright in her seat. She looked around the mostly vacant movie theater, saw the credits rolling, and Leela looking at her with an amused grin. She wasn't surprised she fell asleep given how tired pregnancy had made her, but it was still embarrassing she had dozed off on their date. "I'm so sorry. How much of the movie did I miss?"

"Not too much, and you saw most of the good parts."

"Which good parts did I miss?" she asked as they gathered their things to leave the theater.

"The ragtag group of pseudo-soldiers broke into the mother ship. I'm surprised that didn't wake you up, it was really loud."

"Did it by any chance sound like '*whooom*'?"

"Oh, you did catch part of it then?"

Aurora shook her head. "No, I don't think I did, but," she patted her baby bump, "chickpea did. She told me."

Leela nodded. "Sound does travel faster in a liquid."

CHAPTER FIFTEEN

"GUESS WHAT I did?" Leela asked while she stood over Aurora, who lounged on the couch in her pajamas, enjoying a leisurely Sunday morning. "Go ahead, guess!"

Aurora put down her e-reader and bit her bottom lip. "Um, you finished putting together the changing table?"

"No! Guess again," Leela said as she bounced back-and-forth on her heels.

"Um, you decided my names for chickpea are better than yours," Aurora said with a smile.

"Absolutely not!" Leela grinned from ear to ear. "I got brunch reservations for today at Breakfast in Bend!"

"You did not!" Aurora said, wide-eyed and practically drooling.

"I most certainly did. Since chickpea'll be here soon, I want to take you out on a few proper dates. Our reservation isn't until noon, so you still have some reading-pajama time between now and then."

"Come here, you." Aurora grabbed her hand to pull her closer for a kiss.

"Nothing but the best for you." Leela turned to leave but stopped. "Maybe wear that bluish dress with the flowers?"

"I have to dress up?"

"Please," Leela begged. "I'll dress nice too. It'll be like a real date."

"We went on a date after the meeting with. . . What did you call him?"

"Cock McWaffle, Esquire. But this will be even more fun because of the nostalgia aspect. It's where we first met in real life. What do you say?"

"Okay," Aurora said somewhat skeptically. "If you insist."

"I do insist! Now, I'm going to work on that changing table." Leela left for the nursery and got out her phone to text Tonya. *She bought it!*

Finally, Leela could breathe. The last month had been exhausting. And ridiculous. Not because of the mystical weird, but because of the tradition of marriage and babies. The courthouse wedding and meeting with the adoption attorney were one thing, but the coup de grâce to her patience was planning the surprise baby shower.

After trying to play nice with Tonya, Ani, and her Mom, she had to quit. If there was one more conversation about color palette or invitation wording, she was going to have a full out meltdown. What she could do was get Aurora to the shower. If she had to do more, she would hurt someone, and going to jail would only complicate their lives.

To her surprise, everyone was relieved she stepped away.

Once they left the house, they spent a few minutes discussing new attorneys, but once Aurora's stomach rumbled that topic vanished.

"I think I want the stuffed French toast," Aurora said. "But I could really go for some salty hash browns. What are you getting?"

Leela wanted to say, 'Everything from the buffet and a trip to the dessert bar,' but she settled with, "Pancakes."

"Mmm. Those sound good too."

It really was amazing that they could carry on a discussion about food for as long as they did.

Leela held the door open for Aurora and went to the hostess. "Reservation for Bakshi-Okpik, please."

"Right this way." The hostess led them through the restaurant and to a side room.

Aurora leaned into her ear. "I didn't know they had tab—"

"Surprise!" the crowd of fifteen yelled, which included Aurora's friends from work, a few from her bike club and spin class, Fiona, Jill, and her mom. Oh, yeah, and her mom holding up a tablet showing Ani on video chat.

"Are you surprised?" Tanha asked.

"Very. This is incredible! Hi, Mom." Aurora waved at the screen.

"Hi, boo bear."

Aurora hugged Tanha and took the tablet. "Thank you so much!"

"You're welcome," Tanha said with a laugh. "We had to find a way for Ani to be here."

"Oh, this is the absolute best!" Aurora took her virtual mother around the room to meet her friends.

While Aurora and Ani exchanged pleasantries with the others, her own mother leaned into her ear. "Aurora isn't crying. You said there would be happy tears. You didn't give it away, did you?"

"No, Mom. I was very cool about the whole thing." Leela gave Aurora an impish grin when she turned to her and gladly accepted a kiss on the cheek in thanks.

Tonya walked over to them with a golden bottle in her hand.

Leela smacked her lips together and held the beer Tonya handed her reverently. "Thank you."

"You're welcome. Now, if you don't mind, we're going to steal your wife for food and stupid fun."

The beer was an omen. The party went off without incident. Leela didn't mind making small talk about life, work, chickpea's still undetermined legal name, or how cute Aurora looked. But it was still exhausting.

Aurora had occasionally directed a tired smile toward her, but there was no doubt she was a fan of the event. Especially the dessert bar.

Jill earned all the points for suggesting both the bar and that Aurora should open the gifts at home. Apparently, people who didn't get the gifts weren't into oohing and aahing for over an hour.

Once the party wrapped four hours later—so many games—Leela made several trips from the truck and into the house again, each time with her hands full of pastel-baby-animal-cartoon-cutesy wrapped presents. On her last trip, she rested her back against the door and closed her eyes. Finally, she was at home. The place where she had a comfy bed. The land of naps. Maybe she could squeeze in some shut-eye before Aurora wanted to open the gifts.

"I'm so hopped up on sugar," Aurora said as she beamed a crazed smile. "Can we do the presents now?"

At least her nap dream died a quick death. "Okay. But I need caffeine first."

When Leela came back with her coffee, Aurora was already seated on the couch with a mountain of gifts surrounding her. It was going to take forever. But as long as they went about the gifts in an organized way, they could finish in a reasonable amount time. She just had to be patient and understanding. However, it was difficult to be understanding when she didn't know what Aurora pulled out of a bag or box. Leela had no idea that babies came with such complicated accessories. There were several different suction devices; a few different types of seats for the house, bath, and car; and clothes she didn't know how to put on.

She really should have read the registry more carefully.

"Who is that one from?" Leela asked, her finger ready to snap a photo of Aurora holding the gift.

Aurora lifted the lavender tag on the present. "Portland Cardiology Associates."

Leela rolled her eyes then watched Aurora open the package. She tore the pastel wrapping paper off the box and held up the product with a smile. Leela took the picture, which would be included with their thank you message. "What the hell is that?"

"Not sure." Aurora flipped the box over and read the synopsis. "It's a baby wipe warmer."

"No way. My child will not grow up coddled. Coddling will just lead to chickpea growing up soft."

"Okay, Tanha."

Leela narrowed her eyes. She was sleepy, stressed out, and was just compared to her mother. "That was a low blow."

"I think it was just low enough," Aurora retorted with a wince and then leaned back into the couch cushion to rub her swollen belly.

Aurora's discomfort made Leela push her next retort to the side. "Chickpea's foot reaching for your spine again?"

"Something like that. I don't see how she can get bigger, but I have another six weeks!"

Once Aurora jutted out her lower lip in a dramatic pout, Leela put her phone down, walked to the couch, and directed her attention to the roundness under Aurora's navy blue, floral print dress. "Listen up, chickpea. I know you're comfortable and loving life in the Mama Roar hot tub, but you have to watch the poking. She's not tough like you and me." Leela looked up with a smirk, pleased to see that Aurora's lips were pursed and eyes squinted.

The teasing was back on.

"Not tough? I'll show you not tough." Aurora repositioned herself so she straddled Leela's lap. "I've got you pinned now."

"This is definitely the worst possible position I could ever be in," Leela said dryly and slid her fingers over the outside of Aurora's thighs, feeling the slight braided pattern of her tights. "I hate everything about this."

"You," Aurora lowered her head down, "are such a smart ass." She closed the distance between them and grazed her lips against Leela's.

Leela couldn't pinpoint it, but there was something about Aurora that had made her even more desirable. Her breasts and hips were fuller, and her skin and hair shined with life. She supposed Aurora's heart was bigger too. Every loving personality quirk that caused Leela to fall in love with her was amplified.

When Leela felt one of Aurora's hands grip the hair at the base of her neck, she pressed her lips firmly against Aurora's. A warm rush flowed from her mouth and down. The combination of love and arousal intoxicated her, stimulated her more than any coffee ever could. "How about— Ow!" Leela's hand went from Aurora's ass cheek to her temple. She grimaced and grunted as an intense irritant, like ten thousand nails against a chalkboard, filled her brain.

Chickpea was not happy.

"Might want to prepare yourself," Leela warned. "This is a big one."

Aurora's face skewed in confusion and then to one of pain. She squeezed the cushion beside Leela's head, causing her to sink deeper into the couch.

Leela shook off the vicious rattling inside her mind until she was able to guide Aurora into a reclined position on the couch. The brain rattle stopped, but Aurora's face still twisted in agony. Over the last week, chickpea had been putting up a fight with a high frequency, but it was nothing like this.

Leela tried to embody their yoga teacher the best she could. "Look at me and try to breathe through it."

Aurora's eyes opened, and she inhaled deeply thorough her nose then exhaled a controlled stream of air through her mouth.

After several cycles of rhythmic breaths, Leela took Aurora's hands. "You're doing so great. Even Scout thinks so."

Aurora cracked a smile. "Do you see him?"

Leela craned her neck and, through the window, saw their mysterious eagle perched on a branch. "Yep. You and chickpea have all the protectors right now." She gave Aurora's hand a final pat. "Is the pain subsiding?"

"Yeah." Aurora tried to sit up but gave up and leaned back once more. "Now it's just an aftershock."

It still felt like pieces of Leela's brain tissue had broken off and were trying to escape her skull. She had never experienced anything so intense before, nor did she think Aurora had. "Was that a kick or a cramp?"

"I don't know what that was, but I don't need anymore." Aurora began to awkwardly get up from the couch. "I think I peed a little. I'll be right back."

As Aurora got up to leave, Leela stood. "We need to figure out what just happened! If you go into labor—"

"I'm over a month away from any real signs of labor. And everyone says labor feels like an intense menstrual cramp. I didn't feel that."

"So, it was a kick."

"No. It was like chickpea was grabbing my uterus like it was a blanket and trying to pull it over herself."

"Whoa."

"Yeah, it was terrible. Now, can I change my underwear? I have a very non-sexy wet spot."

"Oh. Um, yeah."

It might not have been labor, but it worried Leela. Chickpea's length fell in the upper range, but Leela didn't understand why chickpea would be that uncomfortable. She picked up her phone and followed Aurora to the bedroom. "I think we should call Fiona."

"I think you're worrying over nothing. Pregnancy is uncomfortable. I think maybe mine is just a little bit more than others." Aurora finished pulling off her tights then gestured to their window. "Scout isn't worried. If he was, he'd be flapping all about and trying to break through the glass like when I burned my hand taking the pizza out of the oven the other day."

Leela glanced through the window. In the trees, the eagle stood still and silent as he kept watch over their home. "I really don't think we should use a bird's agitation level to determine medical advice." Leela pulled out her phone.

"What are you doing?"

"Calling Fiona." She held the phone to her ear. "This is too serious to brush off. I love you and chick—"

"Is everything okay?" Fiona asked as her greeting.

"Hi, Fiona. Sorry to call, but Aurora just had some intense pain and I'm worried. She said it felt like chickpea was folding her organs."

"I did not say that!" Aurora whispered with an edge and yanked a pair of underwear out of a drawer.

Fiona made a few thoughtful sounds. "Did it go away?"

"Yeah, after we did some of that yoga breathing."

"Probably just false labor."

"This soon?" Leela waved Aurora over and put the phone on speaker.

"Braxton Hicks contractions can start as early as the second trimester. I'm surprised Dr. Aguilar didn't warn you this would happen."

"She did," Aurora said. "But this. . . I thought it was supposed to be like a bad menstrual cramp."

Fiona uttered another *hmm*. "And this was more severe than that? Any discharge?"

"Aurora peed herself."

"Leela!" she said with a light arm smack. "Not a lot. Just a dribble, really. Besides, I'm pretty sure Fiona means vaginal, and no. There was none of that."

"That's good. Maybe it's just a reaction from all that food and sugar. I suggest you mark the time it happened. If it happens again within the next half hour, call me and I'll come over. If not, you're in the clear and can focus your efforts on finishing the nursery."

Leela harrumphed. Damn that changing table with its nonsensical instructions and janky pre-drilled holes. Thirty minutes assembly time her ass. "Well, thanks for being on call and we'll touch base if anything else happens."

"And thanks for coming to the shower," Aurora added.

"I had a great time. *Loved* the dessert bar. You two take care."

"Same goes. Bye." Leela disconnected the phone and saw Aurora clad in her bra and taco-themed pregnancy undies. She and chickpea were fine, but she couldn't help but be concerned.

Aurora stood with her hands of her hips. "What? It didn't make sense to keep on my dress."

Leela went to her and wrapped her arms around her. "I need a hug."

Whatever annoyance or tension Aurora may have had seemed gone. She squeezed Leela gently as they rocked back and forth. Leela thought Aurora would have comforted her forever if she needed it.

Gradually, Leela pulled away and moved her hands to Aurora's bare skin bump.

"Thank you for calling Fiona. That was the right thing to do."

Leela nodded. "I don't know if you've noticed, but I take yours and chickpea's safety very seriously. Which is why I guess I should finish putting together the changing table. I don't want it collapsing." She peered out the window and barely made out the tell-tale silhouette of the hooked beak and folded wings. "That'll really piss off Scout."

"We definitely don't want that." Aurora embraced her once more. "I love you so, so much."

Leela stifled a laugh. "You want to finish unwrapping the presents, don't you?"

"Can we?"

#

After a diagram, a few analogies, and, ultimately, a complete redo of the lesson about the financials checklist for sustainability business plans, Aurora felt that Bobby was finally catching on to the system she had created. She deserved an award for her patience.

A reward in the form of dessert.

Aurora sat at the breakroom table and took a brief moment to admire the beauty of her toasted coconut caramel brownie. She cut off a piece and moaned at the gooey sweetness that coated the inside of her mouth.

"You know, if you nuke that, you could make your brownie even more decadent," Tonya said as she poured a coffee.

"You're right!" Aurora pushed herself up and took her treat to the microwave. "Did you have fun at the baby shower?"

Tonya casually leaned against the counter, warming her hands with her coffee. "I did, and I was able to snag a few minutes with Leela. Wowzas, does she have a lot on her mind."

If she only knew. "She's juggling a lot of different balls right now. But thank you for having mercy on her when it came to planning the shower. That gave her one less thing to worry about."

"As soon as the topic of games was broached, you could tell she had hit her breaking point. But she did the most important thing, which was getting you there without spoiling it."

"That she did," Aurora said, hoping her white lie was undetectable.

Aurora deduced they were going to a surprise baby shower the moment Leela suggested they have lunch and dress up because they wouldn't be able to do that once they had a newborn. Leela had never once suggested 'dressing up' when they went out. However, going along with the surprise was fun, and it was cute to watch Leela try to be calm and collected about it. "The party was perfect, thank you very much, because I know you were the one who coordinated most of it since both Mom and Tanha live away."

Tonya waved off the praise. "Social media makes it easy. I have to thank you for whoever came up with the idea of you and Leela opening your presents at home. We dodged that bullet." Tonya took a sip of coffee as the microwaved beeped. "Hopefully, you had fun at home opening everything."

"It was, and so many people got us the cutest things." Aurora took the brownie out of the microwave, brought the plate to her nose, and smelled the warm coconut chocolate. "I know chickpea will love the duckie booties you got her."

"As the thank you note and picture of you holding the booties by your bump suggested. Any surprise gifts?"

"A few. The biggest surprise came in the form of chickpea. She was definitely causing a ruckus later on yesterday, but Fiona said it was false labor and to just monitor her movements."

"Oh," Tonya said with her brow pinched. "Has there been anything else since then?"

With a mouthful of sticky, warm brownie, Aurora shook her head. "Nothing that raises any red flags. Just the usual kicks to the bladder and— Gah!" She grimaced as chickpea seemed to do a pull-up on her rib. "It's just the usual associated discomforts," she said with glassy eyes.

"This doesn't seem usual."

"Welcome to my wo-ah!" Aurora dropped her brownie-covered fork to the ground. The sensation of knives being shot from her womb radiated out and stole her breath. Her upper thighs and seat felt warmer. She tried to speak but couldn't form words through the pain.

Tonya placed a comforting hand on Aurora's shoulder. Her eyes went from kind to fearful as soon as her gaze dropped.

Aurora lowered her gaze to where Tonya stared. A dark red stain grew on her gray maternity pants.

Her eyelids were heavy and she couldn't find the right words. "You need to—"

"Call 9-1-1!" Tonya yelled.

#

Instead of floating effortlessly, Aurora stood with her muscles rigid in the warm water of the natural pool. She watched the colorful lights above her flash with no discernable pattern instead of the graceful swaying dance she was accustomed to. There was no silhouette of chickpea in the distance.

Something wasn't right.

"Chickpea, are you okay?"

The lights continued their chaotic blinking, and the only sound was a distant rumbling.

There were no obvious signs of danger, but that didn't stop Aurora's throat from tightening and pressure inside her chest from building. "It's okay," she said, but she was unsure if it was to reassure chickpea or herself. "I know you're here but can't find me. I'll come to you."

Aurora inhaled deeply before she went under. The sparkly surface lights filtered through the water and provided enough ambient light for her to see chickpea. She was tiny and curled with a mat of hair on her head and fine fuzz covering her body. A small, irregu-

larly shaped patch of darker skin was on her shoulder blade. At the far end of the pool, she kicked with her scrawny leg at what looked like a curved wall. Like they were inside a water balloon.

That was new. Unless...

Instead of the lights, the wall, or chickpea, Aurora focused on herself. She closed her eyes. The stagnant air in her lungs burned and her limbs felt like they defied gravity. That was when she felt the pull and the searing heat at her center. Aurora's hands clutched at her abdomen as though she could stop the ripping. But she couldn't.

She waited for the surge of pain to dissipate into smaller ripples and then waved her hands about, hoping to capture chickpea's attention, but her curled body continued to face the wall.

Chickpea kicked again and the pain returned.

This was a safe, warm place. Why chickpea wanted to change that, she didn't know, but it was dangerous for both of them. When chickpea drew back her tiny leg, poised to kick again, Aurora yelled, "No!" Her air bubble with the muffled scream inside floated away.

The wall slowly indented as chickpea's toes made contact. Then, chickpea's foot went through. The warm water around Aurora started to cool, but she hardly noticed the temperature change, what with the feeling of being ripped apart from the inside.

Chickpea turned, and eyes identical to Leela's stared at her. Aurora didn't understand the silent message she tried to convey, but when chickpea closed her eyes, Aurora did the same.

#

Aurora heard a commotion around her as though she were under water and people were at a pool party. Syllables in slow motion. Blurry shapes and colors moving. Her body lifted as though it were floating. Everything was so relaxing, and she was so, so tired. Surely, she could just close her eyes for a little nap.

"Aurora!"

She was suddenly more alert but even more confused. Loud sounds surrounded her. There was light pressure over her nose and mouth, and as her head lolled to the side, she saw a tube in her arm.

"Aurora!" Tonya's smiling face hovered over hers. "That's good. Look at me. You're in an ambulance. I called Leela and she'll be here as soon as she can."

"Chickpea...?"

"Is fine, and that's why we need to get you to the hospital ASAP, because we want to make sure everything stays that way."

Aurora sensed the activity around her increase once again, and a change in motion. The high-pitched sound stopped, and a bright light and cold air struck her senses.

"Aurora Okpik-Bakshi," said a raspy female voice she didn't recognize. "Thirty-four weeks pregnant, no significant medical history. Membrane ruptures. Possible uterine bleed."

"We got her from here." A bearded face came into view. "Hi, Aurora. Can you squeeze my hand for me?"

"Huh?"

He held her hand up so she could see. "Aurora, please squeeze my hand."

Even though the lights overhead were zipping by, she used most of her energy to focus on that one task.

"That's great," he said to her, but then looked away. "Do you have any idea what caused this?"

"No. She was eating a brownie and telling me she had false labor yesterday."

"No falls?"

"No. She said chickpea—her baby—was poking at her."

"Okay." The doctor's face came back into view. "We're going to take good care of you and chickpea now."

CHAPTER SIXTEEN

TREES WITH NEWLY emerging buds whizzed by Leela as Keith drove her to the hospital, but not fast enough. "Would you step on it!" Leela commanded.

"I'm going nearly twice the limit. If I go faster then I'll definitely get pulled over and you'll be even later getting to the hospital."

"Then let me drive!"

Keith shook his head but kept his gaze glued to the road. "No way. You basically passed out after you clutched your head, and then when you stopped speaking gibberish, you started freaking out! Which makes sense based on the call from Aurora's boss, except it doesn't make sense!" Keith stopped at the signal light and looked over to Leela. "How did you know Aurora was in trouble?"

"Spousal intuition." When Leela and Aurora promised to not tell anyone about the link with chickpea, they meant anyone. However, the visual of Keith's jaw clenching under his thick stubble made her briefly reconsider. "For a few months now, the weird brainwave thing that happened to me when I was in my coma made a resurgence of sorts."

"Are you telling me that your psychically linked to Aurora again?"

Lying protected chickpea. "Yes."

"So, when Aurora's in pain, you're in pain?"

"Yes. And she was in a shit ton of pain so that's why we need to move our asses and get to the hospital." Leela's back pushed into the seat as he increased their speed. "Thank you."

"You two..." He let the idea hang. "So, what do you feel now?"

Leela focused on the pocket of her mind where chickpea had resided for the past few months. There was nothing. No tickle. No scratches. No ripples. The emptiness reached for her heart and squeezed. "I don't feel anything. Why don't I feel anything?" she asked in a panic.

"Calm down. And actually, maybe why you don't feel anything is because Aurora doesn't feel *anything*."

"What are you talking about?"

"Well, unexpected or difficult childbirth isn't uncommon, so maybe they gave her a tranquilizer."

The logical part of Leela wanted to believe that more than anything, but she knew it wasn't true.

"I know you're worried sick," Keith continued. "But they were able to get Aurora to the hospital in five minutes. That's a real good thing."

"I know you're right, but..." Leela pressed her palms to her eyes. "Can you stay?"

"Of course, I'll stay! And before you know it Jill will come, probably with that Fiona lady. We can all be your rocks, because you're going to need to be Aurora's."

Her abused heart paired with her turned stomach. How would she be able to explain what happened? If something happened to chickpea, Aurora would blame herself. She would have to do everything in her power to ensure that she was there for Aurora.

#

The hospital stood in the distance, dwarfing the other building alongside it, and a black shape swooped in circles around it.

"What the hell is that?" Keith asked. "It's not flying like a buzzard."

"It's an eagle."

"Eagles're all over the damn place these days. Got that big one at your house that's been hanging out since fall."

"The fall? You're sure?"

"Sure am. I remember thinking how it was just after Thanksgiving and how 'Merican it was and. . . Never mind." He headed into town, and once they approached the immediate signs for the hospital, Keith decreased his speed to a crawl. "I'm going to pull up outside the ER and let you jump out."

Leela nodded but didn't wait until the car was at a full stop to unbuckle her seatbelt and get out of the truck. Her feet danced as they searched for sure footing after the abrupt change in motion, but she found her balance and ran to the emergency room front desk.

The woman behind the desk looked at her curiously. "Ms. Bakshi?"

She had been so focused on getting to the hospital, she hadn't planned her next steps, but she knew she had to say something. However, to do that, she needed to speak through the rawness that had begun in her throat. "I need to find Aur—" She fought her hardest battle yet to keep her emotions in check. She paused to gain control of her breathes and thought of what Keith had said in the car to comfort her. "I need to find Aurora Okpik-Bakshi. She's pregnant and came in about twenty minutes ago."

The desk nurse nodded and typed furiously on her keyboard. "She's in the OR, fourth floor, wing C. Check in with the desk there and they'll be able to give you more information. Stairs are probably faster than the elevator."

Once the words were spoken, Leela sprinted to the stair entrance and raced up the steps. She ignored the dull ache in her thigh that started once she reached the third floor. She focused on positive thoughts, like Aurora holding chickpea for the first time or when they brought chickpea home. That was the only way she'd get through this.

Leela opened the heavy steel door and found the large waiting room at the end of the hall.

She scanned for the desk.

"Leela!"

She turned and saw Tonya coming toward her from the far corner. "How is she? They! How are they?"

"Since I'm not family they haven't told me anything," Tonya said as she guided Leela passed the children's activity area and to the desk. "The *family* is here now," Tonya said sternly.

"I'm Leela Bakshi-Okpik. I'm looking for Aurora Ok—"

"Just one minute." The registration nurse stood and whispered to a man with rosy cheeks in a long white medical coat.

He appeared to listen very carefully then walked briskly to the desk, tablet in hand. "Please follow me."

She nodded absently and took the first few steps but paused. She didn't want to do this alone. "Can Tonya come too?"

"Yes. That's fine."

Tonya put her arm around Leela's shoulders as they walked to a small room. It wasn't a waiting area. It wasn't really a lounge either. But the tissues on every table indicated that this wasn't a continuation of the children's play area or where much good news was shared.

He gestured to the chairs. "Have a seat while I check her status."

Leela continued to stand and took the tissue Tonya offered her while his finger tapped different parts of the tablet screen.

He flashed a bright smile.

"Things are okay?" Leela asked with a crack in her voice.

"Baby girl Okpik-Bakshi was delivered via caesarian and is currently in the NICU. Despite the premature conditions, she's doing well. I wonder if this is right," he mumbled quietly and poked at the screen some more. "Amazing. She's doing *very well*, in fact."

"Praise Jesus," Tonya said and hugged Leela from the side.

Despite her high intelligence, Leela couldn't believe it. Chickpea was here. She was no longer an idea or mysterious being. She was a person. And Leela was officially a mother. Aurora was a mother. "Aurora's okay?"

"Still in surgery. She's stable and will probably be out of surgery soon." His upturned smile reversed into a frown. "According to the notes, there was uterine bleeding, and the surgeon performed an emergency abdominal hysterectomy."

"They had to do that?"

He nodded. "There was profuse bleeding, based on the amount of blood they gave her. The procedure saved her life."

An image of Aurora bleeding out on a cold table wouldn't leave her.

"She'll be okay, though?" Tonya asked.

"Yes. She'll most likely be in the hospital for a week to ten days and need several weeks to heal after that, but long-term she'll be fine."

Leela wiped away her tears with her sleeve. "She'll be okay," she muttered to herself. Leela felt a mixture of joy and sadness. Aurora narrowly escaped death, but she wasn't going to remember giving birth to chickpea or have the opportunity to carry again. How was she going to tell her that? Leela stood stunned, not sure of what to do next.

"When can Leela see her baby and Aurora?" Tonya asked.

"I can take her to the NICU right now, and the nurses can help you there. They'll also be able to tell you when Aurora's moved into the ICU and ready for visitors."

Leela felt like everything but her was in fast forward. There was too much to process in such a short time. So much to do, but she didn't want to delay seeing chickpea any longer. She started for the door.

"Leela!" Tonya said to grab her attention out of the fog. "Someone has to tell Aurora's parents."

New parts of her began to feel worse. She hadn't even stopped to think about calling anyone else. "You still have her and my mom's contact info from the baby shower?"

"Yeah."

At least she didn't have to rattle off twenty digits. "Good. Please let Ani and Niq know what's happened, and tell them I'll call after I see chickpea. I need to see chickpea," she said, barely keeping her composure.

"I know you do. I'll call your mom after that, okay?"

It had been decades since Leela felt the aching need for parental comfort. "Please."

Tonya nodded and smiled sadly. "Go meet your baby girl."

Grateful for every bit of help she could get, Leela hugged Tonya as tightly as she could possibly hold a person.

Tonya's pressed suit jacket bunched in her arms, but Leela knew she wouldn't care.

"Thank you. I don't know when I can update you, but I will as soon as I learn something."

"I know you will."

#

The doctor led the way to the NICU with a quick pace and looked to his side where Leela met his stride with quick steps. "I know you're scared for your baby and Aurora right now, but they really are in the best hands. When I take you to the NICU, they'll ask you a few questions—luckily, you're in the system already as Aurora's spouse—and a nurse will give you a wristband and tell you what to expect once you're inside."

With the warning of 'what to expect', Leela realized that with all of her science knowledge and doctor parents, the only thing she knew about NICUs was what she had seen on television. Premature babies were skinny, sometimes translucent beings, that could fit in the palm of your hand.

Once they reached the doors of the OB wing, the doctor—who's name she hadn't bothered to learn—went on his way.

Leela entered the doors and was face-to-face with another registration desk and waiting room. Although this waiting room had a positive energy, with its Mylar *Congratulations* balloons tied to different seats.

"Can I help you?" the woman at the desk asked with concern.

Leela realized she had been standing silently for several seconds. She didn't know these next steps. This wasn't in any book she read or a note on her whiteboard. Everything was improvised now. "I'm Leela Bakshi-Okpik. My wife, Aurora, had an emergency c-section and is still in surgery. I think you have my baby registered as baby Okpik-Bakshi." She had no idea how she managed to say those words coherently, but she did. "I'd like to see my baby now." Her voice dissolved into a series of sobs.

A stranger handed her several tissues, and she gave a nod of appreciation as tears streamed down her cheeks.

Everything that happened next had no guesswork on her part. In rapid succession, she was asked to provide a limited list of visitors, given a wristband, and prepped about chickpea's physical appearance. Chickpea was three pounds, had fine hair covering her, a nasogastric tube, a nasal cannula for oxygen, and several different monitors on her body.

But that wasn't the baby Leela pictured meeting.

The baby she imagined was plump, had a head full of dark hair, skin the same color as Aurora's, and screamed, with their umbilical cord still dangling, while she was placed on Aurora's chest by Fiona.

As Leela thoroughly washed her hands with soap and a bristle, she mentally prepared herself to meet her little girl for the first time. To replace her fantasy with reality.

She followed a square-jawed, broad-shouldered nurse whose name tag said Phillip inside the NICU.

The room held the sounds of a few tiny cries and looked more like a laboratory than a nursery. Three glass incubators lined each side of the room, and all had a series of monitors with dozens of wires attached.

Every baby area had a slightly reclined glider too. A nurse sat in one while she held a bundled baby in one arm and a large syringe connected to the tube in her other. It disappeared into the miniature baby's nose. Leela didn't want that to be chickpea's future, even if it was for a short time.

Phillip stopped and gestured to the incubator beside her with his wide, umber hand. "Here she is, Mom."

All Leela could see was a colorful polka dot sheet through the incubator glass. She took another step closer and then saw her. There was chickpea. Her frail little girl attached to numerous tubes and wires while she slept.

She was beautiful.

Leela hiccupped and promptly covered her mouth to cover the loud sob she knew would escape.

"I've been keeping her company since she arrived. She's been napping a few minutes now," Phillip said.

Leela's vision locked in on chickpea's fingers. They were as thin as the smallest twigs. Her skin was as thin as tissue paper.

How on earth could she hold—even touch—chickpea without hurting her? "I want to hold her, but I don't want to hurt her."

"I can help you with that." He went about unlocking the cabinet so that there was a hole for her hand to slip through.

She put her hand through and stroked the back of chickpea's hand with her finger. The pad of her fingertip was almost as large.

"Skin to skin contact is very important," Phillip said. "Whenever you are in here with her you should at the very least do what you are doing now. I'll leave you two be for a few minutes, then we should start the kangaroo care—that's when she lies on the skin of your chest."

"I didn't think I'd be allowed to do that. She's so small," Leela said without taking her gaze away. Of course, she didn't think she'd ever be able to take her gaze away for the rest of her life.

The nurse chuckled. "Normally, I'd agree, but your daughter has a lot in common with her mothers. She's very strong."

"Aurora's the strong one."

"I think you're tied."

Leela turned to him with a questioning look.

"I worked as a nurse in the ER when you came in a few years back. Nobody who worked here will ever forget your story, especially since you married the woman who saved you."

Leela turned back to chickpea, and this time, she touched the mop of black hair that snuck out underneath the white cap on her head. That part of the fantasy was right. As was the falling in love at first sight. "I need to know when I can see Aurora. It's important that she learns everything from me first and that I'm there when she wakes up."

"Absolutely. I'll check the system and then I'll start teaching you a few different things about how to care for your daughter. Even though it may be intimidating, you'll want to do that as much as you can. It's important for your bonding. Talk to her as much as you can, too." He turned and headed to the computer in the corner of the room.

Leela brought her second hand into the incubator to inspect chickpea's toes. She had no idea a pinky toe could be so small. "Rumor has it that you're small but mighty." Leela used her shoulder to wipe away her new tears. "I can't wait to tell your mama Roar all about you. She'll be very sad she couldn't see you right away, but I think we can make it up to her by snapping some pics."

Leela kept one hand on chickpea and took the phone out of her back pocket. As expected, she had five missed calls. "There's a lot of worried people out there, chickpea, but I think I should wait to give them the update until I talk to your mom. Okay, there's this thing we do in our culture where when you get your picture taken, you smile. I understand that you're sleeping and probably don't understand maternal commands yet, so I'm going to smile big for the both of us. Don't let my teeth shock you. You'll get them someday too."

She didn't care that her blood vessels dominated her eyes and her nose ran; there was too much happiness for her to let the memory slip away.

After a few selfies, Leela took dozens of photos where chickpea was the focus. Chickpea's hands, closed eyes, drying umbilical cord stub, feet, monitors, lips, and the crazed hair were all captured. She didn't know when Aurora would be able to see her, so she had to bring as much of the experience to her as possible.

As a finale, Leela started a recording with the camera pointed at herself. "Please don't be offended, but chickpea insists on sleeping, even though you're meeting her for the first time. Anyway, I'd like you to meet chickpea." Leela changed the camera's direction so the lens focused on her daughter. "Chickpea, I'd like you to meet your mama Roar." Leela used the gentlest touch to lift chickpea's wrist so she waved at the camera. The motion caused her to stir and grumble. "I guess she's more into fist bumps. I respect that. Wait, what's that, chickpea? Okay. Chickpea wants me to tell you that she's sorry for causing a ruckus and laying you out, because she loves you and can't wait to meet you."

Leela put the phone on the nearest ledge and looked up when Phillip came to her side.

"I'm sorry I'm late. I got caught up in something I only thought was going to take a few minutes, but I'm sure you know how it goes. Five minutes becomes twenty."

"Seriously?" Leela asked, shocked, then turned to chickpea. "That was one hell of a photoshoot we did."

"Time moves differently in the NICU. Ready for kangaroo care?"

"What about Aurora?"

"Out of surgery but still in recovery. The nurse assigned to her room is a friend, and I've asked that she call me when Aurora starts to come out of her anesthesia. Even when she comes out the first time, she'll be in and out of it for a while, so you'll be right by her side when she'll fully awake."

Leela knew enough to know that Aurora wouldn't be lucid right away. "Yeah, okay. What should I do to be a kangaroo?"

"There are special shirts you can put on in the top drawer there." He turned toward the nurse who finished feeding the baby. "Can you assist with the kangaroo placement?"

Leela heard a 'yes' as she looked through the draw of different shirts. She grabbed a size small and took it out of its packaging.

One of the nurses from the side of the room came closer. "If you're feeling modest, you can—"

Leela stripped off her flannel shirt.

"Never mind."

Leela donned her kangaroo shirt, which had a deep V that went past her breastbone and had an extra piece of material, like a cape, on the shoulder.

"Okay, now stay reclined in the glider. Phillip is going to be gathering the tubing while I place her on your chest and then secure her into place with the wrap at your shoulder. Okay?"

It seemed simple enough, but chickpea was so vulnerable to everything. "You're sure I won't hurt her? She can handle this?"

"She's more like a thirty-seven-week preemie than a thirty-four," Phillip said while he gathered chickpea's tubing and then opened the hatch. "She'll be just fine."

Leela's heart raced as she watched the nurse's hands remove chickpea from her safe, incubated home.

The change of environment caused chickpea to open her lips and release a soft cry.

The typical reaction calmed Leela. Chickpea might have been smaller, but she was just like other babies.

As the nurse hovered chickpea inches from her chest, Leela braced for impact. But nothing prepared her for the feeling of when chickpea was placed on her chest and secured with the blanket wrap.

"Are you comfortable?" Phillip asked.

Not only was Leela physically comfortable, but the part of her mind that had crawled with spiders or was squeezed had been transformed into something utopian. Like an injection of liquid Valium and joy straight into her brain. "Can I stay this way forever?"

"We usually start out with a few times a day, an hour at a time. After the first week, she'll gain weight, you'll feel more comfortable, and we can show you things like how to bathe and change her. Tomorrow you can try feeding her."

"Shouldn't Aurora feed her first?" Leela asked, craning her neck to try to get a glimpse of chickpea's face.

"She probably won't be physically able to come here for a few days. She'll have to pump in her room, once she's able, and then you or whomever can feed her with the breast milk."

Leela was still stuck on 'a few days.' Not only would she have to break the news of the hysterectomy, now she had to tell Aurora she couldn't see their daughter. There had to be something else she could do. "Can you take some pictures of me and chickpea?"

After he took a series of different pictures, he went to the other side of the room and returned with a full length mirror he positioned to face her. "This is so you can watch chickpea's face while you hold her. You can get a sense of what she likes and what she doesn't. I'm going to leave you two be. If you need anything, just give me a holler."

"We're great, thanks," she said without taking her gaze off the reflection of chickpea. The image of her holding her daughter would be engrained in her memories forever. A knowledge poured over her. This was her destiny. Chickpea would do great things, and it was up to her to see that she was protected until that time came.

Leela looked away from the reflection and kissed the top of chickpea's head.

#

Everything in Aurora's body felt fuzzy. She opened her eyes and was blinded. Was she outside? No, it looked like there was a window. Windows were an inside thing, like how her office was inside. She closed her eyes again. Was she at work? The last thing she remembered was. . . It wasn't work. She was with Tonya, and it was so loud.

But now it wasn't Tonya's faraway voice she heard. Whoever it was sounded almost exactly like Leela.

"She's down there now. Well, hospitals are her home away from home, I'm sure she's happier than a pig in shit."

Yeah, that was definitely Leela.

Wait? Hospital?

Aurora cracked her eyelids open again and tried to raise her hand to shield her eyes, but her arm weighed too much. "Hello," she called in the loudest voice she could muster.

"It sounds like Aurora might be awake again. We'll call you later. Bye, Ani."

Footsteps became louder and Leela's smiling face came into view. "Leela? Where am I?"

"Hey, sweets." Leela leaned over her and placed a kiss on her forehead. "You're in the hospital."

"Oh. Did I lose my hand? I can't move it or see it."

Leela picked up Aurora's hand to show it to her. "I promise you have both of your hands, and that you'll feel them again soon. You're coming out of your anesthesia, but I think you might actually stay awake this time."

"Oh." Aurora knew the word anesthesia, and what it was for, but it didn't make sense to her. "Why am I in the hospital?"

"There was a change of plans."

"What plan?"

"The family one. Chickpea decided to come early." She leaned down and kissed Aurora again. "Congratulations. You're a mommy," Leela said in a whisper.

She gave birth? Chickpea was here? "Are you sure?"
"Very sure. She's beautiful just like you, and tough like, well, both of us. A perfect combination."

"I thought I'd remember giving birth," Aurora said and then furrowed her brow. A face came into her memory. "Was Tonya with me when I went into labor?"

"Kind of. You were at work when chickpea slammed down her tiny fist and decided to break out. They brought you to the hospital, and according to Tonya, you slipped in and out of consciousness a few times. Does this make sense so far? Are you following me?"

"I. . . ah…" She was in the breakroom chatting with Tonya and eating a brownie. Then, there was pain.

Leela bowed her head down, rubbed her face, and sniffled loudly. "Once you were here, the doctors learned that the membrane around chickpea ruptured and you had a tear in your uterus. The only way to make sure you and chickpea were safe was to do an emergency C-section."

Aurora's mental fog burned off instantly and motherly instinct kicked in. "Where's chickpea?" She twisted her head to see her baby but couldn't find her. She tried to sit up, and a sharp pain drove through her middle and brought tears to her eyes.

"Careful. Careful." Leela guided her back to the pillows. "You have an incision. You're going to be pretty sore for a while so it's important that you move slowly and use these bed rails here." She tapped on them.

"Where's chickpea?" Aurora demanded to know. "She should be here with us."

"She's in the NICU," Leela assured. "I promise she's safe. I was there with her while you were coming out of surgery and under anesthesia. My mom's with her now."

"You saw her?" Aurora asked in wonder as her eyes started to blur.

Leela brushed a strand of hair from Aurora's forehead. "Yeah, I did. I took hundreds of pictures of her in her incubator—she needs it to stay warm because she's so small. But, even though she's tiny, she's strong enough to be held. I got to hold her for the longest time. Do you want to see?"

Aurora nodded vigorously and tried to sit up again, only to fall back down.

"You relax. I'll bring the pictures down to your level." Leela pulled a chair over and, after her finger danced over her phone, showed Aurora the screen. "This is a video I took for you."

Aurora watched and listened to Leela's introduction with an exuberant smile. When she finally set eyes on her little chickpea, she reached out to bring the phone closer.

Her baby was healthy and in the world.

"She has so much hair," Aurora said with a tearful laugh. "She looks just like she did in my dream. I was practically bald when I was born. Does she have a birthmark on her upper back?"

Leela nodded. "The last dream you had must have been pretty high-def."

"It was." Aurora took the phone and scrolled through the pictures. She marveled over every nose crinkle, arm stretch, and knee bend.

"I may have gone a little nuts with the photo shoot, but I wanted you to see every part of her ten fingers and ten toes."

"Her toes are so tiny." Aurora realized that was an incredibly dumb thing to say but didn't care. This was her chickpea. But the instrumentation around her was unnatural. "What's that tube there?"

"That's how we'll feed her, especially at the beginning, since breastfeeding will be difficult. It'll be tough for you to see her at first and then there's something about latching issues. We can still use your milk though. Although, it might take longer to come in because of the traumatic nature of the delivery." Leela changed her gaze to look out the window. "There's something else I need to tell you…"

"Is it chickpea?"

"No. Chickpea's great. I need to tell you about something else that happened during your surgery." Leela took Aurora's hand and held it against her chest. "Because of the tearing, you started losing blood. A lot of it, actually. To save you, they had to remove your uterus."

"What? Are you sure?"

"Yeah," Leela said sadly, "I am. I'm sorry, sweets."

They talked about having more children. Granted, there were more ways to go about growing their family than through her, but the piece of her that could have provided that was gone. "Did you have any say in that?" Aurora couldn't keep the edge out of her voice.

"No. But I would have, because it saved your life. Chickpea needs both of us."

Aurora knew Leela was right, but that didn't stop the rage from building inside her. There was only one thing that would calm her. "I want to see chickpea, and I want to see her now!" Aurora gripped the side rails and gradually pulled herself up. Something inside her stretched to the point where it felt like she was being ripped apart, but she didn't care. The pain caused beads of sweat to form, but she would not give up. Even Leela screaming her name to lie down wouldn't make her stop. A baby needed their mother, and that was who she was.

"You have to lie down!" Leela begged.

"I will not! I need to see her!"

"I know you do but you're freshly stitched, have an IV, and a catheter. It's dangerous to start yanking all that shit out!" Leela took a deep breath and exhaled slowly. "You hurting yourself, hurts chickpea. I'll get a nurse, but you have to promise to lie down."

Leela's harsh but true words caused her to relax. The pain waned to a discomfort but didn't go away entirely. "I'll calm down, but I need to see her."

"I know, and she needs to see you too," Leela said softly and kissed her. "I'll be back."

Aurora had never felt so many emotions at once. Joy and loss. Excitement and frustration. Love and anger. She'd read that after birth, hormones surged, but she didn't even know if that was to blame. Her uterus was gone. Were her ovaries too? Leela hadn't said, but she didn't really have the chance to explain much further.

A woman Aurora hadn't expected to see came in the room. "Fiona?"

"Hi," she said in a gentle tone and touched one of Aurora's feet through the sheet. "And congratulations."

"Thank you." Aurora managed a tired smile. "But I want to see chickpea. Can you help me do that?"

She sighed. "I spoke to your surgeon, and she wants you to wait until tomorrow."

"I can't wait that long."

"I know. That's why I spoke to your nurse too. The deal is you have to demonstrate you're well enough to keep liquids down and remain lucid. Then, they'll transfer you to a regular bed. If you handle that all right, we can take you to the NICU on a stretcher. But to do all of that, you have to do absolutely *everything* we say. You probably felt the stitches pull when you sat up, but that's only a portion of the possible complications. So, can you play by the rules?"

"I'll do anything."

Leela walked in, along with the nurse who wheeled in a tray with what looked like an adult sippy cup.

"Is this the liquids test?" Aurora asked.

"It is," the nurse confirmed. "Drink slow. Press the button if you need anything." She looked at Leela. "You too."

Aurora watched her leave and shook her head. She reached for the cup and felt a tug.

"Careful," Leela said. "How about I help you with that? Just initially."

Aurora nodded and looked at Fiona. "I guess this changes your post-birth plan for us."

"It does, but we'll figure it out." She cocked her head to the door. "I think I should give you two some more time together. Leela, give me a text if you want me to come back."

"Roger that. And thank you for coming and explaining things to Mom."

Fiona smiled and left them alone again.

Aurora stared at the cup. She knew she should say something, but she didn't know what. Leela by her side was her saving grace. Without her there, she would be truly lost. "Your mom is here?"

Leela nodded. "She's been here about thirty minutes, and with chickpea for twenty-nine of those minutes."

It was good chickpea wasn't alone. Aurora couldn't bear the thought of her daughter, who was only hours old, being isolated from family in an incubator.

Her throat and eyes started to burn.

"Can I see those pictures of chickpea again?"

Through the hundreds of pictures Leela took, Aurora's emotions soared and plummeted. Chickpea was remarkable in every way, and it was an absolute crime they were separated. Her brain understood, but her heart broke piece by piece every minute they were apart. But Leela could be there. She should be there.

"I know you're worried about me, but I want you to be with chickpea as much as you can. I'm sure they'll move me soon."

Leela nodded and pursed her lips. "How about this? I'll give them a kick in the ass to get moving."

"That won't be necessary, Ms. Okpik-Bakshi," the nurse said. "We can transfer you out of ICU now."

She looked up at the acoustic ceiling tiles and thanked the heavens. All she had to do was prove she could handle the move and then she could see chickpea.

"How long will it be before you can assess if I'm well enough to go to the NICU?"

"I have three children," her nurse said seriously. "When you're ready, I'll get you there."

Aurora gave a silent nod of thanks and took Leela's hand. "Please go see chickpea. She needs you as much as she needs me, and while I want to get down there as soon as I can, it'll probably be a little while yet."

Leela leaned down as much as she could to give her the gentlest hug. "I love you so much."

"I love you too." She kissed Leela on the lips. "Go see our baby."

Leela blew her another kiss as she walked out the door.

Aurora hated that she was envious of Leela, but she was glad chickpea could see one of her parents.

"You two are really adorable. I just have to say."

Aurora grinned. "She's my everything. Her and chickpea are my everything."

Her nurse sharply inhaled. "Alright, we need to step on this."

While Aurora was transferred out of ICU, she followed the nurse's advice and didn't look at the time. It wouldn't move fast enough anyway.

Once she was in her new room, she demonstrated—yet again—she could keep down apple juice, then she was on her way to see chickpea.

Slightly reclined on a transport stretcher, Aurora's heart raced when she descended in the elevator to the NICU. Her first visit with her daughter was enough of an incentive for her to ignore the pain she felt when the stretcher went over a slight elevator bump.

The signs leading the way lifted her spirits as high as they would go.

She was pushed through the automatic doors, and while the NICU was a new place, a familiar voice greeted her.

"She clearly doesn't need it, Dr. Brady!" Tanha said in a scrub shirt that redefined v-neck.

"Mom!" Leela reprimanded. "Can you stop for one freaking minute?"

"Please, Dr. Mitra," a man in scrubs implored.

Tanha's face went from a scowl to the broadest grin Aurora had ever seen on her. Even more than when Tanha had learned she was pregnant. She raced toward Aurora and hugged her gently. "My granddaughter is amazing. Come."

The man in scrubs kept his arms folded. It wasn't exactly the welcome she had imagined, but she had a feeling medical staff usually responded that way after a conversation with Tanha.

"Better prepare yourself, sweets," Leela said behind her ear. "Here's our baby."

As Leela pushed her the rest of the way between two incubators, she saw chickpea. Her daughter.

Aurora tried to say 'hello,' but the word was caught.

Chickpea was even more precious than the photographs or video showed.

Aurora had to feel the hair that escaped her cap. She wanted to feel its texture and let it tickle her fingers. Aurora reached forward, but the strain was too much. "Can you get me any closer?" She wiped away tears. "I can't reach."

Leela did as instructed, and Aurora could finally reach out. She gently rubbed her baby's hand with her index finger and thumb. A miniature handshake.

Chickpea's skin was a light bronze, almost a perfect mix of her and Leela's tone, her face was angelic and unobstructed by most of the tubing she saw in the pictures. Her mouth, nose, and ears were so tiny, and she knew behind those closed lids, chickpea had Leela's eyes.

Leela placed her hands on each of her shoulders. "You should introduce yourself. It's never too early to teach stranger danger."

Aurora nodded. She knew chickpea needed to hear her voice. "Hi. I'm your mama Roar. Sorry I'm late."

Leela leaned down beside her. "I think she forgives you."

"Thank you, chickpea, you have such a big heart already." Aurora rubbed a circle on her chest, which was only an inch above her diaper line.

"Her heart is perfect," Tanha said. "Everything is perfect, which is why she doesn't need intervention."

"I'll admit she seems to be doing very well without it," replied the medical worker, who still had his arms crossed.

Leela walked to the other side of the incubator where Tanha stood, still pleased with herself. "I go to the bathroom for three minutes and you take my baby off her oxygen?"

Tanha reached out and gently grabbed Leela by the upper arms. "All of the data here suggested she didn't need it. She has been off it for the last five minutes and her metrics have stayed the same."

"That is correct," he said. "I just can't explain it. I've never seen a preemie like her before. Except for her size, it's like she's not even a preemie."

"And you'll never see anything like her again." Aurora stroked the soft skin at chickpea's knee, causing her leg to twitch.

In the background, Aurora heard bits and pieces of a conversation between Tanha and the man in scrubs, who she assumed was a pediatrician. The medical jargon they spoke about was probably important, but she couldn't take her eyes off her chickpea.

Leela gave her a hug from behind and kissed her temple. "Your mom and dad say they love you and chickpea, and they'll talk to you soon."

Aurora ran her pinky on the outside of chickpea's ear. It was floppier than she'd expected, but she knew it would become firmer with time.

Chickpea just needed a little extra time.

"Sweets, your mom and—"

"Sorry, I got. . . distracted," Aurora said with a smile. "You talked to my parents?"

"Yeah. I talked to them as you started coming out of anesthesia."

"Thank you. Did you tell them everything?"

"I didn't want to, but Ani dragged it out of me."

"Sounds about right." Aurora smirked and then looked around the NICU. "Where did your mom go?"

"You didn't hear? She went to the cafeteria with Dr. Skeptic to buy him coffee. It could be an apology. It could be them writing a paper together about chickpea. Who knows?"

"That also sounds about right." Aurora tried to move so she could touch chickpea with both hands, but her stitches wouldn't let her. All she wanted was to touch her baby with both hands. Something so simple was literally beyond her reach. She began to cry.

"What's wrong?"

Aurora sniffed and wiped at her eyes. "I just want to hold her so bad."

A reel of emotions played over Leela's face. She turned away. "Phillip, we need to kangaroo Aurora."

"Okay," Phillip drawled. The nurse who had been immersed in charts in the back of the room got up from his station. "This isn't the first time this request has happened, but it's not as easy as—"

"I'll do anything!" Aurora blurted. She had started to think that holding her was an impossibility. But if it wasn't easy, was it dangerous for chickpea? "I want this more than anything, but I can't if it's not safe for her."

"Trust me," Phillip said as he got a blanket out of a cabinet. "If it wasn't safe, I wouldn't help." He set the blanket down and took a pair of scissors off a stainless-steel tray with a roll of medical tape beside it. "Skin-to-skin is best, so do you mind if I cut the front of your gown?"

"No. Please, do it." She and Leela traded smiles while he cut her gown. "Can you help me?" she asked Leela.

"I can't say no to a girl in a plunging neckline."

Phillip draped some of the blanket over Aurora's shoulders then sterilized his hands before gathering chickpea's wires and single tube. He skillfully picked chickpea up, causing her to move her lips in some silent protest, and placed her against the skin of

Aurora's chest. "Okay, now use one hand to hold her bottom and the other for her head."

The sensation of this tiny, warm being resting on her was alien. The most valuable part of her life was in her arms. Not even the incision across her lower abdomen could take away her euphoria.

As her hold became more confident, Phillip slid his hands away and placed the blanket over chickpea. "We don't want to expose her to the cold air for very long." He left for the other side of the room.

Aurora heard an object slide against the floor and looked up.

She saw her family's reflection in a mirror. Chickpea's face against her chest, and unlike her and Leela, chickpea's face wasn't stained with tears. "I promise your mama Lee and I don't cry like this all the time. But today is a very special day. Today is your birthday."

"I forgot the cake. I'm a bad mom." Leela kneeled beside them and pulled chickpea's knit cap down.

Chickpea responded by smacking her lips together then exhaling a content sigh.

"Well, I know she's in the coziest place of all of cozyland, but how are you, sweets? Do you need anything?"

Aurora took in the utter completeness and peace she felt. She shook her head. "I don't need anything. I'm perfect."

CHAPTER SEVENTEEN

LEELA PATTED THE Windsor knot of the tie she finished adjusting and straightened Keith's jacket. Oh, how much he'd grown. "Go knock 'em dead. . . Except don't because I actually like them."

"If you like them so much, then why do I have to go over to their office in this ridiculous outfit and ask them for more money?"

Only Keith would think jeans and a sport coat with a tie was dressing up.

"Because I learned they're paying us less money per gallon than any other farm they buy their milk from, and I *know* they only use our milk to make their yogurt. We have the upper hand."

Keith squirmed in his nicest boots. "The vet is one thing, but money is a different ball game. Why can't you go?"

Leela reminded herself it was wrong to yell at people who meant well. She normally wouldn't be this cranky. It was only because of stress. "You're going because my newborn child needs me, and my wife is still recovering from major surgery."

Keith winced. "Yeah, as soon as I said it, I knew it was dumb. I'm sorry."

"I appreciate your self-awareness. And everything you've done the past three weeks. You had to take over sooner than expected."

"That's okay. You had to take over mom duty sooner than expected." He grinned and gave her a friendly side punch to the arm.

"When do you think chickpea'll be able to come home? I'm excited for the name unveiling."

Everyone was excited for the official announcement of chickpea's name, including them. She and Aurora had discussed it ad nauseam, but nothing they could come up with would stick. The only name which fit was chickpea, and her legal name wouldn't be a legume. It just wouldn't.

"We're hoping chickpea can come home tomorrow," Leela said. "She has to pass a few tests before it's deemed safe that she can leave the hospital."

"Tests?" he asked with a frown. "I thought she was basically super baby when it came to her breathing and everything."

"It pretty much comes down to the car seat test. But they also want to make sure she and Aurora have the latching down to a science."

He immediately turned red in the cheeks. "Oh! That's. . . important."

She grinned slyly. "Yeah, kid's gotta eat. So, speaking of the kid, are you good? Because I really need to go. I promised Aurora I'd be at the hospital by nine."

"Say no more. I'll be good. You gave me that sheet with all the data and talking points." He patted his chest pocket.

"Good. I'll see you later today and you can give me a full report of the meeting then." Leela left the farm's office and got into her truck. Once her foot hit the gas, her mindset officially transitioned from business to family. Work was important, but it wasn't her life.

Her family was her life.

Instead of scheduling matrices and product development, Leela's main challenges were trying to maximize her time with chickpea and interpreting the different sensations in her brain to determine what chickpea liked or needed. Leela hadn't felt anything as painful as when chickpea was cooped up inside Aurora, and nothing as so profoundly relaxing as when Aurora breastfed her or when chickpea received a sponge bath.

Chickpea was claustrophobic, liked boobs, and adored spa treatments.

It was like they were twins.

She and Aurora still couldn't get over the similarities she shared with chickpea. According to science, it was impossible, but they chose to believe that they were her parents in every possible way. Unfortunately, because chickpea didn't have a legal name yet, Leela couldn't officially adopt her own daughter. Apparently, in Oregon, a baby had to be born *and* have a name.

Stupid red tape.

After circling the hospital visitor lot, Leela pulled into what had become her spot over the past few weeks. Of course, during the first week her truck had never left. Keith would come in to visit and update her, and her mother and Jill would alternate to bring in fresh food every day.

When she and Aurora came home as a couple one week after Aurora's surgery, it was bittersweet. Aurora was far enough along in her own recovery to leave the hospital, but chickpea wasn't. According to hospital standards. Standards that even her mother called "archaic bullshit." So, for two weeks, she and Aurora would make their visits and come home without their daughter. For two weeks they saw an empty bassinet, tried to sleep in a quiet house, and sat on their couch without a little chickpea weight on their chest.

Leela caught a glimpse of the eagle in the tree nearest to the hospital's entrance doors. "Hey, Scout. I'll give chickpea your best."

She waved as she passed the reception desk. The need to flash her identification bracelet was no longer required since, everyone in the obstetrics wing knew her.

They also knew her mother. She made regular visits to second guess all of chickpea's medical treatments.

Leela was actually very happy her mother was still around. Leela's job was to look after chickpea and Aurora, not herself. If it wasn't for her mom, she'd be hungry and have the worst body odor on the planet. Her father had helped in his own way too, by vowing to stay out of the way until everyone had settled at home. He also planned to provide one of the most generous gifts he ever gave.

She couldn't wait for the surprise unveiling.

The activity within the NICU was low enough for Leela to hear Aurora's voice as she spoke to the nursing coach about feeding schedules.

Aurora caught her eye and gave her a tired smile.

The nurse saw her, took the hint, and left, but Leela still took her time as she walked over. She wanted to prolong the sacred moment where Aurora fed chickpea. She had never seen Aurora so content. "How's my family unit?" Leela asked then kissed Aurora.

"We're doing *very* well. It looks like tomorrow will be the day chickpea can come home."

"Good job, chickpea! Look at you passing car seat tests and latching like a champ! Is it inappropriate to give you both a high five?"

Aurora answered with a cocked brow but raised her hand anyway.

Leela gladly gave her a quiet high five and then tapped the back of chickpea's hand. After the celebration, she sat in the chair beside the glider to fully relish in the blissful brain wash she felt. But the feeling was slowly waning. "I think she's falling asleep."

"You're right about that. Can you take her?"

Because of Aurora's healing incisions, extra help was needed in almost every matter that used core strength. Leela swiftly took chickpea and cradled her in the same position. "There we go, Ruth."

"We are not calling her Ruth, especially when we haven't ruled out the half a dozen other names we actually agreed upon months ago. Besides, she has a temporary legal name. Megis."

Neither she nor Aurora wanted to name her, but they only had so much time to register a birth certificate, get the adoption paperwork rolling, and add her to their insurance. Phillip said their situation was not unique. People waited until the last minute to name their baby, so when the baby came early it put the pressure on. Phillip also said they could change her name later, like they had done when they got married.

Yeah, that was what they'd have to do.

"But RBG was the shit!"

Aurora gave her the look that said it all.

"Okay, fine. Sorry, RBG, I guess your name is too old-timey. At this rate, we should just name her Chickpea."

"We can't do that to her."

"Yes, we can. I was in the Forty Under Forty. That means I'm practically a celebrity, which means we can name our daughter any batshit crazy name we want."

Aurora cracked a smile. "I wonder if anyone else on that list has come up with that excuse?"

"I doubt it. We're special like that," Leela said to her sleeping daughter and kissed the crown of her head. "All jokes aside, we should probably come up with her permanent name before the welcome home party—gathering. Sorry, not a party. Just people close to us who want to eat snacks in our home, who have promised to come in waves, and clean up after themselves or face my shotgun."

"We have good friends."

"The best friends."

#

The clicking cords from the ceiling fan in chickpea's nursery, the wavy air rising from a patch of dry earth, and the suckling of chickpea had lulled Aurora into a meditative state. The negative thoughts that had plagued her all morning took a back seat so her mind could go blank.

Ever since the day she had woken up in the hospital, it seemed like she couldn't escape anxiety and insecurity. Was she doing the right things? When would she finish healing? Why couldn't she and Leela agree on a name? Did her identity change now that she was a mother?

It was the last question that really got to her.

Her place in the world had shifted dramatically. Nine months ago, her only major role was to try to make a positive contribution to the planet: to clean the environment, to spread love and kindness, and see the glass half-full. Now she was a mother. Aurora had a responsibility to continue her previous duties and teach them to her daughter while she nurtured and protected her.

But she knew there was more, especially with a daughter as special as chickpea.

Aurora ached to see her own mother. Not only did she need to meet chickpea, but Aurora wanted advice and to have a heart-to-heart about how she felt now as a woman. Aurora knew she was a woman, but she felt unbalanced knowing that a key piece of how she defined herself as a woman was gone. She knew her mother could relate and would have some piece of wisdom for her to see past it. Or at least come to terms with her loss. Both of them.

She no longer had her dream link to chickpea.

Aurora's mother was also the only one aside from her and Leela who knew about the spiritual origin of her conception. Leela became a believer as soon as she saw chickpea. The physical similarities chickpea had with Leela were undeniable. In fact, when they looked at baby photos, chickpea looked more like Leela than her. The crazy black hair and the big round eyes did not come from her. Aurora knew someday they would have to tell chickpea where she came from, and she hoped she had an answer by then.

An outside force caused Aurora's quasi-mediation to cease. "You're staring again."

"Are you talking to me or to Scout?" Leela asked as she came into the nursery with a sheet of paper and a roll of tape in her hands.

"Both, I suppose." Aurora carefully pointed at Leela without disturbing chickpea. "What's that for?"

"I made a sign. I want to remind everyone they need to wash their hands before they see her. Or you." Leela taped the sign to the door.

"Why me?"

Leela rested her hands on her knees. "You can't risk infection either, sweets. I take pro—"

"Protecting me and chickpea very seriously. Yes, I know. I heard you the first hundred times." Aurora readjusted chickpea and pulled her shirt back down over her breast. "How much time do we have until your dad gets here?"

"Based on his text, about twenty minutes." Leela slung a burping cloth over her shoulder. "Plenty of time for me to put chickpea into the new burrito outfit Stacy got her. Now, gimme the baby." Leela held out her hands playfully.

Aurora handed off chickpea and stood gradually, being mindful not to put too much strain on her wound. "That doesn't really give me time to shower."

Leela bounced slightly at the knee and gave chickpea's back gentle pats. "You did that last night. Just do a once over with a washcloth."

"That feels lazy."

"You slept three hours. Total. You get a pass."

Aurora didn't need any further convincing. She kissed both Leela and chickpea then went across the hall. She took her maternity summer dress from the closet and fresh undergarments from her bureau drawers before taking them all into the bathroom. As she moved from room to room, Aurora could hear Leela talking to chickpea in her newly developed sing-song baby voice. It still amused Aurora that the woman who could occasionally swear like a sailor was the same person who just said, "Burrito baby needs salsa socks for her tootsie feet."

Motherhood definitely changed everyone.

Being mindful not to stretch too much, Aurora cautiously pulled her large t-shirt over her head and pushed her pajama shorts down. The glimpse of short, dark hairs sprouting from her shins made her grumble.

"Everything okay?" Leela yelled.

"I'm fine. I just haven't shaved my legs in forever."

"You're the only one who cares about that, but if it bugs you, I can help. Could be sexy."

Aurora smiled. In a time of healing incisions, and the combination of dried milk and saliva on her nipples, it was reassuring to know Leela still found her attractive.

She wetted and soaped a warm washcloth and enjoyed the momentary luxury of it cleaning her skin.

While she scrubbed, she listened to Leela discuss names with chickpea, waiting for their daughter to react in some way.

She had tried that tactic herself, but nothing stuck.

Before Aurora carefully pulled on her underwear, she examined the six-inch horizontal scar directly above her pubic line. What started as a horrific dark brown line had transitioned into a soft pink. The sharp pain that occurred whenever she moved was now an isolated ache if she pushed herself too hard.

Thanks to Leela, she'd received the best post-surgical wound care and therapy.

Aurora would never, ever tell Leela, but she would have been an excellent doctor.

She finished her quick wash and dry, slid the lilac summer dress over her head, and finished by brushing and rebraiding her hair. She didn't feel one hundred percent—nor did she think she should—but she felt presentable and ready to socialize for a few hours. She left the bathroom and immediately heard a wolf whistle from the direction of the nursery. Aurora peered into the nursery with a smile. "Is that the kind of behavior we want to model for little Megis?"

Leela studied chickpea's scrunched face. "I still don't see a Megis or a Meg in there. Besides, I'd like to keep our association with Megs in the past."

"Part of me is hoping that if I say it enough, it'll fit."

"Chickpea will get her real name. It's not like she's bothered by not having one. The only thing she hates is cold feet and hidden nipples, which I have to say, I agree with on both accounts."

"I don't think you're taking this seriously."

"Fine. I take back the hidden nipple joke, but that doesn't mean I'm not right. I want her to have a name as bad as you do, maybe even more, but it has to be perfect. And the perfect name will only come to us when we're not stressing out about it."

A heavy knock at the front door drew both of their attention away.

Aurora headed for the living room. "I can see your point, but a name is expected. People are coming here—are here—and expect a name."

"If anyone asks about her name, let's just be honest or redirect the conversation to the cake. People like to talk about cake. Are you ready?" Leela asked while she still bounced chickpea.

Aurora wanted to finish the conversation, but she opened the front door for Sid anyway.

"Boo bear!" Ani rushed Aurora and wrapped her arms around her.

"Mom?" Aurora said in disbelief as she was hugged from two directions. "Dad?"

"That's us," Niq said. "We couldn't wait any longer to see you."

Ani pulled away and touched Aurora's check. "Surprised?"

Aurora's mouth hung open despite not saying a word, which was ironic given that she had so many things she wanted to say. "How are you here right now?" She looked over to Leela, who stood with a self-satisfied smirk. "You knew?"

"I may have heard a rumor." Leela readjusted chickpea in her arms and walked toward them. "I don't think you've met this little girl before. She doesn't say much, but she's cool."

Ani took chickpea into her arms, who grumbled from the change. "Shh. It's okay, little one."

Niq smiled broadly and picked up chickpea's hand to shake it. "I'm very pleased to meet you."

Aurora was shell-shocked. Her parents stood in her living room. Chickpea's little head was nuzzled in the crook of her mother's neck while her father spiked her hair. "I can't believe you're here. Oh!" Aurora scrambled to the end table to grab the bottle of hand sanitizer. "Do you mind?"

"Oh, don't worry about that," Ani said without taking her gaze off her granddaughter. "Sid gave us some hand sanitizer in the car."

"Sid? As in Leela's dad, Siddhartha?"

"Yeah!" Niq confirmed. "Interesting guy. He's still in the car because he didn't want you to feel overwhelmed, and he had to call some guy back about a journal submission."

While her parents cooed over chickpea, Aurora embraced Leela. "I can't believe you conspired with your dad to bring my parents here."

"I didn't really do much. Once I mentioned how much they wanted to see chickpea, he offered to fly them here, and then since they were both at the airport—"

"Your dad flew them here?"

"You're a terrible whisperer, Aurora," Niq said with a grin. "In return he just wants a vintage bike fixed up. But yes, Sid's a very generous man."

"He has his moments," Leela said. "He's also extremely socially awkward, so if you don't mind, I'm going to step out to haul his butt in here."

When Leela left, Aurora hugged her father again.

In true fashion, he kissed the top of her forehead and started scanning the interior, no doubt inspecting workmanship. "So, where are these renovations you were going on about?"

"The mudroom is behind the kitchen wall. Nothing too exciting there, but the nursery, which was our old bedroom, is right down here." She led them down the short hall and into the room. "Ta-da!"

"Ah, this is so nice," Ani cooed while she cradled chickpea. "Look at that natural light coming in. Oh, and I see rainforest won the theme."

Aurora picked up a stuffed animal of a panther. "It came down to a coin flip."

"Great view of the mountains," Niq said and walked to the window. He pointed up. "That must be the eagle you were talking about."

"Yeah," Aurora drawled. "I still don't know what to make of Scout other than he wants to be around chickpea. I thought maybe I would have a moment of clarity that explains his purpose, but I haven't."

Niq chortled. "I don't think I had a moment of clarity until you turned five. But if I were you, I wouldn't worry about it."

"Your father's right, and I don't necessarily think you're supposed to make sense of it. I think that's chickpea's job. Isn't it?" She rubbed her nose against chickpea's. "You and Leela have been through a remarkable journey to reach this place, but maybe everything from now on that's incredible is chickpea's journey." She looked down to her granddaughter, who stared up with big brown eyes. "You can guide her like all good parents try to do, but it's up to her to decide what the pieces of her puzzle mean and whether or not to accept her fate."

What would the future of a girl with extraordinary strength, a perfect heart, and who was guarded by an eagle bring? Aurora didn't know, and she was scared to learn.

"What's wrong, boo bear? You have a worry scowl."

"I have a lot on my mind, as I'm sure you can imagine." They both smiled kindly and then brought their attention back to chickpea. Her parents visiting was the greatest surprise—aside from chickpea—she had ever received. "How long are you able to stay?"

"A week," Niq said. "Don't worry though. We found a great house to rent, and we didn't come for you to entertain us. We just want to help in any way we can, whether it's groceries, or advice, or whatever. And if you don't want us here, I can still go fishing with Keith and Jill." He finished with a laugh.

That was the perfect scenario. She would have plenty of time to have a quality conversation with her mother, bike riding with her father might be out due to her healing, but a walk or two outside would be great. Their presence and support meant everything to her. She was a grown woman, but they would never stop being her parents. She hugged her father, breathing in the musky scent of his favorite soap. "I'm so glad you're both here."

Niq held her gently. "We wouldn't have missed this for the world."

"Sid just expedited the process. Didn't he?" Ani asked chickpea.

Aurora turned to the nursery's open door. Where was Sid? Surely, he was excited to see his granddaughter too. "Do you mind if I go check on Leela and Sid? I thought they'd be in here by now."

"Go ahead. I'm going to try to convince your mother to let me hold her."

Aurora smiled and hugged them both again before she left the nursery. She stepped onto the front porch, the breeze causing her dress to swirl around her legs.

Through the tinted glass of Sid's rental car, she saw he and Leela in a tight embrace. Sid's hands clung to her back and his face was contorted with emotion. He briefly opened his eyes and pulled back.

Leela kissed him on the cheek and gave his hand on the steering wheel a pat.

Almost in unison, they opened their separate car doors and walked toward the house, both wiping their cheekbones along the way.

"Hello, Aurora," Sid said with a sniffle and gave her a brief hug. "I do not want to squeeze you too hard. Tanha told me you are still healing."

"I appreciate that. Thank you so much for coming *and* for bringing my parents. That's the best present you could have ever given me."

"You are very welcome." He smiled the biggest and brightest grin. "I cannot believe I get to meet my granddaughter. I am so excited to see her!"

"Chickpea's in the nursery with Mom and Dad." She watched him happily scurry inside. "Wow. I've never seen him like this before."

"I can't believe I'm going to say this, but Dad's feeling a little emotionally overwhelmed right now."

Based on Leela's glassy eyes, he wasn't the only one. "The journal phone call was a lie, wasn't it?"

"Yeah. He needed some time alone." Leela took her hand and a deep breath. "Dad told me he thinks this might be the best day of his entire life. He said that he never thought he'd be a grandfather or that I'd want him in my life ever again or that he and Mom could be friends. Of course, that was after he cry-mumbled. He called chickpea his *karishma* for making all of that happen."

"Karishma," Aurora repeated. The word sounded beautiful and gentle, but at the same time strong and confident. "What does it mean?"

"Miracle," Leela said with a soft smile. "I know you know what I'm thinking."

Aurora had to say it out loud to be sure. "Karishma Megis Okpik-Bakshi does have a fine ring to it."

"Yes!" Leela cradled her face and kissed her until she pulled away with a loud *smack*. "We did it! Let's go tell her."

"I have a feeling chickpea already knows exactly who she is."

ACKNOWLEDGEMENTS

My wife: I know you think you didn't help me in any way shape or form with this novel, but you're wrong. Yeah, I said it. You took me to the big island of Hawaii for our honeymoon. Looking at our pictures helped me piece together the scenery and vibe I wanted to convey. It was great trip down memory lane. You also believe in me. I love that even though you know next to nothing about this book, you still encourage me daily by telling me I'm a great writer. Lastly, I couldn't write about the profound cosmic love Aurora and Leela have if I didn't have you. We are each other's dreamweavers.

This novel contained many experiences I never had, so I had to reach out for help. Thank you Salt and Sage Books and "the moms" who helped me gain perspective. Salt & Sage Books introduced me to Ronkwahrhakónha (Lune) Dube who was an absolute joy to work with when it came to reviewing the Indigenous content. In the areas where I strayed, he was so kind and explained my missteps in detail, so not only did I know that I should make corrections, but why as well. I really cannot thank him enough for his input and kindness. Now, the moms. There's my own mother, and then the quartet of Kelly, Korrie, Lish, and Karyn, who all gave me insights into pregnancy. You were all much more entertaining than those pregnancy blogs I went on. Did you know I still get Facebook advertisements for baby products and pregnancy clothes?

This novel also contained subject matter that required a level of expertise a notch above what I could find or verify. Thank you to Brenda Murphy, Ricky Hirschhorn, and Ana.

Brenda: There are very few people in my circle who could have helped me with the end of this novel. Everyone I knew with an experience even close to what was in the book was either anesthetized or in a waiting room. However, when I reached out to you to take advantage of your years of experience, you didn't hesitate to help me. I am extremely grateful. . . even if I did have to change part of the ending for accuracy. Brenda, in addition helping me, is also an accomplished author. To learn about Brenda's work, please visit her author page, https://www.amazon.com/Brenda-Murphy/e/B072MW3Q5P

Ricky Hirschhorn: My mentor and friend, thank you! I can only imagine what you thought when I said I wanted you to read through my draft to double check my explanations/research for parthenogenesis in humans. (Oh, and also traditional Jewish foods.) I was so happy to get my draft back from you with less comments than my thesis. Many less comments.

Ana: First, I appreciate your patience working with me. I gave you a vague storyline and my general ideas about a bird but you were still able to help me with the raptor integration. Knowledge is power, and you have super raptor power. I also admire the hell out of the work you do (so cool) and I've learned so much. For everyone else who wants to learn more about raptors (and why wouldn't you), go to https://hawkwatch.org/

And lastly, my fabulous editing team across the pond:

Jenn: Thank you for not letting all those little nasty errors getting through and being another line of defense. Nobody deserves to see the same word twice in a row or an 'of' instead of 'off.' Nobody!

Eanna: Commas are stupid and you can't convince me otherwise. Regardless, thank you for your careful eye and ensuring that my novel reads the best way possible. We're going for maximum impact, people! And I am delighted beyond all measure that o-ring versus O-ring was a topic in your editing circles.

Eos and May: As always, you've pulled all of the extra emotional cues, reactions, and dreamy bits out of me to make this the best possible story it could be. I'm so proud to have this book out there in the world with both of our names on it. As a bonus, working on the developmental edits made me smile more than once. Seeing the cover art for the first time did make me science-gasm.

ABOUT THE AUTHOR

Serena J. Bishop is an accidental author. After writing technical, science-based pieces, in 2015 she decided to start turning her daydreams into stories. She writes witty, character-driven novels in the contemporary romance and/or speculative fiction genres. She published her first novel, *Beards*, about chosen family, in 2017, and has since signed with Eos Publishing for her subsequent novels, *Leveled*, *Dreams*, and now, *Miracles*.

When Serena's not writing or attending to her day job as a biomedical scientist, she enjoys cocktails with her wife, being a nerd, time with friends and family, and drinking coffee. Black, no sugar.

She lives in Maryland, USA with her magnificent wife and precious Chihuahua.

You can join her newsletter by going to www.serenajbishop.com or follow her on Instagram, Twitter, or Facebook @SerenaJBishop.

BOOK CLUB QUESTIONS

1. In book 1 of this trilogy, *Dreams*, the majority of the novel showcases Leela as a dream-version of herself. Did you find her real-life personality consistent with that version?

2. Prior to *Miracles*, a short story bundle, *Milestones*, was released which covers Aurora and Leela's first date, first "time," and the first time Leela met Aurora's parents. Given that there is a three-year gap between the end of *Dreams* and the beginning of *Miracles*, what other major events would there have been? How do you think it went down?

3. Hot tub sex. What are your thoughts?

4. For people who have been pregnant (could be yourself), what were the symptoms that gave away you/they were pregnant? Anybody symptom-less?

5. What do you think was the most pivotal moment in the book?

6. Do you think Leela's initial reaction to Aurora's pregnancy was realistic?

7. Aurora's mother, Ani, guesses that Aurora is pregnant. Do you have any closer relatives or friends who have that kind of instinct? Do you have any anecdotes to go along with this?

8. Do you know anyone who has consumed a placenta (probably in pill form) after the birth of their child? Did they elaborate on why?

9. Scout, the eagle, acts as chickpea's guardian. Have you had the experience of an animal not wanting to leave your side when you needed protection?

10. What was harder to suspend disbelief about: human parthenogenesis, a "virgin" pregnancy, or chickpea's super fetal traits (e.g., heart rate, mobility/power)?

11. Was the reveal of Leela and Aurora's psychic links to chickpea a surprise? Or did you see that coming?

12. Baby showers. What are the pros and cons of being an attendee?

13. Leela and chickpea or Aurora and chickpea, which parent meeting resonated with you the most? Why?

14. If you have children (furbabies count), how did you decide their name(s)?

15. Considering there will be a book three, *Heroes,* how did you feel about the ending?

ALSO BY THE AUTHOR

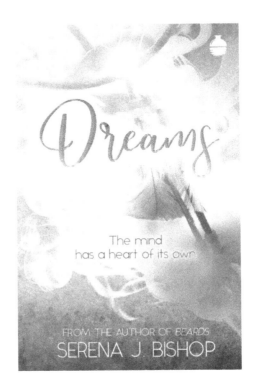

Dreams – Serena J. Bishop

The mind has a heart of its own.

Aurora's life is perfectly mundane. She has a job she hates, an ex that ran her out of her hometown, and the highlight of her week is Monday breakfast with her best friend. That changes when Aurora starts dreaming of a woman who can't remember her own name. A woman who Aurora falls head over heels for. She knows the romance that develops between them isn't real, but the dreams make life so much better that she hurries to bed every night...until she discovers that her dream woman isn't imaginary. Her name is Leela and she is in a coma.

Aurora must risk everything—her job, apartment, friends, and her sanity—to save Leela, a woman she's only ever met in her mind. But in order to help, Aurora must convince Leela's neurologist and parents that she and Leela have a bond that transcends the physical plane.

Can Aurora fight through a progressively nightmarish landscape to wake Leela? And if Leela wakes, will she recognize Aurora as the one who saved her? As the one Leela said she loved? Their dream-relationship might not be real, but if there is any possibility of making her dreams come true, Aurora has to try.

Dreams is a sweet lesfic romance about a love that defies the laws of physics.

ALSO BY THE AUTHOR

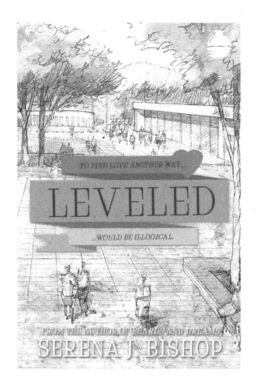

Leveled – Serena J. Bishop

To find love another way would be illogical.

After having her travel papers stolen to research in India, Dr. Persephone 'Perse' Teixeira succumbs to living in her sister's basement and working in retail. Just as she's about ready to hit rock bottom, Perse is offered an opportunity to teach anthropology and history at Chesapeake Bay University. Perse is thrilled; now her only worry is managing her anxiety. However, that changes once she meets a science professor, Dr. Stefanie 'Stef' Blake.

Stef is cute, quick-witted, and a touch neurotic. She's also very interested in dating Perse. When Perse declines her romantic advances because it is imperative that she focuses on her new job, Stef explains she has a relationship system that consists of six levels, which will ensure perfect compatibility before marriage. It's casual, slow, and, really, what are the odds of getting to level six?

Perse is amused, yet intrigued by Stef's analytical approach, and agrees to go out with her. But logic only goes so far and when feelings start to grow, Perse must contend with her anxiety issues, because history has taught her nothing good comes out of falling in love.

Are Perse and Stef compatible enough to get through the levels? Will Perse's past cause her to run before they can find out? Or did Stef create the perfect system for happily ever after?